'ORKNEY'S VERSION

ᛚᚨᛊᛏ
ᛊᚢᛗᛗᛖᚱ
ᚾᛁᚷᚺᛏ

# Last Summer Night

***It's party night in Kirkwall. So, what's the problem?***

A ROMANCE OF MANY DIMENSIONS

## MARK BALLETT

# Last Summer Night

Originally published in Great Britain by MarkB Publishing, a division of MarkB Ltd.

PRINTING HISTORY

First Edition 2021



MarkB Books are published by MarkB Ltd, The Colleens, Lower Cousley Wood, Wadhurst TN5 6HE

Reproduced, printed and bound in Great Britain.

Original cover drawing by Celia Turner. Maps by David Barden.

Typeset in Minion Pro and Univers LT Std

Editing, design and typesetting by UK Book Publishing

ISBN: 978-0-995548-85-5

# About the Author

Mark Ballett was born in Dartmouth, Devon, in 1956, although he has lived most of his life elsewhere. This is his second novel. He lives in East Sussex with his wife Carol, though he often dreams of living in the Northern Isles.

# Also by Mark Ballett

**The Falmouth Son**

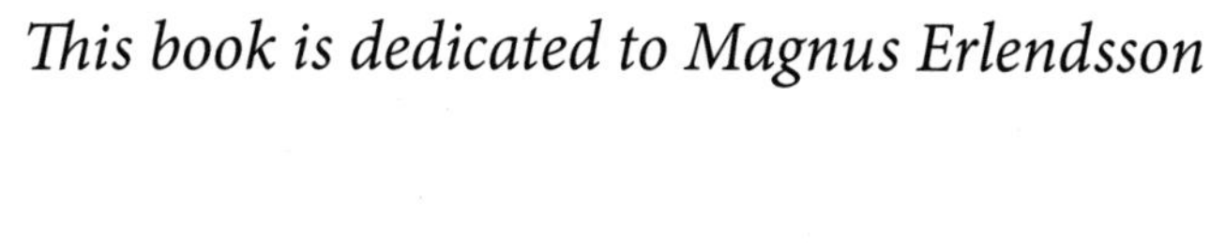

*This book is dedicated to Magnus Erlendsson*

## EXTRACT FROM BLOODY ORKNEY
## by CAPTAIN HAMISH BLAIR RN WWII

*Best bloody place is bloody bed,*
*With bloody ice on bloody head,*

*You might as well be bloody dead,*
*In bloody Orkney.*

# Contents

# Author's Preface

This is the second book in *The Lingering Past* trilogy: individual, stand-alone stories that also try and explore how lives are shaped by the history of three British coastal towns, Falmouth, Kirkwall, and Old Winchelsea. The first, *The Falmouth Son*, was published in 2018.

This story is set in Kirkwall, the capital of Orkney, an archipelago to the north of mainland Scotland that, together with Shetland, make up the Northern Isles. I feel at home in Kirkwall, though I have only visited a few times, but it captured my imagination like few other places. It is littered with relics and everywhere has a memory. If you scratch the ground the past flows like blood from a fresh wound.

This story is about frail human beings dealing with life's pressures, which at times can seem unbearable. Both Aristotle and the Dalai Lama have said, '*The purpose of life is to be happy*', but neither of them said it was going to be easy. Pinning down the meaning of life and why it is worth living at all is a far more difficult problem.

In setting out my story I have taken a few liberties with time and place, but I hope the end result is still recognisable to those who know Kirkwall well, and it makes you want to visit if you don't. Living in the Northern Isles can be hell at times, and you can feel imprisoned there, particularly in winter, but many people who have escaped soon realise that it is a rather special place and there is 'no place like home'.

Like all stories, there are echoes of others, which have shaped how we understand the world. It would be nice if this book adds to that literary tradition and refreshes some of the stories that we all share.

Thanks, once again, to my wife Carol for providing me with the space and support to write, and to Nicola, Richard, Debbie and Bethan who have helped me shape and polish this story.

***Mark Ballett***
*December 2020*
*East Sussex*

# Orkney Islands

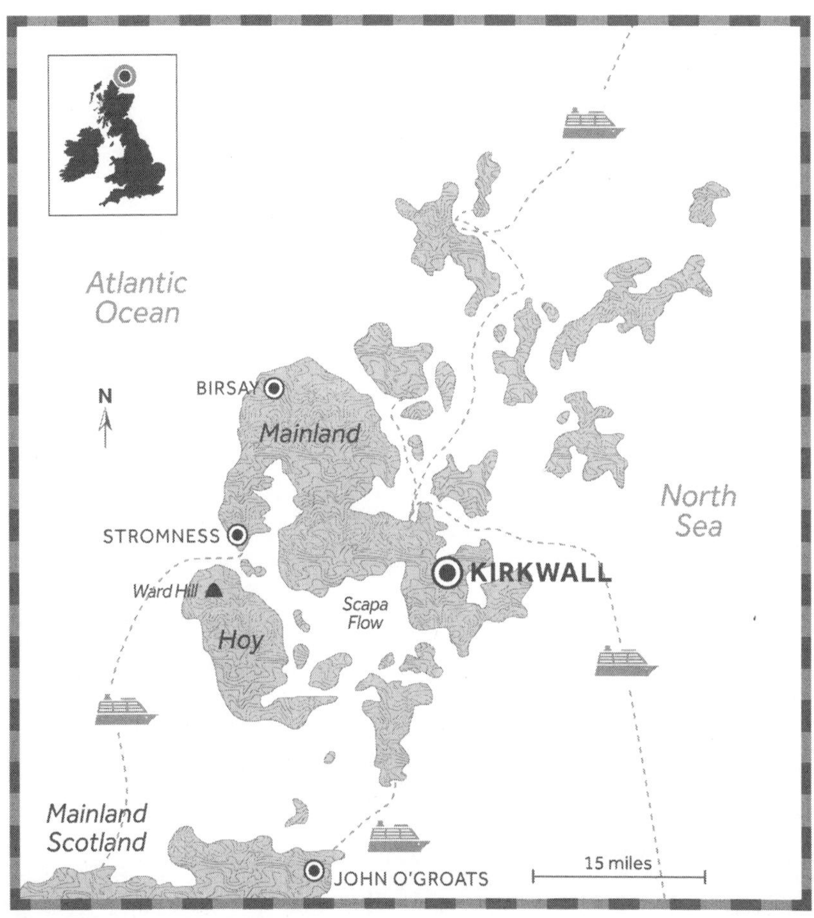

# Kirkwall

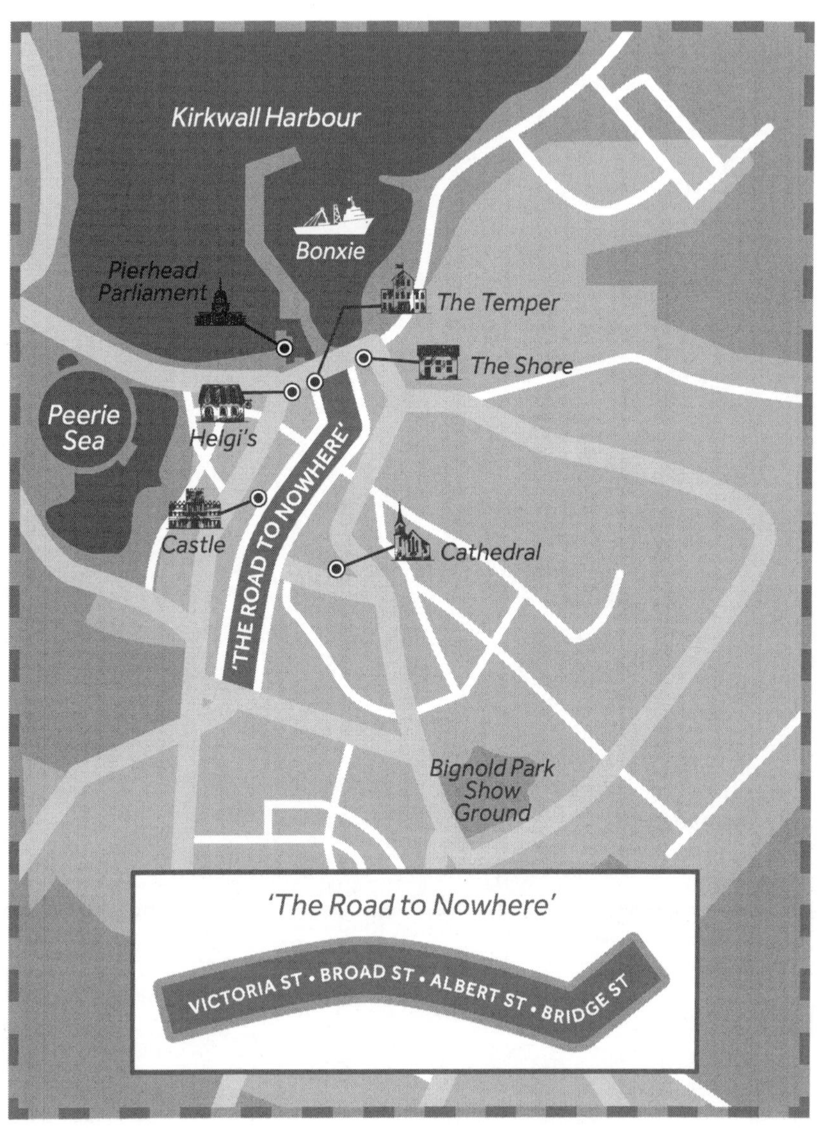

Kirkwall Harbour
Bonxie
Pierhead Parliament
The Temper
The Shore
Peerie Sea
Helgi's
'THE ROAD TO NOWHERE'
Castle
Cathedral
Bignold Park Show Ground
'The Road to Nowhere'
VICTORIA ST • BROAD ST • ALBERT ST • BRIDGE ST

# MY DIARY

# PRIVATE

## NOSY BASTARD, STAY OUT, OR I'LL KILL YOU.

Daddy, why are you reading my diary? You are not welcome here. So, STOP!

Seriously. YOU are the bastard. Did you know that reading private papers was a hanging offence here once? Pity they stopped all that, as they would have spilled your guts and stuffed your privates in your mouth first, if they also knew about the other stuff you've done to me.

Last Summer Night already. Won't be long before the storm monster emerges from the sea again to deadhead summer. Twisting the sky into deadly funnels of wind. Keep us cowering in our hidey-holes for another bloody winter, all eight months of it.

Remember when we first got here and Alex told us to stay inside during a storm – though I think he called it a **skuther o wind**. Thought he was joking until we saw the caravan flying through the air on Xmas Day. You said that it might be Santa's shed and told me to watch out for falling reindeer.

That was the last time I was touched by joy.

My life is pointless and painful and I don't want to do it anymore and **it's all your fault.**

I am going to kill myself at dawn. Throw myself off one of your Special Places. Where purple primroses lip the summer cliffs, and swarms of dumpy 'milk bottle birds' tumble in the updraughts. You know where.

Bringing me here was the worst birthday present a fourteen-year-old could have. All those bloody cakes and jellies you made for my **Welcome to Orkney Birthday** didn't make it any better. Daddy, the party's over. By the time you read this I'll be a messed-up trifle of skin and bones shovelled into a body bag: congealed raspberry jelly blood, mashed brain custard, and broken sponge-finger bones.

What is the point of our absurd existence in this awful place? Or, of life, anywhere?

I might as well be bloody dead, in bloody Orkney.

Good riddance, eh?

Bye Daddy. (No kisses)

---

# Last Summer Night

## Second Saturday in August

(Berkana Reversed. Algiz Reversed. Laguz Reversed)

*'I see a troubled family and a vulnerable child,*
*tempted to take the easy way out.'*

# 1. TIME TO GO

*Going to kill myself at dawn,*
*When the fabled green flash shoots out from the rising sun.*
*Its emerald rays striking me full in the face, so I shatter like crystal.*
*My skull, soft and delicate as a newborn,*
*My brittle bones, like twigs,*
*My heart, already broken.*

Verse, a thing here, back in the day. If you stay here long enough you just pick it up – the rhythm, the sing-song tone, the pretty words. Like we're all infected with Shakespeare. I caught it anyways, whatever it is. Made me treasure beautiful words, which I collect like rare butterflies. I wanted to put 'frangible' in my little death ditty, but I've found they scare people off, words like that.

I think some words may have magic powers, so I use them to cast spells. Perhaps on you. Sometimes I just blurt them out – can't help it. But, for now at least, I need to be careful with my choice of words, as you and I are only just getting acquainted.

I've tried chanting all my spelly words, but it didn't work – I'm still trapped here. So, I choose death over continued captivity. The cliffs my best-worst option. I want to be there in good time, waiting on the cliff-edge, looking north-east by east – where the sun will rise tomorrow; I looked it up.

In the dream world I hide in to help me get through each day, I'd choose something a little more romantic than plunging into the sea. Perhaps a firing squad on Kronos, on the other side of the galaxy. Then my hero, Captain James T Kirk, might rescue me. If I was a member of the Starship Enterprise crew and not a real live girl, I might not have to die.

*The Klingon officer in charge of the firing squad will be watching the horizon to take his cue from the rising sun. I probably won't hear him say 'fire', just feel the force of the ray-guns, set to kill, not stun. I'll fall backwards, my arms splayed back, like in that picture from the Spanish Civil War of the shot guy falling to the ground, though I won't have a rifle, or a ray-gun, of my own.*

*Perhaps James will materialise beside me to stop all this, before it is too late.*

Jim, where are you when I need you?

Anyway, I'll have the Original Series' theme playing on my phone when the sun blasts me at a million miles an hour. With the first tingle of heat I'm going to leap into space and shout 'Beam Me Up, Scotty' at the top of my voice. Just before I get transported out of here. It doesn't bother me that Jim never actually said that. Things like it, but never those exact words. My life a series of misquotations and lies – my death can be too.

If it's cloudy, I'll just turn my music on when it gets light enough and count to nineteen. One second for each year I have suffered. One-potato, two-potatoes, three…you know the rest. Then jump!

***I will be,***
***a trillion glints of stardust,***
***drifting down towards the sea.***

*Snuffed out,*
*one-by-one,*
*by the damp morning chill.*
*A distress maroon arching into the empty ocean.*

All those who should never be allowed out will be out tonight. That's what they say. I'm hoping *my* last summer night will be a distraction; got a few hours to kill before I meet up with my suicide buddy, Brian. Tell him about my cliff idea. Hope he'll be okay with the change of plan. First, I've got to get out of here.

I'm standing in my cosy little room for the last time. Over there, between the door and the window, on the right as you enter, a purple chest of drawers. Darker purple wardrobe opposite. Lavender, the smell of purple, fills the room.

Bed, in the far corner, where I spend most of my time. Black metal frame, black sheets, with white, black, and purple patterned duvet. Tangle of black lace shawls above the bedhead forming an arch, right to the ceiling. I am a supplicant at a Flamenco dancer's feet. She could stamp on me at any moment.

Between the bed and the wardrobe, lots of fairy pictures in junk frames and a shelf of cuddly toys. Yes, I'm a closet Fairy Goth, but no one knows, because no one EVER comes into my bedroom. Well, apart from *him* and now you.

We have shells on the walls of our tiny bathroom opposite my room – Groatie Buckies, little cowrie shells I get from my secret place. Driftwood too. An old red-and-white lifebuoy from the beach, a toilet seat. A puffer fish I bought on eBay hanging on the light string. It's like a prickly balloon made of skin.

Thomas calls our kitchen 'the galley'. Gas ring and oven all we need. We don't have a fridge, or freezer, or dishwasher – like we did before we came here. We're a bit out of step. Not quite 'off grid', but on the edge.

The front room has a nice view of Scapa Flow, but I don't go in there much as it makes me feel sad, seeing her standing still in the field like that, even though I put her there. Anyway, we don't really need it, as I keep my distance from him now and we don't have guests.

Just gone six p.m. Need to get out of here before I get another lecture about my medication. He keeps me drugged up, to stop my sadness overwhelming me. Told him that all I need is the music and my daydreams to help me escape this bloody awful place, this bloody awful life, but he tells me the doctor says I need to take the pills.

BUT YOU DON'T BELIEVE IN SCIENCE! I scream at him. Want to burst his sensitive eardrums, but he can mute me when he wants to. Thomas doesn't go along with what most people think. He enjoys being different. I've been his captive for too long, and tonight, I am breaking free.

In spite of his crazy beliefs, he still makes me take the pills. Told him he is being inconsistent, but he doesn't think much of logic either so there's no point in arguing with him. Says he is my father and has to look after me, even though I am now nineteen.

Tell him he's done a shit job so far, every chance I get.

'Going out?' Thomas says, as I leave my room.

Timed his words to catch me putting my coat on, when I'm not distracted by my music, or episodes of Star Trek playing in my ear. He can see me getting ready in the hallway behind him, even though he's facing the window. The light always on in the hall, so my movements reflected in the glass in front of him.

Seeing me in the distance gives him confidence to speak, which he lacks face-to-face. If he gets too close I regurgitate cruel words, like a Fulmar spitting foul-smelling oil to defend a nest. I have a violent allergic reaction to my father. He dragged me here into outer space and he knows I hate him for it, and the other things he's done.

I can see that his hair has gone on top and what's left is going grey. Is that normal at his age, or a sign that my campaign of hate has worked and I have tonsured him with my corrosive words? He's wearing an old Shetland fisherman's top which accentuates his pregnant stomach and makes him a sad caricature of a local. I can smell Old Spice, which probably means it has been a while since he had a bath.

'Yes,' I say, to the question he asked yonks ago now. My head full of other thoughts. I stumble the few steps towards the front door, tugging my jacket over my head – the bloody zip has jammed again.

Unusually for houses here, the front door faces the prevailing weather and is rarely used. Locked and bolted against the frequent gales. Thomas says I mustn't open this door. It is forbidden. Says that no good will come of it, that bad things will be let loose. I guess he means me.

Tonight, the first time I have tried this door, but he doesn't stop me. He can see I am determined to break his rule. It has always been my emergency exit for when I needed a quick escape, like tonight. But there are no gales tonight. The sky clear, the wind resting, the land annealed during the day by the acetylene sun now radiating back its heat, the flicker of its flame making a mirror of the sea. (*Oops, I'm getting all poetic again. I told you, it's in my nature. Can't help myself.*)

'Be careful,' he says.

*Be careful of what exactly? The bloody door? The chaos of the night ahead? Predatory men? My intended suicide? Be bloody careful how I kill myself? If only he knew what I have in store for him.*

My diary is the only way we communicate these days. All one way, of course, so I never get to know how he feels. Is the truth just too painful to discuss? Anyway, I consider it a form of abuse, reading my diary, so I fill it with filth. I know it troubles him. That is what I want.

At some point tonight, he will be in my room looking for clues. My Flamenco room is, like the rest of this place, packed full of clues. Any detective would soon be able to piece together the fragments of my worthless life, but Thomas will miss them all.

*'Just two sets of prints and DNA in the room. Male and younger female, and they are related,' says the younger of the two detectives I can see in my mind's eye standing in my empty bedroom.*

*'The girl's father?' says the man in charge. He is older, more composed.*

*'Aye, probably. His prints are mostly on the bed and the diary.'*

*The older man nods and looks at the bed.*

*'The bed. Anything in that?' the young detective says.*

*'Aye. It's a possibility. Could be, what with all this sex stuff in the diary. Exaggerated sexuality is a sign of abuse,' the older man says, glancing around the room.*

*'Yes, her diary's full of crazy stuff. Think it's all true?'*

*The older man shrugs his shoulders, then says, 'No signs of forced entry to the house, just the room, but no signs of a struggle.'*

*'Domestic then?' the young man says.*

*'Likely,' his boss says.*

*'Bloody odd room,' the young man says.*

*'Young girl. Bit of a loner. Trying to find herself. Nothing unusual about that. You should see my Lizzy's room,' the older man says, walking to the window to look out on the day. As if nature was his reference for detecting the truth of things.*

*'It's like a child's room, not a nineteen-year-old's. No pin-ups. Teenage girls have pin-ups.'*

*'Unusually tidy, too,' the older man says.*

*'Compulsive type, or has it been cleaned?' the younger detective says.*

*The older detective shrugs his shoulders, turns and hands a piece of paper to his colleague.*

# FUNERAL NOTICE

**The Funeral of the Late**

Miss Pandora Lewis

*Driven to suicide by this Bloody Island and her father.*

**AGED 19**

Scapa View (13), Kirkwall
will take place from
St Magnus Cathedral
to
St Olaf Cemetery
on

**THURSDAY 24TH OF AUGUST AT 10:00 A.M.**

*Friends please accept this intimation and invitation*

WILD FLOOERS ONLY PLEASE
DONATIONS TO ABUSED DAUGHTER SUPPORT
& PRISONERS OF ORKNEY SUPPORT
GRATEFULLY RECEIVED AT CHURCH DOOR

TOMMY MAC – FUNERAL DIRECTOR – KIRKWALL

*'For real, or a cry for help?' the younger man says.*

*The older man shrugs his shoulders, and says, 'Don't know, but the lassie is clearly not happy.'*

Ok, enough of that. Welcome to my world. I'm easily distracted. Don't let it distract you too.

Detectives, just like them, or any half-awake human being, would see my diary was a provocation.

*It's a cry for help, dummy!*

Any reaction would do. But this masochistic, turn the other cheek, passivity is doing my head in. A diary should be a colouring book of emotions, but I only have a charcoal pencil.

*'Fucked-up any ways,' the younger detective says, after flicking through the diary.*

*'Aye, not nice some of it. All this filth in a room full of fairies and cuddly toys. Like a split personality,' the older man says.*

*'Schizophrenic?'*

*'I'm no doctor. Could just be teenage hysteria.'*

*'That an illness then?' the younger detective says, looking at his phone at the same time.*

*'Should be. My lot were all bonkers between the ages of 14 and 20,' the older detective says.*

*'The internet. Porn. Kids see it online and think it's normal, all that stuff,' the younger man says, replying to a text as he talks.*

*'Aye. Maybes,' the older man says, looking at a page in the diary. 'She says here that she killed her mother.'*

*'Aye. Do we know anything about what happened to the mother?' the young detective says, looking up and taking more interest now.*

*'Not yet, but we need to find out.'*

'Show Night is always wild,' Thomas says, now standing behind me in the narrow hallway. His voice breaking the link to the imaginary detective drama taking place in my room. I ignore him and move towards the door. He watches me struggle because the front door hasn't been opened for a while. He is staring at me, as if I am written in ancient Norse graffiti and he can't decipher the runes.

Like most adolescents, right?

Wrong.

I am not like most anybody.

'Aye,' I say, humouring him. Just need a few more seconds to make my escape. But the key won't turn and I know he can sense the pressure building in my head, like it does just before I lose it and begin to scream. He doesn't know what to do then. My scream a freshly sharpened pencil that I thrust into his chest if he gets too close. Just in time, I see what I am doing wrong. I push the key in further, it turns and I squeeze through the narrowest of gaps and run down the long gravel track towards the road.

Sound of the gravel reminds me of the time I ran after the car. Crying and running at the same time and shouting as I ran. I can still hear the engine getting fainter and my screams getting louder and Thomas calling out my name. He was crying too. Sounds and smells the worst for bringing back memories. Smell of bacon frying is unbearable. We don't eat bacon, not now. How can a smell bring back so much pain?

As I let go of the door, I heard the ping of his email. I know that he will go to look straight away. It will mean he will be distracted for a while before he ransacks my room. Oh, he *will* search my room. Won't be able to stop himself. He is a serial abuser, taking advantage of his captive daughter. When he gets around to his sordid ritual, he'll be surprised to find my door locked.

Tonight, I need time to run and hide.

*Outside, surprisingly warm, dry and fragrant,*
*the air.*
*Citrus, mint, and rose musk.*
*Out of the corner of my eye,*
*I catch little flashes of colour and familiar shapes.*
*I want to come back as a meadow flower,*
*if I come back.*
*Or, bits of me to end up in one –*

*A few of my atoms in a Shepherds Purse,*
*or Blue Speedwell.*
*Me, an aerosol of summer.*
*Heaven scent.*

I stop and look around. I'm tempted to twirl, like I did when she was here, to take it all in. There are Cockalowries and Dog Flooers everywhere, and Dog Thistle, and Field Forget-Me-Nots fill the field opposite. Not been grazed for a while. Tishalago clumps no longer in flower, between humps of stinging nettles covered in butterflies. Found rarer things here too, on hunts with Thomas in past years: Field Pansy, Sun Spurge, Corn Spurrey, a Corn Marigold once.

Near the old barn, Rhubarb and Sweet Cicely growing together, as they used to be eaten together. The barn is where we store the past – sometimes I think I can hear it screaming to get out, but that might be the wind. It has a red corrugated roof, which Alex said was painted with red lead, but I think it's just paint. The roof sounds wonderful on a rainy day when solid sticks of rain play it like a drum.

The 'old barn' the closest of three structures that overlap down the slope. All technically our barns, but the others aren't of much use. Sometimes sheep shelter in them on a windy day. The furthest, twenty-five metres away, just the walls left. Alex says it's *unfanndoon*, which around here means in a 'state of imminent collapse'. It is how my life is. The one in-between has the whale ribs of the roof as well, but no covering. When he was a kid, Alex said he saw the roof blow off in the big storm of 1952 – a Tuesday he said it was – when 100,000 Orkney hens were blown away. That's pre-history, archaeology, even light-years, to me. On the other side of the universe with Jim and his crew.

The track to the road marked by a single thin phone line, sagging in the unusual heat between frail-looking poles. Joins us to Alex's house, closer to the road. Just one of the catenary (*love that word*) stitches in the patchwork quilt of our little community, that join people foolish enough to live here and bring the world to us. The wire so fragile and tenuous. It dances and hums in the wind.

Passing Alex's shitty grey house, devoid of life, like a family tomb. Has an upstairs, unlike ours, so more space, though he has lived on his own since his father died. Spends most of his time in his bedroom too and lets the past rest undisturbed in the other rooms. A mouldy corpse of his progenitors in each. Says there isn't any reason to keep the house looking nice. Winter storms suck the life out of everything, even paint.

Three disused tractors in the yard. People used to trundle them off cliffs into the sea, but that's not allowed now. He's hoping some rich visitor will buy them for their gardens. His dad had an old fishing boat in his field for years until some banker guy from Kent took a shine to it and took it home with him. Cost him thousands, but Alex said his dad was happy enough, just amazed at the value of worthless things to folk down there.

Alex's land is an open-air museum, like the rest of this bloody island. Only reason people come here is to wallow in the past. What's the point of clearing it up? Plenty of room. Stuff has been left lying around here for so long Orkney has become a famous dump (*I want to call it a* secular reliquary *but think it may still be too soon to burden you with my vocabulary*).

Thomas doesn't have any friends, so the email he got as I made my escape will be 'work', if you can seriously call it that. Probably an order for one of his 'sacred stones'. His story is, that the reason so many ancient people came to live here in Orkney – they are now saying it was the centre of civilisation in the British Isles in Neolithic times – well, he says they came here because this is where alchemists could find the stone that turned base metals into gold. Don't get me started on how bloody stupid that is, but there are enough mugs out there who want to believe this shit that they actually buy bits of rock from him, online. Yes, he sends them bits of Stromness Granite, otherwise used for building roads, and they send him twenty pounds, plus postage and packing and he charges another ten pounds for that.

Incredible, bloody incredible.

*Fuckwits! If he could turn lead into gold why the fuck would he be selling stones online?*

Evidently, the roads here should be paved with gold.

Looking back down the slope, beyond Alex's mausoleum, our house insignificant in the landscape. My whole world is nothing. Dwarfed by the backdrop of Scapa Flow and mountainous Hoy, with a dragon's breath of flame flaring from the Flotta oil terminal, burning off unwanted gas.

Close to the road now. Old lorry grunts and grinds up the slope, disturbing a flock of herring gulls which lift, as one, in the field nearest to me, dragging themselves reluctantly into the still air. Solitary Glaucous Gull follows them. That's more like me, but I haven't seen one here before. You normally see them in Kirkwall, down by the Peedie Sea.

*Twelve hours to go, or so,*
*Don't really know.*
*No proper night now, just the simmer dim,*
*The night-long twilight.*
*The Orkney summer glow.*

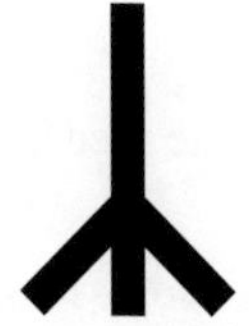

(Algiz Reversed)

*'Is someone deceiving you, or are you misleading yourself?'*

*Why do you want to die?* Brian wrote in his first email. I liked his directness. He said he preferred to write because he had a squeaky voice, like David Beckham. That people laughed at him and thought he was stupid, that he didn't have a brain. Told him I understood and prefer to write too; thought that was a connection.

Writing helps me filter my thoughts and use my best, most powerful, words.

This little eccentricity, his interest in writing, is why I chose Brian. Oh, and his cute photo. Looked younger than me, but he said he was a little older. Anyway, tonight, I get to meet my suicide buddy for the first time. Squeaky-voiced Brian who, like me, is desperate enough to reach out for someone to die with. If his voice is *really* squeaky, I may laugh.

Perhaps I chose Brian because we could keep our distance until the end.

*I don't have anything to live for,* I wrote, when he pushed me.

*Me neither.*

*I just can't bear the pain of existence anymore, of waking and realising I have to live through another excruciating day.*

*Yes, I know.*

*I don't want to be so unhappy and alone.*

*You've got me now,* he wrote. I read this email several times. It felt reassuring, having him. Better than being alone.

He wrote that he was looking for someone to share death together *with helium.*

*Helium?* I tapped out on the Death Buddy Forum.

*Yes, helium.*

*I thought it just made your voice go squeaky,* I wrote, and pressed Send before I remembered what he had told me about his voice.

*Like me?*

*Sorry, didn't think. I wasn't trying to be funny.*

*At first. But then you die.*

*So, we'll both die with squeaky voices,* I wrote, and he went offline. Maybe he thought I was making fun of him after all.

I read up about it, after the first email exchange. Inert gas suicides with helium and suicide bags were popular once, though nitrogen seems to be the way these days.

*Why not do it then?* I wrote, the next time he got in touch, a few days later. *Just do it, stick a bag over your head, breathe some helium and die.*

*I want company.*

I remember thinking, What the fuck? Lonely bastard wants to die because he has no friends and then wants someone to die with. What is that all about? But I know what he means – he doesn't want to be alone at the end.

But aren't we all alone at the end?

He's coming up here from Leeds. The forum's a bit like a dating site, you can choose the most compatible 'buddy'. Wanted someone my age who would be happy to travel. Want to die here, close to Thomas. For him to see my wrecked body, to experience the pain at close hand, like I did.

Meeting at the *noon of the night*, by the Mercat Cross, in front of St Magnus Cathedral. If Kirkwall was an earthquake the market cross would be its epicentre. Time and place my idea. I am drawn to the dark side and the cathedral is a gothic masterpiece that draws you in, like a lodestone, tugging at life. They call it the Light of the North, but it is pitch dark to me. Like the Death Star.

Gone off the idea of helium, but don't want a normal suicide, with pills or rope, and it seems selfish to cause a head-on crash and take others with me, though I've thought about it, even twitched the wheel once or twice towards on-coming lorries, but it seems a selfish way to go. Would have thrown myself in front of a fast-moving train but there are no bloody trains in Orkney. Probably a precaution. The laird knows the track would be littered with corpses after a harsh winter storm. Don't want a normal suicide, but helium just seems weird. Don't want to be found with my head in a plastic bag.

## (Raidho Reversed)

*'It's not the best time to travel, though you may need to.'*

BTS playing in my head as the bus glides towards Kirkwall through the wilderness, between stone walls as straight as steel track. Field Horsetail, Northern Dead Nettle and Creeping Buttercups flicker by. Too windy for trees up here, or any plant higher than the dykes. Grass the colour of mint grazed by glistening cattle still sweating from the day's unusual heat.

Flutterbys everywhere with trembling white wings. A Hooded Crow, like a monk, on a farm gate. Cotton grass and big white blooms of wild Angelica, like Cauliflowers on Rhubarb stalks, beside a stream cutting down a narrow crease in a field. Farmyard with stacked containers and enormous tyre-covered fenders, each the size of a lorry, to protect the tankers in the Flow.

School bus route signs flash by – Be Careful When The Bus Stops. Tell us to Be Prepared. Like Boy Scouts. Not that I ever went to school much, here anyway. Been better if Thomas hadn't decided to home school me, though the visits from the Council's Education Services were hysterical. Thomas explaining his views on science: 'Of course, I teach her science. I also gave her a copy of the Bible to read, but neither religion makes any sense to me.'

I might have known more people if I had gone to school, but I would have learnt less about the birds and the bees and flooers and the trees. In spite of the lies he told the school inspectors, he only really taught me how to read, so 'you can teach yourself about the world'. But every day was a nature walk, until we stopped talking, but my head still crammed full of those early days. Maybe that is why I love words so much – in books, I have found a little peace. For a while, poetry excited me and gave me hope.

*Orkney is the heart of a depression,*
*most of the year.*
*Month after month, week after week.*
*Depression at the heart of Orkney,*
*for people like me.*
*Cyclonic killer of poultry and the weak,*
*blowing them helplessly*
*into the tempestuous sea.*

I doubt if I would have survived this long without the spring and summer bloom. Sometimes, I pretend to be a fly, or a Fairy Flax, because I adore the white flowers on their wiry stems, and the name. They say that if a little girl eats it, she will never grow up; and I did eat it once, just to see.

Bus stops suddenly opposite a sheep track. Two cars and an open-topped orange lorry block the road ahead of us. The main road to Kirkwall, but no one seems to care, and the traffic just waits patiently for the inevitable delay. Locals realise what is going on. Who knows what the tourists think? Anyway, what's the rush?

The highwaymen aren't interested in us. They swarm around a lonely house. Mostly my age, in jeans and t-shirts – one girl in blue overalls. All messed-up, covered in oil and paint.

We watch in silence as a young man is dragged across the road and stripped. Hands tied behind his back, body smeared with something black and sticky and covered in feathers, before being lifted onto the lorry. A young girl, two rows in front of me, films it all on her phone as if it was news. She'll probably upload it to the interworld next.

*Fucking stupid existence, personal isolation and infinite virtual connectivity.*

Although the dude at the centre of all this is now in a mess and struggling, a couple standing at the front door, who appear to be his parents, don't seem too bothered. Alice, who you'll meet later, is taking photographs with her phone before she too jumps on the lorry and it heads off into town, leading a long procession of traffic.

Another bloody Blackening. Stone Age stuff. Anticipating the ordeal of marriage, or something daft like that. What is it that people see in marriage anyway?

The cavalcade of vehicles splits as we slide down the slope into Kirkwall and alternative routes beckon on either side of the road, like hawkers plying for trade. We take a round-about route, passing The Balfour, the brand-new curlicue (yes) of a hospital building, built by an architect who must have lost his mind, or his straight edge. Or, perhaps he just had a sense of humour.

Kirkwall unusually welcoming and spacious in the sunlight. Not like cloudy days, or when the sea fret slips in off the water. Dissolves in the cold sea fog. Shrinks and smells of wet cardboard in the rain.

Get off the bus at the Travel Centre and walk to the harbour. If the Mercat Cross is the epicentre of Kirkwall, the harbour is its heart. Drawn here every time I come into town. I don't want to miss anything tonight.

It is always reassuring to see that my fleet is in.

*The Golden West*, *Seabreeze*, *Libby J*, and my favourite old-fishing-boaty, *Michael J* - K390 – all wooden and curved. *Michael J* looks like it was bent into shape by craftsmen. Black, with a thistle emblem on the bow and a tiny cabin on the starboard side. Behind *Michael J*, industrial-looking *Kraken*, factory-made by robots. Unfair on the fish, or scallops or mermaids, whatever it is they hunt – don't have a chance when *Kraken* throbs towards them at a jaunty angle, on a wobbly sea.

The orange and blue lifeboat opposite, facing the tiny lighthouse at the end of the pier – pointing out to sea, ready for a quick get-away. Saving lives. The lighthouse has piles of creels at its base, which makes it look as if the locals have built a bonfire to burn witches later.

*Three Boys*, K905, a scallop boat, alongside the Corn Slip. They dive for the scallops rather than drag them, or suck them, up from the seabed. Told that three diver-caught scallops can cost twenty-eight pounds as a starter in a smart Mayfair restaurant. Surely that can't be true? That much money could feed us for a week.

Crew of the *Three Boys* filling a white van with their catch. Shells crunch together each time a heavy white mesh sack is moved.

*The boat is bright and colourful;*
*recently painted in poster paint by a child.*
*Deep blue hull and black decks:*
*Tropical sea at sunset and the depths of the ocean.*
*Splashed with orange:*
*Calor Gas bottle on the cabin top;*
*solitary orange fender – just one, the rest are white;*
*waterproof trousers worn by one of the men unloading the boat.*
*Two drysuits, like discarded seal skins, draped over the railings,*
*one black, the other brown.*
*Herring gulls, hopping up and down the slip, hoping for food;*
*they call them White-Maas here.*

From the Corn Slip I can see into the Auld Men's Hut, on the West Pier, where the Pierhead Parliament sits. Looks like they are in session.

(Ansuz)

*'The wisdom of casually spoken words.'*

'Okay, it's time to make a start,' Walli says, calling the Parliament to order.

Five old men sitting around a table covered with books, magazines, and cups. Exclusively men's books: *Nomad, Red Notice, Strike Back*, with authors Ryan and Jo Nesbo. Just one book of photos – The Orkney Islands. Brown tablecloth poking through the gaps, like muddy lakes on the tundra. All casually dressed, wearing jackets, some of them well-worn, but tidy, as if they have made an effort. Mostly clean-shaven, with neat grey haircuts and polished shoes. Working men, not pen-pushers. No longer in their prime.

Windows on three sides of a space no bigger than a stand-alone garage, with a door nearest Harbour Street. Dark blue window frames beginning to rot and in a few places tobacco splinters of wood are visible where the paint has flaked away. 1960s tiled fireplace with a wooden fire grate surround, two electric fires sitting side-by-side, and a radio on the mantelpiece beside a maidenhair fern in a terracotta pot. Twelve chairs in all, sitting on a red vinyl floor.

Fridge with a kettle, cups and milk, in the corner of the room and a plate of biscuits. White clock, that looks a little like an iceberg, in the middle of a flaky duck-blue wall above the fireplace. On the mantel, beneath the clock, picture of a group of men standing on the pier taken a long time ago. Faint smell of damp and diesel fuel. Binoculars standing on end, at the ready, on a corner table as if they have just been put down by a look-out on duty on the bridge of a ship.

Walli notices Panda, sitting on the Corn Slip.

'Time we started, isn't it?' Walli says, tidying some of the books in front of him into small piles.

'It's just seven,' Jock says, looking at his watch. He has to hold it close to his face to see it clearly.

'I didn't know we had a subject for tonight,' Ray says, following Walli's gaze.

'The girl in black is out and about,' Ray says, and all the men look towards the Corn Slip. They are still, staring out of the window at the same time. A fleeting tableau of Orkney life, for old men anyway.

'Aye. Everyone will be out tonight. They'll soon be spilling out of the doors into the road from Skippers,' Tommy says, looking beyond the girl to where Bridge Street and Harbour Street meet, and Kirkwall's two busiest pubs stand side-by-side.

'It's a house of sin,' Alec says.

'Aye. Busy though. What does it say about the young these days?' Jock says.

'More money than sense, if you ask me. There'll be trouble later,' Ray says, turning and walking to the far side of the room, as if he wants to distance himself from the view.

'Well, our subject for tonight is, 'The Harbour o'Owld',' Walli says.

'But it's not what I want to talk about. I think we should talk about the drink,' Alec says.

'The drink?' Tommy says, shaking his head.

'Aye, on a night like the night, don't you think it's time to start a new temperance society?' Alec says, pulling up a chair and sitting down purposefully, resting his gnarled hand on a copy of National Geographic, all about Vikings.

'Folk say we already have one too many dry hotels in town,' Tommy says.

'Young folk just don't know how lucky they are, just being able to eat something, or have a drink when they want,' Ray says, pacing on the spot, behind Tommy.

'Aye, half of them don't know they was born,' Jock says.

'Whit does that mean, Jock?' Walli says, from the other end of the table.

'What?'

'Whit does it mean to say they don't know they was born?' Walli says again.

'It means life has been too easy. Mind what it was like as a lad?' Jock says.

'Aye, just. I do just,' Alec says, sliding another magazine under his hand.

'Food was scarce. Just peat to warm the house. Both me brothers died before they was five,' Tommy says.

'Doctors cost money than,' Ray says, sniffing the diesel in the air as if it was a drug.

'Aye.'

'It's coming back, teetotalling. I guess that not everyone needs drink to be happy,' Walli says.

'Look, whit about the drink?' Alec says.

'Yon wee lassie looks so sad,' Walli says, looking around again to see Panda on the Corn Slip, but she has gone.

'Aye. The thing is, the more folk have the easier it is to be sad. Everywan feels hard done by if they haven't got the latest car,' Jock says, noticing Alex's hand and flexing his own fingers as if to make sure they still work.

'Or phone.'

'Aye. Everyone has too much these days. When I was a kid I didn't realise I was hard done by, it was just normal,' Jock says.

'We was all hard done by,' Tommy says.

'Was a privilege to have shoes,' Ray says, clearly thinking back and remembering.

'We was just living our lives,' Tommy says.

'But what about the drink? Is it just general chit-chat that's the subject the night then?' Alec says, now resting his hand on his lap.

'General who? Never heard of him,' Tommy says.

'Very funny.'

'No, sorry, Alec. Let's talk about the drink than,' Walli says, chuckling to himself.

'Okay. Let's discuss the drink. For a start, why is no drink allowed in here? We have to watch the young folk drinking and we're no allowed?' Tommy says.

## (Fehu)

*'This means wealth, status, position.'*

Marina and Bobby Gunn enter Helgi's and go straight to the window table, to the left of the door, which they booked earlier. They are followed in by Rick and Lynette who they met on the first day of the cruise, soon after joining the ship in Invergordon. They were delighted to find out that they were all from Kansas.

'I know we're missing the lobster on board tonight, but we thought it would be nice to get a little local colour,' Marina says to the other couple as they sit down.

'Still in sight of home. I can see our cabin from here,' Rick says, looking out of Helgi's window at the large white cruise ship, the *Highlander*, moored just five hundred metres away on North Pier.

'Rick, I can see our cabin,' Lynette says. 'We left the lights on.'

'Don't worry, they have generators,' Rick says.

'Can't see any smoke,' Bobby says.

'You know we booked a starboard cabin because we were told that ships are moored with their left sides to the quay and that is why left on a ship is called Port,' Rick says.

They all look and laugh, because the ship is moored right side to.

'I wanted our balcony to always be looking at the sea,' Rick says. 'Now we've got Kirkwall to look at tonight.'

'You've got a good view though, from up there. Us guys in the cheap seats are looking out on a container,' Bobby says.

'I don't think there are any cheap seats,' Lynette says.

'That's true. Anyway, I want some local grub. What is there?' Bobby says, picking up the menu.

'Well, I'm up for an adventure. Something different. Have they got haggis?' Rick says.

'No, but you'll feel right at home. They have ribs.'

(Ehwaz Reversed. Gebo. Wunjo Reversed)

*'You will find help and support but there will be problems and unhappiness ahead in trying to satisfy your craving for change.'*

# 2. AN UNLIKELY VIKING

Walk around the harbour every time I come into Kirkwall. Find it reassuring. Pass a Muslim family praying behind the Orkney Ferry offices. Now, that's a first. Makes me think though, that my routine may be a prayer of my own. Ignore them and walk behind the crane sheds to the pier, past my old boaty friends.

Cars screech round the corner by the entrance to the marina. Heard revving engines approaching, but it was the tyre skid that got my attention. Two of the cars are black: Ford Fiesta and a Renault Clio. Sinister. The other car is blue and noisier – a VW Polo GT Sport. Usually this type you get on the pier. Saw an Audi once. Need two doors and low-profile tyres to qualify for pier cruising. Kirkwall's sad answer to *American Graffiti*.

Boys have mastered the art of racing in slow motion. More about being seen than getting anywhere – *because there is nowhere to go* – and clearly, shrieking tyres maketh men. Perhaps, in the dead of night, they race like James Dean in *Rebel Without A Cause*, playing the Chicken Game on the pier and this is just the start of the night's excitement. Sorry, forgot, this is Kirkwall, so probably not.

Recognise the drivers and their friends. Don't know them. They all laugh when they see me and start talking. Know what they'll be saying about me in the Fiesta.

*'Look out, the crazy Goth is out,' the driver who just looked at me, is probably saying.*

*'Fuck Goff! Get it?' the young boy in the back, squeezed between two girls, says. He laughs at his own joke, with a snort that sounds like a fart.*

*'Not if she was the last one on earth,' the boy with the moustache, in the front passenger seat, says.*

*As they speak the cars seem to travel in slo-mo, their words stretching to breaking point.*

*'What do you mean "one"?' the nearside rear girl says.*

*'Girl, then. Not even if she was the last girl on Earth,' front passenger seat boy says.*

*'That would mean the end of humanity,' driver says. He is shaking his head and smiling, as if he is anticipating a reaction.*

*'Don't care. Still wouldn't.'*

*'What?' offside rear girl says.*

*'If he didn't do her, there'd be no more people on Earth,' middle rear boy says.*

*'What the fuck are you talking about?' nearside rear girl says, leaning forward in her seat and speaking louder to make sure they can hear in the font of the car. Her seat belt squashing her breasts, enhancing her cleavage.*

*'If they were the last people on Earth. Like Adam and Eve,' middle rear boy says.*

*'They were the first people,' driver says.*

*'Yes, but you know what I mean,' middle rear boy says.*

*'No. I don't. I never know what you mean,' nearside rear girl says, sitting back and staring at the boy beside her. They look similar, perhaps related.*

*'Anyway, she probably thinks the same about you,' offside rear girl says.*

*'Splash. I call her Splash,' front passenger boy says.*

*'Why?' nearside rear girl says.*

*'Because someone spilt a glass of red wine o'er her face,' front passenger boy says.*

*'Don't be so cruel, that's a birthmark,' nearside rear girl says.*

*'My dad says it's where the devil licked her,' front passenger boy says, looking up at me as if I am dangerous.*

*'What?' offside rear girl says.*

*'Initiation ceremony. My dad says to stay away from her. Says she's cursed. Don't let anyone lick your face like that, or you'll end up like her,' front passenger boy says, looking straight at me. I could have read his lips, if I wasn't making all this up, like the crazy bitch that I am.*

*'Fuck off. Your dad's bonkers,' nearside rear girl says.*

*'Aye,' offside rear girl says.*

*'Believe me, no Devil is going to lick me, anywhere,' nearside rear girl says, as the car begins to turn and they all concentrate on the driver and the manoeuvre.*

As all this self-inflicted nonsense goes on in my head, Ford executes a sharp one-eighty and slides alongside another Polo, parked and waiting. Renault glides up the other side to make an automobile sandwich – no one in the middle car can now open their doors. Polo GT Sport slides around the island of stationary cars and races off down North Pier. New arrivals rev their engines a few times then turn them off. Comparing lengths of their dicks.

Give them a wide berth. In spite of all the noise and unwanted attention, I'm enjoying my walk. Don't have to start hiding yet, but the clock is ticking. Thomas will take a while to break into my room and find my funeral notice in my diary. Locked door may even stop him this time and the next time he goes in there may be with the police, investigating a crime. Searching my room and reading my diary, just like I imagined it to be.

Haven't made it easy for him. Locked my windows, so he can't climb in that way, but it will be the first thing he'll check – he says he doesn't value logic but still has an accountant's mind. Could climb through the narrow loft space and down through the ceiling hatch in my room, but that will be difficult and messy – loads of mouse droppings up there. Not sure he has that much patience. Think he will break the door, or a window, to get in. Probably the door. But how long will he agonise over doing it?

Sliding into shadow, between some of the pier buildings, I feel like a woodlouse crawling into a crack, though there are more exotic creepy-crawlies around here. Cargo of Italian masonry unloaded here a hundred and fifty years ago. Some venomous yellow-tailed scorpions were stowing-away and decided they liked it here. Must have been the one nice day of the year, like today. They were conned, like Thomas, into thinking it was a northern paradise, but by the time the weather changed – probably the next day – their ship had sailed.

Only find them on south-facing walls. Hide away during the day and come out at night. Can see them more easily as they fluoresce turquoise in UV light. Thomas took me down to see them during our nature studies period. Go when they are growing and you can find their discarded carapaces. Little buggers though, less than an inch long. Maybe bigger down south.

Tanker berth occupied by exotic white and gold ship. First thought – it's the boat from the first *Mamma Mia* film, which I love – just *so* Bollywood. Sailor wearing loose-fitting white pyjamas, with a cutlass, standing at the end of the gangplank, with an absurdly long Danish flag dipping into the water at the stern. No breeze, so the flag is soaking-up seawater like a wick in an oil lamp. *The Orcadian* said something about the Danish Royal Yacht being due in, on its way to the Faroes to take royalty on their holidays.

*Dowager yacht.*
*Bollarded with a bright white rope, which looks new.*
*Skinny curved bow with a*
*Narwhal tusk bowsprit pointing the way ahead,*

*encrusted with gold.*
*The hull, white, and the infrastructure the colour*
*of cream on a pint of Orkney milk,*
*straight from the cow.*
*No blues, or oranges here.*
*It is out of place;*
*A Mediterranean ship lost in Ultima Thule,*
*where, by the natural law of the rainbow,*
*boats should be more colourful.*

'Impignoration,' I say out loud, even though I am on my own.

On North Pier, opposite the ice plant, another 'royal yacht', no more than twenty metres away. *The Highlander.* Posh cruise ship that regularly pops in here on its trips into the wilderness. Port of registration hints at her class – Nassau, it says on her stern. Just above the words there are men and women in fine clothes drinking champagne, looking down on me as if I am a strangely dressed piccaninny (*yes*) not expected here.

Staff serving the drinks above me are liveried, like in Georgian England, but without the extravagant wigs. Old woman is staring down at me. Thin, grey hair, black evening dress, glass of champagne in hand. Shakes her head, turns around and walks away from the starboard handrail, overlooking the quay, and me, towards a small group near the stern.

I know what they'll be saying about me.

*'What were you expecting? Kilts?' her husband might have said, if he had any humour, as she gets closer to them.*

*She makes an exaggerated shudder with her shoulders.*

*'I don't know anymore. Actually, kilts would have been nice. More in keeping with what they had in the brochure and not whatever that is on the quay.'*

*'It's a girl,' her husband says, raising his eyebrows and emptying his glass in one coordinated move, as if it helped him swallow.*

*'It is not a girl. It's an aberration. The world has gone mad. What is wrong with dressing and looking like a woman?' she says, signalling to a waiter that her husband's glass is empty.*

*The other man in the group retraces her steps to see what she is talking about.*

*I wave at him.*

*'I don't think being a woman is quite the same anymore. Haven't you heard that gender is fluid these days. If you want to be a man you just have to declare yourself a man,' her husband says.*

*'If I do that, won't that make you a queer?'*

*'I think she's a Goth,' the man returning to the group says, as he gets close. He is smiling because others are now going to look over the side to see me, the local curiosity.*

*'Didn't they get rid of the Romans?' her husband says.*

*'Post-punk, or something like that. Siouxie and the Banshees and all that,' the other man says.*

*'Oh, my God. Give me another drink. I want to retreat into the past. Where I feel at home,' she says, reaching to exchange her glass for a full one now that the waiter has appeared.*

*'They have a lot of past here,' her husband says.*

*'Yes, but I'm thinking twentieth century, not the Stone Age.'*

*'I think it's mostly Neolithic they're famous for,' her husband says.*

*'Isn't that the same thing?' the other man says.*

*There are now three people looking at me. I wave again, and one of the men waves back.*

*'So, life only began with the invention of the permanent hairdo?' her husband says.*

*'It only began in the Fifties,' she says.*

*'Ah, when you were a delightful debutante,' her husband says, raising his eyebrows again, but this time hoping to stir some long-ago memory in her.*

*'When everything was nicer,' she says, ignoring the cue for intimacy.*

*'That's the problem with old age. The shock of the new,' the other man says.*

*'I wore my mother's wonderful Fortuny dress. No one has ever made a finer dress than him and his secret went to his grave. No one will ever make one like it again,' she says, turning her lower body as if swishing her doubly imaginary dress.*

*'I guess you won't be going ashore here then?' her husband says.*

*'No. Not here. I'm going to save my shore excursions for somewhere more Scottish,' she says.*

*'Next stop is Lerwick,' the other man says. Distracted by a nearby conversation he turns his head slightly to better hear what is being said.*

*'Yes. Isn't that where they have that nice detective?' she says.*

*'And all those murders,' the other man says, speaking and listening at the same time.*

*'It is made up, you know,' her husband says.*

*'What? The murders, or Scotland?' the other man says.*

They started something. Others come over to stare, so I walk back towards town, along the eastern berths full of bigger fishing boats, their hulls at my height as we've just passed high tide. Row of masts in front of me poking up like saplings, some decorated with wicker baskets, others with black cones and one with Xmas lights. Most of the boats I recognise as I pass them. *Albicore* is a regular. Then a work boat that I don't know with an open deck full of cargo including white and blue bags, marked '1000kg Bag,' that have become the temporary roost for a marauding party of 'baakies' – great black-backed gulls.

Getting closer, the gulls squawk loudly and jump from bag to bag, as if engaged in some sort of argument with the sky, perhaps because of the lack of wind. Huge and full of menace, their yellow bills blotched with blood as if they have been picking at a corpse. Could be picking at my corpse the morrow, if they head over to Hoy the night. Huge wings flapping, like malevolent angels, to create a draught. Maybe seeing a dead girl walking spooked them.

## (Gebo)

*'Partnership and gift.'*

Big blue trawler tucked into the elbow of the pier, where it slants west.

*Bonxie*, from Thurso, somehow managed to squeeze into a prime berth. Viking longship tied alongside. Really. The longship's mast lying back along the hull – red and white sails wrapped around a wooden pole. Golden dragon's head atop the prow.

So unexpected, I wonder if this is just another daydream.

Turn off music for a reality check. Chattering kittiwakes free-wheeling above my head on the look-out for food. Splattering the pavement with shit – I'm walking on a Jackson Pollock painting. Sticky, like bubble gum.

Anomalies attract, like kindred spirits. They really do. Often wondered if that is why Thomas gets so many people taking his stupid Flat Earth Tours, or why people stare at me. Stop to watch as four men appear on the trawler's deck and start to load things on the longship.

The men smile at me and then look up together. My eyes follow theirs and I realise that someone is watching me.

'Hello.' A thin, bearded man – though I'm tempted to call him a boy – probably just a little older than me, leans out of the window where they steer the trawler. Men on the deck laughing.

'Hello,' I say and look away.

'Want a tour?' he says.

'Be careful, darling, he'll break your heart,' the older of the men on deck shouts. Don't recognise the accent. I know it isn't from here. They seem to be clearing things away, ready for sea. Untangling the ropes, laying them on the rolled-up sail.

Distracted by the heavy rock from the blackening lorry behind me on Harbour Street. It stops briefly by the bus stop before heading towards us along the pier, following the trail of youth, where it pirouettes a couple of times, then glides around the few islands of parked cars, like a dancer on ice, before heading off again into town. Wedding-train of people following in peeping cars.

Look back at the man-boy but he's gone. Can't help feeling disappointed.

*Can you break a broken heart? That would be a good K-pop title.*

Magically, he appears from the other side of the trawler. 'I'm here,' he says, skipping across the deck onto the pier and walks towards me, smiling, like a long-lost friend. His perfect teeth too big for his delicate lips – hardly seems space for words to escape.

He is wearing a grey t-shirt with four coconuts on it, three standing upright and one lying on its side, and worn blue jeans. Twisted leather bracelet on his left wrist is frayed. Crystal pendant around his neck on a leather strop.

'I'm Sigurd,' he says.

'Like the ferry,' I say, turning and pointing towards the ferry with the same name on the other side of the quay.

He looks then strokes his thin beard, as if he can already see I am a puzzle, and the reassuring touch of his man-fur helps him think.

'Panda,' I say after a suitable pause. He seems eager, so I respond with demurity (*Is that still a word? If it isn't, it should be*) turning my head to the side to better hide my blemish.

'I thought Pandas were extinct in the wild,' he says, looking around as if to say that Orkney is wild, which, of course, it is.

'Pandora,' I say.

Pandora means all-gift. Apparently, her curiosity led her to open a mysterious box, thereby releasing madness into the world and leaving hope. The story is different each time I look it up. You can interpret it any way you like. She was told never to open the box – Thomas told me never to open the front door to our house. Is that the same thing?

*She was the first mortal woman. Ironic really.*

Blue and white ferry is manoeuvring in Kirkwall Bay, behind Sigurd's head. Superstructure slowly drifting across the horizon. It sounds its horn – three blasts. The noise echoing around us.

'It's going backwards,' Sigurd says, turning towards the sound that still clings to the dry air.

I watch his body swivel smoothly on well-oiled hips. His waist, thin and elastic, springing him back to look at me. Is he eager to re-join my gaze? The curious pendant bouncing off his chest changes colour as he turns.

'That ferry. Three blasts on the foghorn like that means "I am operating astern propulsion",' he says.

'I know. I'm a Master Mariner,' I say.

He laughs. 'Really?'

'You a Viking then?' I say, looking back at the longship behind him. If he is, he is an unlikely Viking, the runt of the litter. Eyes like Paul Hollywood's from *Bake Off* – mesmeric and blue and hard to disengage from, but I try not to stare.

'Ganache,' I say.

'What?'

I shake my head.

'Doesn't everyone here have Norse blood?' Sigurd says.

He looks me up and down in a nice way. Nothing lascivious (*yes*), just questioning, as if he is trying to size me up.

Too many ferry-loupers,' I say.

He looks puzzled.

'Incomers. Anyway, do I look like I come from here?'

He looks me up and down again. This time trying to see beneath my clothes with the X-ray eyes that all men have. Then he shrugs.

'Feeling trapped here anyway, trying to make a point,' he says.

'Got life-wrecked here and couldn't escape.'

'What about the ferry?'

Smile and nod.

'A survivor,' he says, after a few moments' reflection. As if that is an adequate label for me. He is cocky but charming. So, I won't try too hard to hide that I like him. Few people on my wonky wavelength, particularly men.

'I'm from Halkirk, on the edge of the Flow country – Scotland's first planned village,' he says.

I laugh out loud. 'Sounds crap.'

'A bit crap, but it's home.'

Sigurd looks back at the longship being prepared below us and my mind slips a gear.

'Limerence,' I say, not intending to, so it comes as a surprise to both of us.

'What does it mean?'

'I don't know,' I say, though I do really. Probably think I said it deliberately, but I didn't.

'Are you a fisherman?' I say, to move us on, though he doesn't look like one.

'No, I'm at university. My uncle's boat, and my dad is a farmer. Family gathering going on and I've been dragged along. In fact, every man-child in my extended family is here. That's why we have all the cars,' he says, looking towards an orderly row of newish 4x4s, parked opposite on the pier.

'What are you reading? Isn't that what they say on University Challenge?' I ask.

'You watch University Challenge?'

'TV and old films is all there is in the winter. If I was at uni, I'd study classic movies, or *Star Trek*. Can you study that?'

'These days, who knows?'

'I think *Star Trek*, the Original Series, is the greatest work of drama ever. Better than Shakespeare.'

'Really? Well, you can study most things these days, but not where I am.'

Don't say anything. Just wait for him to tell me.

'Edinburgh,' he says, proudly.

'And you're not studying *Star Trek*?'

'Philosophy.'

'I'm not impressed,' I say, but I am really. I don't know anyone at uni. I think my friend Martin went but we don't talk about it.

'Okay,' he says, more amused than annoyed by my comments.

'So, what's all this about then?' I say, raising my arms in exasperation at life.

He shakes his head. He doesn't understand. Probably means he's happy with his lot.

'This fucking shitty existence we all have to endure,' I say.

'Ah. Well, big subject that. I think the jury's still out.'

He seems to be thinking, trying to remember all the stuff he's been taught. Not expecting to share a discourse on the meaning of life with me.

'So, what brings a philosopher to Ultima Thule?'

He looks puzzled again, as if I am speaking in a language he doesn't quite understand.

'What the Greeks and Romans called the furthest north place on any map,' I say.

*He doesn't seem to know much.*

'My uncle said they needed muscle power.'

His thin arms don't look like they have much power. The muscles on his right arm slightly more pronounced. *Too much wanking*, I think, and laugh to myself as I look back at the longship.

'How about a drink?' he says. 'After I show you around *Dreki*, our dragon ship.'

'Do you race it?' I say, still smiling to myself.

'Her.'

'Everyone is so sensitive about pronouns these days.'

'Are they? Anyway, it's not that sort of dragon ship,' he says, leading the way across the trawler's spotless steel deck. Smells of fish paste, like we had on sandwiches as a child, when things were normal – she was with us still, my dad was an accountant, and I was sane.

Sigurd helps me cross to the longship, which turns out to be narrower and shorter than I thought. Men getting on with their work, ignoring us, showing us a soft respect. It seems old. As they say on those antique programmes on TV I watch when I am feeling low, it feels *right.* It could have been excavated from an Orkney burial mound. Vikings may have sailed it across the wild waters from Norway.

Sigurd says something to the men and they make way for him so he can lead me to where they are fixing the mast.

'Look,' he says, pointing to two small coins at the bottom of the slot, where the mast is just about to go. Bend down and can see one of them has a bird on it.

'One is a Raven Penny, the other is a Raven Banner Penny. Old Viking coins. It's a tradition to have them under a mast, when you raise it,' Sigurd says.

'Are they real?'

Sigurd nods.

'They say that the raven is the bird of death, that's why it is associated with a warship like this,' he says.

'Well, they eat dead things around here, rabbits mostly.'

*It must be an omen.*

The men set to work again as we walk to the bow and I climb up onto a narrow platform to look at the striking dragon figurehead. It is covered in gold leaf. Its blue eyes are more like Sigurd's than Paul Hollywood's.

'I love the way you do that with your hair,' he says, standing just below me. He is such a flirt, but I like it.

'They call it a compulsive disorder, chewing my hair. I'm mad, you know. If I don't take my pills anything can happen.'

He laughs again, as if he thinks that what I am saying is repartee, not a warning.

'Intriguing. You're the first mad person I've met.'

'I doubt it, we mad people are good at pretending we are sane. You should read *The Lunatic at Large*. Written by an Orkney man – J Storer Clouston – over a hundred years ago. That's me, a lunatic at large.'

'Read a lot?'

'You don't have to be stupid to dress like this. I'm super articulate, when I want to be.'

'I like articulation in my women.'

I laugh at this, but I think I am blushing too. It is nice to feel wanted, even in jest. Martin told me that the most attractive thing about another human being is them being attracted to you. Maybe she's right.

'*Your* women? Really? Anyway, you *are* my first Viking.'

'How do you know? You might meet Vikings every day.'

'Bit of a home bod. I rarely meet anyone. My best friends live in novels.'

He looks interested.

'Frankie Adams, John Grady Cole, Quoyle and Petal Bear, Francis Beverage and, of course, all the Lisbon girls. You should read more,' I say.

He shrugs his shoulders as if the idea of reading is new to him.

'*The Member of The Wedding* might be a good place to start. It's where I met Frankie. It's beautiful. Or, *The Shipping News*, Quoyle and Petal Bear are the best and worst sort of people, but I like Petal in spite of herself. Francis is the Lunatic at Large; that's me tonight.'

'I'll start with the Lunatic book. Though I'm not sure you'd get away with a title like that these days,' Sigurd says.

I watch as the mast is raised without much effort and one of the men brings a rope to tie to a wooden post beside us to hold it up. He smiles conspiratorially at Sigurd.

'Actually, this is the first conversation I have had with a real live boy in a long time,' I say.

'If you spend all your life in an imaginary world, you might miss the point of living.'

'Which is?'

'Making the most of it.'

'Fictional relationships are easier.'

'Have you read the *Orkenyinga Saga*?' Sigurd asks.

Shake my head.

'It's the only Norse Saga about a part of the British Isles. It's just about Orkney and the men who ruled it – some of them were my ancestors. There is a line in it about girls who have hair like yours.'

'Really? So, what do the Vikings say about girls with hair like mine?'

'I don't think I know you well enough to say.'

'Why exactly did you bring a Viking longship to Kirkwall? And where are they going at this time of night?'

Before he can answer, a man appears on the narrow platform that sticks out from the side of the trawler, so that it projects over the sea and is overhanging us, nearly touching the longship's mast now that it has been raised. A box with a red light, just below him. Above him two flags flying, a Saltire and a Norwegian flag, of equal size. The physical resemblance to Sigurd is strong so I guess it is his uncle. The men unravelling the sail stop work and look up.

The new man makes this verse:

*Lightning-felled timber built*
*and bloody-waked,*
*to Orkney, land-greedy.*
*The Earl's banner,*
*storm-ripped, battle proud,*
*marks just claim.*
*Tugged over stony-sea,*

*banner-high, over Earl's head,*
*muscle-straining, sails over land.*
*Death cannot undo oak-keeled tracks.*
*Elders reminded of ancient rights,*
*land voyages in dead of night.*

The man scans me, as if making a copy, then looks at Sigurd and says, 'Don't be late', and leaves. I smile at Sigurd who raises his eyebrows and shrugs his shoulders as if to excuse his family.

'Demesne,' I say, then smile and shake my head by way of an apology.

'Time to go,' the older man on the longship says and we get off and stand on the trawler as they begin to undo the ropes. Surprising just how quickly they prepared the boat. Sail now unfurled and ready to be hoisted. Man standing ready with a rope in his hand, taking the weight of the sail, until they are ready to pull it up the mast.

'Okay,' the man at the back, the one who seems to be in charge, says, and the ropes are pulled free by the crew at each end of the boat, and they push her off. Man closest to us is short and stocky, his arms thick and covered in ginger bristles. Reminds me of rigid and hairy Hogweed stems – Thomas used to make them into peashooters for me.

Small outboard engine on the back is either powerful, or the Viking war machine is lighter than it seems, as they spin it around easily enough and make their way out between the pier extension and the breakwater. Unfurling the sail as they go. It bobbles as if it were made of balsa wood. The older man at the helm turns once to wave to Sigurd.

'Where are they going?' I ask.

'If I told you I'd have to kill you.'

'You'd be doing me a favour.'

He looks puzzled.

'Going to kill myself at dawn,' I say.

He laughs again. If I had been trying to amuse him I don't think I could have been more successful.

'Why would you do that?' Sigurd says.

'"Making the most of it", isn't enough for me.'

'Really? That's sad, but pretty much in tune with Albert Camus. He thought that judging whether life is, or is not, worth living was the most fundamental problem in Philosophy.'

'What *is* the meaning of all this?' I say, turning to look around me, my arms raised again, as if what I could see of Kirkwall in this moment was the limit of any possible human experience.

'Camus thought that life was absurd as human beings are searching for meaning in a meaningless universe and the only logical options open to us are to commit suicide, find hope, or embrace the absurdity.'

'My father doesn't believe in logic. He says rationality is a prison for the mind. I think he's mad,' I say.

He shrugs.

'So, did Camus kill himself?' I ask.

'No, I think he died in a car accident, but he didn't really propose that suicide was the answer, just one option. He favoured just putting up with it.'

'So, is that where your "making the most of it" comes from then?'

'Maybe. I don't know. I'm a good man but a pretty bad philosopher. Anyway, how about a last drink? It's not much, but something to hang on for.'

'Maybe, later,' I say. 'It all depends if they have caught me by then. I might have to hide.'

'Who are you hiding from?' he asks. I can see it in his face, the first hint of doubt.

I hide behind my hair, wait for him to speak.

'Good, well, assuming they don't catch you, why don't we meet at 10:00? Over there,' he says, pointing to the entrance of the Towers Temperance Hotel.

'You'll not get much of a drink in there,' I say.

'My Kirkwall uncle doesn't approve of drink.'

'Some Viking.' I laugh at the thought of a Viking who doesn't drink.

'My grandfather made him take The Pledge after he lost his eye in a drunken fight with my father. Said if he didn't, he wouldn't get his share of the family wealth when he died,' Sigurd says.

'The Pledge?' I say.

'Used to be a big thing a hundred years ago. You made a public pledge not to touch alcohol and your friends and neighbours kept an eye on you, to make sure you didn't. My uncle says that only two bars in Kirkwall served booze then,' Sigurd says.

'I can guess which two they were,' I say. The dull throb of laughter and loud voices coming from the two bars at the top of Bridge Street.

'I've got to eat with my family first, so that should work out well,' he says.

Sigurd smiles as I turn away, clearly assuming a 'yes' to his invitation. Helps me off the boat, touching my hand. His fingers soft and warm like baby sparrows. Wonder if it is a secret sign.

Sigurd bends a little to climb onto the quay. His pendant spins, changing colour from white to grey, and then goes a dull red. He notices me staring at it.

'It's a sunstone,' he says. 'Vikings used it to navigate. It's polarised so you can use it to locate the sun on a cloudy day. Helped them find their way in the wilderness.'

'Honey bees do that too,' I say.

Sigurd shrugs.

'It's always cloudy here. Not like today which is a rather special day,' I say.

'Yes, after meeting you I think so too.'

'Stop it,' I say, but can't hold back the smile. Martin is right. He seems pleased with himself. His teeth fully on display.

'Sonder,' I say, and he just smiles, already used to ignoring my outbursts.

'I hope you can outsmart whoever is chasing you and don't go killing yourself before we have that drink. I want the chance to break your heart.' He giggles, completely unaware that he was mistaking a mad woman for a tease.

*Can you break a broken heart?*

I turn away, unsure of what to do, or say.

*How can he be so happy and so easy to amuse?*

Walk around the harbour, along the path below Cromwell Road that leads to the breakwater. The longship is sailing across the bay, passing in front of a schooner at anchor. Sail curved and buffeted by the sea breeze, tipping the mast over a little with each shallow puff. Sail has LX in the middle of it. Would have been a frightening sight when boats like this appeared in the bay.

They say Vikings were brutal men, who took what they wanted, but Sigurd seems gentle and kind. Maybe he is a direct descendent of St Magnus who gave his name to the cathedral and wanted to pacify the Viking hordes, and some say has the power to work miracles to this day. Wonder if Sigurd can work miracles too.

Putting my music on, I realise just how long it has been silent. Is Sigurd really who he seems? He may be tricking me. He may be evil.

*I see wickedness in men, that others don't see.*

Perhaps, you should never trust a Viking, even an unlikely one.

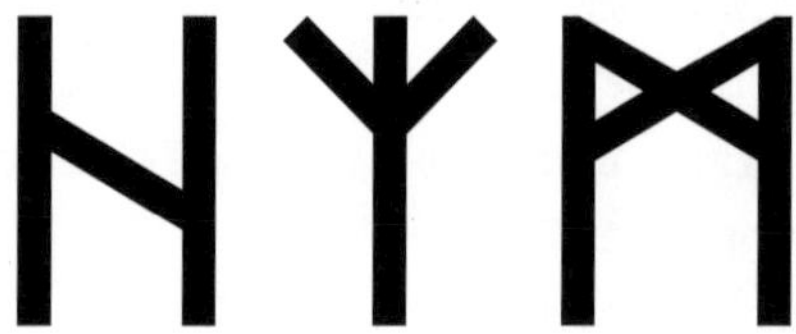

(Hagalax. Algiz. Mannaz)

*'Be on the lookout for unexpected influences providing you with assistance and teamwork, your Guardian Angel is hovering.'*

# 3. GETTING READY

'We could be in Oslo now,' a middle-aged woman with a North American accent says to a man about her own age sitting beside her at the bar in Helgi's, on Harbour Street, opposite the Corn Slip. It is the first time she has spoken since they entered the bar ten minutes earlier.

The bar takes its inspiration from Kirkwall's Viking past, and the woman has spent most of her time reading the menu which tells about the eponymous Helgi, his voyages, and the battle of Clantarf.

They are both wearing dull gold wedding bands. His hand is slim, but hers is swollen and her ring is buried in a deep trough of flesh. He is distracted, trying to order a drink, but the bar is busy and he has to wait. She scans the walls decorated with Helgi's sagas, but she is also watching her husband staring at the barmaid, apparently willing her to turn to notice him. They are no more than a hundred metres from where Panda is taking her leave of Sigurd, with the echo of the verse still in her head; climbing the ladder, Panda and Sigurd's hands have just touched. The word 'sonder' is just forming in her mouth.

*Oh shut-up and enjoy yourself,* the man, Lionel, thinks. It has been a tiring day and he now wants to relax but he can tell that his wife won't let him and that the evening will not end well. It never does when she gets started on something.

The couple are sitting at the bar, the only seats available; the tables either reserved, or full of people eating when they arrived. Before he can order, two police officers enter and exchange a few words with the young barmaid. The blonde policewoman catches Lionel's eye and she smiles at him, which makes him feel better about the wait. He doesn't know it yet but this is PC Sarah McTravers and they will meet again later, in rather different circumstances. She is standing to one side and just behind a male colleague with three stripes on his arm. That's Sergeant Terry Maitland and Lionel will meet him later too. Lionel is not alone in trying to get the barmaid's attention, several people are watching the exchange with the police, all with money in their hands like flags of surrender on a battlefield, competing for her attention, trying to buy a drink.

'Lot of police around tonight,' Lionel says, when the barmaid eventually gets around to him after, rather unfairly, he thinks, serving two locals before him, even though he had his money-flag out first.

'Aye, Show Night can be a bit wild. They'll be just letting everyone know they're around and about.'

'It sounds exciting,' he says, but his wife, Lillian, doesn't look happy.

'It'll be that right enough. It's the one night of the year when all those who should never be allowed out are let out. What can I get you?'

'I thought that everyone drank straight Scotch in Scotland, but someone told me yesterday that most locals drink vodka, is that right?' Lionel says.

'Oh, they drink all sorts. We sell enough whisky though.'

'I'd like a Manhattan,' Lillian, says.

'Okay, will that be two?'

'No, I'd like to try one of the Orkney beers. Let me have an *Orkney Blast* please.'

Lionel smiles at the barmaid then looks at his wife who is obviously annoyed with him.

'We could have had our gold pins before we got home. We just need one more territory,' she says.

Lionel isn't listening; he recognises the carping tone and sharp edge to her words. He is expecting a lecture, again, about his decision to drag her screaming to Orkney. So, in trying to shut her out, he finds himself thinking back a few days to his meeting with Kito, the day after they arrived in Kirkwall.

He had instructions to meet at Kito's farm and the GPS in the hire car made it easy. He was excited to see the famous Scapa Flow, filling the horizon behind the house, as he turned off the main road and looked down the slope. It was set a hundred metres back from the road, past another solitary farmstead, surrounded by fields. The grass had faint striations, the fading memory of the plough, which gave the impression that the buildings were sitting on a plump green corduroy cushion.

The house was modest, low-lying with some outbuildings, mostly in disrepair. Piles of rubbish littered the adjacent land, as if it had been scattered by a naughty puppy that had stolen random trinkets from the house and then dropped them, like discarded toys, whenever it got bored. It was untidy and uncared for, and he wondered why farmers here didn't bother to dispose of things properly. Once-useful-things were just left to rot on the side of the lane, or propped up alongside the barns, now partly overgrown with weeds.

It crossed his mind that the uncovered rafters of one of the barns ahead were ribs and the old plough and the other rotting agriculture machinery he could just see through a hole in the wall were the petrified internal organs of its agrarian past. He thought that, in another setting, the view out of his car window could be a work of dystopian, found art.

A flock of small birds darted by that he couldn't easily identify, but there was a green smudge in the air where they had been, so, they were greenfinches, he thought. Then a seagull appeared being chased by a great skua, which he did recognise. He knew them to be pirates of the northern air, stealing food from flying birds rather than catching it themselves. They would also attack peat cutters in the fields. They call them Bonxies here, he thought. The Bonxies reminded him of vultures on a more familiar prairie searching for carrion, back home.

It was a landscape with a memory. It felt really wild and different to his normal life, where they built over yesterday at regular intervals, leaving nothing of what had gone before. As he got closer to the house, he saw a group of statues standing in the field looking out across the water. Life-size terracotta bodies, female, all naked.

Lionel parked near the front door, beside the sign that said Flat Earth Tours Start Here. It stood just five metres from a sign that said Orkney Nature Tours Start Here. He got out and walked across the small parking space to see the figures better. He had a strong urge to climb the fence to see them up close but thought better of it.

'Hello.' A young woman appeared beside his car. He hadn't seen, or heard, her approach. She had long red hair and was dressed in black, knee-length black socks and chunky leather boots with silver straps and something silver on a chain around her neck. Her presence reached out and touched him, prickling his skin. She looked anxiously behind, towards the house, and then came quickly towards him and put a note in his hand. 'Hide this,' she said, 'read it later.' She then walked back to where she was when he first saw her, at a respectful distance.

Lionel was surprised but did as he was instructed and put the note in his pocket. As he did so he noticed the strawberry birthmark on her face; it was like she had a permanent lop-sided blush.

'Yes, okay, I will. Hello. Sorry, just couldn't take my eyes off the statues in the field,' he said, gesticulating in that direction.

'My mother.'

'Is she a sculptor?'

'Sculpture,' the girl said.

'I mean, did she make them?'

'Yes, I know what you mean. But she is not a sculptor. She is the sculpture,' the girl said.

'Sorry?'

'If you find my accent difficult to understand you're going to have a hell of a time here,' the girl said.

'Yes, I'm still getting used to being a foreigner. I find I have to repeat myself a lot. No one expects my accent. But I'm still a bit lost about your mother,' Lionel said.

'That's her body. The sculptor, me, as it happens, has sculpted her in clay, to make the sculpture you see before you,' the girl said.

'Oh, okay,' Lionel said, still a bit puzzled, but pleased that he now understood.

The girl is hiding behind dark sunglasses and playing with her shiny red hair.

'Oh, really…well, I wasn't expecting to see …'

'She's dead,' the girl said.

'I'm sorry. Look, I'm just here to take a tour,' Lionel said.

'Birds and flooers, or nonsense?'

'Flat Earth,' he said, pointing to the sign. 'I'm looking for someone called Kito.'

'You mean Thomas. But let me save you your money. He's a charlatan. I know because Doubting Thomas is my father and I also know, like just about every other sensible person on this bloody planet, that the Earth is not fucking flat.'

'Well, I can see you aren't a believer, but let's just say I have an open mind,' Lionel said.

'It's mostly Americans we get here and…are you from the cruise ship that's just come in?'

'No, we're not on a cruise. And it's Canadian, actually.'

'No matter, you're all so bloody gullible. God protect us from people who voted in Trump, or that wimpy child-man Trudeau, and eat maple syrup for breakfast.'

'Panda. Stop it.' A man with a military demeanour was skipping towards them trying to get his boots on at the same time. He had short hair and an athletic build, with a Middle Eastern looking scarf around his neck as if he sweated a lot and needed a mop, or he wanted to relive his gap year.

'Excuse my daughter. She hates me.'

'They say there is a thin line between love and hate?' Lionel said.

Panda shook her head and headed back into the house, leaving the two men face-to-face. Lionel looked at her arse. He couldn't help himself.

'Are you here for the Flat Earth Tour?'

'Yes, Thomas, that's me. I'm Lionel.'

'Good. It's been a while since I did one of those, mostly people want nature tours. In spite of what my daughter says, my name's not Thomas, it's Kito. I'm sorry about her, but she lives in another world and likes to create as much trouble as she can in this one.'

'It's okay, Kito, I have children too. I know how it is.'

## (Hagalaz)

*'Beware, the forces at work are outside your control.'*

Sergeant Maitland and PC McTravers are now in Bridge Street, heading north, at one end of the main route through Kirkwall, which once skirted the sea before land was reclaimed to the east. 'The Road to Nowhere,' as it is called by some, is made up of Bridge, Albert, Broad and Victoria Streets, joined end-to-end. Mostly paved with flagstones that look like giant bricks. It is Kirkwall's spine.

They are passing Trek & Travel, just across from the vacant plot where Wisebuys used to be, heading towards the harbour. The Anchor Buildings are ahead of them on their right, opposite Scapa Travel, where the street narrows to little more than a lane. The road is mainly for pedestrians but is still used by cars and vans for access, mostly during the day.

The height of the buildings on either side is exaggerated by the narrowness of the gap between them. A deep railway cutting with blue-grey stone rails heading towards the sea. The shade filling the narrow trough of a street makes the sky ahead, above the harbour, look brighter, as if they are walking into a new day.

It is still early but already a raggle-taggle band of men have spilled out of the Tauvaig Inn and Skipper's Bar opposite, to clog this arterial route connecting the harbour to the centre of the town. A number of them still in t-shirts even though the air trapped in this narrow trench is beginning to cool. The scent of beer and vaping is drifting towards the approaching police patrol on the scant breeze. The slabs beneath the drinkers are wet, as if a wave has recently washed ashore and then withdrawn again, or the men ahead have been spilling their beer, or pissing in the street.

'I feel like I'm walking into a movie,' Sergeant Maitland says.

'Sorry?' PC McTravers says.

'They wet the roads to make them darker, in films.'

'Do they?'

'You look next time,' the Sergeant says.

'*Alice in Wonderland*,' PC McTravers says.

'What?' the Sergeant says, turning to look at her.

'My dad's favourite film. He made me watch it over and over as a kid. The one with Fiona Fullerton as Alice.'

The sergeant shakes his head.

'I'd want to be Alice. If we were walking into a movie. You could be the Mad Hatter, like Johnny Depp,' PC McTravers says.

'If it has to be fantasy, I'd choose the *Wizard Of Oz*,' Sergeant Maitland says.

'Whatever,' PC McTravers says, watching as a white transit van appears at the end of Bridge Street and begins to ease its way through the crowd towards them. Behind the van, the Bay Takeaway is doing good business at the end of Bridge Street, and they can smell chips frying.

Sergeant Maitland and PC McTravers look nervous as they walk along Bridge Street towards the harbour on their tour of the local pubs. Their boss, Inspector Tomilty, or Bagpuss, as he is known behind his back, told them that on Show Night it is their presence on the streets that is important. They need to be seen, but they also need to take great care.

During their briefing earlier, the Inspector pointed out that there had been 10,000 people at the show so it would be a busy night. He said that they were a deterrent, just like the fusion bomb had been in the Cold War. Although Sergeant Maitland, PC McTravers, and most of their colleagues thought it was both a bad and dated choice of simile, they knew they were important in keeping the Kirkwall peace. When PC Butcher, aka Blobby, asked what would happen if the deterrent didn't work, Bagpuss didn't have much of an answer, but as they were leaving the room he seemed to find his focus again.

'Don't forget, we are the thin blue line that separates order and chaos,' he said.

So, all of 'The K Team,' as Bagpuss called them, were a little nervy about Show Night, as they understood that the limited resources of the Orkney constabulary were never meant to be tested in anger, and that it was the night of the year most likely to kick-off and spiral hopelessly out of control. It was a heavy responsibility.

'I hate coming down here,' the Sergeant says. 'I don't mind the drunks. It's the pill-poppers, who don't smell of alcohol and have starey eyes, that scare me.'

'I'm not so worried. Maybe because I'm a girl. I might be worried if I was a man.'

'Aye, it was a smart move to get women as bouncers in these places. Brute force is less effective when they are off their heads than a little female persuasion,' the Sergeant says, looking at a sturdy blonde lady with Doc Marten boots outside Skippers.

'Aye, reminds them of their mams,' PC McTravers says, as the wall of men and boys in front of them cracks open to let them pass. The sergeant nods to one or two of the people he knows professionally and they nod back.

'It's when they start giving lip, it's hard to react and keep it all under control. I remember it going well wrong a few years back,' Sergeant Maitland says.

'Did Bagpuss have to push the nuclear button?'

'Sadly, no. There is no button. If we can't stop it, it will just keep going.'

'A chain reaction.'

'Aye, and we're the weakest link,' Sergeant Maitland says.

As he speaks, a message comes over his radio about a gang of kids in hoodies, wearing Donald Trump masks, in Broad Street. They have been seen cementing up the recessed screw holes on either side of the shopfront windows. All the shops have them, so they can board-up their windows for the Ba Games in the winter.

'It's begun,' he says, as they turn around and head back to investigate, following the weak but still visible track through the bodies, which parts with seconds to spare. The crowd's timing goading them like life was a bull fight and they were the angry bull.

(Tiewaz)

*'Just pure male energies.'*

Ewan is standing naked in front of the mirror in his bedroom. The large room is sparsely furnished: bed, chest of drawers, chair, and the mirror.

The bed is opposite the window, which overlooks a field of black oats swaying a little in the occasional breath drifting in off the sea, like the sky is sighing. A traditional Orkney box bed, it has doors, making it look like a big square wardrobe. Ewan calls his bed Narnia because, as a child, he read about children who entered a fantasy world through a wardrobe. Like them, he leads a more exciting life behind those closed doors, but there are no witches or fawns, or lions in his world, just women on his laptop screen.

When he was younger, girls would allow him back into their beds often enough. *Running in the night* they call it here, but his vanity and his 'appetites' – as his mother calls them – put them off these days, and there are not many women left on the Mainland willing to give him a go. Too often, his passions have overcome him and led to trouble, and these days he is something of a recluse and most of his encounters with the opposite sex are virtual. So, tonight is one of his few chances to see if he still has what it takes; if he can find someone who doesn't know his reputation, or who just doesn't care.

In contrast to the box bed that has sat in the same room for a hundred and fifty years and clearly belongs, the mirror looks out of place. It is six feet tall and stands in the corner of the room, behind the door. It has a gold, oval frame, and could have come straight out of the Belle Epoch, or the Evil Queen's bedroom in Snow White. It was expensive, but that didn't matter because Ewan values how he looks enough to want the best reflection and he was prepared to pay for it.

He has been standing like this for some time and he turns slowly and cranes his neck around to see all of him. He is happy because, as far as he can see, he is perfect. The look on his face suggesting what he is thinking – *Girls, look at what you are missing* – something like that.

'Your tea's ready,' his mother, Muriel, shouts from the kitchen, though 'kitchen' may be too grand a description for this small room

– scullery might be better. It is so small it acts like a soundbox, amplifying her words to exactly the right volume required to get her son's attention when he is in his room. She knows, from many years of practice, that if it sounds to her like her voice is thin and squeaky, Ewan will hear her.

In spite of its aural eccentricities, she likes this small domestic space, mainly because it is warm in the winter, when it is icy cold in the rest of the house. Like the other rooms, it only has feeble storage radiators, so most of the winter heat comes from cooking. During the short dark days, she stands by the cooker staring out across the fields, watching her son tending the cattle.

She is leaning against the worn worktop beside the sink. There is a small microwave and two electric hobs in the corner, a red table just big enough for two in the centre, and flowery cushion flooring under foot. The table is laid for one, with unmatched patterned crockery and bone-handled cutlery.

'Okay, just a meenit,' Ewan says, turning to face the mirror one last time and spreading his legs a little before looking down at his cock.

'Two meenits,' his mother says.

'Aye, coming,' Ewan says, quickly putting on the red underpants he keeps for special occasions and his 'leisure suit'. His clothes are thin and lightweight to show off his body, which has been finely honed by manual labour on the farm. He knows he'll be cold later but that doesn't bother him, even though he feels the cold badly. He thinks that dealing with cold is a test of his manhood. Didn't he work in the fields naked sometimes too? Even once in the snow for a while until his mother fetched him inside. But tonight, he isn't worried about the cold, his first priority is how he looks.

When he gets to the kitchen his tea is on the table waiting for him, as it is every night of the year. His mother cooks all his meals and he eats them here on his own. Muriel thinks it is her duty to wait on him; she eats on her own later, when Ewan loses himself online searching for women, real, or imaginary, depending on his mood.

'It's your going-oot tea,' Muriel says, smiling at him as he sits down. She has already placed a clean tea towel on the table so he can use it as a bib, which he tucks into the neck of his shirt.

'Thanks, Ma,' he says, picking up his knife and fork and holding them briefly above the plate, as if the anticipation of eating was exciting him as much as the sex he expected later on.

'I'll just be buttering some bread,' Muriel says, placing her freshly baked loaf on the table, so that Ewan sees it before she cuts him two thick slices and slobbers them with butter already softened by the stove.

As he eats, Ewan admires the fried food in front of him. He always has a fry-up when going out on the town. In fact, it is the only time he has a fry-up and as he only goes out once a year, it is something of a special occasion and he looks forward to his 'going-oot tea'.

'It might be warm now but I expect it'll be cold later, so I don't want to hear of any of your silly antics. I don't want trouble with the police, not like last year. I never do understand why you just can't get drunk, fight, and be sick in the street like the others,' Muriel says.

Ewan nods, shovelling fried potatoes into his mouth as if he hasn't eaten for a week.

'How many times have I told you not to eat so quick, you'll get indigestion,' Muriel says. She has said the same thing every day for the past twenty years. It is part of their feeding ritual and the way they both smile suggests that neither of them would have been satisfied with a meal that missed it out.

He nods again and smiles, his mouth too full to speak.

'Maybe you should hang around after the show next time. Why rush home to get all dressed up on Show Night?' Muriel says, tidying around the cooker, keeping busy while Ewan eats.

'Me going-oot tea, Ma. I come back for me going-oot tea.'

'Don't think I mind being here on my own. It's only the one night of the year, after all. It's good to have you out of the house for a change. Gives me a bit of space.'

'Aye.'

'Do you have plans?'

'Said I'd meet up with Sammy. Though he'll just be going on about them fellas from Birsay winning his class,' Ewan says.

'They was nice-looking beasts. I'm not surprised they won. No favouritism at the show, you know,' Muriel says.

'See that Limousin-cross steer calf that got best beast, won by the bloke from Sebay? And the Aberdeen Angus Cow Champion. Had great legs and head. I'd have liked to see some of the stots a wee bit stronger, but it was great to see such lovely kye,' Ewan says, pausing briefly from his feast.

Muriel smiles at her son's enthusiasm for cattle. It pleases her, because it is his life.

'I cud hardly move fur people. Had to keep popping under cover because of the showers though. Why dis people in queues no make way for you? Everyone queuing for their burgers and chips. I was wanting one of them lobster rolls they were selling but they were six pounds,' Muriel says.

'I got me lunch for free. I just sat down with Sammy for a chat at some sort of cooperative. Caithness ting, I think. They asked if I was a member and I said "Aye". They had a few tables and a peedie lass brought us some sandwiches,' Ewan says.

'Must have mistaken you fur someone important, or was you using your charm on the wee girl?' Muriel says.

'You see them Up Helly Aa fellas, from Lerwick? All dressed up as Vikings and silly folk,' Ewan says.

'I always wanted to go to see them parading round with burning torches and catching fire that Viking ship, but the ferry is too rough for me in January,' Muriel says.

Ewan smiles and chews his food a little more, to please her.

'You see them silly men dressed-up as girls?' Muriel says.

'Aye, that's as they only allow men. Didn't they used to say that the day of the parade in Lerwick was Transvestite Tuesday?'

'Aye, strange folk them Shetlanders, but dressed as girls or no, them Lerwick boys can be a handful with a drink in them. So, stay out of their way the night,' Muriel says.

Ewan nods, his mouth full of food again.

'I met up with Gladys when they were judging best horse in show,' Muriel says.

'Oh, aye, that Clydesdale mare, Downhill Snowflake; the sort of name that sticks in your head, you see Smithy jump up when he got it?'

'Aye, I did. Lovely dog won Champion Dog too. Afterwards, Gladys and I, well, we gut talking.'

'You're a gossip, Ma,' he says, before stuffing more food into his mouth.

'I'm an oral historian,' Muriel says, giggling to herself.

Ewan laughs, nearly choking on his food.

'Gladys said she heard it on the radio, that's how it used to be afore books and the like. People told each other stories to keep them alive, to give the next generation some of their wisdom.'

'You wise then, Ma?'

'Aye, all old folk is, just you youngens don't see it.'

'What history was it then, Ma?'

'No all history, we were speakin' about her readings; she wants me to let her do another reading.'

'Is it runes, or tea leaves she's doing these days?'

'She says the runes are the better way, they hold more truth than tea leaves.'

'Gladys will just tell you what you want to hear.'

'Maybe and maybe that's no all bad. Anyway, it's no 'his' class. Sammy's. Maybes make him try harder next year.'

'Ma, that's me done. Good tea. It's set me up for the night.'

Ewan stands and walks towards his mother. He kisses her on the forehead, holding her shoulders, and she puts her hands on his hips. She smiles as he turns and walks out into the hall and slips on his lumberjack's coat before thinking better of it and replacing it with a thin cotton jacket.

'It'll be cold later,' Muriel says.

Ewan nods and puts the thin jacket on anyway before opening the front door of the small cottage. Outside the air smells of toasted grass and the sky is full of exuberant swallows in the middle of an insect feeding frenzy.

It is three miles into Kirkwall and Ewan always walks. He knows the folk who live in the houses he passes and they know him. He recognises all the faces who drive by, except the visitors of course, and there were a lot of them at this time of the year, but all the locals know him too. He knows the beasts in the field and who owns them, and he has his opinions on how well they are looked after.

As he gets to Kevin's farm gate, just where the brow of the hill breaks, Kirkwall begins to spread out in front of him and he pauses to take in the glorious view. The sky is bigger than normal. Like it is when you lie on your back and look straight up. He feels giddy with the curve of the earth, the pull of the ground fighting against the fright of the infinite space above his head, beyond the thin evening clouds. He gasps at the wonder of it all and feels a pang of mortality that makes him think of God.

*Fine bod*, he thinks, as he starts walking again, remembering his reflection from the mirror earlier and imagining himself dripping with water.

Just the thought of it makes him go hard.

(Jera)

*'I see good karma and good harvest, so be patient.'*

'Ever eaten swan before?' Alastair asks Pavel, the Polish kitchen hand taken on for the summer in the Towers Temperance Hotel. The hotel is on Harbour Street opposite the Inner Harbour, just along from Helgi's.

The kitchen looks like it has been hollowed out of a solid block of steel. Apart from the sheen of grey metal, the only colours visible are the red terracotta floor tiles and the blue chequered trousers of the two men working there. It is surprisingly cramped and mostly empty. You would hardly believe it was the height of the tourist season and this was the biggest hotel in town, but not everyone was comfortable with the idea of staying in a hotel which didn't sell booze.

'We eat everything in Poland. Swan, yes. We like what you call goldfish too,' Pavel says, as he slides between the stoves carrying a box of spring greens.

'We call them carp,' Alastair says.

'We cook it with 'black sauce' made from dark beer and fish blood. We eat on Xmas Eve. Much like, so we have to buy fish early. We keep it in the bath till the day before.'

'Really?' Alastair says, looking up from his chopping board.

'We don't bath the days before Xmas. Stand-up wash. My father is fond of stand-up wash, he says he never had a bath as a boy. Not one.'

'We didn't eat much fish, as a kid. Not much. Just fish and chips.'

'Ah, yes, Scottish fish and chips. But carp, that is good fish. We like that much. Do you know that in Germany they eat this fish with bread and ginger?'

'Really?' Alastair says, looking puzzled.

'Yes, you know, like they make the houses, the bread and ginger houses – Hansel & Gretel.'

'Oh, gingerbread. It's a sort of biscuit,' Alastair says, selecting another onion from his pile and starting to chop again.

'Ah, it is bread, gingerbread. But how can bread be a biscuit?'

'We don't eat swans, not normal people anyway. My mother told me that it was treason 'cos all the swans were owned by the Queen.'

'The Queen owns the swans? How can you own a wild thing?'

'I don't know, but the Earl family want them, so they get them. Maybe the Queen lets them. Bit of a family gathering, so six of the buggers to cook. Every year I say you have to let them hang otherwise they are going to taste like shite and I get "Vikings never hung their meat" crap. Of course they did. I looked it up, online. They dried fish on the rigging. They salted, smoked and preserved all sort of things, but the bloody Earls know best.'

'I like it, swan,' Pavel says, crouching down and looking into one of the ovens which contains two browning birds. 'Yes, lovely. They look done to me.'

'Yes, should be done by now. Take them out and cover them. If we let them sit a while it might make them edible.'

'Okey, dokey,' Pavel says, reaching for the dish towel.

'Too bloody fishy for me. Wild swans just taste like fishy pheasant,' Alastair says, swiping the onions from his board with his knife into a large steel tray.

'Oh, not like ours. Not of fish. Polish swans more like pig, but we leave them to hung for a long time, we don't eat them just a few days after they have been shot.'

'Pavel, I know, but that's what they want. Look, mate, when you've done that, do them haggis will you? It's the starter. Stick them by the sink to cool.'

'Okey, dokey. Gingerbread is a biscuit, huh,' Pavel says, reaching for the steaming pot of haggis at the back of the stove.

(Dagaz)

*'You have an inner strength that can be used during difficult times.'*

A grey-haired man is walking past the front of the hotel, not more than fifteen metres from where Alastair and Pavel are working. A young woman with a buggy is chugging past him, like a harbour tug pushing its charge into port. There is a gentle hum of a ship's generator in the distance. Overhead, Herring Gulls wheel around in the still air that carries the faint perfume of ships and the sea.

The old guy has his sleeves rolled-up to reveal smudged tattoos on both forearms. Like a decrepit Popeye. He is a photocopy of a younger man from a machine with a failing printer head. His body still retaining a hint of its former strength, with a solid torso and thick, strong legs. A bull-head. He looks tired but determined and, on the lookout, as if he has lost someone.

'You on holiday then,' he says, to a couple walking towards him. There are tables on the wide pavement in front of the hotel, leaving only a narrow passageway close to the road and so he is able to head them off; they have no choice but to stop.

'No, we live here. Can we help you? Are you looking for something?'

'I'm visiting. Been here three days now. Staying at the Youth Hostel on Old Scapa Road. My daughter, Angie, rang me when I was on the ferry from Aberdeen. She said, "Dad, Mike and I are thinking of coming over to see you." You'll have an expensive visit, mind, I said to her, as I'm not at home, I'm on the ferry to Orkney. She didn't believe me, so I said to this bloke opposite me, I says, can you talk to my daughter on the phone and can you tell her where I am? He does and she says that I am like a gypsy. She said I was a gypsy. Me and my trips,' the old bloke says.

'Well, have a nice stay. You have the weather for it,' the woman says.

'I don't mind weather. Used to work outside. As a boy, I worked on the Blair Athol estate. Out in all weathers I was. They said I could stay and have a cottage and everything; I was only 18 – some time ago, right – but I had itchy feet. Wanted to move on. You know the Duke is the only person in Britain allowed to raise a private army?

Not just that, but the village water is provided by them railway people. British Rail is their water company,' Davey says.

'Really? Well nice to meet you but we must be going. Hope you have a good time,' she says.

'Aye, I will. Sitting around at home is not for me. Too dull. Need an adventure, to help me feel again. You know how you can lose the feelings in your fingers on a cold day. Well, I've lost the feeling in my heart. Everything gets dull when you get old and I think travel may be a cure. I'm off to Shetland next week,' he says, as the couple edge past him and walk off towards the Marina carpark.

'Davey, Davey MacDonald,' he says under his breath as they disappear down Harbour Street.

'I'm Davey MacDonald,' he says out loud, but nobody appears to hear.

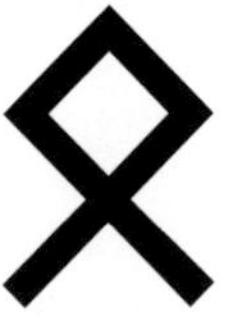

## (Othala)

*'Beware of the burden of property and legacies.'*

As Davey stands outside on the pavement, considering his next move, Alastair and Pavel are busy in the kitchen, and the first of the Earl party enter the function room next door.

The carpet has been removed to reveal a patchy brown wood floor and the furniture replaced with garden tables and benches. There are tapestries on the walls with flaming torches hanging between them in places deputising for the unlit chandelier above their heads. Axes and shields are leaning against the far wall. Stripped of modernity and decorated for the occasion to be a Viking Hall.

Tommy Earl, aka 'Swift Eye', enters first. A delicate ferret of a chap with a patch over his left eye. His one good eye working overtime, darting from side-to-side as if he expects to be jumped by robbers at any moment. He is wearing a dinner jacket with a tartan bow tie. His wife, Rosy, follows above and behind him. A clear foot taller, her head sitting on top of his, like they were Siamese twins.

'Sir, can I get you both a drink?' the young waiter says.

'Campari and soda for me, and coke for him,' Rosy says.

'I'm sorry but...'

'Oh, bloody hell, each year I forget. That'll be two cokes then. How can we do this without alcohol?' Rosy says.

'We all need to keep a clear head. Don't you remember why we have this feast?' Swift Eye says.

'That was thirty years ago,' Rosy says.

'Aye, it was, but it was alcohol that lost me my eye,' Swift Eye says, turning to his three grown-up children who have followed them into the room. He invites them with his multi-functional eye to order too, although it is hard to believe that he is the father of the first one to speak.

'Magners, pint,' a monstrous lump of a man growls.

'Sorry, sir, but we don't sell alcohol,' the waiter says wearily, as if he has to repeat these words all day, every day, to guests.

'Coke then,' he says.

'Coke, ice, lime,' Patrick's tiny brother Malcolm says, without being asked, but a little too loudly. Patrick pushes in front of him as he is speaking, for no apparent reason.

'Watch it, numbskull,' Malcolm says.

'Now, boys,' Rosy says.

'Can I have a quadruple vodka and single tonic please?' Lizzy, their daughter, says, moving closer to her father and putting her arm in his. She is dressed rather provocatively in a short dress with a halter top and little else.

'She'll have a pint of tonic,' Rosy says.

'Ice and lemon, madam?'

'Yep,' Lizzy says, smiling up at her father and catching his monocular gaze momentarily as it scans the room like the beam from a lighthouse. She, a tiny fishing smack alone at sea.

Other family members now enter the room and approach Swift Eye. As they get close they put their hands together, as if in silent prayer; the normal mark of respect and allegiance from a liegeman.

# MY DIARY

---

PRIVATE. YOU REALLY SHOULDN'T BE READING THIS.

# YOU HAVE BEEN WARNED.

## VIRGINICHY

I fucked him, earlier today, after school. Of course, I don't go to school, not like everyone else, so I had to pretend. He 'finished' before me, but he kept going and he tried to please me. That's what he said, that he was trying to please me.

Afterwards, I thought, 'Is that it?'. Not really what I was expecting, but he seemed to enjoy himself. Couldn't believe his luck when I went up to him in the park in my schoolgirl disguise and asked him if he wanted a shag. I've tried it before with other men but they were too scared. This old fart didn't seem to care though, just took me to his place and we did it.

Now that I am officially a woman, I'd like to dedicate this to you, Thomas, for all the heartache you caused me during my childhood. The pain and deception and anguish and alienation and for bringing me to this bloody place. Why Orkney? You told me that Mum said she wanted to visit Skara Brae and that was enough for you to uproot us from the real world, but I think you got seduced by a sunny day.

Orkney is a tart in a see-through negligee on a sunny day and, like me today, irresistible.

My life is surreal. One minute I'm watching Star Trek, or antiques programmes on TV, and the next I'm being fucked by some old codger in a home. Yes, he was podgy old. Hardly a man anymore, though he had a stiff enough cock.

Why are you putting me through all this misery? Surely life isn't meant to be like this. I want those celestial spheres above our heads that you love so much to crack open, so we can get a glimpse of the puppet-master up there pulling all the strings, like the fucking Wizard of Oz.

'Hey mate,' I'd like to say to him, 'stop being such a cunt with my life and leave me alone.'

Ah well, that's my 16th birthday over with. It was a present to myself and better than the crap you bought me. When it comes to presents you need to start thinking woman, not girl. I'll probably try Alex next, he's always leching after me. Dirty bastards, men. Don't they know we can see what they're thinking?

I scratched my pubescent itch and it's gone away for now. I wonder if I'll get pregnant. Wouldn't that make you proud? If the old bloke did the right thing by me, my child's grandfather younger than its dad.

I'm glad I did it but I already miss what it was like before.

I was never innocent, but something is now lost.

Virginichy no more!

---

(Berkana. Ehwaz. Mannaz)

*'When families get together, strive for good judgement.'*

# 4. BLACKED GIRL

Sigrid singing *Strangers* in my head as I meander back along the 'Road to Nowhere', into the approaching gloom. *Strangers... falling head over heels.... just like in the movies.* Still feel Sigurd's glow, like the lingering warmth of the setting sun.

Walking in a trance, contemplating death. How are you meant to live, knowing that you are going to die? The terrifying destiny that awaits us all. Jumbo the fucking elephant in every room.

Not knowing when, that's the hard bit.

Well, I know.

Wake up in Albert Street as it runs into Broad Street. Castle Street off to the right, opposite The Reel, where in a bar on the ground floor of the local music centre, locals of a certain age are celebrating Show Night in their own particular way.

Kirkwall Fiddle and Accordion Orchestra in full flow, repeating notes and phrases as only they can. A Faroese jumper knitted in sound. Drones on, but there is a sort of progression that can be mesmerising. Music seeping out into the street, sucking you in, making it hard to pass by.

Stop and look in the window. Fifty people sitting, all playing the same tune. Synchronised swimmers with instruments. I am glued to the view when a couple of tourists ask if they can go in, and I nod, because I know they can, even though I never have.

A lady in the middle of the room catches my eye and smiles. I know what she is thinking.

*Oh my. Johnny, Johnny, Johnny, for the love of Christ, if you're going to tap your foot to the music tap it in time. You are why I normally sit in the front row, so I don't have to watch your foot-tapping, which is not only out of time but irregular. A beat should be steady, particularly for this tune. If Fred got back from the show when he said, I would be in my front row seat, but Eileen took great delight in being there before me, the night. She'd do anything to sit next to Derek, but I don't think Derek is into women, not any more anyway and not old women – who is?*

*Now, where are we? Oh yes, the dumpty, dumpty, doodly bit.*

*Ok, I know it's your thing, the jazzy, slurring interpretations you do. I know you say it's your signature, your 'groove', but you're hardly one of the Wrigley Sisters. Anyway, seventy-year-olds don't have 'grooves,' unless you're talking about the creases on your forehead.*

*Not that the Rose of Allandale needs much time keeping. It's the ploddy-est tune we play.*

*My granddaughter, Lilly, says it sounds like we are playing the same thing over and over again. She says that Ed Sheeran does that. He records loops of music and then plays over them. Backing tracks. She said it would be good if we played something over half of the tunes we play, to make them more interesting. She says we are just playing backing tracks.*

*I stopped tapping my foot when I was a girl. When I was a rose too. Just like you, dear. Yes, you, staring at me; stuck to the window like a sucker fish. All girls are roses, even if you think you are a weed.*

*Thorny, petalled and perfumed, that's what it should be like to be a girl.*

*My mother said I smelled as pretty as a rose, but the boys preferred Kathleen better. She was less feared of the wrath of the Lord, and her parents, than me. She was the Rose of Kirkwall in her day, but look at her now. She is sitting three rows in front of me and her hair is thin and grey and her arms are like sticks.*

*I think I've become more of a rose as I have aged and she has become more of a weed.*

Why I don't belong here. We are not of the same blood. Don't have interwoven memories of Kirkwall tartan. Nothing that ties me to these people, or the ghosts in the Kirk graveyard dancing to these familiar tunes in the smouldering shadows of a summer's night. Bobbly bobbly repetition, the hypnotic sound of identity, opens their sleeping eyes. A dance macabre, summoning the dead, bringing them together again.

I turn away and look up at the cathedral behind me. Battenburg cake of red and yellow sandstone blocks, crudely buttressed with spotlights, like the sky above London in the Battle of Britain.

Golden delicious lightbulbs wrapped around the trunks of roadside trees, like they are on fire, as if Orcadians burn trees like the Ku Klux Clan burn crosses. The entrance to the graveyard lit too, opposite the Mercat Cross. But, in spite of all these lights, we are still some way from dusk. Candle of day is still flickering. Dark blue silk sheet covers the earth, lightened at its edges where it touches the western horizon, grading through purple, to pink, to white at the end of the world.

Alone in this wilderness. An erratic brought here from the glaciation of my heart. I am naked in front of the cathedral, the centre of eternity and antithetical to life and living.

Wrong; I do have company after all. Young woman, covered in treacle and feathers, is standing tied to the Mercat Cross in front of St Magnus Cathedral. I didn't notice her at first because she is standing so still, like any other crucifixion outside a church. What better camouflage could you have? Layer upon layer of cling-film wrapping her in place, unravelling a little at the bottom, creating a tattered hem to her plastic dress.

Curfew bell sounds just as I notice her, as it does at one minute to eight every night. Could be the 15th century and she could be a witch at the stake, ready to be burned alive, though then there would have been more of a crowd. I have stepped back in time, or nothing has changed here for centuries.

'You okay?' I say to the girl as I get closer.

'Aye, I'm fine. Bit cold though. I should maybe have had more drink.' Her face and hair are dark brown from the treacle, flour, and feathers that have been poured over her head. Looks like she is wearing a bikini under her t-shirt, but it is hard to see through the layers of plastic wrap. Wonderful emerald green eyes, like gemstones.

'You look like you're a chicken wrapped up ready to go into the oven,' I say, and she smiles.

Bits of her flesh not covered in cling film have been brailed (*yes*) by the chilly air emanating from the cathedral. Walking into its shadow is like opening the door of a fridge. Have an urge to touch her, to read what is printed on her skin. Find out what it is like to be grown up, or just be some happier person, and part of things and partake of traditions, like this. Snake tattoo on her left arm, the head just visible at the wrist.

'What do you do if you need a wee?' I say.

'Scream. Come to think of it, it's probably a good job I didn't have no more drink,' she laughs.

'Saw your chap getting taken from his house earlier. I thought he looked like a messed-up parrot.'

'His mates know he hates feathers. I think he's still on the lorry. It'll be back around here soon enough. You're the Flat Earth Girl, aren't you?'

'My father's madness, not mine.'

'The Red Goth then. Isn't that what they call you?'

'I think some people call me "Splash",' I say, instinctively turning my face away to hide my imperfection.

'Aye, cruel that. Must be good to be different though. Not like me.'

'You'd be surprised how much I'd like to be you. Anything to set me free and get me away from my fucking father. He's bonkers,'

I say, moving around her to inspect her from the side. She is tied so tightly that there is no gap and she could have been carved from the same piece of rock as the ancient cross.

'Mine too. Spends all his time out in his wee boat fishing, but never catches a thing.'

'Sure he's fishing?' Thomas has taught me to doubt everything.

'Oh, aye. He's just shite at it. Went a bit bonkers when my mother killed herself.'

'Oh, I'm sorry.'

'He thinks that people who kill themselves go to hell. Blames himself because he's always gone on about suicides, thinks they're not serious, just want attention. So, he told Mum to get on with it after she threatened to do it.'

'And she did?'

'Aye.'

'Bloody hell.'

What would I do if Thomas did that?

*'I'm fed up with all your histrionics (nice word by the way). If you're going to do it, do it and get it over with,' Thomas says, standing beside me as I look down at the sea 1283 feet below my toes.*

*'You have driven me to this. You and this bloody place,' I say.*

*'Yes, you've said,' he says, impatiently tapping his hand on his trouser pocket.*

*'Don't you care that you will have murdered your only daughter? First your wife and now your daughter.'*

*'Pandora, I'm tired of all this. In a way, it will be a relief for both of us if you just jump. I'll get a bit of peace and you'll be free of all your worries.'*

*'Oh, so this is a mercy killing, is it?'*

*'If you really want to jump, then jump. Do it, so that I can get home and get on with my life.' Behind him Fulmars swoop through the air. If we stand here much longer they may attack and try and swoosh us away.*

*'Oh, sorry. Am I interrupting something? Do you want to get back to watch TV? You could find a repeat of Captain James T Kirk tackling another moral dilemma on an alien world? He should have come here. He might have saved us, from this.'*

*'Pandora, don't be silly.'*

*'Silly? The only reason the Starship Enterprise never came here was that our lives are too far-fetched. No one would believe that a place like this could exist in the universe. Our storyline wouldn't get past the most junior script editor.'*

*'I now have no idea what you are talking about.'*

*'You never have.'*

*'I'm sorry,' Thomas says, turning away, as if I am lost to him.*

*'So, that's it, is it? Shall I do it?'*

*'If you want to,' he says, turning back to look at me, one last time.*

*'Bastard,' I scream as I lean forward and begin to feel the air rush past me, blowing my hair back from my face, to reveal a rose.*

*'Pandora,' I hear him shout, but it is too late. He has left it too late to come to my aid.*

'You okay?' the cling-filmed girl says.

'Sorry, just got distracted.'

'Mum's death is what started him fishing. I don't think he's really trying to catch anything. It's a sort of penance. If he'd been a Catholic he'd probably be given a dozen Hail Marys and Rosary to do, and that would be the end of it, but he goes fishing instead.'

It takes me a while to get the thought of Thomas saying those things out of my mind.

'Flagellation, that's what Catholics do,' I say, after the pause.

'Really? Sounds kinky. I thought they fished for souls?'

'Cod, Ling, Pollack, Torsk, Wolf Fish, Dab, Skate, Lesser Spotted Dogfish, Spur-Dog, Coalfish, Conger Eel, but not soles.'

She shakes her head, puzzled.

'The fish you can catch around here,' I say.

'Really, well, he has never caught any. How do you know all that?'

'I'm a whizz at nature, me.'

No longer alone. Others have now arrived on Broad Street, most of them looking at us. It's another anomaly, a girl on a cross. She may have gone unnoticed if I hadn't talked to her. Am I her Judas?

Martin is slinking past the shops on the other side of Broad Street, pretending not to see me, but I know where she is heading.

'You're a mad bitch, but you're cute,' Martin said, when we first met and I told her that I had given her a new name. Likes to sit on the castle ruins, Peedie Sea side of the Castle Hotel. It's her favourite place, looking out over the water.

'Friend of yours?' the girl says, noticing me watching her.

'Comely,' I say. 'Martin. Yes, she is a friend of mine.'

'Funny name for a girl.'

'Funny girl,' I say, not wanting to explain why Cathleen is now Martin, at least to me.

'Brave though, getting married,' I say, looking back at the girl on the cross. 'I'm going to my grave a spinster.'

'I thought that too till I kept getting asked. Two proposals on the same night. Maybe, it's just my time, I thought. Don't they say that marriage is more about timing than anything else. I was ripe for marriage,' she says.

'Ripeness is all.'

She looks puzzled again, but she is happy enough to humour me.

'Oh, just a book thing. I like books,' I say.

She nods.

'Two proposals?' I say, mulling the idea over in my head.

'Aye, two different blokes on the same night. One of them has been chasing me since we were at school, but the other one was a surprise because he was the keenest of the two. We had a bit of a fling a few years ago, but hardly seen him since. Said he's been admiring me from afar.'

'How did you choose?'

'Took the first one who asked, my old school buddy. I think he knew the other one was on my scent and he pounced first.'

'A pre-emptive strike.'

'If you say so. Could have gone either way though, because the other one had a softer side to him. I had to choose if I wanted a hard centre or a soft centre and I guess I'm a traditionalist and think that men should be hard inside.'

'Really? You make them sound like boiled sweets.'

'Not really picky, me. Either would have done really. You make the best of marriage, don't you? Whatever you start with, you have to make the best of it.'

To the left, just inside the graveyard, something moves and we are both distracted. A large fox has skipped up onto a tomb and is staring at us, its eyes reflecting all the lights.

'Red fox,' I say.

'Didn't know we had any on Orkney.'

'We don't, basically they don't exist here.'

'That one does.'

'It could be a sign. My neighbour, Alex, says that sighting rare animals is an intimation of approaching death, that they are the souls of those who went before coming to guide you to the other side.'

'Bloody hell, I'm no planning to die. I'm getting married.'

'Aye, well, he also told me once that if a fox crosses your path it means that you'll encounter a significant gain in life.'

'A superstition for every occasion.'

'Silly sod nailed a fox's head he'd brought back from down south to our front door once. Thought we might be cursed and it would help.'

'Funny folk out there.'

'Out there? You mean not living in the metropolis of Kirkwall?' I say, and we both laugh. 'Living in the past more like. The further you go out of the town, the further you go back in time.'

Our voices didn't seem to bother the fox but after a while it gets fed up and scampers towards the back of the graveyard. We are silent for a minute or two. Watching, to see if it will come back.

'What did the other suitor say? The one you turned down,' I say, after a while.

'He cried. Said he couldn't live without me and he'd make me change my mind. He cries a lot. He's emotional and soft as shit.'

'Blimey, didn't know the blokes round here could be that romantic.'

The girl laughs. She seems pleased with herself in spite of the mess in her hair and the restraints.

'And he wasn't even drunk,' she says.

'Come to think of it, I've just been chatted up by a softy too.'

The girl opens her eyes, wide.

'Seeing him later. I liked him, but always fear the worst in men. Are you sure you're okay?'

'Aye.'

'Don't need a wee?'

'No, but don't keep talking about it, and give him a chance; they aren't all bad, men,' she says.

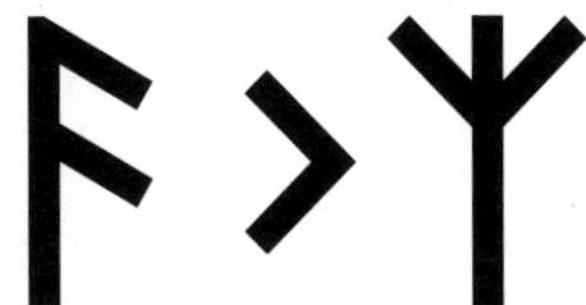

(Ansuz. Kenaz Reversed. Algiz)

*'I see good Advice and a protective influence but going separate ways.'*

# 5. GENDER BENDER

Cross and girl in deep shade now. She looks cold, but happy enough, so I slip away. Walk back down Broad Street till I get to Castle Street, crossing over to the hotel side and the ruins. Sure enough, Martin is in her favourite spot. In front of her, herring gulls hopping around, still hopeful for food at the water's edge.

'Still here then?' she calls out, watching me circumnavigate a pile of stones, all that's left of the long-gone castle roof.

She is sitting opposite a break in the curtain wall of the castle. Remains of the east gate which led to the dungeons. Above her, what is left of the star chamber window, just a frame for some sky now, beside an indentation from a cannon ball. Surrounded by clusters of marble-sized musket holes like constellations of stars.

I tiptoe though the ancient battleground, not wanting to disturb the dead. Wondering if there is any petrified flesh amongst the stones. Slow-release fertiliser for the tiny white stars of Arvo and Common Chickweed that are poking up amongst the rubble, along with Pineapple Weed, and Rat's Tail.

'Hello. Anyone there?' Martin says.

'Aye,' I say, after turning the page on my thoughts.

Can't help smiling. Normal reaction to the intensity of her stare. Sees something in me that I don't, or she is also searching for the clue that explains me.

'I thought you were going to kill yourself,' she says, as I get closer. She moves to one side to let me sit down. Might be my friend but I don't really know her that well. Only one I speak to about things like that though.

'Aye, the night,' I say.

'The night?'

Doubt in her voice. As if she is thinking, 'Well, you said that before and here you still are.'

'Aye,' I say.

A sparrow hawk circling overhead with bulging and rounded wings. Seen one here before, hunting starlings at dusk on their way to nest in the sycamores. Perhaps it is the lingering tincture of death that attracts them.

'I've heard pills and booze work well, but not that paracetamol crap, just buggers you up,' Martin says.

I shrug because I don't want to get into that.

'Got myself a date first though,' I say.

'Who, Bigsy? He fancies you.'

'No, some guy up for the show. Meeting him later. Called Sigurd, he's a student, says he is studying philosophy.'

'He know your plans, for later?'

I nod.

'Seemed to think it was a joke. Whenever I say something serious, he laughs,' I say.

'He might be the ONE then?'

'No, if you still want to know if I have done *it* yet, the answer is still no, not properly.'

'Properly? There's nothing proper about doing it.'

'Not under my own volition.'

'You and your fancy fucking words.'

'Volition,' I say. Slowly slurring all the syllables into a streak of sound. That makes her laugh.

'Did someone force you? It isn't that mad bugger of a father of yours, is it? Has he been…?'

I shrug and look away.

'What is it with you and your dad?'

'I don't want to talk about it.'

'If he does, you need to get out of there.'

'Tonight is the night,' I say, looking up at the sky. Wonder if I'll end up in heaven.

'You're a crazy bitch.'

'Aye, that's what the meds are for, to keep me sane.'

'Got any to spare?' Martin says, but this time I ignore her craving for narcotics, even though I do have my stash with me.

'I've been thinking about what it's like, afterwards. They say your life is supposed to flash in front of your eyes and you can see the future, the closer you are to death the more you understand,' I say.

'Who says?'

'I watched my gran die. Just before she went, she said she understood everything. She was smiling and then she breathed out for the last time. That's what death is – one long last breath. It smelled sweet. Like her soul was made of candyfloss.'

'Shit, you're not expecting to find yourself in Heaven, are you?'

'When you die the light goes out in your eyes.'

'When was this?'

'Oh, before we came here. My dad went to make a cup of tea and she passed. When he came back, she was gone and he dropped the tea and hugged her. I'd never seen him hug her when she was alive.'

'So, you think death is going to be a revelation?'

'I think you find out what life is all about.'

'You're the only person I believe when they say they'll do it, you know.'

'Who else do you know planning to kill themselves?'

'Plenty in the winter, when it's so fucking bleak and seems to be going on forever.'

'Last Summer Night, winter's coming; next thing you'll know it will be Christmas.'

Martin looks at me. Until now she could have been talking to the birds.

'Want a drink?' she says.

I nod.

'Stay here, I'll be back with a charge.'

'Moiety,' I say.

Feel cool in the shade. Is it a poltergeist passing? Do ghosts stay where they died, or where they were buried, or where they lived, or do we all have to go to live in the catacombs below the cathedral? If ghosts can move around then the castle and the cathedral and Broad Street behind us must be swimming with restless souls.

Is that why it is cold in Kirkwall? Nothing to do with being so far north, just the density of the dead, sucking the heat from the sun. Is Alex right about why I see birds and plants in all the wrong places? Are they dead people showing themselves to be my guide on my final journey?

I have always been aware of ghosts.

*I have tied a plastic wastepaper bin to my back with string and I am holding the brush and tube of the vacuum cleaner in my arms, when Thomas enters the room.*

*'Hello,' he says nicely. It was before, so it was okay and easy to be nice.*

*'What are you doing?'*

*'I'm a Ghostbuster,' I say.*

*'Oh, like in the film,' he says, and I nod my head.*

*'I didn't know that we had ghosts.'*

*'So, it worked,' I say, and we both laugh.*

*'Are they friendly?'*

*'There are ghosts everywhere,' I say, even before I knew that to be true.*

*'Oh,' he says, leaving the room so that I could carry on hunting for ghosts, only to come back a few minutes later with a white sheet over his head.*

*I killed him, the ghost, and he died and then he tickled me and we both laughed.*

Laughing when Martin returns.

'What?' she says, as she gets closer.

'My head is full of shit.'

'Well, it seems to have cheered you up,' Martin says. She is carrying two, two-litre bottles of dry cider.

She passes me one of the bottles and I take a deep swallow.

'I thought about it, you know. Killing myself. I thought about it but then remembered what a shit childhood I had and didn't want to load all that on Alba,' Martin says.

'Patriotic calling her after the Gaelic name for Scotland,' I say.

'She's named after a white wrinkled rose my mother has in her garden. Rugosa Alba, they call it. It smells beautiful, like a newborn baby and Alba wrinkles her nose when she cries. It seemed heaven sent, or even scent, with a 'c'.'

Martin reaches down for her bag and pulls out her purse which contains a little money but also some light blue pills.

'Want one?' she says, popping a couple into her mouth and sluicing them down with cider.

'No, not tonight. You and your little blue pills.'

'Aye, pill-popping keeps me sane. It's my alternative to topping myself. If you can't face reality you have to choose, it seems to me, end it all, or change it.'

'Must be expensive.'

'Perk of my little sideline.'

I swig the drink and wait. Doesn't normally open up like this and I am curious. Martin takes a deep slurp of cider and burps deliberately loudly. She looks out across the Peedie Sea and then turns to me again.

'Once a month I take a little ferry trip down to Aberdeen and come back a day later,' Martin says.

'That's a job?'

'Aye, pays well and I get some of these thrown in.'

Martin takes out a bag of pills and lets me peep inside. They are mostly blue, but one or two of them are pink.

'In fact, I have to go tomorrow night.'

'Your mum look after Alba?'

'Yep. I don't want my mum to know, so I tell her I'm staying with a friend. She thinks I've got me a new man and wants me to find a dad for Alba.'

'Is the drug baron dad material then?'

'As it happens, he is, but he's not really my type.'

'Aren't you worried about what happens to Alba if you get caught?'

'My boss says there's no chance of that.'

'Easy for him to say. Do you trust him?'

'Actually, he's a nice guy. Not the sort of guy you'd expect to be into this stuff really. He likes kids. Asks after Alba a lot. I think he might be a bit broody.'

'OMG, he's not Alba's father, is he?'

Martin looks away and then laughs to herself, before looking back at me.

'No, kept that in the family. Nearly incest, but not quite. There, bet that surprised you, but it's all you're getting. Even for a lass who is on her way out the night.'

'Does your mum know?'

'Aye, but she pretends not to. Doesn't want to believe it, but she knows what he's like.'

'Shit. I thought my life was a mess.'

'What the fuck do you have to worry about. No inbred kids, no criminal entanglements and you're kind of cute too.'

I shake my head. Feeling sorry for myself.

'Your problem is you need to get out more. You spend too much time brooding in that wee house of yours, clinging to the past. No fucking point. It's gone. Let it go. If you only knew more people, you'd realise that most of us have problems and anxieties and troubles that we struggle with.'

I don't need a lecture. Not now.

'I don't want you to die,' she says.

I shrug. Have nothing else to say.

ᚺ ᚹ ᚷ

(Hagalaz. Wunjo Reversed. Gebo)

*'There will be an unexpected disruption, expect to be depressed and dissatisfied, but a partnership is in sight.'*

# 6. AY UP ME DUCKS

There is a knock on the door of the Auld Men's Hut. The five men around the table stop talking and look surprised, as if they don't often get visitors. They turn towards the door as Davey walks in and looks around the room.

'Ay up me ducks,' Davey says. He is silhouetted in the doorway until he turns to close the door and the table dwellers see him more clearly in the penumbra of light that skirts the room. He moves sideways to stand beside the red fire extinguisher behind the door, as if he is standing beside a little red boy, his son.

Tommy, with his back to the door, struggles to maintain the twist that allows him to see the intruder.

'Can we help you?' Tommy says, scraping his chair around to see who he is talking to.

'Aye, I'm tired and need to sit,' Davey says, and walks around the table to a spare chair in front of the fire.

'That's Stan's chair,' Alec says.

'Well, he's no here, is he,' Davey says.

'Actually, we're in the middle of something,' Walli says.

'Aye, me too. I'm travelling. I'm eighty-four and still exploring. My daughter says I'm a gypsy. I'm off to Shetland next week. Well, boys, don't let me stop you,' Davey says.

'This is a private meeting,' Jock says.

'Hardly business-like, is it?' he says, glancing at the books and magazines strewn across the table, with empty cups in front of each man. An archipelago of ceramic mugs.

'I'm afraid you can't stay here,' Walli says.

'Is that so, me ducks? Bloke in the street there told me it was for old men to sit and rest,' Davey says.

'Well, yes, if you are from Kirkwall, it is,' Walli says.

'Me, I'm fae Wigton, but I stay in Corby now. Have lived in the same house for sixty years, but still haven't been in all the houses in the street. Tube works. Steelman, me. Bloke I met told me that the only qualification to come in here was to have balls and be over 65 and you can grab 'em to see if you like.'

Tommy and Walli laugh.

'That's what'll be than, making all the noise, those steel balls of yours,' Jock says.

Everyone laughs at this, including Davey.

'Ball bearings,' Ray says, catching up on the conversation.

'I like it here at this end of the country. What's the world coming to though when Lands' End is owned by Yanks?' Davey says.

'Is it?' Walli says.

The five men around the table exchange glances and then start speaking, but Davey can't understand it all as they have slipped into a heavy Orkney dialect. He takes this opportunity to pull out Stan's chair and sit down. He waits for a while before speaking.

'Enough of this bollocks,' he says, angrily. 'I can speak a few tongues that you would na understand too. Speak so I can understand you.'

Tommy and Jock look surprised, but Walli smiles.

'Davey, sorry for that, we don't mean to be rude. I guess most tourists don't know about the Pierhead Parliament,' Walli says.

'Pierhead Parliament? I like it. Get more sense from you lot than we do from those other buggers. That's it. I'm thinking we should have a parliament on every pier in the country. How many's that then?' Davey says.

'Aberdeen,' Walli says.

'Invergordon and Grangemouth,' Tommy says.

'Fraserburgh, Rosyth, Leith,' Alec says.

'What about huts?' Ray says.

'Well, yes. Look, piers are no the subject for the night. We can do piers another time. Look, Davey, you are welcome to rest here for a while, if you don't mind us droning on. And we'll speak clear Queen's English too, so you can hear what we are talking about,' Walli says, while beginning to tidy the magazines in front of him to regain order and assert his authority as the putative chair.

Davey smiles, nods his head, and notices a picture of the young Queen Elizabeth on the wall.

'I met the Queen. Well, I nearly bumped into the Queen once. I was working at Balmoral and I was strong then. In those days, they had big bags of coal and us youngsters had to do all the lifting. I got it on my shoulder and staggered around the corner and this wee woman was there. Nearly bumped into her then noticed who it was. "Pardon, Ma'am," I says.'

'What did she say?' Jock says.

'Nothing, she just smiled. She never smiled much, not to us, but then she did. I think she was a bit embarrassed.'

There was a long pause, everyone watching Davey smiling to himself as he was lost in an earlier time, another life.

'On you own, now, Davey?' Tommy says.

'Aye. My wife went ten years ago. Motor neurone disease. Made her sound like she was a car needed a service.'

'Well, I've got a classic car, not sure if she is a vintage or a veteran, but she is still going strong. Matured into a dragon though. I married a wee girl fifty-three year ago that was pretty and soft and nice to me. She's now made of stone and breathes fire,' Tommy says.

'I miss her,' Davey says.

'Aye. I'm sure I would too if Helen weren't around,' Tommy says.

'You'd be lost without a car, where you live,' Walli says, and they all laugh, except for Ray, who doesn't get the joke.

'I saw one of them hit a mine in the war, you know?' Davey says, looking out towards the fishing boats in the basin and the others follow his gaze.

'And one of them fast RAF boats, that used to go out and pick up pilots. Just went 'bang' and blew up in a big cloud of water. Off Newcastle. I was there then,' Davey says.

'That was a long time ago, you must have been wee then,' Tommy says.

'Aye, I've seen a lot. We was off to see Wales play in a football match and came over a hill and it was like that old TV programme, *Quartermass*, searchlights everywhere, it didn't look real. All them children killed,' Davey says, staring at the water.

'Aberfan?' Walli says.

'Aye.'

'When you get to our age, you have a lot of memories, don't you?' Tommy says.

'Aye, if you haven't gone dotty with that Alzheimer's. Keeps coming back. All these things I've done. They keep coming back,' Davey says. 'Trouble is, I don't remember how it feels. All me emotions seem to have been used up. Is that a thing? Does your heart shrink with age?'

This left the Pierhead Parliament silent, and deep in thought.

(Thurisaz Reversed)

*'Be careful to check Every angle.'*

'I feel honoured to get to visit the family home,' Sandy says, smiling, when Kito opens the front door and steps forward to kiss her on the cheek.

'We don't normally use this door,' Kito says. He seems preoccupied, almost annoyed at the inconvenience, even though he invited her to come over.

'Oh, sorry. You'll need a sign then. I saw your tour signs, but not one that said Entrance.'

'I normally hear people coming and get to them before they get this far,' Kito says.

'I parked up the lane.'

'That'll be it then. Anyway, I'm a bit distracted tonight. Come in.'

'Am I the distraction?'

'Sorry, but I'm worried about something,' he says, ignoring her question.

'Tell me more,' Sandy says, squeezing past Kito into the narrow hallway. He is staring past her down the drive, lost in thought.

'It's the second time tonight that this door has been opened,' he says.

Sandy looks puzzled.

'I said I'd never open it. I thought it would bring bad luck.'

'Oh, okay. Anyway, it's brought me. I hope I'm not bad luck. So, what's up? Clearly, it's not just you longing to see me again?'

'I need your help,' Kito says. 'I'll tell you inside.'

As they move along the mimosa-scented corridor, little does Sandy know it is the smell of the past. Panda's mother's sweet perfumed scarf still hanging on its hook. Kito leads her into the front room, passing the broken doorframe into Panda's bedroom. The door open and her bedside light still on.

The front room has two windows looking out over the fields towards Scapa Flow, whose surface tonight is made of tweed. On closer inspection, the few imperfections in the weave are ships at anchor, all pointing in the same direction. A long dark fold in the cloth is a super-tanker waiting to take on oil at the Flotta terminal.

'What are all those things in the field?' Sandy says, pointing to the ring of clay figures in the middle distance.

'My daughter made them and she won't let me get rid of them.'

'They look great. She's very talented. Why would you want to get rid of them?'

Kito looks uncomfortable and anxious, as if this wasn't why he had asked her to come around and he'd rather not talk about it.

'They are statues of her mother.'

Sandy frowns and turns to look at him.

'A sort of memorial?' Sandy says. 'When did she die?'

'I don't really want to get into this right now, but I haven't been completely honest about that.'

'You told me she was dead.'

'Yes. It seemed the easiest explanation.'

'I don't see why you need to lie about it.'

'Can I explain another time? I'm worried about my daughter and I need your help now.'

'Not exactly evidence of having let go of the past and being free to move on either, is it? Sandy says.

'I'm not sure I am ready to move on.'

'I came to that conclusion too,' she says, still staring at the terracotta army of past wives as something rushes by, and this makes her pause for a few seconds and he notices.

'Brown Hare. It's one of the Orkney Five: Hen Harrier; Barnacle Goose; Grey Seal; Damsel Butterfly; and Brown Hare. They feature in my Orkney Big Game Tour,' he says.

'Sorry, but I'm still on the statues. I think it's a bit bloody weird,' Sandy says.

'Don't worry, it might be weird but I'm not dangerous.'

'I didn't think you were, but I'm still computing all this. Anyway, I've told Margaret where I am.'

'Vote of confidence then?'

'Kito, I hardly know you. You tell me you don't want me to come to your house because of your daughter,' she says, looking back towards the statues in the field, 'and maybe even this odd hobby of hers, and my best friend has told me to stay away from incomers like you,' Sandy says.

'Really?'

'Yes, I showed her your profile picture on Match.com and she said that you were far too cute not to have a partner, so beware. Oh, and she looked at your flat earth website which, frankly, should put anyone off.'

'But you weren't.'

Sandy shrugs and looks back at him as if he might have an ulterior motive for getting her into his house and she is trying to work out if she should worry after all.

'I don't have anyone else to turn to,' he says, in tears. The sight of his pain makes her sit down opposite him, turning her back on the view and the statues.

'Actually, that's pretty sad, having to turn to me, but what's so urgent?'

'My daughter has run off.'

'How long ago?' Sandy says. Her arms across her chest, her legs crossed.

'An hour, or so.'

'Don't you mean she's gone out?'

'She doesn't go out much, not at night, and she never locks her bedroom door,' he says, shifting forward a little in the saggy chair that looks like it is trying to eat him and he is struggling to resist being swallowed.

'Has she taken anything? Clothes, money, a suitcase, that sort of thing?'

He shakes his head.

'How old is she?'

'Nineteen.'

'She's an adult. I don't know what you're so worried about.'

'Yes, but she's not well.'

The dull thrum of an aeroplane engine can now be heard in the room. It gets louder and becomes a distraction. It only takes a minute to pass, but they both seem to share the desire to pause and it is a convenient excuse. Brian, high above them, is looking down on Mainland, anticipating his imminent demise.

'What's wrong with her?' Sandy says.

'Depression mostly. She's on medication for that. But she's also a bit of dreamer. Gets lost all the time in her music and some fantastic world, where everything is set to music and Orkney and I don't exist. Oh, and she has a form of Tourette's Syndrome.'

'Is that where people say rude things all the time?'

'Yes, but only a small proportion of people with Tourette's do that. It's what gets them on TV, but she just shouts out random and often pretty obscure words.'

'Why?'

'She likes nice sounding words. Bit of a poet as it happens. It's like a tic. A word comes into her head and she can't suppress it.'

Sandy looks puzzled.

'Petrichor, she says that a lot,' Kito says.

'What does it mean?'

'It's the smell you get just after a rain shower on a hot afternoon. I only know because I find myself looking up her words and I like that one.'

'Has she run off before?'

'No, she doesn't get out much. We lead a pretty cut-off life.'

'Might do her good to get out then,' Sandy says, looking around the sparsely furnished room that feels damp and surprisingly cold for such a bright evening. The sort of chill you get in Pickaquoy Tesco; even on the warmest days it feels cold in the food aisle near the chillers.

Kito picks up a notebook from the table beside his chair, opens it, and hands it to Sandy.

'Read that.'

'What is it?'

'It's Panda's diary.'

'I'm not sure either of us should be reading her diary.'

'Please. You'll see why I am worried.'

'No, I don't want to do that. Diaries are private. Didn't anyone ever tell you that?' she says, handing him back the book.

'Can I read you a bit? I think it's important. I'm worried about her.'

Sandy sits back in the chair and shrugs, and Kito reads.

'I've killed myself, just now, or an hour ago, this morning, or yesterday. It really depends when you get around to reading this,' he says, reading the diary entry slowly and shaking his head, as if he is still trying to take it in, before scanning the page and continuing. 'I hope you are now crippled with doubt, blame, and self-hatred for the rest of your life,' he says, looking up at Sandy and closing the diary on his lap.

'Well, what do you think?' he says, after a minute or so.

Sandy takes her time before replying, as if she is listening to an echo.

'I'm trying to work out where to start,' she says, shaking her head.

'I think she writes these things to hurt me.'

'Only if you read her diary. She doesn't seem to think much of you.'

'I told you we didn't get on well.'

'Yes, but I wasn't expecting this.'

'Well, what do you think?'

'Well, if we skip the bit about why the hell you are reading her diary in the first place. Is that what all that mess in the hall is about? Did you break into her room to get it?'

Kito nods. 'There's more,' he says, gesturing towards the diary.

'I don't want to hear any more of it,' Sandy says, leaning forward in her chair.

Kito closes the diary and hugs it to his chest.

'She clearly needs help. I'd say you need to find her before she does something stupid.'

'How?'

'Kito, how do I know? I run a B&B, not a clinic. All I know is this is awful, your life with her is a mess and you need to do something about it.' She stands up and looks back out of the window and shakes her head.

'This,' she says, 'isn't just weird, it's criminal,' pointing towards the statues. 'Her mother has gone or died, or something, and you let her make pottery versions of her?'

'I thought it might help.'

'Well, did it?'

'We named her Pandora, because we thought she would bring us hope and Pandora was formed out of clay by the gods. She really isn't well and sometimes I think she thinks she can mould another mother from the soil. She looks at them as if they will one day start to breathe and walk back to her.'

'How the hell do you think that is going to help? Does she think they'll replace her? You said you home schooled her too. What the hell did you teach her? All this flat earth stuff and mythical mumbo-jumbo? No wonder she's depressed, anyone would be. You've made her feel that she is different at a time when adolescents most need to feel the same.'

'Sounds like you might run a clinic after all.'

'Don't you remember what it was like to be that age? You need to belong, to feel secure,' she says, raising her voice.

'I didn't mean to make you angry.'

'I'm frustrated. I just don't understand how anyone could be so stupid.'

Kito bursts into tears and his body crumples. He is sobbing and moaning and hugging himself, rocking back and forward on the edge of his chair. Sandy sits down opposite and lets him cry. It is a while before he is able to speak again.

'I haven't been myself,' Kito says.

'If I thought for one second you had been, you wouldn't see me for dust.'

'I think I've been going through some sort of slow-motion breakdown, but tonight it has speeded up.'

Sandy stands and looks out of the window at the terracotta shadows in the slowly dissolving summer's day and then turns around to look at him. He is crying, silently. His body bent forward, arms and legs crossed, still hugging the diary. She doesn't say anything for a bit, then shakes her head.

'I now see why a cute guy like you is on his own.'

Kito brushes the tears from his eyes to see her more clearly. Looking up at her, childlike.

'Look, I have enough problems of my own, but I'll do what I can,' she says.

Kito stands up quickly and Sandy takes a step back, her face registering concern, which Kito sees immediately.

'Sorry, I didn't mean to startle you. Thank you. Really, thank you.'

'My night on the town with the girls would have been an ordeal anyway. I think I'm past my drinking prime.'

'Thank you.'

'It's okay. We'll need a recent picture of her.'

'Okay.'

'Posters. Can you print off twenty or so with your mobile number on it and we'll put them up around town. No, 50. Print 50 before we go. You should ring the police.'

ᛒᛖᛚ

(Berkana Reversed. Ehwaz Reversed. Laguz Reversed)

*'Expect domestic trouble, you'll be restless and confined, and entering a period of confusion.'*

# 7. THE FEAST

Swift Eye spots Sigurd as soon as he enters the function room, now a replica Viking dining hall. The burning torches are effective, though just iPads attached to the wall with short videos on replay that Rosy took at the Up Helly Aa celebrations in Lerwick some years before. He is standing in the middle of the room with her and Sigurd's uncle from Bonxie, Billy, who is known within the family as Hooky.

'Siggy, good to see you,' he says moving towards Sigurd, towing the others behind him. 'Hooky tells me that you've taken to university. Where is it you stay?' Swift Eye says, shaking him vigorously by the hand.

Sigurd, nods, almost bows, to the smaller man. 'Hello, uncle. It's Marchmont.'

'Posh place that, Marchmont. I went into a deli there once and nearly fell over with the price of everything. Mind, it must be fifteen years since we've been to Edinburgh.'

'Travel can be dangerous. You go away and then people take what is yours,' Rognald, Sigurd's father, says as he joins them.

Rather pointedly, he doesn't show the customary sign of respect to his brother.

'It is hard to leave. As you get older you lose the urge to go off on trips,' Swift Eye says.

'What would our ancestors say about that? Wasn't our fortune the result of a summer expedition? Didn't some hairy-arsed blokes come and bang the rightful owners of the land on the head and take it from them?' Rosy says.

'They say so, they say they took the land and somehow, over the years, our family has managed to keep it,' Swift Eye says.

'Thank Valhalla, we don't have to fight for it anymore,' Rosy says, just as a phone rings on the table by the door and several men rush over to see if it is theirs. The ringing soon stops.

'Oh, we do, but it's a different sort of fighting. Instead of warriors we have solicitors,' Swift Eye says, looking around the room to judge by the mood and the intensity of conversation if it is time to sit down.

'Bloody hell, I never thought of lawyers as modern-day Vikings,' Hooky says.

'Lawyers only exist to make sure that people like you keep what you've got,' Rognald says to his brother.

'People like us, actually. We have both benefited, over the years. In England, old money came from slaves, here we just took what we wanted and defended it. Still doing that today. Did you hear the trouble we've had over the land out at Car Ness?'

'Where you plan to build twenty houses?' Rognald says.

'That's it. Great spot right by the water. Get a good price, I reckon.'

'Aye, as I recall, half of the land was left to me in the old way, so I don't know how you seem to think it is yours to do with as you like,' Rognald says, smiling at Rosy, who looks away.

'I am the one who stayed. You left this place in disgrace with me maimed and our family broken and stranded. It is me and my family who have had to defend it from the high hills to the sea,' Swift

Eye says.

'It is half my land by rights, ancient rights,' Rognald says.

'Not anymore. Anyway, you used to tell me that people belonged to the land and it didn't belong to people?'

'The ancient laws can't be changed by you alone. I have come to shout out my rights to the land. I want it back. It is then up to me what I do with it,' Rognald says, raising his voice a little. Sigurd looks uncomfortable even though he knew what his father was going to say.

'I don't see the others paying you homage. I am standing on the mountain now.'

'Be careful, brother, if you don't do as I say, don't be surprised if the valley comes to the mountain.'

'Boys, this is not the time and place to fight over land. Don't you remember why we are here and what happened the last time you two fought?' Rosy says, talking to her husband and ignoring Rognald's stare.

'When and where would be the right place?' Rognald says.

'Let's eat. It is time to start the family feast. We have swan,' Swift Eye says, turning and raising his arm in a gesture that invites others to follow him. The chat-chat stops and people begin to make their way to their allotted seats.

'Great, love swan,' says Sigurd, walking beside Hooky to the far table.

'I hate it too,' he says, as he looks for his place and turns to sit down.

Thirty people sit in a big square, like they have done for generations. Fruit juice is served and then the staff leave and the door is locked.

'I call on my brother and honoured guest, Rognald,' Swift Eye says, raising his glass.

Rognald gets to his feet and makes this verse:

*We share this talon-gripped earth,*
*battle-scarred and fed with*
*elders' blood. Keel-dug trenches*
*show the way.*
*Each voyage line cut deep into the Jarl's*
*heart.*
*No rightful claim lost, just stored*
*for those to reassert, for fear of*
*battle-fury being loosed again.*

'To our father and his father and his father, to whom we owe our lives. To their memory and their rule of law which we are bound to keep. To their honour, we now drink.'

Rognald drinks orange squash from his *auroch* horn and the others follow. Those with ancient drinking horns place them carefully back on the table, but some of the young men have pewter mugs which they toss onto the floor. By the mess it makes, it appears that not everyone drank it all. Some of them laugh at the tinny sound of metal on the wooden floor and the sight of the pile of dented pewter cups, which look like they are sitting in a pool of piss. The elders ignore the ritual that they have now outgrown and ponder the meaning and intent of Rognald's verse.

Swift Eye bangs the table, the doors are unlocked and opened, and in comes the first course.

'What would our ancestors think of a feast in a temperance hotel?' Sigurd says to his uncle, who is sitting beside him.

'They'd think we'd taken leave of our senses.'

'Oh great, Haggis,' Sigurd says, when he sees the plates being carried to the head table, to serve Swift Eye first.

'Yes, I hate it too.'

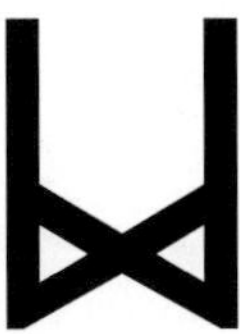

## (Mannaz Reversed)

*'You will feel isolated and lonely.'*

'What you dreaming about?' Martin says, after draining her cider bottle. Mine still half full.

'Just reliving my fictitious sex life,' I have been thinking about what I wrote in my diary. Wondering if I had gone too far. An old bloke walked by and I thought of sex. Why I associate the two things in my mind is beyond me. Do they both offer a kind of security that I crave?

Martin shrugs and takes another drink, exposing a new-looking rose tattoo on her right forearm.

'That must be an Alba rose. Let me see the others.'

Martin rolls up her shirt sleeve to show me that her arm is covered with tattoos. She then undoes the front of blouse and there are tattoos on the top of her breasts too.

'Wow.'

'You like my tits?' she says.

'I was admiring your tats.'

Take off my jacket and roll up my shirt sleeves to show her my arms.

'Fuck. What a mess.'

She reaches out and touches the scars. Lets her fingers linger for a while on the most recent scabs.

'How did you do that?'

'Walls of a house in School Place. It's nothing. The sandstone scratches rather than cuts. I do this when I'm happy. If I want to hurt myself I find a cement wall, but if I'm really unhappy, I use that pebble dash shit that is everywhere on houses here.'

'They call it harl.'

'If you rub hard it cuts deep down into the flesh and it burns like hell. Blood, skin and bubbly fat everywhere. It flays you alive.'

'Why?' Martin says, shaking her head and grimacing.

'I get these intense feelings of anxiety. When everything, my skin, my clothes and even my lovely bedroom are hateful and I have to get rid of them. But it's mostly my skin. I feel that if I can change my skin, all the pain will go away.'

'Does this happen often?'

'Often enough to know where all the good walls are, where you get a good burn and you can't be seen.'

'Who's that? Boyfriend?' she says, pointing to my forearm where I have carved the letter S with a kitchen knife.

'My mother.' These simple words release the tears and Martin puts her arm around me and holds me tight until I stop crying. My head sinks into the satin cushions of her tattooed breasts that smell faintly of flooers.

'She's dead. I killed her.'

Sit still together for a while. Don't need to say anything else. She knows that she can't trust everything I say, but the graffiti on my skin tells the story of my unhappiness.

The noise coming from Broad Street, behind us, suggests the night is getting started.

'Come, let's see what's up,' she says, and tugs me off the wall, pulling me behind her like a puppy on a lead. I like it, not having to make up my own mind about what we are going to do next. Often the biggest problem, what to do next? I never know which of the terrible options is better. She leads me to the corner of the park and we stash my half-finished cider behind the overflowing rubbish bins and head back into town.

The park grass is knee high. Wild meadow where once children played. On the edge of the tall grasses a lovely yellow patch of

Lady's Bedstraw, and tall purply Sticky Buttons, that remind me of thistles, taking advantage in the break in cultivation. I wonder what Mainland would look like with no farming, if it was allowed to go wild again. Better still, if there were no people; only me and the birds and the bees. I remembered playing with *her* in a park like this, but with short grass; it seems even further away now, as if the past has retreated another step.

'Watch out. Rex is on the prowl,' Martin says, nodding to the right where Rex, dressed in his familiar leather waistcoat, is walking towards us. Sleeves rolled up to show off his tattoos of ships, anchors and girls' names, even though they say he has never left Kirkwall.

'He's either got a colostomy bag down his trousers or the biggest balls I've ever seen,' Martin says and I laugh.

Bulge at the top of his right leg that makes him walk like a bandy-legged cowboy.

'Girls,' is all he says as he passes us. He glances disapprovingly at my arms, so I cover them up.

'How long do you think before the first fight?' Martin says.

'I'd give him half an hour. Depends what pub he chooses.'

'I see him a lot in The Ship, so maybe there,' Martin says, as we both watch him walk down the road. His distinctive swagger interesting to watch.

'Mean bastard. I wouldn't want to fight him.'

'Perfect night for him, the boys'll be so pissed they'll be more inclined to take him on.'

'Scary bastard, that one. Like an alligator ready to pounce.'

'Can't hear no clock ticking,' Martin says, still watching him shrink into the distance, though I have turned away.

'No, sadly, we are not in a fairy tale.'

'I'm not sure about that.'

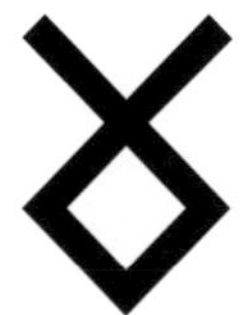

## (Othala Reversed)

*'The rune tells of a lost possession.'*

In Broad Street, the blackening lorry has stopped in front of the Town Hall, surrounded by a noisy gang. We pass a window full of funeral notices and mine is at the top, in pride of place, or at least it should be. I pull Martin over to the window to show her.

'Mine will be up there tomorrow.'

Martin frowns and shakes her head, and we walk back towards the lorry.

'Did you know that anyone living in Broad Street can't be buried in the cathedral?'

'Why?' she says.

'Because they are still alive.'

Martin shakes her head.

The bride-to-be has just been released from the cross and replaced with her two bridesmaids, shrieking with delight as they are wrapped into place. I now know her name because 'Jenny' is written in big letters on the back of the truck where she is standing in her cling film wrap-around dress. She is looking down at a man in the crowd.

'I told you I love you, didn't I?' A young man standing on the road is crying, looking up and pleading with her. She sees me approaching, raises her eyebrows and smiles. Cars slow down as they pass to watch what is going on.

'Johnno, not here. I'm getting married tomorrow and if Fran turns up he'll kill you,' Jenny says.

'He can try,' he says. A grown man crying over love, but no one is making fun of him; they all seem to share his pain.

'I'm getting married the morrow to Fran and that's it. You're a lovely guy but I told you 'no', didn't I?' Jenny says.

'Johnno, you'd better go, mate. Fran'll be here soon. We said we'd all go for a drink,' a friend says, holding him by the arm and trying to drag him away from the lorry.

'I'm no scared of him. I'll fight him for you?' he says, looking at Jenny, who seems bewildered but clearly pleased that he should feel so strongly.

We watch as Johnno persists in his quest, even though he is told several times that Fran is coming. Martin looks concerned, as if he has connected with her. Something has made her thoughtful. Maybe the unusual outflowing of passion from a man. Hard not to get drawn into such genuine and unexpected emotion.

Sure enough, Fran soon appears with a small entourage, still covered in feathers like an Aztec nobleman. Gets a cheer from the assembled crowd as the blackened groom jumps up on the back of the lorry to stand beside his bride-to-be.

'What's up?' Fran says.

'I challenge you to a duel,' Johnno says.

'Been drinking?' Fran smiling to himself but directing his comment to the audience.

'Stone cold fucking sober.'

'Yes, like as much. Piss off, man, you had your chance and she said no.'

Fran looks at Jenny. 'Well, didn't you?'

'Aye.'

'I'll fight you for her hand, you can choose the weapons,' Johnno says.

'Don't I get a say in this. I'm nobody's property, ye naes,' she says to him.

'Can someone take this wanker out of here before I hit him?' Fran says, and a few of Johnno's friends grab him and pull him away.

'I'll be back,' Johnno shouts as he is led off. 'You've not heard the last of me the night.'

'Bloody hell, girl, you do pick them, don't you?' Fran says to Jenny.

'You can talk. I picked you, didn't I?'

The crowd begins to disintegrate, so we break off and head back towards the harbour.

'Fancy a proper drink?' Martin says.

'Why not.' Not really sure where we'll find a 'proper drink', but sense it will involve a less familiar pub this time. Happy enough in the Castle, even The Ship, but Skippers and Tauvaig bars are too rowdy, particularly on Show Night. Full of men who seem threatened by someone like me.

'They're all out the night,' Martin says, pointing at Ewan passing the old Customs House, already without his top, walking along Albert Street, towards the harbour with another man.

'Oh God, not Nobby too, did you see him last year?'

'No, this is my first proper Show Night, but I heard. You?'

'Yes, I've seen him do it over the years. It just comes naturally to him. Oh my God, look,' Martin points to a side street opposite, where Ewan's mother, carrying a laundry bag, is peeking around the corner spying on her son.

'What is he, forty? She only lets him out on Show Night and now she's following him around,' Martin says.

'To be fair, from what I hear, he probably does need looking after.'

'The night is still young.'

# WHY YOU HATE HONEYSUCKLE

*You are standing on the wobbly bench by the big smelly hedgerow, covered in whirly yellow flowers, watching as your mother heads for the car. She seems angry, as if you have done something wrong. She is wearing the coat you found. Your father is crying, standing in front of the car, as if he is a tree and he knows that cars can't drive through trees.*

*When you grow up to be a big girl, you'll realise that the flowers all around you are called Woodbine, or Honeysuckle, and people wore them to avert bad things happening, but they didn't work that day.*

*You hear her say those words and then she notices you standing there, now crying too. Her face blank, as if she can't see you at all.*

*When she drives off you run after the car, crying. The gravel clinkering under your feet but you can't catch it and it dissolves in the air right in front of your eyes.*

(Laguz Reversed. Ehwaz Reversed. Isa)

*'You feel like you are in a rut, restless and confined, put your plans on hold for a while.'*

# 8. LOLITA

'Are you listening to me?' Lillian says, still sitting at the bar in Helgi's. She is on her fifth cocktail. It is busier now, with a second row of people standing behind the bar stools, occasionally leaning between them to order drinks. The Americans: Marina, her husband and Rick and his wife now drinking coffee in the window corner.

'Sorry, I was miles away,' Lionel says.

'You were staring at the barmaid's backside again.'

'Was I? If I was, I wasn't thinking about it. I was thinking about this guy I met the other day.'

'The flat earth guy? The guy whose daughter gave you that silly note?'

Lionel nods.

'Has it been worth missing our gold pins?'

'We can get them in the Fall. Let's go on another trip then. You can choose where we go.'

'Was it worth it, meeting this guy?' Lillian says, after a pause to finish her drink.

'He lives with his unhappy daughter and his wife is made of clay.'

'You sound envious.'

'No, she really is made of clay. She's dead and the girl has made these life-size models of her in their field,' Lionel says.

'She sounds like she has a screw loose to me.'

'No doubt about it.'

'Well, will you get a blog article out of it?' Lillian says, as a man pushes between them to pick up some drinks.

'Maybe a story about dealing with unbearable grief.'

Lillian shrugs, as if that hardly seemed newsworthy to her.

'This is a weird place. Have you seen that lorry driving past with the people covered in paint?' Lillian says, distracted by the passage of the lorry across the front windows of the bar.

'You do it here the day before you get married.'

'Really? I just went out to dinner with Beth and the girls at the Deer and Almond.'

As she is speaking she follows Lionel's gaze to the barmaid's backside, again. She can see the outline of her thong beneath her thin cotton skirt.

'You are looking at that girl as if you could eat her.'

'Am I?' Lionel says, looking back at his wife.

'Everywhere we go you stare at young women.'

Lionel shakes his head and picks up his beer.

'What is it you want from them? We both know you have passed your prime in the sack, dear. So, now you do it in your head? When was the last time we did it?'

'Really, you want to get into this again, now and here?'

'Why not? This is where you seem to want to be staring at girls.'

Lionel shakes his head and looks towards the front of the bar. Anything but look at the barmaid, whom he knows is listening. Through the plate glass window, above Marina's head, to the right of the door, he sees Panda and he smiles at her. She recognises him and shakes her head before moving on.

'You seem to be addicted to the attention of young women. Don't you know, they just see a dirty old man?' Lillian says, following Panda as she moves away from the window while she stands and picks up her bag.

'It's Kito's daughter, the girl who gave me the note.'

'You're as bad as each other, addicted to romance. I've had enough of this nonsense. I'm going back. Enjoy your evening in dreamland,' Lillian says, as she pushes her way through a knot of giggly girls.

Lionel watches his wife leave and turns back towards the bar. The barmaid is looking at him.

'Jet lag,' Lionel says.

'Aye, is that what they call it in America?'

'Canada.'

'Another drink?' the barmaid is trying to look sympathetic but failing; not able to hide the fact that she clearly finds Lionel's predicament funny.

Lionel nods his head and sighs. Turning around, he watches as Lillian slips through the front door and he sees a man collecting money in a tin decorated with a raven flag coming towards him. Unlike the Salvation Army collector, and the guy with the roses, who were both in the bar earlier, he is being much more successful. Everyone he asks puts money in, and folding money too, not just coins, but he skips the obvious tourists, like the Americans in the window.

'Can anyone contribute?' Lionel says, as the man passes.

'Aye, you can, but it is more of a Kirkwall thing and we don't ask holiday folk to contribute to the levy.'

'The levy? What is it for?'

'To buy a bulldozer,' he says, looking around the room, planning his collecting route through the crowd.

'Why do you want a bulldozer?'

'I don't want a bulldozer, but my family have collected levies in Kirkwall for generations and when the laird asks for contributions it is me who gets the job. Bars are a good place to start, particularly the night, as most folk come out on Show Night.'

'Why does the laird want a bulldozer?'

'That will be for the new houses he is building at Car Ness, opposite the old battery. He is a developer and needs a new dozer.'

'And he wants you to pay for it?'

'It is our way. When the laird asks us to pay a levy it is just what we do. It is just what we have always done. In the olden days, it would be money for ships and rations for his fighting men who went out on expeditions, but now, well, it is just a tradition.'

'It sounds like a feudal tax,' Lionel says, shaking his head.

'Aye, maybes, but we don't bother, we just pay up.'

'Can I contribute?'

'Aye, you can. It will be unusual, mind, but if you want to you certainly can. I'm told that dozers are no cheap.'

Lionel takes a twenty pound note out of his wallet and puts it in the tin and the man smiles and moves to the table in the corner of the bar where everyone has money out ready. They all smile at Lionel when he turns to look at them.

At that moment, Mathew and friends from the youth hostel enter the bar. They don't have to stay long to see it is packed and there isn't room for them, but they are there long enough for Marina to jump up from her table by the door to introduce herself and shake his hand.

'You're from the dig. We saw you earlier. How exciting! Meeting a real-life archaeologist,' she says, grabbing his arm and pulling him to one side. The others follow, soaking up the spare space like a dry sponge in a wet glass.

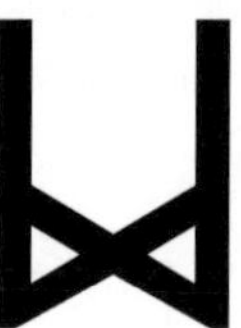

(Mannaz Reversed)

*'There is no help available'.*

Jenny, still covered in cling film, is at the bar in the Queens Hotel on Shore Street, just down from The Bay Takeaway and across the road from the ferry terminal. She is with Fran and his mates when someone shouts, 'Lady of the Mists,' and everyone surges out of the door and on to the pavement to watch as a middle-aged woman in what looks like a white wedding dress rides by, bareback, on a big white horse. They all cheer and the woman turns and waves regally. The horse takes this in its stride, even when cars hoot as they pass her.

'They say it's lucky to see her on Show Night,' Fran's mate Malcy says.

When she has gone most people go back inside, leaving Jenny alone on the pavement deep in thought. Maybe she is thinking about her white dress, wrapped-up neatly in her room, ready for tomorrow.

There are just a few sailors with bell-bottomed pants left with her on the pavement. She smiles at them and they smile back, but don't approach her. They have probably been warned just how incendiary chatting up local women is in a place like this. She is enjoying her cigarette when a Volvo estate drives up and stops beside her. It is Johnno's car and he is driving. Tony, Robin and Mick get out of the car and grab her.

'It's okay, mate, just crazy local traditions,' Johnno says to the sailors from the driver's seat.

'Boys, enough. I've had enough excitement for one night and I now need to get pissed,' Jenny says, laughing as they carry her to the car and squash her between Tony and Robin in the back seat.

'Johnno, I'm knackered, I've been paraded round for the last three hours and need a break. Where are we going now?'

'Just come to collect my bride.'

'You don't get it, do you? I said NO. Know what that means? It means NO. I am not marrying you. I am marrying Fran.'

'We'll see about that, won't we, boys?' Johnno says, as he speeds up Harbour Street and heads out across the Ayre.

A few minutes later, Fran comes out of the pub to find his bride-to-be.

'They've taken her,' says an old guy he recognises as coming from North Ronaldsay, one of the show crowd.

'Who has?' Fran says.

'Some lads in a blue Volvo.'

Fran walks into the road, looking as far as he can to the west, down Shore Street.

'T'other way,' the old guy says, and Fran spins on the spot, but Harbour Street ahead and Shore Street behind him are as empty as if cars had never been invented. The dollop of horse shit in front of him seems to confirm that impression. There isn't even a taxi on the rank.

'You know, blackenings weren't so much fun in my day. My mother told me that it all started out with foot washing,' the old guy says.

'What?'

'Blackenings never used to be this much fun and they never did girls, just the lads. Equal opportunities it will be. Bridesmaids too these days.'

Fran shakes his head.

'What's up?' Malcy says, coming out of the bar with two pints in his hand.

'Johnno, the bastard. He's got Jen,' Fran says, then he makes this verse, to Malcy, the old guy, and the matelots watching all this:

*With the setting sun*
*the cunning fox drags*
*its love-prey to cover.*
*We dogs of war must not*
*tarry, in our search.*
*Help me recover our dear bride before*
*the villains spoil her, for our*
*love-wrenched heart, is*
*hot with bone-crushing flares*
*that only her gentle hand can quench.*

(Ehwaz)

*'Expect movement and changes.'*

Groups of noisy lads passing by on Harbour Street have distracted the old men in the hut. The parliamentary conversation about 'the drink' has faded away and been replaced with random gossip, watching the night's theatre unfold in front of them.

'These boys are amateur drinkers,' Davey says, looking down the road towards the Queens Hotel to see if the lady on the horse is coming back.

'They seem to do okay at it,' Tommy says.

'It's a disgrace, all this drinking,' Alec says.

'I liked the lass on the white horse,' Davey says.

'Lass? I went to school with her. Bonny enough, but bonkers. People like to see her ride around. There is some folk story about mystical riders and the like, and it sort of fits, you know,' Ray says.

'Mystical? I think you mean mythical,' Walli says.

'Whatever. People like her doing it, especially on Show Night,' Ray says.

'Mad Margaret showing off again,' Tommy says.

'That dress makes me think back to when me and the missus was first married,' Davey says.

'Young'uns will think it odd, but we never did, you know, not until our wedding night,' Tommy says.

'Used to be a stud me, so me wife said, "Davey, you're a stallion of a man," she said.'

'Those were the days, eh?' Tommy says.

Walking towards the Auld Men's Hut, on the harbour side of the road, is a man carrying a barbecue. It's Brian. Panda, now sitting on her own at a table outside the Kirkwall Hotel would have seen him if she had looked in that direction, but she didn't.

'Not exactly what most folk carry on their night out, is it?' Jock says, pointing to the man and they laugh just as he looks up at them. Their attention seems to deflate him and he quickly crosses the road to the Girnel.

'Amateurs. I could drink twelve pint of seventy-shilling once and be none the worse for wear,' Davey says.

'Heavy. We called it heavy,' Tommy says.

'Aye, that too. I could drink it like it was water when I was a lad. Not now, though. Don't take it now. Whisky from time-to-time, but no beer. Goes straight through me. They should have a bar in the toilet for old folk, then we could drink and piss it out at the same time,' Davey says.

'I don't even drink whisky now, just smell it. I like to sit and smell it,' Ray says.

'Got me into trouble though. I was a mod. Had the hair and suits and my scooter had twenty-eight mirrors. We used to go down to

Brighton to fight the rockers. Me wife, she said I was belligerent,' Davey says.

'I can see that. "Cut the bollocks" is hardly how most people start a conversation,' Tommy says.

'Seen too much to stand for any bullshit.'

'That's true, you have lived. "Seen it all", that's what you should have on your gravestone when you go,' Walli says.

'Seen more than most, but I'm no planning on going any time soon.'

'Can come as a bit of a surprise, mind. The good Lord don't give you much warning of your time,' Alec says.

'I know that right enough. I watched a man get blown off a dam once. We was building a dam, up north. Bloody great thing and we had these steel shutter things for setting the concrete in sections. It was a windy day and this old bloke – well, he seemed old then – he may have been sixty; he just got blown off and smashed up on the rocks at the bottom of the dam. Made some noise. More than you'd think. A loud thud. Often wondered what went through his mind as he fell. Did he have time to think back?' Davey says.

'Think back?' Walli says.

'Aye, take stock. Add up all your victories and count all your losses. See who won, Him, or t'others.'

'You talk as if your life has been a string of battles,' Tommy says.

'Aye. Life is a fight to the last breath. You have to earn the right to keep going. If you take your eyes off the ball for one minute they'll get you,' Davey says, looking out of the window again and seeing Mathew and friends from the youth hostel coming out of Helgi's.

'My fellow Youth Hostellers,' he says, pointing to them. 'Look, I'm off. Thanks for your hospitality. Probably be glad to get rid of me. Got a second breath of wind. I'm off to see what the night has in store.'

Davey quickly gets to his feet and leaves the hut. The old men all watch him as he crosses Harbour Street without looking. A taxi has to break hard to avoid hitting him.

'He didn't see that coming,' Alec says.

They watch as Davey approaches the young people on the other side of the street and starts speaking, turning to point back to them as he does so. They are then joined by the Americans and after Davey has introduced himself to them, they turn towards Bridge Street and set off and, after just a beat or two, Davey sets off in pursuit.

'It's a bastard getting old,' Tommy says.

'Aye,' Ray says.

(Algiz)

*'A fortunate influence will enter your life.'*

Soon as Martin and I got to The Ship, we were pounced on by two farmers from Caithness. Martin was up for it, but I wasn't, so I made myself objectionable and slipped away. Now on my own, people-watching, at a table outside the Kirkwall Hotel. Just along from the Temper and Helgi's. Staff, mostly my age, know I don't want to buy anything, so they leave me alone.

A group, with an old guy in tow, just left Helgi's and are coming this way. Closely followed by the crazy Canadian who took the flatty with Thomas the other day.

Must be archaeologists because, as they get closer, I can see that their t-shirts all mention 'digs' of one sort or another. An old guy following looks a bit like a body builder gone to seed: solid jelly, where muscle used to be. The archys look like they are trying to shake him off. Perhaps he's not the sort of past they want to associate with. Pretty spry though, for an old guy.

The Canadian bloke has spotted me and comes over.

'Panda. I'm Lionel, we met at your house, couple days ago.'

'Never seen you before.'

'You gave me a note,' Lionel says, laughing, as if I was making a joke.

I shrug and look away, watching the archys walk past.

'Can I sit down?'

I ignore him.

'Trouble?' he says, nodding towards a commotion some way down the road where the police are dealing with a drunk.

Seems to think I want company and he sits down anyway.

The waitress looks bored, like most of the teenagers incarcerated here, but she is programmed to serve.

'Beer please, anything local.'

'We've got Scapa Ale,' she says.

'Okay, that'll be fine. Would you like a drink?' he says to me, as if this is some sort of date.

'Rum and coke.' Decide to humour him if I can get a free drink. Girl serving us was at the school I went to briefly before Thomas pulled me out. Used to go out with Bigsy. Wonder if she knows he's got the hots for me now?

'Just wanted to apologise. My wife says I stare at young women. She got angry with me for smiling at you in the window, just now. If I did, I'm sorry,' he says, once the waitress has gone.

'We're used to it. You'd think half the men in this place had never seen a woman before.'

He seems pleased that I haven't chased him away and it's nice to have someone to talk to.

'So, did my crazy dad convince you that the earth was flat?'

'He got me thinking.'

Just wait for him to tell me more. I can see he wants to.

'We didn't spend much time on the flat earth stuff, we ended up talking about what has happened to him and you. About why he is so unhappy.'

'Did you pay him, or did he pay you?'

'I said I'd pray for him.'

'Do you think he can be saved?' I say, in jest, but he seems in a serious frame of mind.

'Anyone can be saved if they are truly repentant.'

'He's got a lot to repent for,' I say, unable to stop anger seeping out into my mouth: sometimes the past makes me retch wicked words.

'Do you want to talk about it?'

Shake my head.

'He told me enough about what happened to your mother to see why he is so troubled. But I'm not sure he wants to get over it. My pastor helped me see that grief and mud are pretty similar, if you wallow in them for long enough they are hard to wash off.'

'He lives in Orkney, his wife ran off with his best friend, and he has a daughter who hates him. Wouldn't you be unhappy.'

Lionel looks puzzled. He sips his beer, which has just arrived.

'He told me that she died, your mother died because of a wrongly diagnosed cancer.'

I shrug my shoulders and sip my drink.

'So, that's not true?' Lionel says, seeing the doubt in my face.

'Does it really have anything to do with you?'

'You did give me that note. I thought you might need help.'

*Where were you five years ago?*

Lionel takes a longer, more thoughtful, sip of beer. He puts the glass back and looks down at his hands which he clasps together on the table, as if he is about to pray.

'My first wife died so it touched me, his story. Once you have been through difficult times you tend to be more sympathetic to others.'

I shake my head.

'Maybe he's trying to prove that what we think is true is false with this flat earth thing, because he doesn't want to accept the truth.'

'You a psychologist then?'

'I spent a lot of time with my pastor after my wife died. He was a wise man,' Lionel pauses, leaving time for his thoughts to settle.

'When Norma died I was pretty mixed up. I felt guilty that I could have lived with someone for so long without recognising that there was anything wrong, that she was so sad.'

'Is that when you sought solace in The Lord?' I say, unable to camouflage the sarcasm.

'It gave me hope. I felt that there was no point in going on without her, but The Lord saved me.'

'So, you simply invented God so you wouldn't have to kill yourself?'

'I didn't invent him. I just saw his healing light.'

'You're as big a charlatan as Thomas. No wonder you wanted to take a flatty.'

'It was good to talk to someone who has heard it all before.'

'Who? God?'

'My pastor, but maybe yes, God too.'

'Is that what the priest told you, that a shared burden isn't as heavy?'

'No, it was more how he understood me. I just had a sense of His loving power. That it could help me.'

I take a deep breath. A Herring Gull lands on the pavement beside us and waddles up to the table, looking for food. It takes Lionel by surprise.

'Confident buggers, aren't they?' Lionel says.

We both watch the gull as it wanders off.

'Just talking about it with my pastor helped. Someone who isn't judging you but just lets you get it out. In my head, it was squashed into a tight ball, but in his room, I could see everything more clearly.'

'Pellucid,' I say, but he ignores me. He's preoccupied with his speech.

'He told me that what happened to me was normal, it was okay, and most of all it wasn't my fault,' Lionel says.

'And you believed him?'

'It doesn't work like that. He helped me to work out what I believed, something a lot more helpful.'

'I know it was my fault that we lost Mummy.'

'Well, Dr Swartz told me that if you discard the beliefs that are limiting your happiness the world looks a far more attractive place.'

'Did you tell Thomas all this?'

He nods, gulping his beer now as if his sermon has dried him out.

'Did you tell him it's okay for him to believe the Earth is flat?'

'I'm not sure it is helping him. It just distances him further from the real problem of coming to terms with loss.'

*Is that what is happening to me. Am I still coming to terms with her loss?*

'I told him that the first time you let yourself go and share the thoughts that overwhelm you, you will feel differently about your life,' Lionel says.

'Epiphany.'

'Something like that.'

'I don't want to keep living like this. In so much pain. Knowing that I am going to die, but not when,' I say, pushing my chair back and standing up.

'You're right, we're all going to die, but we have the blessing of life first and the future is uncertain – anything can happen – and it might be wonderful,' his voice full of enthusiasm and joy.

I shake my head and run across the road without looking and a car beeps its horn at me.

*How could I explain to him how I feel? How could he understand my sorrow? How could anyone?*

Out of the corner of my eye I notice that two police officers are looking at me from further down the road. The sight of the law makes me nervous, and I remember that I am now a fugitive and need to run and hide.

# DEAR EDITH, 1

Dear Edith,

I have news. I've done something terrible, but it was SO good I just have to tell you and I can't wait until we get back. Destroy this email after you have read it. There can't be any audit trail of my misdeeds and DON'T tell Sam!

We are not in Norway. We're in Orkney – look it up on Google Maps, it's nowhere – chasing Lionel's long-lost relatives. His great-great-grandfather worked for the Hudson Bay Company. It seems lots of Orkney folk ended up in Canada. Their boats stopped for victuals in Stromness – a little village not far from here – on their way north, and they recruited the local men. It's how *we* tamed the north.

Anyway, he pestered me to change our plans so much that in the end I gave in and here we are instead of heading over to Norway to get our Gold Pins. You know how much I want a Gold Pin, just like Tracey and Bob. Tracey is going to be such a bitch when we get back without the magic number 100. We've missed Norway, but Lionel says we can go away in the Fall and I can choose where.

The first thing Lionel did when we got here was to sign up for some silly Flat Earth Tour. You know how easily distracted he is. Thought it would make a story for his blog, which is doing rather well. Today, he went off to Stromness on his quest for distant relatives, but I needed a break from his whims and his passion for heritage. So, I was left on my own and I went to the county show. It's a big thing here, but it would be a sideshow at the Calgary Stampede. Day out for everyone though. The show was busy and quaint. And old, like it has happened every year, forever, just like this.

I'm back in my room because, although we've only been away a week, Lionel is up to his old tricks again. I am so *over* the male menopause, or is it just boredom after all those years? Or maybe it's me. Until today I think I had forgotten what we saw in all that sex stuff. I was even contemplating life on my own again, but that *is* a scary thought. Anyway, I've just left Lionel in a bar ogling young girls and I am now back in my room. They don't exactly have Holiday Inns in Orkney, so we went ethnic and we're staying in a little place. They have hot water bottles beside the bed. You put hot water in to warm you up and you need them even in summer! Really, it is like they have never heard of comfort heating.

The weather is strange here. Mostly warm, but then you get rain showers that feel like ice water, as wintery clouds sweep overhead. The gaps overhead full of runny sunshine; golden, like Lucerne honey, dripping over the edge of the clouds to remind everyone it is summer, still. Remember how my brandy bottle full of honey goes solid in the winter and runny in the summer? That's what I was thinking of.

To get out of the rain I ran into a tent with a bar and drank red wine in the middle of the day, just listening to people speak. I was in a sea of beautiful voices. The people here speak like they are singing, but I didn't understand it all and whenever I speak they look at me as if I am an alien. They aren't expecting my accent and it takes them a while to tune in, so I repeat myself a lot.

They have several showing rings. It's a bit like a rodeo in someone's back yard, but with farm produce and cattle. Here's a programme link, so you can see what you're missing in far-flung Manitoba! Anyways, what is it they say about cats being away and mice playing? The show wasn't just cattle and burgers, there were plenty men on show and I had an ADVENTURE of my own. Can't wait to tell someone about it, but this is Top Secret – FOR YOUR EYES ONLY.

We like to think we have kept ourselves in good shape, don't we? That we might still be attractive. Don't we all? So, what would you do when a good-looking man, young enough to be your son, and wearing a kilt! starts chatting you up? Zander his name. Storyteller his game. Really, people do that here. In the corner of the field a pagoda with a circle of chairs and every hour he told stories. It was crowded so I went to watch. Mums with kids buzzing around him like bees and it didn't take long to understand why. Yummy, yummy, yummy.

I have to admit that I had a few stories of my own flying around in my head, but I was able to concentrate enough to hear some of what he said. Folklore and myths. Stuff that kids love. He told stories about giants flinging rocks about and Viking raiders and Earls fighting Bishops and the simple folk who lived here. He said that in a way they still live here. That they are looking on, watching what we do. Dramatic. He raced around making his stories come to life. Lots of body language going on. Not sure if I was captivated by the stories, his body, or his beautiful eyes: I think he may have hypnotised me!

'Ladies and gentlemen,' he said. Isn't that so British, *Ladies and Gentlemen*? He said, 'Please accept my apologies if I stumble a bit, but I've been tripping up ever since I arrived in Kirkwall. What it is, my problem with walking upright? I am tripping over the past. Orkney is littered with history and as soon as you begin to recognise it, it trips you up, it gets in your way.' He said that visitors normally didn't notice and locals were acclimatised, but people like him – incomers – who move here, have to adjust to living so intimately with the past. How romantic is that? 'Living with the dead,' he said, how creepy.

After the second show. Yes, I went back! He came up to me and asked me where I was from as he had heard me talking to an American lady from a cruise ship sitting next to me. He asked me if I wanted to go for a drink but I said 'No,' and he just smiled and looked over towards a gaggle of drooling milfs waiting to talk to him. I know that's what they call them. I know I've past that stage, but I got myself excited for a minute or two. Forgot my age. Forgot everything actually.

Oh my god, I was tingling all over because it was SO obvious that he knew I fancied him and that I was flattered with it all. I think he liked the fact that he had me in his power. If he had touched me I just couldn't have stopped him. I was energised with the tingle of it all. Is that a thing, a *tingle*? Oh my god, it was like an electric current. Sparks flew!! I was feeling myself getting pulled into him so I said something stupid and walked off, but I knew he was watching me as I walked around the show. Each time I passed him telling stories he looked over and smiled. Yes, I kept walking past him! I couldn't resist it. I was in his orbit. Caught by his gravitational pull.

I think that is why I got so annoyed with Lionel tonight. It's the guilt. I keep going on at him when he is distracted by a pretty face and I'm doing it now!

ᚠᚢᚱ

(Fehu. Uruz. Raidho)

*'I see a legacy and prosperity, men with strong emotions, and travel with pleasure.'*

# 9. CASTLEGREEN

Back at the The Ship. Police reminded me that I'm on the run. It's exciting, the thought of being chased. Closest I have felt to being wanted for a while now, but I want to check in on Martin.

'Welcome back,' Martin says, as I sit down. 'Remember Arthur?' she says, teasing the one remaining farmer by stroking his thigh with her long nails.

'Hi, Arthur,' I say, but he hardly notices me. Martin has him under her spell. She winks at me.

'Drink?' she says, reaching for her bag, but I shake my head and Arthur looks pleased, sensing that I am not going to stay long before I realise it myself.

Mistake, coming back, as all I can think of is my death. Not in the mood for all this, or a rum and coke with a sour apple chaser, the drink of the moment for people my age. I'm high enough already. Not sure if it is my medication, or the chase, or Sigurd, or just the electric hum of the night, which is getting louder as each minute passes. Sound of a bicycle wheel as you accelerate downhill; the burr of the spokes building the faster you go.

'I have to go,' I say.

'You've just got here. Off to see your philosopher?'

'Aye.'

'Will I see you ever again?'

I shake my head.

'Where you off to?' Arthur says.

'Backpacking in Japan,' I say, and he looks impressed. Doubt he's ever been much further than Edinburgh. Mind, nor have I.

Martin gets up and comes over to me. She is now standing so close that I can see pools of obsidian sadness in her eyes.

'Sure about this?'

'Aye.'

'You really aren't alone, you know. We all feel crap at times.'

'Try all the time.'

'Try little blue pills.'

I shake my head and let the hair fall from my mouth. I have been sucking it now for some time.

'Well in that case, sayonara, my friend.'

She raises her hand high above her head and everyone in the pub goes quiet as she makes this verse:

*Warrior fight death*
*challenge the angry man.*
*Breath deep, till skin-torn,*
*flesh-slashed, skull-smashed.*
*Squirt your heart-blood in his face.*

*Man's destiny is death*
*forgive the guilty one.*
*Embrace him.*
*Give him your compassion,*
*shame him with your love.*

*Carry my love-kiss,*
*I will miss you.*
*Journey far, but*
*remember me.*

'Polynya,' I say, and Martin laughs.

She leans forward and kisses me gently on the lips, much to Arthur's surprise and to the huddle of men next to us. Make noises that suggest that two girls kissing makes them feel uncomfortable. She lingers and I don't pull away.

This is fragile ice for both for us.

'Martin, that was unexpected.'

'For me too,' she says, as I notice my reflection in her eyes, far away, falling into deep coal-shafts that possibly reach the centre of the earth.

'Martin?' Arthur says.

'Transgender,' I say, and laugh out loud.

As I leave, I am being paid more attention. A purple bougainvillea under a white-hot sun. An anomaly, here. To be fair, not many exotic flowers do bloom in Kirkwall, or trees, except the Tree of Life in the High Street and salt tolerant sycamores, hiding behind walls.

(Thurisaz)

*'It will be life changing.'*

Short walk to the Temper. The boys on Bridge Street too far gone to notice me. I wait by the front door, as arranged, but it's quite a while before Sigurd appears.

'Sorry, I forgot we all had to speak. It's a family tradition,' he says.

'What did you say?'

'I made a verse about the sea.'

'Everyone's a poet tonight.'

'You asked earlier where *Dreki* was going. Do you want to come and see?'

'Are you trying to get out of buying me a drink?'

Sigurd shows me a bottle of wine he has in his coat pocket and I shrug.

'Where are we going?'

'I forgot I have to help. I was only invited for my muscles, such as they are. What do you think?'

'Puny,' I say, looking at his arms.

'Yes.' He smiles and flexes his bicep until a small plum appears beneath the skin. He seems to be waiting for me to touch it, but I shake my head.

'So, you up for a bit of my family's madness?'

'Why not?'

'Great, we could walk there – it's about a mile and a half out of town, along the coast – but I'm feeling lazy. Let's get a taxi.'

'This isn't a trick to lure me away to break my heart, is it?'

'Why should you care? Aren't you planning to kill yourself sometime tonight?'

'Not till dawn.'

'Is anything you say true?'

'How does anyone know what is true?'

'This conversation is getting too close to my philosophy lectures for comfort. Anyway, my family can trump any of your mad inventions,' Sigurd says, grabbing my arm.

Taxis waiting in a neat white line, beside a parallel row of moored boats in the inner harbour just five metres away. The road buzzy with busy cars, red brake lights flashing too much. Skeins of young men, like migrating geese, spreading out on the pavement, as if getting ready for the Ba Game. Couple of visitors looking down from their bedroom window in the Kirkwall Hotel, staring at the spectacle, which is just sufficiently frenetic to make it unusual and interesting. The sky blushing pink above a teal sea.

'Pretty, isn't it?' Taxi driver says, drawing deeply on his vape while leaning on his cab and looking out to sea.

'The sun never sets here in the summer, she just dips below the horizon and we have twilight all the night. Can work in the fields till the early hours if you want.'

'Or, drive taxis,' Sigurd says.

'Oh, aye, that too,' the driver says, putting his vape away. 'Where you off to then?'

'Can you take us out to Castlegreen?'

'Not a lot there, mate.'

'Yes, I know.'

'Sure, you know. Of course, you know. Romance. I was young once,' he says, doing up his seat belt. The residual smog of his vape filling the car with sandalwood and myrrh, like incense for Baby Jesus.

Head north, skirting the bay, looking back at the town and the ships at anchor. Cruise ship in the bay dressed overall with strands of diamante lights. On the upper deck, a pile of spangles (*what oh!)* from a crystal rainbow that has shattered and fallen on them at dusk: party time. The single white light high-up in the mast, like the star of Bethlehem, has punched a hole through the thin mauve sky. Makes me wonder if, tonight, my death will be balanced by another miracle birth.

Why all this religious mumbo-jumbo in my head? Perhaps I'm hoping for a miracle too. To be raised from the dead, or reborn, happy.

'Atlantis,' I say.

Sigurd just looks at me and smiles, waiting for my next announcement.

'It was the name of the only child born on the *Mayflower* crossing the Atlantic Ocean.'

Sigurd laughs. 'Of course it was. Actually, that I believe, but what has that got to do with anything?'

'I don't know.'

'Your mind is a mystery to me.'

Road now runs along the coast; just some grass and a thin beach between us and the waves. Can't see the long ship anywhere. The road turns inland, turns again, struggling to find a way through. A few more twists and the tarmac gives up and we come to a dead end. Stop near a house sitting on its own, as if it is lost.

'This will do,' Sigurd says.

Taken less than five minutes so the driver doesn't seem too impressed with his fare. Sigurd doesn't give him a tip. Get out and watch as the taxi turns and drones away. No lights in the house and it feels isolated, even though we can still see the glare of Kirkwall in the distance. Don't feel comfortable watching receding cars.

'Bit gloomy, isn't it,' he says, looking around, trying to decipher the shadowy patterns in the landscape.

'It's always gloomy in Orkney,' I say. 'Even on the brightest day.'

*Ok, some days, like today, can be something else, but often 'gloomy' is the right adjective, if you've said 'bloody' too many times that day.*

Climb over a locked gate and walk down towards the water's edge, scrambling over a few rocks first. Sigurd bends down and picks up a stone and gives it to me.

'Any good at throwing?'

I shrug, feeling the smoothness of the rock. Rounded by the waves so that it feels soft and comforting.

'Throw this rock as far as you can out in the water.'

'This stone?' I say, trying out an alternative word. The trouble is, they can often both sound right.

'Yes.'

I throw it so hard I get a twinge in my upper arm, but the splash is no more than five metres away, just beyond the small breaking waves limping on to the shore.

'My family would say that you now have a claim on all the land between here and the splash.'

'I own it?'

'Land ownership rights around here still reflect Udal law which has some pretty daft ideas. My uncle Swift Eye is always doing battle with lawyers over it.'

'Swift Eye?'

Sigurd shrugs.

'My uncle was called Charlie.'

'Was?'

'We don't see him anymore.'

'Well, your uncle probably wasn't a descendent of one of the Earls of Orkney, like Swift Eye and my dad.'

'Was he the guy on the boat earlier?'

'No, that's my mum's brother, but he loves all the Viking stuff. Swift Eye is my dad's elder brother.'

'Landed gentry.'

'Landed but not gentrified. The family is always fighting over land. That's what tonight's adventure is all about.'

'Don't know much about families. Just me and my dad, and I hate him.'

He laughs again, but this time he seems less sure that I am joking. 'That's a strong word.'

*It's a strong feeling.*

At the far end of the field a herd of thirty or so shorthorn cattle sidle up to us, like ghostly apparitions. Do we seem like ghosts to them? One of them snorts and some of the spittle hits me in the face.

'Ugh,' I say.

'Bloody things scare the shit out of me. Any one of them could crush us both to death in seconds,' Sigurd says.

'Would save me the bother later.'

'Yes, but it isn't part of my plan for tonight.'

'No, well, don't go wandering through fields of wild beasts at night then.'

'Twilight,' he says.

'I don't think they'd appreciate the distinction, do you?'

Make our way carefully through the minefield of cows and over the fence before we take a breath. It's not just my increasing anxiety, but they stink too. Half expecting an explosion of shit as we pass astern of them. My heart beating faster. Although I'm planning to die soon, I don't want to die like that.

The lights of Wideford Hill's communications mast in the distance, above and beyond the cruise liner. The dark outline of a salmon farm closer to the shore. As I catch my breath, I hear men talking ahead of us and recognise the tone and cadence of their voices. We walk towards them and on the other side of a low promontory we see their silhouettes on the beach all busy at work. A large field beside the water is all that now separates us.

I can see that there are two or three 4x4s down by the water and *Dreki* with its crew just offshore. The men on the beach are unloading what looks like tree trunks from the trailers. As we get closer, a few of the men turn to look at us. One is the poetic man from the trawler earlier; he walks towards us before we get down to the beach, though it isn't clear how he knew we were there. Goths disappear completely under the cloak of night, like they never existed, or they have been reabsorbed by the negative of day.

'Panda, this is Fish Hook, my uncle.' Sigurd says, as the man approaches.

'I liked your poem earlier,' I say.

'Thanks. It was more of a rallying cry than a poem.'

'I can't call you Fish Hook,' I say, laughing.

'Okay, fair enough. You can call me Hooky. I'm afraid you'll have to let Sigurd help us for a little while. We have a difficult task ahead of us and it will need all the men here.'

'Where's Dad?' Sigurd says.

'Split is with the men. They have just got the rope attached to *Dreki*. We'll need you in a few minutes,' he says, before he turns and walks back to the beach.

'Your dad is called Split?'

'He's known as Skull Splitter, but they call him Split. Some people call him Rognald. I call him Dad.'

'Okay, I get it, but why does your family have these crazy Viking names?'

'My dad says it's a homage to the past. People pass Christian names down the generations, don't they; this is the Viking equivalent.'

'But I guess he wasn't christened Skull Splitter?'

'Magnus.'

'So, what do they call you? Sigurd, Heart Breaker?'

'Siggy.'

'Stardust?'

Sigurd smiles and holds my hand and kisses me mostly on the cheek, but his lips overlap a little with mine. Never been kissed, so unexpectedly, twice on the same day. Reminds me of Jenny and her proposals of marriage. How odd, and romantic, to make that connection.

'My mother used to say that things come in threes,' I say, but Sigurd just shrugs, not knowing what I mean, and walks off.

(Wunjo)

*'I see, success, joy, happiness.'*

Sitting on a large rock in the middle of the field, looking out to sea. Kito told me there are skerries just offshore, a haul-out site for Harbour Seals. I can hear them barking in the distance. Probably been disturbed by this Viking invasion, and wondering if the men that slaughtered them here in the 1960s have returned.

Sigurd has made his way to the beach where three men are now removing the field fence. He looks spindly in silhouette. Others are laying out the tree trunks to form a path.

I realise what they are doing and smile.

Doesn't take long to get *Dreki*'s bows on the beach, the crew standing in the water holding her straight as she is pulled onto the log rollers, moving forward easily even though the beach slopes a little.

At the top of the beach the men go silent as one of them climbs on board and goes to the stern. He is carrying a banner and seems to be steering the boat, even though it is now out of the water. At his signal, the men begin to pull again and the boat turns towards me and the gap in the fence. The log carriers moving logs from the stern to bow, as soon as the boat has slid across them. Building a moving road that leads right across the field.

I laugh out loud, almost forgetting once again that I am soon to die. My mirth soon swallowed by the sibilant insistency of the gentle surf, and I remember.

# HIM

(Hagalaz. Isa. Ehwaz)

*'There will be unexpected disruptions, so put your plans on hold for a while and be ready for movement and changes.'*

## 10. SCENT

'You can sit here,' Johnno says, after guiding Jenny into his parents' bedroom at the front of the house. He spreads a towel on the bed and she sits on it. She seems comfortable in his presence and happy enough to go along with all this. The large bay window has a heavily patterned net curtain that looks like an intricate doily until Johnno turns the lights on and it becomes a blank white sheet. He closes the second layer of shiny cream curtains which cut out the residual glow from the outside world. The sharpness of the artificial light makes Jenny squint, like she has soap in her eyes.

The dressing table is covered in perfume bottles and the room smells sweetly of flowers and musk.

'I think she might be an addict, Mum,' Johnno says, seeing Jenny staring at the dressing table and the bottles.

'I didn't notice it, before. You know…' Jenny says.

Johnno smiles. 'You remember then?'

'That was a mistake. Anyway, we were just kids,' she says, looking a little embarrassed.

'Was I too young for you? Or just not cool enough?' he says, but she ignores him.

'She wears four at a time, puts different ones behind each ear and on each wrist.'

'No one smells like your mum,' Jenny says, inhaling the pungent air.

'I think she does it to annoy Dad.'

'Your dad can be a bit sweaty.'

'Aye. I think he does that to annoy her.' Johnno takes a deeper breath than normal as if to check he wasn't sweaty too.

'Marriage bliss, eh?'

'Marry the right bloke. That's the secret of a great marriage.'

'I am. Anyway, Johnno, why have you brought me here?'

'Remember when we did it here?' Johnno moves to the foot of the bed and sits down so their eyes are now at the same height, and their bodies just a pillow width apart.

'Aye, I do, but don't get any ideas. That was a while ago, but I do remember our lovely one-night stand. I'm getting married in the morning, do you remember that?' Jenny instinctively moving her hands onto her lap to create a little more distance between them.

'Not if I can help it.'

'Well, you can't help it, you soft sod.'

'I can, because you're my prisoner,' Johnno says, standing up and moving back to the door.

Jenny gets up and goes to inspect the perfume bottles on the dressing table, sitting on the stool in front of it. Johnno, watching her, is reflected in the dressing table mirror. Bits of him missing where the reflective layer has peeled off. The thick old glass giving him a greeny-gold tan.

'Vikings only kidnapped the most beautiful women. That's why them Scandinavian girls are so bonny,' Johnno's reflection says.

'Is that so?' Jenny says, smiling at him in the mirror.

'I'm holding you prisoner here until I talk to Fran.'

'Are you now?' Jenny says, turning to look at him.

'I believe in fighting for what I want,' Johnno says, guarding the door.

'He'll go fucking looney tunes when he finds out. Have you seen him and his mates when they go off on one?' Jenny says, standing up and walking towards Johnno. They are now face-to-face.

'I have mates too.'

'What, Batman and Robin?' Jenny says, turning away and smirking. The moment has passed.

'He's called Mick, and there's Tony.'

'Okay, Mick, Robin, and Tony then. They'll run a mile when Fran and his lot come looking for you.'

Johnno smiles nervously.

'It's your funeral. Don't say I didn't warn you.'

'If it's not worth fighting for, it's not worth having. Look, do you want a drink?'

'Aye, if we're playing your daft game, I need something to take the edge off reality for a while. Got any rum?' Jenny moves back to the bed, lying down this time, closing her eyes.

'Johnno, Johnno, there's two cars outside. They've just pulled up and one of them is Fran's,' Mick shouts up the stairs.

Johnno turns towards the voice and then back to Jenny, who now has her arms behind her head.

'Trouble's brewing,' Jenny says, hearing him open the door. 'Don't forget my drink.'

Johnno locks the bedroom door and goes downstairs, where Tony, Robin, and Mick are waiting. They look uncomfortable.

'What about my rum?' Jenny shouts through the bedroom door as he gets to the bottom of the stairs, but Johnno ignores her. He walks to the front window. Two cars are slewed across the road with their headlights on full beam shining at the house.

'It's just like those old police films with James Cagney. The ones that end up with the house being riddled with machine gun bullets and the hero dying in front of the girl he loves after he opens the door and walks out to surrender,' Mick says to himself, but loud enough for everyone to hear.

Fran is clearly visible from the hall window, silhouetted by the lights.

'He'd be an easy shot from here,' Mick says.

'Shut up, Mick,' Alice says.

Johnno's sister, Alice, is trying to watch television in the front room behind him. She has been with Fran's party most of the day – she was the girl taking photographs outside Fran's house when he was captured earlier – but now she just wants a break and is trying to lose herself in mindless TV.

'Ally, take Jen up a rum and coke, will you? But make sure you lock the door afterwards,' Johnno says.

'Why can't you do it?'

'Ally, please.'

Alice shakes her head and heads towards the kitchen.

'Think he wants to parley,' Tony says, looking over Johnno's shoulder and interpreting the fact that Fran is now standing at the garden gate as an invitation to talk.

Johnno opens the front door and takes three paces towards Fran, along the yellow bricked garden path that his dad is so proud of. 'It took me three days to do that. Hardcore, membrane, then cemented them all in place. Herringbone pattern that is,' he would say, every time they were in the garden together, and the words now seemed to be imprinted on the air. Johnno stops were the path kinks a little to the right – 'Gives it a bit of character, the curvy bit,' his dad would say.

'What the fuck, Johnno? I'm getting married tomorrow and I don't want to end up in a cell, but you've taken a step too far, man. I'm going to give you ten minutes to let her go, before we come to get her,' Fran says, also standing on the path, just inside the blacksmith-crafted gate that is now ajar behind him. His voice is calm, but sure.

The two men are connected with bricks, like they are on the same journey only going in opposite directions, but they have come to an impasse, literally, as there is nowhere for them to pass without stepping on the grass and the grass is too dangerous to stand on. The neat lawn is really full of alligators, or it is electric – 10,000 volts. That's what Johnno's dad says to stop people walking on it. 'It's why I built the path', he'd say angrily if anyone strayed.

'Who's to say she wants to come with you?' Johnno says.

'Johnno, listen to yersel, man. You grabbed her and brought her here. If she wants to stay, fine, but she'll need to come and tell me herself. No, fuck it, I'm no having this crap. You got ten minutes, then we're coming in. Your dad will not be happy with the state of the house, and his precious garden, by the time we're finished with it.' Fran turns to his men, standing in line politely on the path, who all nod.

There is a minute of indecision, with both men staring at each other, waiting to see who will blink first. In the end, they turn and walk away at much the same time. Their movements coordinated as if pacing out a duel. A hubbub of voices as Johnno re-enters the house and locks the door behind him.

'It's like the fucking wild west,' Mick says.

Alice shakes her head and carries on up the stairs. The ice clinks in the glass with each step. The boys are talking loudly behind her and the TV is droning on in the background. From time-to-time canned laughter breaks out. The smell of her mother's perfume is stronger than normal as she unlocks the green door and opens it to find Jenny sprawled out on the bed. She sits up as soon as she sees that her drink has arrived.

'Ally, my girl. Thank you. I need that. Hope it's strong,' Jenny says.

'You stink. Mum will go mad when she gets back. No one is allowed to touch her scents. Why did he put you in here?'

'I think it's nostalgia. He wants me to remember the good times we had together, in here.'

'Jesus. On Mum's bed?'

'That would be telling. Anyway, what's a girl to do, locked up and surrounded with perfume? I feel like I'm in a brothel.'

'Did you wash in it?'

'Got a bit carried away, I don't normally have real perfume, just that toilet water crap. It's strong, isn't it? I love the No 5 stuff.'

'Classic, Mum calls it. It's what she wore when she first met Dad, but she said it was cheaper then. It's mad now.'

Leaving the door open Alice sits down on the bed beside Jenny and hands her the glass. She drinks half of it in one gulp and Alice laughs.

'Bloody hell, steady, lot of rum in that, not like a pub. Anyway, how have you managed to get two men fighting over you?'

'I think I must be irresistible. Johnno says I'm beautiful.'

Alice moves to the window, pushes the curtains open and looks down on Fran and his gang. They are huddled together in the campfire headlights, deep in conversation, planning their next steps.

'Don't tell my mad brother, but you made the right choice though,' Alice says, still staring out of the window. She then turns and looks at Jenny. 'I had a thing for Fran. Tried to get him a couple of times but he was too nice.'

'What you mean?'

'I was too young really. It was a kindness to tell me 'no' then. If you didn't have him, I think I'd try again.'

'Is that why you're always hanging round him and his boys?'

'They humour me, though they all tried it on at some stage.'

'But not Fran?'

'He is a gentleman. Just like his father.'

'Well, you missed your chance, he's mine now, but I'll be keeping my eye on you from now on,' Jenny says, smiling.

'What do you think he'll do?' Alice says, looking at the window.

Jenny shrugs and finishes her drink.

'He can be a mad bugger at times.'

'Exciting, isn't it?'

'Aye, you got any more rum?' Jenny says, holding up her empty glass and clinking the ice. She picks out the lime, sucks it and grimaces.

'Ugh.'

## (Kenaz)

*'This says you will have strength, energy and power.'*

'Guinness please,' Lionel says, when the barman in The Shore becomes free.

It takes longer than he anticipates getting his drink; he'd forgotten you have to wait for it to settle. It gives him time to look around the room and he sees two men in the corner he thinks he recognises.

A short, grey-haired man in his late sixties comes and sits beside him and orders a whisky which he soon knocks back.

'I have to pay for mine,' Lionel says, noticing that no money had changed hands.

'Aye, well you're no from around here and I have a special arrangement with my wife. I'm only allowed out on Show Night if I don't take any money and she comes around tomorrow to settle my tabs.'

'You wouldn't get away with that in Winnipeg,' Lionel says.

'Well, I doubt much that I'll ever get to Winnipeg.'

'You might have relatives there. That's why I'm here, tracing my ancestors.'

The man orders another whisky with a gentle nod of his head when the barman looks at him.

'Hi, Jacko. What odds would you give me on it raining tomorrow, before dawn?' A young man has come up from the noisy group sitting in the corner of the bar, just to ask the question.

Lionel's new drinking partner doesn't answer, but reaches into his jacket pocket, takes out a card and gives it to the young man.

'Aye, I know she's banned you from betting but she's no here, is she?'

'I would feel bad taking your money, son.'

'I want to tell me old man I took some money off DQ Jack.'

'It will rain on Sunday, at sunrise, but I'll no bet on it.'

'Go on, fifty pounds says it doesn't.'

'You'll be just throwing your money away, son.'

Jacko shakes his head and sips his whisky. At no time during the exchange has he looked at the young man, who raises his eyebrows and returns to his friends.

Lionel turns back to finish his drink and sees that behind the bar there are some old game shooting prints, one of a dog with a bird dangling from his mouth beside his master with a broken shotgun. It reminds him where he has seen the men in the corner table before.

'You know those lads over there?' Lionel asks Jacko.

'Aye. Well, I know who they are. I'd no say they were friends, or such. But I know most their parents.'

'I'm afraid I'm going to have to speak to them.'

'Aye,' Jacko says, staring at his empty glass, as if he was weighing up the pros and cons of ordering another drink.

Lionel, drink in hand, gets up and walks across the room.

'Can I help you?' a big guy says after his first tactic, of ignoring him, seems to have failed.

'It's him I want to talk to.'

They all follow Lionel's gaze and the young man being stared at turns to look at Lionel.

'Do I know you?' he says, still smiling from what was said before.

'No, but I recognise you from the other day.'

The man shakes his head and smiles at his friends.

'You shot some swans on the beach.'

'Sorry, mate, lost me on that one,' he says, dismissively turning away.

'You shot two swans then drove off in an inflatable boat,' Lionel says, then leans over and taps him on the arm. 'Yes. Same shirt.'

The man looks down at his arm and up at Lionel, smile now gone.

'Look, mate, less of the touching. Anyway, even if I did, I can't see what it has to do with you.'

'Wot, you from the RSPCA?' one of the party says, and another says, 'He's pissed. Fuck off, will you.'

'Well, was it you?' Lionel says.

The young man turns away again and starts speaking to the man beside him, pointedly ignoring Lionel and his question. The others scoff as he stands there, outside the circle once again.

Lionel admitted to his pastor, much later – after many hours of prayer to repent his sins – that what he did next was probably a mistake.

## (Hagalaz)

*'There will be unexpected disruptions.'*

The Americans and archaeologists, with Davey still in tow, have also drifted along Harbour Street, in the same direction as Lionel, but it has taken them longer to arrive outside The Shore. They had made it halfway back to the *royal yacht* before changing their minds and heading into town again and Davey, like a sea anchor, slowed them down with his anecdotes: he wasn't able to talk and walk at the same time.

'It's good to walk,' Marina says.

'I'd rather be cruising with one of those bad boys,' Lynette says, as a small, sporty car passes, window open and loud music playing.

'They're just children.'

'You're showing your age. I think we're supposed to be Cougars.'

'Not sure there'd be room in a tiny thing like that for, you know,' Marina says, shaking her head.

Lynette laughs, and roars like she thinks a cougar would roar.

They have just arrived outside The Shore when it kicks-off inside. A surprisingly loud noise, that later Rick would describe to his friends back home as 'the sound of a football team in a clothes dryer', exploded out of the front door, right into their faces.

'Wow,' Mathew says, stepping off the pavement into the road, pushed there by the shock wave. Lynette screams and the rest move together, instinctively forming a shoal. The look on Rick's face asks two questions: 1. Has it had been a big mistake after all to forsake the luxury and security of our floating palace for this little adventure in a foreign port? 2. Are Orcadians less civilised than they had been told at the welcome drinks?

'Bobby, I'm not sure about this,' Marina says, after the noise dies down a little.

'Just a bit of rough-housing. You can tell you are in a tough pub when they give you beer in plastic glasses,' Davey says, looking towards some discarded plastic on the windowsill.

'I thought that was so you could take your drinks outside,' Sharon, one of the archaeologists, says.

'Used to be to stop you glassing someone,' Davey says.

'Glassing someone?'

'Aye, smashing a glass in your face. I've been in many a dockyard pub where you'd get glassed for just looking at someone the wrong way.'

'How barbaric,' Patsy, another archaeologist, says.

'Dear girl, as some new friends reminded me earlier, you young folk don't know you've been born. There's more to life than brushing the ground to find wee bits of pottery.'

'More likely to use knives now,' Mathew says.

'Chivs' always been popular, but not as immediate. A glass in your face is more of an emotional reaction. Beware of emotional bastards when they get pissed. I was emotional once, but it sort of fades with age.'

'At home, they just shoot you,' Bobby says.

'Aye, Cowboys. Yanks always shoot from the hip,' Davey says.

'Do we?' Rick says.

'I suppose you think you know best because you're old,' Patsy says to Davey.

'Because I'm old I know that you young folk live in a fairy-tale land and have no idea just how tough life can be.'

'We're archaeologists. We study tough living,' Andrew, another one of Mathew's group, says.

'But you have no experience of living it.'

'Some people's lives are hard, even today,' Marina, says.

'You're both right. Life can be tough, but not for us, I'm glad to say,' Bobby says.

'Want to see the remains of Kirkwall Castle? Lot of history went on there when life was really tough, but just some of the walls left, in the Castle Hotel grounds,' Davey says.

'They mentioned the castle in our lecture, but I thought there wasn't anything left to see,' Rick says.

'That sounds fascinating. Rick, can we?' Lynette says.

(Thurisaz Reversed. Raidho. Kenaz)

*'Be cautious with changes and decisions, You'll go on a journey, the start of something new.'*

# 11. TEA & RUNES

'We're ready to go, just thought we should have a cup of tea first, it helps me relax before a casting. Here you are, in my special cups,' Gladys says, placing the bone china cup and saucer in front of Muriel who looks at it before picking up a biscuit and dunking it.

They are sitting in the front room of Gladys' boarding house on Bridge Street, which has been in business now for over a hundred years. Muriel looks across to the table in the bay window already set up for the rune casting. Gladys' familiar yellow rune cloth in the middle of the table and her orange rune pouch, tied at the top with red string, placed right in the centre.

'Ewan out tonight?'

'Had to let him come. He's a good boy really, just has his mad side that comes out from time-to-time.'

'Hardly a boy.'

'I thought if I came too, I could be there if it all kicked-off and maybes protect him from his instincts.'

'More tea?' Gladys says, one hand on the pot, ready to pour, even though she has yet to touch hers and Muriel has only drunk half a cup.

'I can't stay long, but I couldn't resist a reading. Would you tell me what you see?' Muriel says, gulping down what's left of her tea.

'Aye, I will, the runes are ready but let's not waste your cup,' Gladys says reaching across to get Muriel's teacup.

'Is it very different for you, the runes and the tea leaves?'

'Divination is a gift and I have a strong picture in my head about what things mean from where they appear on the cloth, or on the bottom of the cup. Tarot cards, they are similar too,' Gladys says, picking up Muriel's cup and saucer, swilling what liquid is left in the cup around a few times and then pouring it into the saucer, leaving a pattern of tea leaves on the bottom of the cup.

'It is going to be a good night,' Gladys says, after a short inspection of the tea leaves.

'Oh, really?'

'Someone, maybes your Ewan, is going to fall in love.'

'Well it won't be me. I'm done with all that nonsense.'

'He is going to meet his match tonight. Someone who will be able to control his instincts.'

'That will be a miracle.'

'Don't they say that Last Summer Night is the night for wishes and miracles?'

'Aye, they say a lot about the night. Well, I wish someone would control his instincts.'

Gladys puts the cup down and leads Muriel over to the table in the window.

'Muriel, sit here,' Gladys says, pointing to the chair facing into the room. She sits opposite her and undoes her blouse, pulling out three runes from the cup of her skin-tone brassiere.

'I have runes on me at all times. It builds a bond if they are touching my skin. It helps me understand their meaning,' she says, as she opens the top of the rune pouch and puts them back in.

'Will it be a full casting or I,3,5 or 9 selection?'

'I like it when you just select three, but I don't have a clear question tonight. So, a casting please. Isn't that what gives you the most to go on?'

'It is less specific, so if you don't have a clear question, it can be more powerful,' Gladys says, picking up the open pouch and shaking it. The solid wooden runes making clunky music in the bag.

'Muriel, what are you seeking from my sacred runes?' Gladys asks, adopting a reverential tone.

'I want you to use your gift to tell me about the future.'

Gladys stops shaking the bag and casts the twenty-five wooden blocks on the cloth in front of her. Some of them are the right way up, others turned over. Some of them are 'naturals' and others are reversed. All of them have meaning to Gladys, as does their relative position on the cloth.

'I can see flames and paintings and tattoos on people's bodies,' Gladys says, immediately, taking a deep breath as if she is shocked by the clarity of the image.

'Nothing would surprise me on Show Night.'

'Tattoos protect us from evils spirits that inhabit the underworld.' Gladys lifts the hem of her blouse to show Muriel a row of Viking runes tattooed on her ribs.

'Gladys, I've known you for fifty years and I never knew you had those.'

'Used to have to keep it a secret, didn't we? But it seems more acceptable now. Don't we all have a mark to protect us from the devil,' she says, and Muriel touches the top of her leg where her secret lies.

Gladys tucks her blouse back into the top of her skirt and looks back at her runes.

'What?' Muriel says, seeing Gladys' face change.

'I also see death.'

'That will be Mrs Tucker, they say she's close now. Tonight, or tomorrow is when she'll pass.'

'No, this is a man. A man with a beard.'

'Not Ewan then?' Muriel says, and Gladys shakes her head. She looks relieved, briefly.

'I hope there's not going to be another killing?' Muriel says.

'Another? When was the last time there was a murder on the Mainland?'

'Mumutaz shooting in 1994, and before that Vikings probably.'

'Funny you should say that, but I see Vikings too. It's going to be a night of flames and pictures on naked bodies and Vikings.'

'Oh, my. Can you see Ewan?'

'It's not Ewan.'

'Well, that's a relief. I was worried that Ewan would get arrested again.'

'No, tonight Ewan will find real love. I see it here too, in the same place in the circle as the tea leaves.'

'Here too?'

'There is no stronger reading than when you see the same thing in both rune and cup.'

'Gladys, if that is true I'll buy you dinner at Helgi's, that I will. Here, have this,' Muriel says, passing a Scottish ten-pound note across the table.

Rather than take the money straight away, Gladys frowns and leaves Muriel's arm hanging in the air. She is still peering at a rune she has just turned over and musing on the pattern it now makes with the other runes around it, some of them touching, which seems to mean something to her.

'What is it?'

'Isn't it terrible when a man does it with a child?' Gladys says.

'Terrible, but it seems to be in them, some evil that makes them do it. Do you remember the Tozer boy?'

'Aye, it goes on all the time, but tonight I see a young girl trying to escape from her abuser.'

Muriel shakes her head and makes the sign of the cross.

'It's her father and she is desperate.' Gladys covering the runes with the cloth bag to bring the reading to an end. She shakes her head and sighs, looking tired, as if all this has drained her of energy.

'It must be a burden for you to have such a gift.'

'It is hard to accept that God condones the wickedness in the world.'

Muriel leaves Gladys happy about her son, but troubled to think that somewhere in Kirkwall there is an abused child trying to escape from her wicked father.

## (Kenaz Reversed)

*An ending of some sort.*

I am cloaked in the sweet scent of Strandby, which attracts Meadow Brown butterflies in the warmth of the day; it is too cold for them now. But the Vikings have attracted some followers. Small crowd gathered by the track at the edge of the field that leads to the disused camp site. Clustering around the billboard advertising the planned development of new executive style homes. Just a dark rectangular hole in the mauve sky to me.

*Hardly brim-full of homeless executives, is it? Kirkwall.*

The longship is moving faster now, but I am getting bored. My phone vibrates – death is calling.

'Hello, it's Brian.'

'Welcome to Orkney.'

'Are you still there?' Brian says, after a pause.

'Yes, I'm just a bit puzzled by your voice.'

'I'm a bit bunged up, so my squeak has deserted me. I'm in the church in the centre of town.'

'The cathedral.'

'I wandered around for a bit but kept ending up back here.'

'The longer you live here the stronger the pull.'

'Well, I'm in the churchyard. I thought I'd have a quiet time before, well, you know.'

'The cathedral. It's bigger than a church.'

'Doesn't look big to me. Anyway, look, I couldn't get any helium. Not really something you get on the High Street,' Brian says.

'I was never too sure about the helium.'

'Expensive too,' he says, as if that should matter to a man about to die.

'You're right. So, what's the plan?' I watch the progress of the longship across the field. Though it looked flimsy on the water earlier, it is now made of lead. I can see why they need Sigurd's muscles.

'I've bought a charcoal burner. A bit like a barbecue,' Brian says.

'And how exactly are we going to kill ourselves with a barbecue?'

'I've been reading that you just need a confined space, like a car, and it sort of eats up all the oxygen. It's big in Japan. They call it 'death by hibachi'. You're meant to use a traditional Japanese heating bowl, but I couldn't get a real one, not in Leeds.'

'I don't have a car.'

'Oh, well, maybe we can break into a car.'

'Bloody hell, Brian, can you imagine some poor little wifey taking the kids to the kirk in the morning and finding two cooked bodies in her car?'

'We won't be cooked, just suffocated.'

'Have you no heard of an Arbroath Smokie?' I say, and can't stop myself from laughing.

'Pandora, it isn't a laughing matter.'

'Anyway, you're early. I'm tied up at the moment.'

'What are you doing?'

'Brian, you really wouldn't believe me if I told you. It's even more ridiculous than death by barbecue. See you at midnight. Oh, by the way how are you with heights?'

It isn't until Brian has gone that I remember that Kim Jong-hyun, a member of the KPOP group SHINee, killed himself by burning charcoal in a frying pan. That makes the idea more appealing somehow. Following him on the path to the underworld. Still favour the cliff though.

*Dreki* has made some progress across the soon-to-be housing development site in front of me, pulled by a gang of men with a pirate at the helm. He is holding a banner which I now see has a raven on it. Wonder how exactly I could have explained all this to Brian, from Leeds, who wants to die by barbecue, or anyone else for that matter, and I laugh again.

*Oh my god, what is happening to me? Laughter is a sign of madness, right? That's all right then.*

Thomas appears, on the road with a woman I haven't seen before, moving along the line of spectators showing them something. Reminds me I'm a fugitive.

*He must have read my diary and for the first time taken me seriously. I wonder why?*

'Don't look at me,' I say, from my hiding place behind the rock, when Sigurd comes over to talk to me.

'Who are you hiding from here?'

'My father, he's over there, on the road, with a suspicious looking woman. They're after me.'

'Why?'

'I was abducted at birth and held captive as his plaything until now, but he now thinks I'm so attached to him that I wouldn't run away. Tonight is his test of my loyalty.'

'Hasn't gone so well for him then.'

'Who is the guy with the banner?' I say, and we both turn around to look at *Dreki*.

'My dad,' he says. He sounds proud.

'Don't look at me, you'll give me away,' I say, when Sigurd turns back.

'This is how we used to make a claim on a piece of land. Normally an island though. If you sailed around it or pulled your boat across the land it gave you claim to it,' Sigurd says, looking straight ahead at the passing longship.

'I thought you were making a porn film and wanted me to be the ravaged local.'

'You have some imagination'. He smiles at me, as if it doesn't really matter what I say. I can't shock him and he likes me anyway.

*Why do I try to shock the men in my life?*

'My father feels the need to reassert his claim on this land, which was left to him and his brother, but his brother seems to think it is his now.'

The longship is getting close. 'Look, enough of this, we're halfway there and I have to get back,' he says.

He jogs across to help keep the boat steadily moving forward. As he gets there a group of four men run ahead to remove the fence on the other side of the field, which leads down towards another beach fifty metres away.

Sit in silence, exploring the soil with my fingers. I can feel Oysterplant and Dead Men's Bells, and the stickiness of Goosegrass. I watch as the boat crawls across the ground in front of me on its agricultural voyage and wonder what plants it is crushing as it goes – Oraches, Moors, Silverweed, Sea Chickweed, Sea Sandwort.

Wooden hull creaks. Does it do that at sea as it rolls on the waves, ploughing the ocean? Can smell ships and the sea, but I am imagining that. Rolling logs leaving a hatched track on the grass as if a tank has passed by and we are on a battlefield. Ground is moving and I am a fishing float, bobbing up and down on each cresting wave.

## (Ansuz)

*'Time to acquire wisdom.'*

I peek out and Thomas and the woman seem to have gone, so I get up and sit on the rock again.

'I'm here,' I shout, but no one hears me, my words comingled with a chant from the men pulling the boat, in a tongue I don't recognise. Like a sea shanty but different: older.

Only takes them another twenty minutes to get across the field and push *Dreki* back into the tide, where it sits bathing in the gentle wash of the bay.

'Come on,' Sigurd says, grabbing my hand and pulling me towards the beach through stands of Bullwan, with its crinkly tobacco leaves. Wonder if I am helping nature, by spreading their seeds as we brush past them. 'Put this on,' he says, handing me a lifejacket, as we run into the water and he lifts me up over the side of the boat.

'I didn't realise Vikings were so safety conscious. Am I your plunder? Am I being kidnapped after a violent raid; being taken back to Norway to be your bride?'

'Just helping you escape from the posse of desperados on your trail. Or are they bounty hunters?'

'All I know is they are licensed to kill,' I say.

'And seduce beautiful women,' Sigurd says.

'I shall be all right then.'

'Don't be so sure, danger of that sort is lurking everywhere.'

'I think they've gone, but I'm not sure that two people can constitute a posse.'

'Okay, then, Miss Grammatical Precision, then I'm rescuing you from yourself.' He is laughing as the men on the beach push off and turn us so that the crew can hoist the sail. I notice, again, roman number LX in the middle of the sail.

'Sixty what? I say nodding to the sail.

'My dad's birthday present to himself when he was sixty. He says he's now 'gusting sixty', just like they say in the shipping forecast when there is a gale.'

'Full of wind?'

'Full of wild destructive power, when he has a mind to be. That's how my uncle lost his eye. My dad went mad and hit him with a chair.'

'Does he do that often?'

'They were fighting over a girl and she chose my uncle; after that my dad had to leave.'

'Banished. How romantic. Force of nature then, your dad?'

Sigurd nods and stares ahead into the darkness. Boat tilts and a swishing sound comes from the bow cutting through the water, like a sigh of relief; the hull glad to get back in its element and wash away the soil.

'What was all that about?' I say.

'My father wants his share of the land back.'

'From your uncle, the guy who wants to build new homes for the hordes of homeless executives you see in the bars of Kirkwall of a Saturday night?' I say, laughing to myself.

'Aye, that's him. He likes traditions that suit him, but not when it comes to owning land.'

Light flares at the stern. Sigurd's father, Split, is standing with blazing torch in his hand, which he brings forward and hands to me. Still not completely dark but as he approaches I notice the navigation lights on the mast are also on.

'Dad, this is Panda.'

*He looks like Captain Kirk. Has he come to my rescue after all?*

'We need you to guide us through the treacherous reefs ahead,' Split says, and nods towards the prow of the boat, where the dragon's head rears up above the sea. Spray from the sloppy waves washing its face. Now holding *Dreki*'s fire-breath in my hands.

Sigurd and I stand close together, arms around the dragon's neck to counteract the gentle roll of the boat. Hold the flaming torch above my head as it is hot and the higher it is the more of the passing waves are visible ahead.

'This would make a great setting for a porn film,' I say.

'More like bloody Titanic, if you ask me. Look at that big bugger,' Sigurd says, pointing at the cruise liner ahead of us. 'I wouldn't want to be on it when it sinks. It's like a fancy iceberg.'

'Last Summer Night. There'll probably be icebergs here tomorrow,' I say.

'You'll miss them.'

'All I need now is for Jim to tie himself to the mast to resist the siren's call and save me and my last night on earth will be complete.'

'Jim?'

'Captain James Tiberius Kirk of the Starship Enterprise. Kirkwall was named after him.'

Sigurd laughs out loud.

'Well, it should have been.'

The torch flares and I pull it back towards us and it illuminates Sigurd's beautiful eyes and I see he is still wearing his t-shirt.

'What are the coconuts all about?'

'My philosophy of life in a picture.'

'What, eat four coconuts a day, or something?' I say, looking back at the sea ahead of us as the first dolphin flashes past and takes up station with two others, cresting the bow wave. Keeping pace with the boat and leaping clear of the water, leaving a trail of mist droplets in the air. Beneath the surface, they leave streaks of light as excited plankton are pushed aside by their bulk.

'Look, porpoises,' Sigurd says, clearly excited and wiping the spray from his face.

'Dolphins, actually, Risso's dolphin, sometimes called grampus.'

'It's like having David Attenborough with you.'

'Wish I knew how to enjoy life like that,' I say, staring at the grampus and lowering my torch over the bows to see them better. Then they go, as quickly as they came, and the sea is empty again, made of thick green moulded glass, like old coke bottles.

'Tell me about the coconuts,' I say, turning back to Sigurd.

'A few years ago, when I was unhappy.'

'I can't imagine you being unhappy.'

'Try being part of a family that lives in the Dark Ages, it's not always this much fun. It can be miserable. Anyway, I went to a fun fair with some friends and there was a coconut shy. My mates all missed, but I threw four balls in about 20 seconds and each ball hit a coconut, right plumb in the middle, and all four coconuts fell to the ground. I thought they had nails to hold them in, but they all fell to the ground.'

'Impressive, but how do you construct a philosophy of life from that?'

'I realised that for those twenty seconds I was completely focused on hitting those coconuts. I was living totally in the moment and something just clicked and I was not only able to hit one of them but to do it four times in a row. During that twenty seconds, I was so focussed on what I was doing I forgot I was unhappy.'

'Live for now, right? It's what all the self-help books say.'

'Right now, this instance, and make the most of it.'

'I do the opposite,' I say, turning away, looking into the darkness ahead, 'I don't do things, I imagine them.'

'What sort of things?'

'Sad things mostly.'

'No wonder you want to kill yourself.'

I smile and put my hair in my mouth and Sigurd puts his arm around my waist as the boat surges towards the harbour on each gust of wind.

'You know that I said that your hair reminded me of a bit from a saga,' Sigurd says, looking at my face, now almost covered with hair.

'Oh, yes – "girls with hair like that" – is what you said. I remember. Do you now know me well enough to tell me what it was?'

Sigurd makes this verse:

*Silken-haired maid*
*summoned the serpent in me,*
*when she caressed her locks.*
*Enchantress, stroking up a spell*
*to bind my heart,*
*bewitching me with her*
*coy act of love.*

'Oh,' I say.

'It's very sexy. It came to mind the first time I saw you.'

I shake my head and look back at the sea.

It feels good to be here with Sigurd. He's right, all I can think of is what is happening to me now, the madness of my abduction, and my voyage across the sea with this handsome man.

I have completely forgotten why I was so sad.

(Hagalaz)

*Unexpected disruptions*

Another burning torch, this time in Fran's hand, with Bobby, Nige, Malcy and Hal standing with him on the electric grass. They are facing Johnno's front door, daring it to move. Fran takes a few steps forward just as the door opens and Alice comes out, leaving him stranded mid-lawn.

'Fucking hell, Fran, what do you think you're doing?' Alice says.

'If he won't let her go, we'll burn him out of the house.'

'Don't be such a twat. I was trying to watch *Dancing On Ice* until all this started.'

'You can't just kidnap someone without repercussions.'

'Put those out,' Johnno says, as he joins his sister, just as a police car arrives. Its blue pulsing light illuminating the faces in the windows opposite, peering out between the curtains.

'Oh fuck,' Alice says.

'Hello,' Sergeant Maitland says, as he walks into the front garden, past Fran and his mates.

'Hi, Alice. Everything all right here?' PC McTravers says, just a few paces behind.

'Hi Sarah. It's just a friend's blackening,' Alice says, directing her words towards the policewoman.

'You know her?' Johnno says to Alice but looking at the policewoman.

'Aye, Sarah's my lifesaving coach, down at the Pickaquoy sports centre.'

'Blackenings must have come on a bit since my time. We didn't have incendiary gangs in quiet residential streets,' Sergeant Maitland says.

'Or kidnappings,' Fran says.

'No, we had them. Isn't that why you are all covered in paint and feathers?' Sergeant Maitland says.

'Yes, but that was just the blackening, now this bawbag has kidnapped my bride-to-be for real and we're here to get her back,' Fran says, staring at Johnno with intent.

'And what are the flames for? Don't you have a phone?' PC McTravers says, as she approaches them.

'We wanted to scare that bastard,' Fran says, pointing to Johnno in the doorway.

'Alice, is this true?' PC McTravers says.

'Don't ask me, I've just been having a drink with Jenny upstairs,' Alice says.

'Jenny?' Sergeant Maitland says.

'My bride,' Fran says, taking possession of her with his firm voice by emphasising the first word.

'If I've got her, you'll no be wedding her,' Johnno says.

'See, he admits it,' Fran says, looking to the policeman as if asking a referee for a free kick.

'It's Jenny you're marrying, right?' Sergeant Maitland says to Fran.

'Aye, it is.'

'No, it's not, she's not marrying him. She is going to marry me,' Johnno says, from the front door.

'Johnno, for fuck's sake,' Alice says. 'He's mad. Unrequited love and vodka don't mix.'

PC McTravers takes a step forward.

'Alice, where is the lucky lady with so many suitors?'

'She's inside, shall I get her?'

'Yes, that might be a good idea,' PC McTravers says, and Alice goes into the house.

'Oh, fuck.' Hal drops his torch which has now burnt down so far the flames have reached his hand.

'You'll want to run that under a cold tap,' PC McTravers says.

'Lads, maybe you should all do that. Let's get rid of the fireworks, shall we?' Sergeant Maitland says.

It is surprisingly difficult to put the flames out so Malcy douses his in the fish pond.

'Malcy, what the fuck? My father will go ape-shit if you've killed his bloody newts,' Johnno says.

'Newts?' The sergeant says, looking impressed. 'Great crested, or common?'

'How am I supposed to know?' Johnno says.

With the torches out, it seems much darker, just the streetlights and the pulsing blue light from the police car.

'Flaming torches are popular tonight,' Sergeant Maitland says, looking at the smouldering torch.

'What?' Fran says.

'The Harbour Master is on the warpath. Someone with a torch like yours sailing round the bay and heading for the harbour.'

'That's Show Night for you,' Malcy says.

'Brings out the Viking spirit,' Nige says.

Alice leads Jenny out of the front door and she stands with her in front of the two police officers. She has a blue Camberwick bedspread wrapped around her shoulders.

'Sorry, officers, the blackening just got a bit out of hand,' Jenny says.

'Are you being kept here against your will?' Sergeant Maitland says.

Jenny looks around the front garden and smiles. 'God, no. Alice and me, just having a bit of drink upstairs.'

'What about these guys?' Sergeant Maitland says.

'Some sort of man game. Trial of wills,' Jenny says.

'Trial of willies more like,' Alice says.

'Beyond me,' Jenny says.

'Come on, everyone, the party's inside,' Alice says, leading everyone into the house except the two police officers.

'Alice, what are you doing?' Johnno says.

'Just smile, will you, until they've gone and the neighbours all get back to their telly,' she says, quietly to her brother.

'One last thing,' Sergeant Maitland says, before they leave. 'Have you seen this girl?'

Both sides of the argument turn and crowd around the sergeant's phone to look at the photo.

'Yes, I have,' Jenny says. 'Saw her earlier in front of the Kirk.'

'When was that?' Sergeant Maitland says.

'Earlier this evening, by the Mercat Cross as the curfew bell went. What's wrong?' Jenny says.

'We're a bit concerned about her and want to make sure she is okay. Do you know where she might be?'

'Said she had a date with a softy. Bit like you, Johnno,' Jenny says.

'Do you know who?'

'No,' Jenny says.

'I might be sensitive but I'm no soft,' Johnno says.

'Yes, you are,' Jenny says.

'That's why she chose me. Wants a man not a girl,' Fran says, and immediately Johnno has to be restrained by Robin and Mick.

'Johnno, stop it. He'll kill you,' Jenny says.

'Please, the last thing we want is a murder to deal with. Will you not all calm down?' PC McTravers says.

'Aye, Sarah, we will. Come on, everyone. Let's have a two-hour truce so we can have a drink,' Alice says, leading them all into the house and leaving the brace of police officers standing on the path, side-by-side, staring at their departing backs.

'And I thought getting the car off Blobby would make the night a bit easier,' Sergeant Maitland says. PC McTravers laughs as they walk back up the path to the garden gate.

# MY DIARY

## I'VE TOLD YOU BEFORE.

# YOU SHOULDN'T BE READING THIS

## ABOUT A MURDER

I take full responsibility for her passing. All the guilt I feel is justified. It was me who took her life. I feel it as deeply as if I had slashed her throat. I dream of doing it. It seems so real. It is true. Is it true?

I wasn't expecting the spurt of blood that shot up into the air. The geyser of red champagne released with a tiny razor blade as the cork popped out of the bottle. I knew that there was a big artery in the neck but it was a hit and miss thing, I hadn't looked up the anatomy of the slash, just hit out.

'Oh,' she said. The surprise on her face. She really wasn't expecting me to do that. Shout at her, yes, she knew I'd do that, but not cut her. If she had stayed still she would just have got branded on the face, maybe across her nose, but she moved and I lunged forward and all of a sudden her neck was where her cheek had been.

She was the first person I have killed. But she won't be the last. You will be next. For tormenting me and all the abuse. I'm going to kill you in your sleep. Snuff you out like a candle. Your last squeezed breath will be a release for both of us.

I was surprised how much pleasure it gave me. It put me in control. I was no longer the weak one, fearing others. Now I was someone to be feared. I saw that change of status on her face as she fell to the ground. The blood squirting out of her was a bit like air being released from a balloon. It made a slurping sound and she deflated as it covered the wall and some of it got up as far as the ceiling.

From the stuff I have seen on TV, this will be an easy crime to crack as I'm sure to be covered in blood splatter. I think that is the term. Splattered with my mother's blood; a bit like birth again, but different. Don't they say that the main cause of death is birth? I am reborn and you can only be reborn when your parents die. One down, one to go.

I know I've now given you another reason to hate me, as you've only just decorated the room.

---

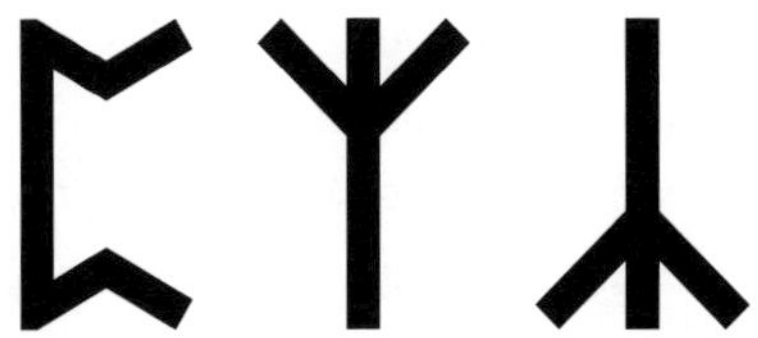

(Perthro. Algiz. Algiz Reversed)

*'Things that are hidden are about to come to light.
Someone has been deceiving you.'*

# 12. BREACH OF THE PEACE

The police officers had just got back to their car when they get a call to say there was a fight in The Shore. It is no more than a mile away so they are soon there and arrive just as Mathew, Davey and the Americans set off towards Bridge Street. The police see Rex standing outside with a group of sailors and immediately decide he must be involved.

'No me, man, not tonight,' he says, as they approach him. 'Some mad yank in there attacked Andy.'

They enter to find most people standing with two men being corralled at opposite ends of the room. Jacko still sitting quietly watching from his perch at the bar.

'Jacko,' the sergeant says as he enters and Jacko nods.

'Andy, what's going on?' the sergeant says, approaching the younger man first.

'Mad bastard tried to arrest him,' the fat guy says. Andy just shrugs his shoulders.

'Said it was a citizen's arrest and when Andy would no go with him, he poured a Guinness over his head. I'd say that was assault, with a deadly weapon.'

'Beer?' Sergeant Maitland says.

'The glass. He was going to do him.'

'It's plastic,' Sergeant Maitland says, picking up the empty 'glass'.

'Aye, but plastic can do damage too.'

'Right, you stay here,' Sergeant Maitland says, and he walks over to Lionel on the other side of the room and leads him outside and into the backseat of the police car.

'Your name?' the Sergeant says once he has got into the front seat of the car.

'Lionel Hartman.'

'You no from round here?' Sergeant Maitland says.

'Just here for a short holiday.'

PC McTravers joins them in the car, sitting in the front passenger seat.

'Man in there says you were attempting to carry out a citizen's arrest,' PC McTravers says.

'I saw him a couple of days ago shooting swans for some rich guy's dinner and that can't be legal, can it?'

'Shooting swans?' Sergeant Maitland says.

'Yes, he was shooting them because apparently some guy called Earl likes to eat them.'

'How do you know that?' PC McTravers says.

'I was on a Flat Earth tour when I saw him do it and my guide told me,' Lionel says.

'In Kirkwall?' Sergeant Maitland says, looking as if this is new to him and, in his job, very little is new to him.

'No, beside Scapa Flow.'

'Earl, you say?' Sergeant Maitland says.

'Yes, do you know him?'

'Aye, I do. His family have a bit of feast at the Temper on the night of the show, but I didn't know they ate swan,' he says to his younger colleague who doesn't seem to have heard this before.

'Yes, they were mute swans and I looked it up online. It said it was against the law, as they all belong to the Queen. Not sure if that is theft or treason, or both, but it must be serious.'

'Assault is a more serious thing, though the law is a wee bit different up here about swans,' Sergeant Maitland says.

'What do you mean?'

'Well, swans don't belong to the Queen up here. Not sure they do in most of England really, though some breeds are protected, but not up here. Here they belong to everyone and although it isn't encouraged, it isn't against the law to shoot them.'

'It doesn't matter, he was resisting arrest. Anyway, he is in his twenties with a gang of friends, and I was on my own with a pint of Guinness and I am 62 years old.'

'You maybe should have come to us,' Sergeant Maitland says.

'What would you have done about it? I bet the Earls have you in their pocket. Isn't it how it works in a little place like this?'

'Mr Hartman, I think you may be a little overwrought.'

'Sorry, but I haven't been arrested before.'

'For what it is worth, no, it isn't how it works here. We will talk to Andy and get to the bottom of this, and you will need to pop into the station to give us a few details before you leave Orkney.'

Sergeant Maitland stops talking, distracted by a noise outside, further up the road. The others follow his gaze up Shore Street. Five shaggy highland cattle with huge horns are charging towards them followed by a running man. The cattle head straight for the car but then veer off to one side and out towards the Ayre. No one watching seems inclined to get in their way, or to try and stop them, they just watch this latest Show Night act.

'There're going to kill me. Help me, they are going to kill me,' the running man says, as he passes them, clearly not seeing the two police officers, or even the police car parked in front of the bar.

A gang of ten or so men come running after him, and the beasts, but when they see the police car they all stop running and walk nonchalantly towards Skippers Bar, like a herd of cows off to be milked.

Sergeant Maitland looks at PC McTravers and shakes his head before turning his attention back to Lionel.

'I'm not being arrested then?' Lionel says.

'No, not yet, but I'd advise you to keep your head down the night. Where are you staying?' Sergeant Maitland says.

'I can't remember the name, but I can show you where it is.'

'Right, we'll drive you back there after we've had another wee chat with Andy. You wait here,' the Sergeant says to Lionel, before turning to PC McTravers. 'Go and find out what the hell that was about, will you?' he says, looking back towards the ruffle of deep breathing men now trying to squeeze themselves into the busy bar.

As Sergeant Maitland enters the front door of the pub again he turns to a grey-haired man now standing on the pavement. 'Willy, will you do something about those beasts for me?'

'Aye, Terry. I will. No problem, I will.'

(Ehwaz)

*'Expect movements and changes.'*

There are two reception parties waiting for us as we enter harbour.

'You lot, I've been watching you sailing across the bay. Put that bloody flame out, that's the fuel bowser beside you.' Man with white cap is shouting at us from the end of the harbour wall. Sigurd looks back at Spit and then takes the torch from me and drops it into the water. It sizzles as the flame is extinguished. Cloud of black smoke drifts across the water like a thin veil of mist from the underworld.

Several posh folk looking down from the bows of the *Highlander* as we pass. Have drinks in their hands, like they did earlier, as if glasses are essential life-saving equipment that have to be carried at all times while on board. Applaud as if we were entertainment put on for their benefit alone. As we turn towards the quay the sail flaps in the wind and we drift alongside, our landing judged to perfection by Split, so much so that someone cheers. Three purring GTXs pull up just before we arrive, like puppies welcoming us home.

'My uncle, Swift Eye,' Sigurd says, pointing towards a group of men waiting on the quay, as we kiss the jetty and two men jump ashore with ropes.

'The developer of executive homes?'

'Not if my dad has anything to do with it.'

Swift Eye, followed by his retinue, move towards the edge of the quay. Carrying broom handles like they were swords. It is now past high water, but the sides of the boat are still level with the quay and Split and he are at the same height.

Swift Eye steps forward to speak just as half a dozen cattle come racing along Harbour Street behind him. The commotion disturbs him briefly before he composes himself and makes this verse:

*When the sharp dawn blade*
*cuts the night-skin*
*all must be settled.*
*If not, then honour and custom*
*leave us no choice,*
*but to fight.*

*I call a Ting.*
*To see if, one last time*
*words can prevent*
*the blood-drenched*
*coat. The loss of eye and limb.*

Split nods his ascent to this challenge to talk once more. Seems a bit silly really, but everyone is taking it seriously. Does he mean it? Do they all know that if they can't agree by dawn, blood will be shed in the Earl family one more time and it might be their blood?

Always known when midnight arrives. Can feel the click from one day to the next, as the spring winds down and day begins again. I often wake. So, I know it is time.

'I have to go,' I say.

'Why? Don't let my uncle frighten you. They can't do much damage with a broomstick.'

'It's the noon of night and I have to go.'

'Cinderella, is it?'

I take off my boots and give Sigurd one. 'Here,' I say, and throw the other into the water. No idea why.

He laughs, holding a black Doc Marten in his hand. It is so far removed from being a glass slipper as I am from being a princess.

'You'll hurt your feet.'

'Aye,' I say, as I skip off the boat, passing a serious but now surprised Swift Eye and run along the quay.

'It's called flow,' Sigurd shouts at me.

'What is?' I say, turning back to hear what he is saying.

'When you concentrate on what is happening so much you forget everything else. It's how I stay sane.'

'Imbroglio,' I say, and smile and turn away.

'It's not another man, is it?' Sigurd calls out after me, much to the amusement of everyone. My departure has disturbed the proceedings, introducing a well needed pause before the verbal skirmishes commence.

Turn again and wave before heading for the kirk. 'May the best man win,' I shout as I run. Away from the bright trawler lights I dive into a pool of icy shade. Shocks me awake and I remember my destiny. Feel the chill of death, even though it is a warm night by the standards of this bloody place.

Brian and the death pact. My thoughts now return to my sad life, forgotten since leaving the site of the new executive homes, less than an hour earlier.

# DEAR EDITH, 2

'So, you're a cattle enthusiast?' Zander said, looking at the bull in front of me with the most enormous *things*. As you can imagine, I went red when I realised what I had been staring at all this time, trying not to watch as he made his way over. But I guess it must have been obvious that I was loitering with intent.

I just smiled, not really sure what to say.

'I'm a tour guide, of sorts. Want a tour?' he said.

He didn't wait for me to reply, just started speaking.

'From Bignold Park here we can walk down to the town where my Kirkwall History Walk begins. It goes along Palace Road, Broad Street, Albert Street, Bridge Street, to the sea – the backbone of the town.
It used to be a beach and everything on the side opposite the cathedral was water. The bay that used to be there was called the Oyce, but all that is left is the Peedie Sea.'

'You mean that funny circle of water, on the edge of town?'

'Just a tiny memory of what it used to be. Peedie means small around here.'

'I thought it was a boating lake,' I said, as he launched off into his script again, this time about Vikings.

*The first men ashore were the youngest, as the bows of the long ships crunched into the pebbly beach they jumped into the shallow water and splashed their way to dry land. Long hair and ragged beards, dressed in layers of cloth. Some of them shouted as they ran up the beach towards the huts on the shore.*

*The women and girls who had gathered to watch them approach turned and ran at the first howls from the men. Fleeing to the clusters of huts just back from the water. Older men and children stood their ground and watched as the women giggled and scattered. It was always the same after the summer expedition. When the men came home they went wild. They ate, drank and celebrated their successes, but first they fucked their women silly. Wives, girls and concubines all knew what was coming when their men returned. If they returned. There were normally some women spared the warriors' return and one or two new pretty girls dragged ashore.*

I was staring down at Kirkwall, lost in thought. The way Zander described it made it easy to imagine. I could have been standing there amongst them waiting for my man, and I have to admit it was an exciting thought.

'My four tour streets, joined end-to-end, is what defines Kirkwall. Some call it The Road To Nowhere, but I like to think of it as the Road To The Past,' he said. His words nudging me out of my daydream. 'Let me show you how the past and present are intertwined, zipped together on this fantastic road.'

Of course, I said 'no', that I didn't think that would be wise, but he was persistent and asked me why.

'You're young enough to be my son,' I said, aware that I was on a slippery slope and having second thoughts about all this.

'So?' he said, teasing me.

'You know.'

'Are you worried about immersing yourself in Kirkwall's colourful past?'

'Yes, that must be it. Thank you but, not this time,' I said, but he just laughed at me and took my hand; he led me off and I didn't stop him. Can you believe that? I was powerless.

'I said, no,' I said, as we left the showground, but he ignored me again and we walked side-by-side down the hill towards the town.

My heart beating so fast I could hardly breathe.

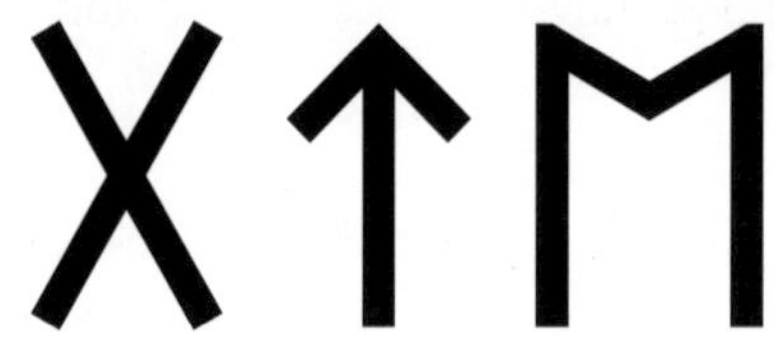

(Gebo. Tiewaz. Ehwaz)

*'Partnership and fighting for what you believe in can lead to a change for the better.'*

# 13. TIME TO TALK

'Fuck,' I say, approaching the gate to the graveyard, beside the cathedral. Even from the centre of Broad Street I can see I have been tricked.

'Brian?' I say, as I get closer.

*It must be him.*

'Pandora?' he says.

Looks a bit sheepish now that we are face-to-face.

'If I'm honest, I'm not surprised,' I say.

Brian is old enough to be my grandfather. Sitting on a large flat tomb. Unpacked his rucksack and laid out his possessions.

'I knew it had to be you when I saw that,' I say, pointing at the charcoal burner by his side.

'Sorry.'

'You told me you were twenty-two.'

I'm annoyed, but not really that surprised.

'I thought if I told you my real age you'd think I was some dirty old man just wanting... Well, you know.'

Raise my eyes and look at him, but he is looking down. Looks up at me again, after a while.

'So, how old are you?'

'Fifty-eight.'

'Shouldn't have believed your stories about having no credit and not getting Skype working.'

'Well, we're here now,' Brian says, as if that was it. Thinks I have no choice but to go along with him, to the end.

*He's given me the perfect excuse to back out. Do I want to back out? I don't think I can do it on my own.*

'You said you'd tried this before,' I say, remembering his emails when he seemed reluctant to go into detail.

'Third time lucky.'

'Did you keep on getting reincarnated?' I say. Laugh out loud.

*That is fucking funny.*

He doesn't laugh, just thinks about it for a while.

'So, what happened?'

'Just didn't work out. Don't have a brain, not really. Don't seem to be able to do it on my own.'

'Wouldn't reincarnation really piss you off if you'd killed yourself?' I say, still smiling to myself.

'I guess it depends what you come back as.'

'I think you just get a short time to contemplate your life and then you're gone, forever.'

'I'd like to come back as a hydrangea,' Brian says, looking at a hydrangea bush beside him, up against the churchyard wall.

'I'm not coming back.'

There is a rustling noise behind me, and I turn and see Sigurd and his father walking along Broad Street, at the head of thirty or so men. Sigurd sees me and waves, though he looks a bit puzzled when he sees Brian. Behind them, a blind man with a white stick is tapping his way along the pavement.

'Friends of yours?' Brian says.

'Family feud that is just about to erupt into open warfare. They seem to be heading back to the Temperance Hotel.'

'What's that?'

'They don't serve alcohol. It's where the word temper comes from.'

I can't resist it.

He looks puzzled, but he waits while I make myself comfortable on the tomb opposite.

'The word temper comes for the temperance movement. They thought that it was alcohol that led to trouble. If you didn't drink alcohol you had a better chance of staying calm. Not losing your temper.'

'Really? I thought it was Latin, something to do with time,' Brian says.

'*Tempus fugit*,' I say.

Brian still looks puzzled.

'Time flies.'

'It only seems a day or so since we first met online,' he says.

'I wondered why I couldn't find you on Facebook,' I say, shaking my head. Amazed at my own stupidity.

*Maybes I didn't want to know the truth.*

'Don't do social media.'

Still shaking my head, still crushed. See Charlie, with his white stick, on his own, of course.

'Now, Charlie there, only comes out on special nights and walks around the kirk. Doing penance for his sins.'

'What sins?' Brian says.

'Stole some silver from the altar. As he ran out of the cathedral he was struck by lightning on a perfectly clear night, which blinded him. They say it was St Magnus's curse. Why no one here works on his saint's day, April 16th, for fear of something similar happening.'

'Impressive for someone who has been dead all this time.'

'People here don't believe that makes him any less of a threat,' I say, as we watch Charlie walk by, not aware we are only a few metres away and staring at him.

'Still a source of inspiration and the odd miracle,' I say, once Charlie has gone.

'Miracles?'

'He appears in a ball of light and does good things for people, so they keep coming here to ask for his help. Used to lie outside the front of the cathedral and pray for his intervention in their lives. These days, they just sit and pray inside.'

'Well, are we still on?' Brian says.

I shrug and nod.

*Do I have a choice?*

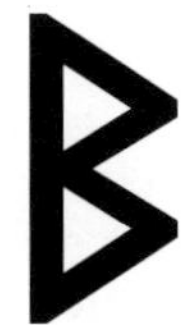

(Berkana)

*'New beginnings.'*

Fran's gang are watching *Top Gear* in the sitting room, sipping beers that Alice has put in their hands, and Johnno's men are in the kitchen with Alice, who is making herself a banana sandwich. Jenny has gone back upstairs with the remaining rum and a couple of cokes.

'She says she is happy here for now. She just wants a bit of rest and a drink,' Alice says.

'Good, gives us time to talk. Hey, guys, help me move this table,' Johnno says.

Johnno, Mick and Robin move the table from the small dining room and put it in the middle of the sitting room, right in front of the telly.

'I'm watching that,' Hal says.

'Tough, we need to talk. I'm calling a parley,' Johnno says, as he pulls some of the dining room chairs around the table.

'Another one?' Alice says.

'I thought this was a truce,' Fran says.

'We can parley during a truce,' Johnno says. 'Isn't that what truces are for?'

'There is nothing to talk about,' Fran says.

'Fran, you and Bobby sit there, me and Alice will sit here.'

'Don't you drag me any further into this,' Alice says.

'You're already in this, sit down will you,' Johnno says.

'We've got nowt to talk about,' Fran says.

'Well, if you won't settle this like men and accept my *holmgang*, we'll have to come to some arrangement,' Johnno says.

'What the fuck?' Fran says.

'Old Norse duel,' Johnno says.

'Oh, for God's sake, humour him. Sit down and let's get this over with,' Alice says.

The two parties are now sitting on opposite sides of the table, with *Top Gear* still playing on the TV. Hal and Robin are perched on the wings of their chairs so they can keep following the motorised action. They are completely oblivious to the negotiations about to start in the middle of the room and the fact that they are in opposing camps.

'Turn the sound down, it's just cars,' Alice says.

'I'll give you ten thousand pounds for her,' Johnno says, once the sound of screeching tyres has died away and the talking has stopped.

'What?' Alice says. 'You can't buy a bride.'

'Isn't that what a dowry is?' Johnno says.

'They used to call it a *toucher*,' Malcy says.

'What?'

'They used to say it was a *toucher*-less marriage if there was no dowry.'

Fran shrugs.

'We don't have dowries any more in Orkney and anyway the money normally goes to the husband, not the jilted bridegroom in return for leaving her at the altar,' Alice says.

'Ten thousand pounds, is that all you think I'm worth?' Jenny says, from the doorway. She is a little unsteady on her feet, so she sits down at the head of the table. A zephyr of multi-coloured perfume, like a smelly rainbow, has followed her into the room and everyone notices.

'What a pong,' Alice says.

'If I was selling my wife you'd be the last man in Orkney I'd sell her to,' Fran says.

'I'm not your wife, yet, and I'm not for bloody sale. Anyway, if I marry you, wouldn't that be our money you're giving him?' Jenny says to Johnno.

'You're not marrying him, you're marrying me, tomorrow. The Legion's booked and I've got them making prawn bloody cocktails for you,' Fran says.

'Okay, twenty thousand pounds and I'll throw in my sister, she has always had a thing for you,' Johnno says.

'What?! Who the fucking fuck do you think you are? I'm not being sold to anybody either,' Alice says, standing up, but Johnno grabs her hand and makes her sit down again.

'Everyone knows you like him,' Hal says, from the sidelines.

'Shut up,' Alice says.

'Does she?' Robin says.

'Aye, everyone knows she's had a thing for you, Fran,' Malcy says from the settee.

'I didn't,' Robin says, and Jenny shakes her head.

'Anyways, where do you think you are going to get twenty thousand pounds from?' Fran says.

'Little nest egg I've been saving,' Johnno says.

'What? To buy a bride?' Alice says.

'Think about it. Fran. You and Alice would be good together and you'd have twenty thousand pounds to boot. You can have my car too,' Johnno says.

Fran smiles and turns towards the now silent TV screen just as a sports car races a cheetah across a frozen lake.

'What about us? We'd be bloody skint. And how do we get to Tesco? I only went with you that time because of your car,' Jenny says, getting up from her seat and moving to Johnno's side of the table.

'You never told me about that,' Fran says.

'Thought you knew,' Jenny says.

'Everyone knows about Jenny and Johnno's night of passion,' Hal says.

'Don't worry about the car, we'll have each other,' Johnno says, when he catches Jenny's eye.

'Bloody Nora. That's just fine. What a deal: I get you and they get twenty thousand pounds and the Volvo,' Jenny says.

'What are you talking about? I'm not having anything. We're getting married in the morning?' Fran says.

'Are we? I saw the way you looked at Alice when Johnno suggested you take her and the money, and that was before the car was thrown into the deal. Men, bloody men, you just can't trust them,' Jenny says, bursting into tears. She runs out of the room and back upstairs, carrying her mostly finished bottle of rum with her.

'And you've never told me I was beautiful,' Jenny shouts, from the top of the stairs.

(Othala)

*'Inheritance.'*

'Sorry about all that,' Swift Eye says, back in the Temper. He has just returned to the head man's chair. The room in disarray with tables uncleared and the swan carcases still on serving dishes.

'I thought our discussion would be better held in the masonic hall. We Freemasons are about promoting harmony, after all, but I forgot the key. I thought it was in my bag. Anyway, it is an interesting night for a walk through town. '

'Lairding it over all your vassals,' Split says.

'Brother, I thought you wanted to avoid a fight?' Swift Eye says, as the last few take their seats.

'Before we fight, I accept the ruling of this Ting, our family court, to decide what is right,' Split says.

'It is your right,' said Swift Eye. 'What is your claim?'

'Sven, Long Arms, my ancestor and direct bloodline descendent claimed the land by the crooked stream. Being the youngest son of his descendant, I now have rightful claim on this my share, as it is split between brothers. I was taught the verses of claim and my son Sigurd, he too can declaim the verse, that will prove it is rightfully ours. The land needs to breathe, we do not want it swamped with houses. My family has sworn that we will do everything to stop that happening. Tonight, we re-traced our claim, so that the earth and the people will remember it.'

(Agiz)

*'A fortunate new influence.'*

*Although*
*way past*
*the Noon of Night,*
*the sky is still soft with its*
*summery,*
*half-awake,*
*tone.*

Brian and I make our way towards the harbour along St Catherine's Place. A tour party is coming the other way, led by the old guy from earlier, telling stories as he goes. Chasing them when I saw him last time. Now seems to be in charge.

'Steel works is a bloody hot place to work. Even on the tube side of things. It's like hell in the blast furnaces, but tubes was a bit more refined. A lot of Scots in British Steel, then. All gone now, of course. In Corby, every Saturday to this day you see coaches taking folk back to see family in Glasgow. Young men headed south for work: Glasgow, Consett, Teesside, and then Corby. The Iron Trail.'

'Did you know that one million people a year commit suicide?' Brian says, after we have passed them.

'Seems a lot.'

'Globally, one million people. That's one every forty seconds. So, one's probably going just now,' Brian says, looking down at his watch.

'And for everyone that dies there are twenty who try.'

*There's a lot of sad people out there.*

'So, I reckon we have a 1 in 20 chance of dying tonight?' Brian says.

We have reached the mini-roundabout opposite the car park, where they have the memorial to the ship. We cross the road, ferry terminal side, to give the end of Bridge Street a wide berth, but no one notices us.

'If you've tried before, does it alter the odds?' I say.

Brian shrugs and looks at his watch again. 'There goes another one and twenty ones who failed.'

*Clearly, some of us are more determined than others.*

As we get closer to the Corn Slip, see Lionel standing in front of the Temperance Hotel, on the other side of the street. Looks a bit pissed. Waves and makes his way across the road.

'Oh, hello,' he says, skipping the last few metres to avoid a taxi approaching the rank.

'Brian, this is the genius who paid my father good money to find out why the earth was flat.'

'Is it?' Brian says.

'Fuck no. It isn't,' I say.

'Lionel,' he says, introducing himself. He curtseys, laughs at the idea, and stumbles around a bit as if there was something we couldn't see in his way.

'I'm in the doghouse,' Lionel says.

'Why?'

'Ogling barmaids, fighting in a pub, getting picked up by the police, coming to Orkney in the first place and missing out on our gold pins.'

'What gold pins?'

'We belong to this club and if we visit 100 countries we get a gold pin. We've stuck on 99.'

I shake my head at this.

Lionel shrugs his shoulders. 'Just something my wife wanted to do.'

'Is this a country then?' Brian says.

'Scotland, yes, it's a country,' I say.

'No, I mean, Orkney?'

'What the fuck. No, it's part of Norway,' I say in jest, pointing towards a Norwegian flag conveniently flying on a pole beside the Auld Men's Hut, but Brian takes me seriously.

'Okay, so I've been to three countries then: England, Scotland and now Norway,' Brian says.

'Really?' Lionel says, shaking his head and giggling.

'I spent most of my life in Leeds,' Brian says, as if that should excuse his ignorance.

Lionel opens his eyes wide. 'Off for a barbecue then?'

'We have an appointment,' Brian says.

'Boris Karloff,' I say.

'What?' Brian says.

'I was astonished to see him in Baghdad, for I had an appointment with him tonight in Samarra,' I say. 'It's a quote from an old movie about a guy who thought he was running away from an appointment with Death, only to meet him where he was expected,' I say.

'I'm not running away,' Brian says, looking a bit more puzzled than usual.

'You might live then,' I say.

'Nice night for a barbecue. Could do with a burger to soak up all this booze. Can I join you? I've got a bottle of whisky,' Lionel says, staring at his half empty bottle.

*This is what a flat earth tour does to you. It addles your brain. Wonder what his God would think?*

With Lionel now in tow, we walk on past the Auld Men's Hut and the Shapinsay Ferry slip, towards the touristy silhouette of a pile of lobster pots in the car park. Brian and I seem to have accepted that it is still too soon to go, and I am in no rush, the night still young. Lionel comes and sits down with us, so I am now sandwiched between the two men.

'What really happened to your mother?' Lionel says, as if Brian wasn't there.

*I'm not in the mood for this.*

'You and your father seem to be suffering.'

'We live in bloody Orkney.'

'I think it's nice here,' Brian says, looking out over the water, rippling back and forth against the pier in the moonlight.

*The tinkle of falling water,*
*like shards of glass*
*being swept*
*with a brush.*

'Supposed to be the smell of dawn in Paradise,' I say, taking a deep breath through my nose.

Lionel asks a question with his eyes.

'Tae grise. Fill your lungs,' I say.

'All I can smell is thyme,' Brian says, sniffing the air.

'Aye, that's it,' I say.

'I wouldn't go that far, Paradise, like, but I do like it here,' Brian says.

'I hate the place. But I don't mind that smell,' I say.

'I love all the rare birds you have here. When I was with your father I saw five red-throated divers, up real close,' Lionel says.

Brian smiles at this and then looks at me.

'Your mother. Is that why you want to...you know?' Brian says.

'Want to what?' Lionel says.

'Brian and I have a death pact. He's my suicide buddy,' I say.

'That's why I've got this,' Brian says, pointing to the charcoal burner in his bag.

'You're going to barbecue yourselves to death then?' Lionel says, and starts to laugh uncontrollably, as if he has just inhaled laughing gas rather than aromatic sea air. Brian and I just look out into the shallow darkness where the sparkly wavelets flash and curl.

'Anyway, you still haven't told me what is so bad about your life,' Lionel says, after he recovers. The laughing seems to have sobered him up a little.

'We found my mother hanging from a tree in the garden,' I say, looking at Lionel.

He stops laughing and shakes his head.

'I'm sorry.'

'Sometimes I wonder if suicides aren't in fact sad guardians of the meaning of life,' Brian says.

'What?' Lionel says.

'You don't sound like a bloke without a brain,' I say.

'Heard it on the radio. Makes me feel that killing myself will help others,' Brian says.

'I need a burger,' Lionel says.

'We don't have any burgers,' Brian says.

'What?' Lionel says, seemingly incapable of comprehending that you could have a barbecue without a burger.

A couple holding hands walk up behind us. They are laughing and seem happy enough until they see me. Man stops and looks at the woman and then walks toward us, towing her along, as if she were holding back a little, sensing his unease.

'The police are looking for you,' he says.

'Aye, I gather that,' I say.

'You okay, love?' the woman says.

'Yes, I'm fine. My father is bit protective. He thinks I should be at home rather than out on the town with these reprobates. Haven't the police got better things to do than take me home?' I say, looking at my two new friends. Brian smiles and Lionel stands up and takes a bow.

'Last thing I saw them rounding up cattle,' the man says.

'Sounds about right. I'm fine. Thanks for asking though,' I say.

'Having a barbecue?' the girl says.

'We're going to cook up a few of our ribs on the beach,' I say, and this sets Lionel off laughing again, and even Brian can see the funny side of it and his face cracks into a tiny smile.

'You sure you're okay?' the man says, as Lionel is laughing hysterically again, out of control.

'Has he taken something?' the woman asks.

I shrug and wonder if he has.

'You just don't know how funny the ribs thing is. I need a laugh after being arrested and locked out of my room by my wife.'

'Arrested?' the woman says.

'Yes, I tried to carry out a citizen's arrest on the bloke who shot some swans for the Earl's dinner and it didn't go as I expected.'

'Sigurd told me about that. Must be the ones he's having for his dinner in the Temper,' I say, looking across the road.

'Bastards,' Lionel says, gets up and walks away, back towards Harbour Street.

'Yes, bonkers, but they are my friends and I'm fine, really,' I say to the concerned couple. They smile politely and walk back towards the road too but are soon on the phone and I know it is time to move on. Pull Brian to his feet and we follow in wobbly Lionel's tracks.

'Come here.' I pull Brian over to the wall of the pier, get my phone out and turn the light on. Lean down and look into a long dark crack in the stone and there are three scorpions, looking back at us.

'Bloody hell,' Brian says. 'Are they scorpions?'

I nod, though I'm not sure he notices.

'Thought you only got them in deserts.'

'Exactly.'

(Hagalaz)

*'Unexpected interruptions.'*

Lionel stops at the water's edge ahead of us and undoes his trousers. Piss arching out in front of him, through the crisscrossed mooring lines of two fishing boats, The *Misty Isle* and the *Odette*, clinging to the harbour wall just outside the Auld Men's Hut.

'Should arrest him for violating the penal code,' Brian says, and we both laugh.

Hang back and watch as he struggles to get dressed again. Still noticeably drunk but walking now with more of a purpose, diagonally across the road, towards the Temper. Goes in the front door, but before we get there he comes out again and walks around to the side door where I met Sigurd earlier.

'Oh shit,' I say.

Follow Lionel into the hotel's function room. There seems to be a meeting in progress. Lionel standing just in front of us, everyone looking at him.

'Can we help you?' the man I recognise as Swift Eye, at the head of the table, says, looking at Lionel and then at Brian and me.

'Who's the Earl around here?' Lionel says.

'I'm Earl.'

'Well, if you are the bastard responsible for having those swans killed,' he says, pointing to the swan carcasses.

The sight of the skeletal swans is a surprise.

'I want you to come outside right now, as I am going to kick the crap out of you,' Lionel says.

'I think there must be some misunderstanding,' Swift Eye says, looking concerned, as if he had evolved beyond violence to resolve things.

Lionel looks at the food debris on the table. Goes across and picks up a swan carcass and walks over to Swift Eye and puts it on the table in front of him. Sigurd smiles at me from his place beside his father who seems like he is about to intervene. I can see that there is a gale brewing in him.

'Why in God's name are you eating swans?' Lionel says.

'Enough of this,' Split says, standing. A cumulonimbus towering above the plains below, threatening to release a tornado to rip across the Kansas prairie.

'I wasn't talking to you,' Lionel says.

'Well, we are all family here and we stand together when we are under attack,' Split says.

Swift Eye laughs at this.

'Not man enough to fight your own battles?' Lionel says to Swift Eye, who is now looking even more uncomfortable. Searching with his eponymous eye for an escape route.

I walk up to Lionel. 'Come on, let's go. You don't want to get into any more trouble.'

'Always considered myself a coward, but maybe some things are worth fighting for,' he says, picking up the nearest chair and running towards Earl, screaming at the top of his voice, just as two police officers enter the room.

Swift Eye ducks out of the way but the chair still catches him a glancing blow. Split, Sigurd and Hooky all move to catch him but he is surprisingly elusive and manages to dodge around the tables and prepare for another charge at Swift Eye who is now cowering behind the serving table.

'Stop!' the policeman you already know as Sergeant Maitland shouts, as he bangs the wooden door with his stick. The noise a magic spell: they all become trolls caught in the open at dawn.

'Now sit down all of you,' the sergeant says, and most do, but Lionel loses the game of musical chairs and has to remain standing.

'Fortunately, we were passing when the night receptionist warned us that you were on the loose again and headed here. Didn't we tell you earlier to stay in your room for the rest of the night?' Sergeant Maitland says.

'My wife wouldn't let me in.'

'Well that's no reason for harassing these good people,' the sergeant says.

PC McTravers looks at me and I can see she knows who I am.

'Good people don't eat swans. Are you going to arrest them this time? That Earl over there is the ringleader,' Lionel says.

'Mr Earl,' the sergeant says, with the slightest hint of a bow, as I take the opportunity to slip away.

ᚠ

## (Fehu Reversed)

*'Some sort of failure'.*

'I'm sorry to have dragged you into all this,' Kito says to Sandy outside the Castle Hotel. They have just spent twenty minutes showing passers-by Panda's picture, but no one has seen her. Most of them were drunk, mourning the death of summer.

'What did you do to her to make her so angry?'

'When her mother left I couldn't really cope and I wasn't there for her. I just wanted to run away too. I guess you could say I abandoned her.'

Sandy lets the silence invite him to say more.

'I lost faith in everything. I drank too much, had panic attacks. I didn't know how to behave.'

'How old was she?

'Ten.'

'Did she have anyone else? Family, or friends?'

'Sally had all the friends.'

'Has it always been like this?'

'We spent a few years plodding on, trying to pretend that life was still worth living. Then we came here, five years ago, when she was fourteen.'

'What exactly did happen to your wife?'

'That's when she made those statues,' Kito says, distracted by some lingering thought.

'You need to get rid of them. It isn't healthy.'

Kito shrugs and sighs.

'You didn't answer my question about what happened to your wife?'

'I mostly tell people she was told she had terminal liver cancer and she killed herself.'

'But you told me she wasn't dead.'

'It's just what I tell people. Panda and I, we both have different stories and they change with our mood. The truth is, I don't really know. She just went away.'

Kito pauses and Sandy looks down at her hands.

'She just left?'

Kito nods.

'Hard thing for a mother to do.'

Kito looks off into the distance, as if he is looking for an explanation of what really happened.

'Panda must think it was her fault. She's blaming herself and she's angry with you, and the only way she knows is to take it out on you is in her dairy,' Sandy says.

'Perhaps you're right.'

Sandy shakes her head.

'The rest of her diary is full of extravagant claims. I think they are intended to shock me,' Kito says

'Have you read it all?'

'She won't talk to me so I read it when she goes out. I thought I was inured to it but tonight seems different. I think it was the door, her locking the door.'

Sandy looks down at her phone which she has just felt vibrating in her handbag. It is a while before she speaks.

'Margaret says a friend of hers saw her in Harbour Street, a few minutes ago. She's with two older men,' she says, still looking at her phone, thinking.

'What?' Kito says, seeing there is something else.

'She told Margaret that you have something to hide and I should be careful. What do you have to hide, Kito? What is there you haven't told me?'

'Nothing, and probably everything. I don't know what that is. You can ask her when we catch up with her. Come on,' he says, walking off quickly towards the harbour.

Sandy thinks for a few seconds but then follows.

# ROAD KILL

*You are watching as your mother takes her last breath. It is long and deep and hollow. The exhaled air is warm on your cheek. Then there is silence and she is still. When you are older and it goes quiet, your mother lying on the blacktop comes back to you. You can taste the sweet smell of blood, and other things pooling around her. You know immediately that she has gone. You know that the body you are holding in your arms is just a body, it is no longer your mother.*

*One day you will dream of killing her and you will write about it in your diary for your father to find, but now you just feel lost. You saw the car that hit her but she pushed you away so that you were safe and she took the full impact. You are surprised at the contents of her head now lying in the road. You didn't know that thoughts were mushy and grey. Hers were normally so colourful.*

*You are now alone. After today, you will feel alone when you are with your father and your mother isn't there. Maybe this is what really happened; she didn't just drive off and say those words.*

ᚱᚾᛏ

(Raidho. Nauthiz. Tiewaz)

*'Follow your soul's path. Delays, be patient, face your fears. Victory will come if you fight for what you believe in.'*

# 14. BLACK & WHITE GAME

'Ah, the rockers are back,' Davey says, interrupting the story about his amateur boxing as a young man. He is now in the Auld Men's Hut with his entourage – he led them there and, finding it empty and the door open, invited everyone in – when he sees Panda and Sigurd, outside the hotel across the street.

'What?' Marina says.

'That girl's leather jacket. It brings back memories.'

'Everything seems to do that,' Rick says.

'My life is a flipping daisy-chain of memories. But it needs something to set me off. That leather jacket. *On the Waterfront.* Marlon Brando. Fights on Brighton sea front. Bloody great it was. The lot of rowdies you have up here are nothing, I'd jump through the lot of them. We was on the front page of every paper because they thought we'd bring the country down. The papers said we was a national disgrace. Me, I was The Ace Face. Took me hours to gab up of a night.'

'I guess that makes you a Mod. I'd have had you down as more of a Rocker,' Mathew says.

'Nope. The real deal, me. Nothing seven and six about me.'

'Haven't you heard of the Mods and Rockers?' Davey says to the others, as they don't appear to know what he is talking about.

Marina shakes her head, but some of the young archaeologists smile as if they have.

'What is it they say? If you can remember the Sixties, you weren't there. Or something like that. Well, that is wrong. To remember something properly you had to be there. You need a picture in your head, or it isn't a memory, it's just a story you've learned. You youngsters don't have the same experiences, so you don't see things the same way.'

'So, does that mean that if you can't remember it, you didn't experience it, it is less true?' Mathew says.

'Heck, lad, that's too bloody deep for me. But you can only guess what them broken bits of pot you find were all about. You can only guess what it was to live in the olden days.'

'But you know,' Patsy says.

'Aye, I do. I do bloody know and you youngsters need to show us old folk more respect, because we are windows on the past that will soon be closed and you can learn a lot from the past. I know about the Mods and Rockers because I was there.'

'And I guess you're going to tell us about them too,' Rick says.

'I was a rather dashing Mod,' Davey says. 'Just wish I could feel it too. I used to have a big heart, but it seems to have shrivelled up, like my...well, like other things do at my age.'

'You've got good eyesight,' Marina says, looking down Harbour Street where Panda, Sigurd and Brian are now talking.

'Just can't read anything up close without these,' Davey says, clutching his tired looking glasses. 'Haven't been able to for twenty years.'

'I think she's a Goth,' Mathew says, looking at Panda on the pavement.

'Well, she's a Rocker to me. Mods and Rockers was all about the music. And fighting, we loved fighting.'

'What music did the Mods like, Davey?' Marina says.

'The Who, The Yardbirds, The Small Faces.'

'Never heard of the Small Faces,' Mathew says.

'*Psychedelic Baby*, *Itchycoo Park*, *Lazy Sunday*. I'd sing them, but you wouldn't like my voice. Not now, but once I had a good voice. And you should have seen my suit. Purple-brown it was. They called it puce then.'

## (Thurisaz)

*'Protection and luck are on your side'.*

Sigurd is standing beside me on the pavement, when Brian comes out.

'Police are talking to the guy with the eye patch about the swans,' Brian says, as he gets closer.

Boys a little awkward, face-to-face for the first time.

'Sigurd, this is Brian. My suicide buddy.'

'Brian, Panda has told me so many things in the short time I've known her, that I don't know what to believe.'

'It's true. We are…well, yes. I wanted company,' Brian says.

'Really? Why?' Sigurd says, looking troubled.

'I'm young and unhappy and had enough of life.'

Sigurd looks puzzled.

'Brian's advert online. Only found out at midnight that he was old enough to be my grandad.'

Sigurd shakes his head. He looks angry and frustrated at the way the conversation is going.

'I feel old and unhappy,' Brian says.

'Just because your life has been shite so far, it doesn't mean it needs to be in the future. Some people have happy lives too, you know,' Sigurd says.

'Like you?' I say.

'Just because you haven't experienced it yet, doesn't mean you can't.'

'Lionel tells me that if I believe good things will happen to me, they will. Says I need to welcome God into my life, so that I have a reason to hope.'

'Lionel – is he the mad guy in there who was swinging the chair at my uncle?' Sigurd says.

I nod and look towards the door into the function room, but no sign of anyone else coming out.

'Not how most Christians behave, is it?' Sigurd says.

'Zealots,' I say and shrug my shoulders.

*Ironic really, that we only need God because we are all going to die, and now we are talking of him saving us.*

Sigurd walks away and I watch as he lights a cigarette in a shower of yellow sherbet from the light above his head. He seems frustrated and wants to distance himself from our madness.

'Anyway, what's the plan?' Brian says, taking advantage of Sigurd being out of earshot, raising his voice to make sure he has my full attention. I seem to be in charge.

'I was going to suggest a cliff,' I say.

Brian thinks about it for a while, turning around to make sure that no one is listening.

'I told you I'm not very good at this sort of thing. So, I don't want to find myself still alive with all my bones broken. I want to go straight away. Light on. Light off. Know what I mean?' Brian says.

'I'm not sure death is like that. I know you get time to look back, but I'm sure you're not in pain.'

'What makes you think that?'

'My Gran. Her pain left her. She talked to me on her deathbed, from the other side. She said she could still see me.'

Brian doesn't look convinced but he humours me.

'She met up with her mother again. She said that she understood everything. She found peace after all the heartbreak of her life.'

Brian listening now.

'I want to know why we have to put up with all this crap,' I say.

'If you're right, we'll soon find out, won't we?' Brian says.

'Did you know we have the highest vertical cliff in Great Britain?'

'How high?' Brian says, looking up as if that will help.

'Nearly thirteen hundred feet.'

'No one could survive a fall like that, right? Anyway, the charcoal burner might be a bit of a faff,' Brian says, looking at the bulky charcoal burner in his bag.

'It will take us three hours to get there. My dad has a boat at Stromness; we can take it, but it will be a hike across Hoy in the dark.'

'The exercise will do us good,' he says, then laughs when he realises what he has said.

'Do you need to be fit to kill yourself?'

'Strong. I think you need to be strong,' Brian says.

'We'll need to leave here at three a.m. We can get a taxi to Stromness and maybes steal a car on Hoy. There's always cars parked by the lifeboat.'

'Taxi? Why not steal a car here too? On your last night the law of the land doesn't apply. What other crimes can we commit?' Brian says.

'What crimes do you want to commit?'

'Don't know. I'm a law-abiding person, me. I don't think I could have killed myself when it was still illegal.'

'When was it illegal?' I say.

'Until the early 1960s, I think.'

'What did they do to you, lock up your coffin if you were successful?'

'I don't want to do anything wrong,' Brian says.

'Lionel says that suicide is wrong and it's a crime against God. He says it's sinful. An act of blasphemy.'

Brian looks puzzled.

'An insult to God,' I say.

'I hope he'll forgive us,' Brian says.

'Lionel?'

'No. God. When we see Him later, we'll have to apologise,' Brian says.

'You religious then?'

'Perhaps the approach of death makes you think of God,' Brian says.

I look at Sigurd again and sense that, unlike Brian, hope is stirring in my breast, like a fledgling about to leap into the unknown and try to fly unaided for the first time.

'Anyway, what do we do until we head off to Hoy?' Brian says.

'I'm going with Sigurd.' I'm not sure why. It surprises me that I have enthusiasm for anything.

'Three's a crowd, I know,' Brian says, looking toward Sigurd.

'I hardly know him,' I say.

'Or me,' Brian says.

*Perhaps you don't need long to get to know someone.*

'I think I'll wait and see what happens to Lionel. He may need a hand,' Brian says.

'Be careful, he may convert you,' I say.

'He can try.'

'Okay, three a.m. in front of the cathedral,' I say, and watch as he and Sigurd walk in opposite directions, crossing paths halfway and ignoring each other's stare, like a prisoner exchange in an old film.

The longer the night goes on, the more I feel like an actor in a drama.

A pretty fanciful one.

## (Berkana)

*'New Beginnings.'*

Sigurd has his arm around my waist as we walk across the road to the inner harbour and we sidle up to my old friend *Michael J K390.* Nudges me gently towards the black iron railings at the edge of the quay. Stare at the smudge left in the sky by the sun, now in hiding below the horizon, though some light still seeps out to back-light Halston pier. Flashes from the occasional passing car reflect off the windows of *Michael*'s little cabin, like a signal-light, sending a message we can't read.

'Jesus, is that a rat?' Sigurd says, as a small animal walks along the white painted strip on the other side of the railings.

'*Wind in The Willows*,' I say.

'Never read it.'

'It's a vole: an Orkney vole. Normally live in grassy banks along roads and ditches, or in rubble. First time I've seen one here.'

It stands up on its two back legs, looks around and then jumps into the water and swims away. People here used to think that death was just a transformation into another form of life and that animals were drawn to those about to die. They say that old folk see more wildlife than youngens do.

'Wow,' Sigurd says.

'I knew they could swim, but not in the sea,' I say.

'Perhaps it's a lemming and suicidal, like you.'

'We have only just met,' I say; his arm has tightened around my waist during our brief encounter with 'Ratty'.

He looks at me as if to say, 'So?'

'Rather intimate, the arm.'

'I put my arm around you on *Dreki* earlier.'

'I thought you were just making sure I didn't fall into the sea.'

'It just feels right. Anyway, it's just a precaution. The police won't be looking for a couple, will they?' It did feel right. His arm around me.

Wander back to the road, turn right towards the Corn Slip. He is holding my hand now.

'Is it always like this here?' Sigurd says.

'No, just the night. All the looneys are let out of the asylum. Including me.'

'You seem more normal to me than half the people I have seen out tonight,' Sigurd says, as we get close to the Auld Men's Hut again. Something going on under the lighthouse at the end of the pier.

*Thomas might have something with this Pandora thing. I break free and all the madness in the world seems to have escaped with me.*

Nobby, standing on the edge completely naked, about to jump in. A small huddle of people is encouraging him and laughing too. We are too far back to see what is causing all the amusement, but I have heard about this and would be embarrassed if Sigurd saw, so I am glad 'it' is out of sight. The water still deep enough and calm, though it looks cold.

Ten-second countdown and Nobby jumps from behind the crab pots with a scream. Everyone claps. Watch as he swims around a bit and clambers up the ladder – has to squeeze in between the wall and a trawler to get out.

'Ma, what you doing here?' he says, to his mother waiting on the quay with a bag of towels and dry clothes. She hands him a towel and shakes her head. Onlookers laugh.

'Nobby. We call him that because he jumps into the sea naked every time he gets aroused,' I say.

'Is that often?'

'Only once a year, in public anyways.'

'The cold water will put an end to that.'

'I think that's the idea. Best not to look though, may make you feel inadequate,' I say, and regret it. I don't want to be cruel to Sigurd, but I am so used to being cruel to Thomas that it just slipped out.

'Ouch.'

'Sorry, I can be a bitch. He got arrested last year for indecent exposure. Police too busy tonight. They say he is often seen working on his farm naked.'

'At least he's got his mother to look after him.'

'He's lucky, mine's dead.'

'Sorry to hear that. Come, let's have a drink on *Bonxie*. We've got the place to ourselves.'

Turn back toward Harbour Street and I see Jenny from the blackening by the Corn Slip, now dressed in jeans and a jumper, walking along hand-in-hand with a man, but it isn't the man I was expecting.

'Jennifer, isn't it?' I say, as we get closer.

'Jen will do.'

'What's all the commotion about?' The man you already know as Johnno, says.

'Nobby,' I say.

'I guess I've missed it for another year,' Jenny says.

'Missed what?' Johnno says.

'Nobby, doing what his name suggests?' I say, looking at Jenny for support.

'What?' Johnno says.

'I think you must be an alien body double of Johnno because you don't seem to know nothing about your hometown and what goes on in it,' Jenny says.

'Hey, haven't you got the wrong man?' I say.

'In the end, I had to go for the one who was willing to fight for me, didn't I? In spite of the fact that he knows nought about anything,' Jenny says.

'Aye, I'm not the wrong guy – Mr Right, me. It didn't come to a duel in the end, I paid him off.'

'Twenty thousand pounds, and his bloody car. No one has done nothing like that for me before,' Jenny says.

'And me sister,' he says.

'What do you mean?' Sigurd says.

'I threw my sister into the deal. She's worth it,' he says, clutching Jenny's hand and pulling her closer to him. Smiles, looks happy, finding a man who wants her so deeply.

I shake my head.

'The police are looking for you,' Jenny says.

'Told you,' I say, looking at Sigurd.

'They put posters up, over there,' Johnno says, pointing to a nearby lamppost.

I nod and look at Sigurd.

'Why they looking for you?' Johnno says.

'I'm a drug mule,' I say, thinking of Martin. 'I bring little blue pills back to Mainland from Aberdeen on the ferry every month and sell them to the kids at the Grammar School and Stromness Academy.'

'Fuck off,' Johnno says, dropping Jenny's hand and taking a step back.

He looks surprised. Jenny just shakes her head and smiles at him.

'Sorry, but I just don't like to hear about stuff like that,' he says.

'He's sensitive,' Jenny says, reaching back and holding his hand again.

'You haven't offered me any of your little blue pills,' Sigurd says to me.

'Oh, bless. He looks hurt,' Jenny says. 'Looks like we've both fallen for the softies then?' she says, as they turn, still holding hands.

'Yours is a generous softy,' I say.

'It was my nest egg; I can do with it what I want. Anyway, she's worth it.'

'Says he's a budding entrepreneur,' Jenny says, as they walk away.

'I'm no soft,' Johnno says, loud enough so that we can hear too.

'What was that all about?' Sigurd says.

I shrug, but I think it has something to do with love.

'She seems to think that Johnno and I are soft in some way,' Sigurd says.

'Aye, strange that, isn't it?'

He looks puzzled.

'She told me she wasn't picky, unlike me.'

'So, I'm lucky you're here then?'

Nod at him and catch a kingfisher flash in his eyes from a shooting star, as the police car appears for real in the distance. It is like the universe is warning us.

'Quick,' I say, pushing him against the Auld Men's' Hut, which is now in darkness.

'Wait for them to go,' I say. Me now pressing him up against the side of the building.

'You never did tell me what you are running from,' he says.

'Shadows.'

He shakes his head and looks down at me like my father used to when I was a small girl.

I kiss him.

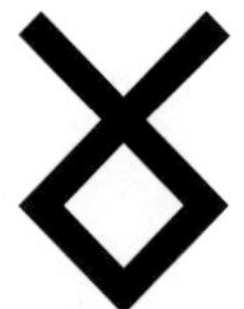

## (Othala Reversed)

*'Frustrated inheritance.'*

'Brother, I do not want to fight but I don't see how we will ever agree on the land,' Swift Eye says, looking around the room still full of his followers, though most of them now look tired and bored.

'It is custom that if we do not agree and say the oaths before dawn the only recourse is with arms,' Split says, alert and still clearly determined to see this through.

'It is custom, but old custom and I have no intention of fighting you again. It didn't work out well for me last time,' Swift Eye says, instinctively touching his eye patch.

'Then I will take what is mine,' Split says.

'My lord might not fight, but we will,' Swift Eye's bull of a son, Patrick, stands up and proclaims. 'We will fight to protect our property.' His diminutive brother, Malcolm, still carrying the broom handle from earlier at the harbour, looks less sure. Lizzy is asleep beside her father, her head resting on the table between the dirty plates. Rosy is no longer there.

'There is the black and white board,' Malcolm says. 'Let the ancestors decide on the outcome of this, and then there will be no need to shed blood.'

'Aye, there is the board,' Swift Eye says, his eye darting back and forth between Split and Hooky to judge their reaction.

Hooky whispers in Split's ear and there is a short period of deliberation before Split speaks.

'We agree to abide by the decision of our ancestors with the outcome of the black and white board,' Split says, pushing his chair back and standing.

'So do I,' Swift Eye says. 'I will play. Who will play for your rights and honour and ownership of the land?'

'I will,' says Hooky, looking at Split, who nods his agreement.

'Then it is settled. Where is Rosy? She will have to go and fetch the sacred board so we can summon our ancestors to help us decide on the truth of things,' Swift Eye says, as he stands too and scans the room for his wife as if she may be hiding in the shadows waiting to be summoned for a task such as this. But Rosy is nowhere to be seen.

(Algiz. Laguz. Dagaz)

*'A fortunate new influence. Follow your intuition. Dawning of a new day – slow and steady growth and progress.'*

# 15. JOCK & THE HUT

'What do you think is going on here?' Jock says, opening the door to the Auld Men's Hut and turning on the light.

Davey stops talking and smiles. 'Aye up, me ducks,' he says, squinting.

'Aye up to you too,' Jock says.

'Jock my man. Just resting my bones. I'm old you knows,' Davey says.

'Aye, I know, you said earlier. Who are your friends?'

Jock enters the hut and looks at Mathew for ten seconds before he gets the message that he needs to move to give Jock his seat. He sits down and looks at the full bottle of whisky on the table in front of him.

'Would you like a drink?' Marina says.

'Aye, I would. But you mustn't be telling anyone. It's no allowed,' Jock says.

He watches as Marina pours.

'Forgot to lock up, so came back. Get hell from Walli if he found out I'd left it open,' Jock says.

'Never know who'll come in,' Mathew says.

Jock grunts and picks up his glass, resting it on his upper lip to inhale the bouquet.

'Seeing you sitting in the dark made me think they might have sabotaged the lighting here too?' Jock says.

'What do you mean?' Rick says.

'You no heard? Some lads fused all the lights at the Show Gala Dinner. Some rascals going around town causing all manner of havoc the night,' Jock says.

'We're just keeping a low profile,' Rick says.

'Anarchy and discontent. That's what you get with an easy life,' Jock says.

'Davey has been taking us on a grand tour of Kirkwall,' Marina says.

'Really? Davey. What exactly do you know about Kirkwall?' Jock says.

'Well, to be more accurate he has walked us around town telling us about his fascinating life,' Marina says.

'That sounds more like the Davey I have come to know the night,' Jock says.

'So, do you have the real inside track on Kirkwall?' Rick says.

'Well, do you see that police car?' Jock says, looking over toward the car still parked in front of the Temper.

'Yes.'

'It is outside a hotel we call The Temper, because it is our one and only remaining Temperance Hotel.'

'You mean a bit like prohibition, no booze?' Rick says.

'Aye, a bit like that.'

'Really, a lot has changed then,' Bobby says.

'Aye, young folk today don't know they was born, right enough,' Jock says.

'We do,' Patsy says.

Davey stands up and walks towards Jock as he speaks, picks up his whisky glass and smells it before walking back to the other end of the room.

'What about the police car?' Bobby says.

'There has been a bit of a disturbance at the Earls' dinner,' Jock says.

'You still have Earls?' Lynette says.

'No really, but there is a certain order to things. I don't rightly know about titles but everyone understands their place,' Jock says.

'How British,' Marina says.

'We don't feel British. Not here. You're confusing us with the Hebrides,' Jock says.

'I don't know where that is,' Marina says, looking at her husband.

'In Britain,' Jock says. 'There is a local family called Earl. Each year the younger brother pays for a rather odd dinner on Show Night. They say it was part of an agreement they had when they were younger in part settlement of an injury.'

'Injury?' Rick says.

'Aye, the brothers got into a fight over a woman and one of them lost an eye. The other was banished down south but pays for a feast each year as part of the deal.'

'Why would you have a dinner every year to commemorate it?' Mathew says.

'It's what the Vikings did and they make a big thing about their ancestry and traditions.'

'Did he go to jail?'

'No. The police weren't involved, but it seems there has been some trouble tonight,' Jock says.

'We saw that young Goth girl coming out of the place just after the police arrived,' Bobby says.

'We saw more than that. Voyeurs we was, not fifteen minutes ago? She was snogging some bloke pressed right up against that window,' Davey says, pointing to the middle window overlooking the inner harbour.

'And she didn't see yous all sitting here?' Jock says.

'No, we were too embarrassed once they got started. We didn't really know what to do,' Lynette says.

'Ay, well, that is maybes a good sign though,' Jock says.

'Rocker. I still say she looks like a rocker to me,' Davey says.

'Lot of folk looking for her tonight. They say that she is planning to kill herself,' Jock says.

'She didn't look like she was about to kill herself just now,' Bobby says.

'No? Well, let's hope she's no going to kill herself. She's only a wee thing. Hardly got going in life, eh, Davey?' Jock says.

'When I was her age I was down the pit,' Davey says. 'Nottinghamshire coal fields. Shireoaks Colliery, next to rail track. Bloody hard work. Too hard, even for me. I was strong as an ox at yon girl's age but it was too hard for me. Worked Top Hard and Barnsley Bed seams. Still cough to this day and when I get a cold you can see coal dust in my hanky.'

'Davey, I can hardly believe that one man could have done so much in his life,' Marina says.

'I'm not sure I do,' Mathew says.

'Ah well, your prerogative, young man. Working man me. Worked all me bloody life. Long life too.'

'Davey, yes, I know. It's remarkable, really. But Jock, I hope you're right and all that kissing is a good sign and the girl is okay. I didn't know so much could be going on in one place at the same time, or that anyone's life could be so full and interesting as Davey's, but I'm getting tired. It's well past my bedtime. Lynette, I'm really weary now and want to go back,' Rick says.

'Yes, okay. Let's go,' Lynette says.

'We'll walk you back to your yacht,' Davey says. 'Never been able to say that before. You're the first people I've met who live on a yacht.'

(Ansuz. Isa. Laguz)

*'Listen, learn, take advice. On hold, wait for improvements. Follow your intuition'.*

'Sarah,' old guy on the quay shouts down to us. On *Bonxie*'s main deck watching pollock in the water. About to tell him that he must have made a mistake when he starts to speak this verse:

*Aye up me ducks.*

*Death does not hunt the young,*
*they search it out,*
*lost in life's icy blizzard.*

*It isn't calling them,*
*the pain-drenched agony of life*
*is a test.*

*Each step a memory slash of burnished steel,*
*each life a daisy chain of scars.*

*Whose blossom shines on age-crinkled skin,*
*like the scalding breath of the roaring sun.*

*Keep going,*
*reflection the reward.*

So unexpected there is a long pause. Replaying the words, trying to decipher them.

'I can tell you don't stay in Orkney,' I say, and he smiles. The guy talking about steel furnaces and tubes in Broad Street earlier looks satisfied with his verse, turns and walks further out along the pier where his friends are waiting for him. Walks purposefully and in a straight line – he doesn't look drunk.

Sigurd and I both laugh as he shuffles away. But his words have touched me. Think he said it is good to grow old.

*Is that what we live for? To grow old.*

Sigurd leads me down some steps into *Bonxie*'s guts. Narrow corridor of cold iron skinned with cream paint that froths, blisters, and bubbles with hidden corrosion. Like the walls have melted. Shitty rust streaks, like stained underpants. Invitingly varnished cabin doors with bright steel handles and hooks to hold them open. All closed. The boat seems empty. Hum of distant equipment, as if we have entered a fridge.

Steps up to the place where thy steer it from, where Sigurd was when we first met. Just one or two small instrument lights below wrap-around windows showing a panorama of the harbour: a curve of streetlights, like a jewelled necklace. Taxis coming and going from the rank. Kirkwall Hotel still has lights in several rooms.

Sigurd gently pushes me back against the faux-leather chair fixed in the centre, where the king must have his throne. Don't resist as he comes closer and kisses me. His mouth urging my lips apart and his prominent teeth clashing with mine. His face pushing into me though the rest of him is holding back.

'Number three, or is it four? I'm losing track of all the kisses,' I say, after our lips part.

'Do you always number your kisses?' Sigurd says.

'My first real kiss was earlier tonight from my friend Martin.'

'Boyfriend?'

I decide to keep him guessing.

'It seems everyone wants to kiss me tonight.' Pull my hair across my face and chew the ends and he smooths his beard in sympathy. Different voices saying the same thing.

Sigurd leans forward again but I gently stop him by putting my hand to my lips.

'I find it hard to resist you.'

'If you knew more about me you might find it easier. I've already decided that I am going to my grave a virgin. A kiss is just the start of a chain of events that can lead to tragedy.'

'The old guy on the pier said life, with all its challenges, was worth it,' Sigurd says, then quotes part of the verse we have just heard:

*The pain-drenched agony of life*
*is a test.*

*Each step a memory slash of burnished steel,*
*each life a daisy chain of scars.*

*Whose blossom shines on age-crinkled skin,*
*like the scalding breath of the roaring sun.*

*Keep going,*
*reflection the reward.*

*How did he remember that?*

'My gran said you have to die to be rewarded.'

'You might have the wrong end of the stick on that one?'

'My mother used to kiss me.'

Sigurd looks puzzled, unable to see the connection. He sits on the stool on the other side of what I now understand is called the bridge and points at the skipper's chair, as if he is offering me a seat.

'Is that a throne?'

'If you like, it can be your throne.'

'I feel like Zebedee, or Tigger,' I say, jumping up and down on it.

'Here,' he says, passing me a can of coke. Pile of them in front of him. He has one too.

'I keep having this day-dream that I have killed myself and I am looking back, trying to work out what happened, what it was all about.'

'Over the past few centuries my philosopher colleagues haven't got far with that one, but maybe that old guy on the quay has the answer. How did you leave it with Brian?'

'I said we'd meet at three a.m. and throw ourselves off a cliff at dawn, but the cliff I've chosen is miles away, probably take three hours to get there.'

'Do you think all these obstacles – leaving it till dawn, the barbecue, the three-hour journey, not doing it without a buddy – are signs you aren't serious?'

*Maybe he's on to me.*

Sigurd picks up an almanac in front of him and turns a few pages.

'It says here that dawn is at five-twenty and you said you'd meet him at three and if there is a three-hour journey – you won't get there in time.'

'It's springy,' I say, bouncing up and down on the chair.

'You need that when it's rough, or you wouldn't be able to sit there for hours on end.'

'That must be nice, sitting here for hours on end, watching the waves,' I say.

'I'm happy enough sitting here watching you.'

I can't help giggling tiny bubbles of pleasure.

'Even without the other stuff, all this sex fuss someone my age is supposed to put up with to keep their man?' I say.

A spark of streetlight strikes his eyes again and I see the sharp blue of it. Deep liquid sockets, so profound they drown all other colours.

'Am I your man?'

'I think you've misjudged me. You laugh at what I say as if you think I don't mean it.'

'Are you really going to kill yourself?'

'Me and Brian are both so unhappy he's come all the way from Leeds so we can have company at the end.'

'You didn't seem unhappy earlier on *Dreki* coming into harbour, you were laughing. You didn't seem unhappy when I kissed you. You don't seem unhappy now.'

I think about this for a while and of course he is right. I keep regurgitating the bad stuff and ignore the good times, and young chicks never prosper on foul food.

*You've distracted me.*

'My life is empty and there is no chance that it can get better. I am stuck here in this awful place with a madman for a father, being made to take all these bloody pills,' I say, but then I feel inspired.

Reach into my bag, searching with my fingers until I find what I want. Undo the top of my medicine bottle and walk across to the door beside Sigurd, take a step outside and sprinkle them on the water. A few of these colourful narcotics land on the deck and Sigurd leans down to pick one up. Beetroot red with 40mg printed on it.

'If I don't take my citalopram I'll go mad. My alter ego takes over and I do bad things. I am as unstable as nitroglycerin and can detonate at the slightest touch. I am not someone you would want to kiss too often.'

'Don't know about that. Anyway, I'm not a great believer in pills.'

'So, depression is part of the Philosophy syllabus, is it?'

'My mother used to take lots of pills and spent most of her life in bed. Now she does wild swimming and she's human again. She reconnected with humanity.'

I shrug.

'Perhaps tonight you have reconnected too.'

'Siggy, you are a breath of fresh air. Sitting here now I don't want to die. I want to live. I actually want to kiss you again, but I know it won't last. I know I'll wake up tomorrow and remember what I did, what I can't live with.'

'What could be so bad?'

Get up and walk around the bridge until I am as far away as this tiny space allows. Look out of the window and put my hair in my mouth before speaking.

'I killed my mother.'

Sigurd waits for the deep silence to dissipate and then walks across and puts his arms around me. Crying quietly. Turn and look up at him and rest my head on his shoulder. Stand like this for a while before I pull away and sit on the throne again.

'Would you like some tea?' he says.

I watch him disappear down into the deck through a stairwell that is glowing like you see on those films where there is a treasure chest full of gold. Disappointed when he comes back without a fistful of doubloons, but he has a bottle of brandy and two mugs of tea.

'I've put honey in the tea,' he says, pouring me an inch of brandy in a tumbler at the same time as he hands me the mug.

I wonder if I am doing the right thing, opening up to him.

'She hung herself from a tree in our garden and I found her when I came home, dangling in the bright summer sky. In deep silhouette with the sun behind her.'

Sigurd doesn't say anything, he just drinks his tea and watches me as if I am sloughing off my skin like a moulting snake.

'She was hit by a car. We were crossing a road and she threw me out of the way. She sacrificed herself to save me. I heard her last breath leave her body as her brains pooled around her head.'

Sigurd sniffs, stands up and walks to the side of the bridge next to the quay and looks out of the window, as if he wants to distance himself from what I am saying. I stand too, but don't move and I watch him as he follows the progress of a caricature drunk man along the quay.

'I slashed her throat with a razor blade and she bled to death. I didn't mean to do it. I just wanted to disfigure her so that my father would love me more than he loved her.' I raise my voice to try to get his attention again.

It works, and Sigurd turns towards me quickly, as if I am a little girl again and I have done something naughty. I have pushed my mother too far and she has snapped.

'And you are a master mariner, with three children, who probably smokes a pipe in secret.' His words shoot out like they have come from a machine gun that I never knew he had, and I can see he is annoyed with me.

'Yes, that's me.' I try to brazen it out but am a little taken aback. It is the first time I have seen him like this. The first time he has attacked me with metal words.

He turns back towards the quay and doesn't say anything else, as if he is my boss and I have been dismissed.

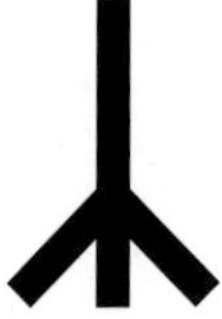

## (Algiz Reversed)

*'Be on your guard.'*

'Are you any the wiser now that I have revealed all of my secrets?' I say, after a long pause. I was hoping he'd speak first but I can't wait any longer. Don't want us to fall out. Want to make amends.

He turns towards me again and smiles, though he looks exasperated.

'I think you're mad.'

'I told you that yonks ago.'

'But I don't think you're mentally ill, just mad. You're angry mad, not mad, mad. You know what? That's just normal. It's normal to be trying to make sense of the world at our age. It's normal to be disoriented by sex and sexuality. It's normal to want more control and to think that your parents don't know what they are talking about and that their opinions and values are out of date. It's even normal these days to have to deal with having just one parent. It might be tough, but you're not alone.'

*So, I'm normal, am I?*

'There's a fucking huge range of Normal and you are in there somewhere, believe me. Everyone struggles with growing up. It's normal,' Sigurd says.

'Is that why you are annoyed with me? Do you feel superior to me? Because you can see that and I can't?'

'I don't feel superior, in fact, I'm a bit in awe of you.'

I shake my head. I don't know what to say.

'Yes, sort of wonder but less joyous. I'm surprised by you but also a bit scared. It's a surprisingly attractive mix.'

'You must be a pervert.'

'No, just fairly normal actually. That's why I didn't believe you when you said you were going to kill yourself. I don't think you believe it either. No wonder your father doubts everything. You camouflage the truth with drama.' Sigurd walks across the bridge behind me. I have clearly wound him up.

*If only Thomas would challenge me and respond like this.*

'Thomas says I'm a drama queen.'

'He sounds like a wiser man than you give him credit for. You need to act less and be yourself more.'

'My father and I have lots of stories to try and explain what happened, but none of them are true, because I don't know what happened. I just know that she is gone and it is all my fault.'

Notice I am crying. Been a while since I cried so freely. I lean forward and kiss Sigurd gently on the lips and then move away.

'Tell me, is sex like you see in porn movies. I have only lost my virginity in my head and it wasn't much fun,' I say.

Sigurd raises his eyebrows in that way that can mean so many different things.

'That wasn't an invitation.'

'I know, but if you aren't going to do it tonight with me, you'd better not kill yourself. Wait at least until you find out what all the *sex fuss* is about.'

'Sigurd, thank you. Tonight, has been one of the best days of my life.'

## (Kenaz)

*'Strength and energy through spiritual enlightenment.'*

Something has happened. The storm clouds have been cleared by Sigurd's thunder and lightning. Must take after his dad after all. There is now calm.

'Here comes your American friend,' Sigurd says, looking down at the quay. 'I didn't recognise him just now staggering about. He's drunk.'

'Canadian.'

'Is there a difference?'

I follow Sigurd onto one of the tiny platforms that stick out on each side of the bridge.

'One of them says coke, the other soda, and I think Canadians take off their shoes when they enter a house, Americans don't,' I say, as Lionel looks up and sees us.

'Hello, young lovers, shouldn't one of you be up on the balcony and other one down here?' Lionel says, walking out of the charcoal grey into the lemon drizzle of a dockside light.

Neither of us say anything.

'Didn't you do Shakespeare at school?' Lionel says.

'Shakespeare is shite,' I say.

'*Romeo and Juliet*,' he says.

'Yes, I know, but it's still shite. *Star Trek, the Original Series*, is better.'

'Police let you go then,' Sigurd says.

'Yes, I got cautioned again, and I have to go back to the police station tomorrow.'

'Where's Brian?' I say, looking back down the pier towards Harbour Street, but there is no-one there.

'Said he wanted to give you some space. I think he's gone back to the cathedral.'

'How did you find us?' I say.

'Your father mentioned the trawler to the police. Have you got any coffee? My body needs a break from the alcohol,' Lionel says to Sigurd.

'Instant, or tea. Always plenty of tea on a trawler.'

I am so engrossed watching Lionel, and amused by his drunkenness, I hardly notice the others arrive.

'Aye up, me ducks,' the old guy from earlier says, as he leads his chorus line onto the illuminated dock that now looks a bit like a stage.

'Thank you for your verse earlier,' I say.

The old bloke nods his head. 'I'm Davey, Davey MacDonald,' he says.

'He's dragged us back here. Says he's worried about you,' a big American bloke says.

'I've only been in the Orkneys for a day and I get to meet the rocker everyone is looking for,' Davey says.

'Orkney, you don't say Orkneys. If anyone hears you, you'll be castrated and thrown into the sea. Anyway, I'm not a rocker, I'm Pandora, but you can call me Panda.'

'They say you're going to kill yourself,' Davey says.

Raise my eyebrows, but doubt anyone can see.

'I just want to tell you not to be so silly. I'm squeezing every drop of life out of every second. I don't want to close my eyes in case all this disappears and I don't get to be here anymore. The problem with young folk is you don't see the obvious. Life is a blessing, it's bloody marvellous. So, don't throw it away.'

'Davey, yes, I've got that. It took till tonight and maybe until I heard your verse, but I've got that now,' I say.

Davey looks pleased with himself but he has something else he wants to say.

'I've known three who did it. One got fed up of being old, one was ill, and the other just went a bit mad.'

'I'm the mad one, but I think I might have changed my mind.'

'Oh, that is good news,' a woman with an American accent says, hugging the big guy's arm.

'Staying awake like this helps,' another American male voice says. 'Sleep deprivation is a cure for depression. I've just been reading a paper on it.'

'Excuse my husband, psychologists never have holidays. We were worried. We wanted to make sure you were okay.' Another female American voice this time.

'You aren't the King and Queen of Denmark, are you?' I say.

'No, just rich,' the big American man says.

'I just love Kirkwall,' the woman clinging to his arm says, as she tugs him away and they all move towards North Pier again, as if in a ballet and each step is choreographed.

'Have a good life,' one of the American ladies says.

'No need to be good, just enjoy it. I have. Still am. I'm off to Shetland next week,' Davey says, as they slip back into the gloom.

(Ansuz)

*'Listen, learn, take advice.'*

Sigurd, Lionel, and I make our way down below. Fire extinguishers and hieroglyphic safety signs decorate the narrow corridor like they are exhibits in a quirky gallery.

'It's called a mess on a ship,' Sigurd says, as he leads us into a small canteen.

'Tidiest mess I've ever seen,' Lionel says, taking his shoes off as he enters.

'You look a lot happier than you did earlier,' Lionel says, now standing beside me.

'Sigurd tells me that my anger at life is normal at my age, and Davey has inspired me.'

'Each life a daisy chain of scars whose blossom shines on age-crinkled skin like the scalding breath of the roaring sun. Keep going. Reflection the reward,' Sigurd says.

'If the people I've met tonight are normal, so am I,' I say.

'Perhaps The Lord has come into your life,' Lionel says.

'I was hoping it was me,' Sigurd says.

'You two, Davey, meeting Brian, sleep deprivation, the magic of this special night, who knows?'

'What about Brian?' Sigurd says.

'He says he wants time on his own, so he went back to the cathedral,' Lionel says.

'You've made one convert tonight then,' I say.

'Brian says he's tried twice before, on his own, but both went wrong. Thinks he's stupid, that he doesn't have a brain. So, he wants to get it right this time. His stories are hilarious. The first time he jumped off a bridge and was rescued by a group of scouts on a kayaking trip. He was dazed from hitting the water and they were so pleased with themselves, rescuing him, that he didn't have the heart to stop them,' Lionel says.

'Should be a suicide rescuer's badge,' Sigurd says.

'The second time is even more unlikely. The anti-terrorist police were called because he took a shotgun into the park,' Lionel says.

'Why the park?'

'No idea. Anyway, he said it took him a while to get up the courage to shoot and when the police arrived it got complicated. They shouted at him that they would shoot him if he didn't put down the gun.'

'A perfect suicide,' Sigurd says.

'Yes, you would have thought so, wouldn't you? But then a young policeman decided he would come forward and talk him out of it and he was so busy trying to explain that he wasn't a terrorist that the young man overpowered him before either he, or they, got around to shooting,' Lionel says.

'What can go wrong throwing yourself off a cliff?' I say.

'It sounds like he'd probably sprout wings, or be plucked out of the sky by an albatross or sea-eagle,' Lionel says.

Sigurd laughs out loud. 'What makes him think that death by barbecue was going to work out any better?'

'I've been planning to jump from a cliff. I wrote about it in my diary, so my dad will probably be on his way to Hoy in his wee rubber boat by now to try and stop me.'

'You left a trail then. Another clue to your lack of intent?' Sigurd says.

'I think you are too hard on your father,' Lionel says.

*What does he know about anything?*

'You only met him for the first time a few days ago on that bloody flat earth tour of his,' I say.

'You think my family are strange, and your father runs flat earth tours?' Sigurd says, surprise and laughter in his voice.

'Yes, my father is mad too, just in a different way. Lionel thinks he is hiding from the world by pretending it doesn't exist.'

Sigurd looks at Lionel who shrugs before speaking.

'You are both giving up on life as most people see it. Your choice is just more dramatic,' Lionel says.

'She's a Drama Queen,' Sigurd says.

'There's no point talking to you – aren't you drunk?' I say.

Lionel puts on a more serious face. 'My first wife killed herself. Overdose. I found her on the floor in the kitchen when I got home from work. We had underfloor heating so her body was still warm and it took me a while to realise she was dead. The note she left was written by a person I had never met,' Lionel says.

He sips his tea and then stirs in three sugar cubes, one at a time.

'She said that she felt her life had been a failure.'

'I'm sorry,' I say.

'I wish I'd known then that you need to believe that things can get better, but it took her death for me to understand. I've never been very brave with relationships.'

'Brave enough to attack my uncle,' Sigurd says.

'I think I was drunk. With one-to-one emotional stuff, I'm a cowardly lion.'

'Is that when you found The Lord?' I say.

'I think he's on the lookout for people who can't cope.'

'Not found me yet, unless one of you two is Jesus Christ,' I say.

Both men point at each other and smile.

'Did you blame yourself for her death?' Sigurd says.

'No, I didn't know how she felt. I guess she didn't think I could do anything to help.'

'We didn't know either, about what she was going to do. Mummy. It happened so quickly, just like she had been living a lie and then one day, she was true to herself,' I say.

'What happened?'

'She just shrank. As the car drove away she got smaller and smaller until I couldn't see her anymore.' Seeing it all again through younger eyes.

'Come on, enough of this. Let's have another drink,' Sigurd says.

# DEAR EDITH, 3

'Kirkjuvagr,' Zander said, pointing down the hill towards the town, releasing my hand. It wasn't that he was holding it tightly, I could have pulled it away at any time, but I didn't. He just guided me, giving me confidence to come with him. Do you know how long it has been since I have held another man's hand? It was just that he now released it, symbolically setting me free. He stretched both arms out and embraced the view, like he was welcoming his beloved.

'That's what the Norsemen called this place. It means *Church Bay*, but not this church,' he said, pointing to the cathedral down the hill. 'That came later. People settled here because it was a safe place to launch their boats.' He pointed beyond the cathedral to the water.

'The Oyce, down there,' he said.

'Ah yes, where the Vikings ravished their women folk,' I said.

'It was that little bay that attracted people, the Picts and then Norsemen.'

'I said 'no',' I said, after he had finished speaking.

He didn't seem to hear me.

'I'm married.'

'Lucky man,' he said, looking at me and smiling, and the way he said it made my legs go weak.

We walked on in silence, with him on the roadside.

'It's polite for the gentleman to be close to the road,' he said. 'In case you get splashed by a passing Hansom Cab.'

'What?'

'My London-born grandmother used to tell me that whenever we went out together.'

I shook my head and walked on, ignoring his Freudian slip. I am probably old enough to be his grandmother.

'We are passing a dark and deadly place,' he said.

I shook my head, as it was clear this was more of a performance than a discussion.

'That triangle of grass with the bush is called Gallows Ha'. In the cathedral, there is still a double ladder used by the hangman and the condemned. They climbed the ladder side-by-side, but only one of them came down again. They just took the ladder away and let them suffocate, wriggling in the air. No 'drop' to break their necks. If you were lucky someone would pull you down by your legs, to speed things up, but they risked getting pissed on.'

'Ugh,' I said.

'Where the bushes are, that is where the hangman used to live. When the body had been left hanging long enough, he took it down and kept it with him in his cottage until it could be buried.'

'I guess he wasn't married,' I said.

'They were social outcasts. Busy though, there were over two hundred capital offences at one time.'

'How awful,' I said. 'How could anyone do that for a living?'

'Maybe dead people turned them on.'

'That's perverse. Is it haunted or something? Is that why they haven't built on it?'

'Oh, lots of folk think that Kirkwall is haunted, not just that little bit of grass. St Magnus is famous for his miracles,' Zander said.

'How do you know all this?'

'A local history book written in 1900 by a guy called Buckham Hugh Hossack. Full of interesting stuff and I have a photographic memory. Ask me anything in Hossack and I'll tell you about it.'

'Not just a pretty face then?'

'Thank you, I'll take that as a compliment. Anyway, a perversion is just something that doesn't appeal to you?'

'What?'

'You brought it up.'

'Did I?' I walked on, behind him, as if I was on an invisible lead.

'The road on the right is named after a man who liked to slip laxatives into people's champagne and dress up as a sailor. He also fined his servants if they did anything wrong.'

'Is that all you need to do to become a celebrity in this town?'

'Well, his eccentricities were easily overlooked when he left all his money to rebuild the cathedral. Without his fortune, it wouldn't be what you see today. For over a hundred years it didn't have a roof. They carried out trials of witches there too and then dragged the poor wretches up the hill to the head of the Clay Loan to burn at the stake over there, though in Hossack they say they were "worried at the stake".'

'Did Kirkwall have many witches?'

'There are records of sixteen or seventeen, something like that, mostly women but one man.'

'The Wizard of Kirkwall,' I said.

'You didn't need to do much to be thought as a witch, or a wizard. If someone wanted your land they may accuse you. Just refusing to fuck a powerful man would probably be enough, or if you refused *droit du seigneur*.'

'What's that?'

'The right of the lord of the manor to fuck the bride on her wedding day,' Zander said.

'You just made that up.'

'They say it happened. Anyway, these days women have a choice.'

I laughed.

As he spoke, I could easily imagine the hangman and his prisoner beside him, crying, while Vikings were splashing ashore after their summer expedition, just in front of the cathedral. Chasing all the women to satisfy their lust.

'That house over there used to be a brothel, though they didn't call it that. Famous 'guesthouse' in its day. Money would buy you any perversion you could think of.'

'Okay, I get it. I'm being treated to the salacious version of your history walk. Is that why you told me that story of the Vikings' return? Are you trying to excite me?'

'Are you getting excited?'

I didn't answer him, but the answer was 'yes' and I knew that he knew it.

'Can you hear the screams and the debauchery?' he said, looking down the hill towards the Earl's Palace, as if trying to hear something.

'They had all sorts of fancy torture equipment in there. You didn't want to get on the wrong side of the Earl. He was the worst kind of Bond villain.'

At the bottom of the hill, we stood, side-by-side, by the tollbooth, on the corner of Palace Road and Broad Street. There was a lot of commotion in the scene Zander described. The Town Guard were causing trouble, riding their horses in and out of the cathedral and getting into fights. The Llambas Fair was in progress on Church Green, a penitent was tied to the Mercat Cross, and amongst it all there were soldiers running about firing guns and chasing a group of men who seemed to want to seek sanctuary in the cathedral. In the background, cannons were pounding the castle walls. Noise, smoke and a strange mixture of laughter and terror in the air. Different events from the past all happening at once.

'You might be surprised about some of the goings on then. Earl Patrick was a sex machine. He had orgies in the Castle. They say he had thirteen illegitimate children and he bedded any woman he pleased. If you refused, he would make life hard for your family.'

'Ah, the witch thing.'

He nodded, though he seemed distracted, lost in the past too.

'Are you trying to seduce me?' I said, but he either didn't hear, or decided to ignore me. We stood side-by-side in silence for a while. Both of us lost in space and time.

'You're good at this,' I said.

'At what?'

'Making the past come alive. I can see it all.'

'I think that's what belonging is – a shared memory of the past.'

'I saw the musket holes on the wall by the cathedral door.'

'They call them vernacular memorials.'

'Really,' I said, and laughed at all his nonsense. He could have been making it up for all I knew. Isn't history mostly made up by the people who want to control the present? But, know what? I didn't care. He had got into my head and I think I lost touch with reality for a while. It was like I was hallucinating. The few times I tried microdots. Golly, remember those? It was like that.

'I feel like someone spiked my drink.'

'That's Kirkwall for you.'

He then looked at me and smiled and gently picked-up my hand again and led me though the melee in Broad Street, dodging bullets and dying soldiers, moving past the seemingly impregnable castle walls still being bombarded with cannon fire and into Albert Street, where the smoke of battle dissipated, and I could see clearly again.

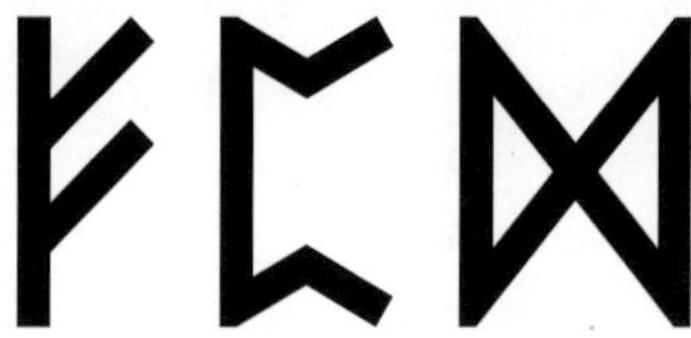

(Fehu. Perthro. Dagaz)

*Success, attainment, prosperity. Mystery, secrets, the occult – a revelation is coming. Dawn of a new day.*

# 16. TED

I wake in Sigurd's arms.

Brass ship's clock on the bulkhead says it is three a.m. and time to meet Brian. The three of us must have dozed off on the cosy mess room benches. Lionel and Sigurd still asleep. Lionel fell asleep first so didn't see us kissing and Siggy petting me like a puppy. Nice. Safe and warm.

*'Ladies & Gentlemen,' I say, when I arrive centre-stage to give my long-awaited TED talk about the night that changed my life. Pause to collect my thoughts; I don't have a script. Lights are so bright I can't see the audience. The gentle susurration of the air, and the peep I took ten minutes earlier, tell me it is full. Incredibly, all these people have come to hear what I have to say.*

*'A lifetime ago, I woke up on a trawler at three a.m. in Kirkwall harbour in my first lover's arms. I couldn't remember the last time I had been awake so early in the morning, but it didn't feel late, or early. I wasn't even tired. I was wide awake for the first time in years. My head no longer full of pressure and about to explode, as it was just a few hours earlier.*

*'I was Cinderella, waking from a horrible dream, which was how my life had seemed until that moment.*

*'Earlier, on that Last Summer Night all those years ago, I really thought that I had no choice but to end it all. I really thought I meant what I said to my suicide buddy, Brian, that I was committed to going through with our pact, because I couldn't see an alternative. But, looking back at the child I was then, maybe I didn't. Maybe I just wanted attention. To be honest, I don't know what is true after all these years.*

*Kirkwall, and the amazing people I met that night, saved me. I saw for the first time that I was special: an invaluable link in the chain of existence, because there had never been anyone like me before. No two lives are the same and each of our perspectives on life is as rare and valuable as any work of art. But rather than galleries and museums, the way we save it is by passing on our experiences. I believe it is why we are here. I met an old guy called Davey that night and he taught me that, and Kirkwall taught me that who we are today depends upon who went before. I wouldn't be me if it weren't for the multitudes that live on in the collective unconscious of mankind.*

*'Humanity is a concatenation of utterly unique lives, and each of us have a duty to live a long and full life, to make the best contribution we can to what comes next. A duty to both the past and the future. It was a revelation, for me. So strong, I almost started to believe in God, like my other new friend Lionel wanted me to.*

*'I wondered if it was Lionel's wise words, Davey's spell, Kirkwall's leaky past, falling in love, or one of St Magnus' miracles, that had done this to me. Maybe it was a heady mix of all of them.*

*'Lying in Sigurd's arms, I understood for the first time that life, even my shitty life, was better than death. That might sound obvious to most of you, but I know that many of you are here today because you have had dark thoughts and contemplated giving up on life. My message to you is a simple – don't.*

*'It is my sincere conviction that happiness is more a question of acceptance of who you are, and where you find yourself, than anything*

*else. You just need confidence to accept your destiny and make the most of life. Like I have.*

*'The purpose of life is to inform the future and we all have something uniquely valuable to say.*

*'Thank you.'*

'Hello,' Sigurd says, after he opens his eyes to see me looking at his face, smiling.

'Hello,' I say, touching his face to make sure he is real.

'Been staring at me long?'

'Just long enough to practise my TED talk.'

'Oh, yes, do you give many TED talks?' Sigurd says, chuckling.

'My first, as it happens. When I'm old and famous.'

'Did it go well?'

'You and your philosopher friends would have been proud of me. I think I've come to terms with existence.'

'About time,' he says and sits up, rubbing his eyes. Both look at Lionel snoring opposite, knowing we have to wake him to tell him it is time to go.

## (Kenaz)

*'The spirt moves in mysterious ways. New strength and energy from the spirit world.'*

Bridge Street is empty, though the tang of people and beer swills around us and we can hear the mumble of the night's discarded words slumbering on the flagstones beneath our feet, disturbed by our passing.

Arm-in-arm down Albert Street and into Broad Street, like gunslingers about to face the bad guys, me in the middle with my compadres on both sides. Are they my Sad Guardians, here to stop me doing something stupid? Hands on hips, ready to draw at the least provocation from a suicidal thought.

Brian standing on the pavement looking up at the cathedral. Makes the sign of the cross, as if he has just finished his prayers.

'Sorry to disturb your devotions,' Lionel says.

'It's okay, just thought I'd give it a go. You know. The Lord and all that. It's kind of reassuring.'

'Your father said that religion was just a question of belief. He's right. So, you can either believe or not, right? But why believe in the least attractive option – it's pure masochism,' Lionel says, talking to me.

'Did you pray to get saved?' I say to Brian.

'No, I prayed to have a painless death.'

'So, you're still going through with this?' Lionel says to Brian.

'Yes, I am. What about you?' Brian says looking at me, though I think he can already tell that I am going to let him down.

Both Lionel and Sigurd look at me too, but Brian speaks again before I am able to find the right words.

'You don't need to say anything, I can see it in your eyes,' he says, sounding disappointed and alone, as if I have denied knowing him at all, like Peter denied Jesus.

'I feel like I've been reborn.' Tears flow done my face from a spring of hope.

'You shouldn't have brought me all this way, if it was just a stupid game,' Brian says.

*I'm sorry.* I think to myself but don't say it out loud.

'It's okay,' he says, after a beat, as if he understands. 'I'm glad I got to Orkney before, you know. I feel closer to death here and it will be easier to leave.'

I wipe away the tears with my free hand. Sigurd is holding the other one.

'Will you show me where you wanted us to jump?' Brian says, poking me with a cattle-prod stare.

Tears still rolling down my cheek and for the first time I feel scared.

'Don't think I've really tried to live, not properly. More of an existence so far. I have been so angry. It has been too easy to blame my father for my misery, rather than doing anything about it,' I say.

'What can you do?' Brian says.

'Live,' I say. 'And stop the self-pity,' I say, paraphrasing something that Sigurd said earlier.

'Suicide just transfers the misery to those you leave behind,' Lionel says, moving closer to me. Drawn to me by the surface tension of my tears.

'I don't have anyone to leave behind,' Brian says.

'You have us,' I say, before Lionel has a chance to speak.

'I'm still going through with it,' Brian says.

'Well, if you are, I'm coming with you,' Sigurd says.

'Me too,' Lionel says.

'I lead a life of utter loneliness and then I get three death buddies.'

'Brian, you now have three friends. You can keep going without being so alone if you want. The future is uncertain – anything can happen – and it might be wonderful,' Lionel says.

'It's his strap line,' I say.

'You won't stop me.'

'Okay, but we still want to come,' Sigurd says.

'Okay, thanks. I don't want to die alone. Let's go. But I don't need this,' he says, lifting his charcoal burner bag to show everyone he still has it. He turns around as if he is going to leave it on a gravestone and then stares at the cathedral.

'You see that? Over there, look,' he says, still carrying his bag and walking slowly towards the building.

There are purple flashes coming from the deep shade close to the wall, like excited plankton in an oceanic trench I've seen on TV.

'Fireflies,' Sigurd says.

'Don't get fireflies in Orkney. Glowworms but no fireflies,' I say, 'Though I do keep seeing animals that aren't meant to be here. So, maybe it's another sign that the dead are watching us.'

A figure is standing by a side door. It is a man and he is glowing, like there is a light inside him trying to get out.

'It's a man and he's on fire,' Brian says, sounding concerned.

We all walk towards the purple man to see what is going on, but before we get too close he raises his hand, which is red hot too, like the Star of Bethlehem.

'Cool,' Sigurd says, but no one else says anything.

'I grant you each a wish before dawn,' the figure says, but the voice is of a young boy.

We are all silent and still, staring at the apparition.

'My name is Man and this is my house,' he says, before turning and opening the door behind him and disappearing into the cathedral. There is giggling inside and the sound of running feet and a group of boys in hoodies run out on to Broad Street.

'Losers,' one of them shouts at the top of his voice. 'Fucking losers.'

We are all quiet for a while, trying to work out what just happened.

'I thought that that saint bloke had come, you know, the miracle guy,' Brian says.

'St Magnus. Did you think your prayers had been answered?' I say, as Brian turns back towards us. There is a look of wonder on his face, as if he has been reborn too.

'Stupid, but I did. Told you I didn't have a brain,' Brian says.

'Bloody kids, they had me going too, just at first. How did they do the light thing?' Lionel says.

'Well, maybe St Magnus chose them to speak to us,' Brian says.

'So, you think that was a miracle,' I say. Can't help wondering if what has happened to me was one of Magnus' miracles too.

'Don't know. What is supposed to happen in a miracle?' Sigurd says.

'Statues cry, the blind see again, the lame can walk,' I say.

'Or the dead are brought back to life,' Lionel says.

*Does he mean me?*

'It was a miracle: that we fell for it,' Sigurd says.

'But we did, didn't we? For a few seconds, we hoped,' I say.

Lionel laughs. 'It did seem special when I first saw it. This place helps. Anything could happen here. Let's all wish and see if any of our wishes comes true.'

'Think I've already had my wish,' I say, because I am suddenly feeling overwhelmed with this great positive feeling, that lifts my feet off the floor. I didn't think the night could get any better but now I am buoyed-up with hope, that we have been chosen, that something special has happened and it wasn't just a schoolboy prank.

'What are you going to wish for?' I say.

'Not sure, I'm going to think about it first, just in case,' Brian says.

We stare at each other and giggle like school children. Something has happened, but we aren't sure what. Maybe we were just all taken in at once and that gave us a sense of joint enterprise and we are all guilty of unblemished hope.

(Raidho)

*'Travel, movement, a pleasant journey – follow your soul's path.'*

The 'miracle' a cue to move on. No one says anything, we are all lost in our own prayery thoughts. Bridge Street's flagstones splashed with yellow light from the waxing moon. Just the soft percussion of feet until Brian walks on a rattly drain cover.

Viking, a real one this time, dressed-up with shield and sword is walking towards us, arm-in arm with Gloria Gaynor, and Dorothy from the Wizard of Oz. They are much the worse for wear and holding each other up, singing *Over The Rainbow.*

'I think they may be the Up Helly Aa guys, from Shetland. They told me about them in the Tourist Office,' Lionel says.

Brian looks bemused as they walk past, unaware we are there.

'Biggest fire ceremony in Europe,' Lionel says.

'I get the Viking, but what about Gloria Gaynor and the short fat guy dressed as Dorothy?' Sigurd says.

'Thousand men with flaming torches and they only have a few Viking costumes. The others get to choose what they wear,' I say.

'They don't get dressed up like that in Leeds,' Brian says.

'It's different here in Norway,' I say.

Brian nods. Lionel laughs. Sigurd shakes his head.

'Bloody hell, we don't even have to wait,' Sigurd says, when we turn the corner into Harbour Street and find a taxi waiting.

'Shit, there's my bloody wish gone,' Lionel says, laughing to himself.

'You can't have the barbecue in the car,' the taxi driver says as we get closer and it is obvious we want a ride.

'It's a charcoal burner,' Brian says, though he seems surprised that he still has it with him.

'I don't care what you call it, you can't have it in the car. It'll have to go in the boot,' he says, getting out of the car and walking to the back and we follow.

The boot is already full, with a spare tyre and a fish box labelled R. Groat, Stronsay. A tangy smell wafts out of the boot as the lid is opened.

'No room, mate. Sorry, you'll have to leave it if you want a ride,' the taxi driver says.

Brian stands looking at the taxi and then at me.

'I don't want to leave it, so I think I'll stick with the charcoal. Never that keen on falling, if I'm honest.'

'I know the perfect place for a breakfast barbecue,' I say.

'Me, too – Hawaii,' Sigurd says.

'Inganess,' I say.

ᚦᚷᛚ

(Thurisaz. Gebo. Laguz)

*'Protection and luck is on your side. Partnership and gift of love, peace and contentment. Follow your intuition.'*

# 17. HIS KINGDOM

Davey is sitting in a golden chair on the balcony of Rick's suite on the *Highlander*, sipping a glass of champagne. The delicate glass awkward in his wrench-like fist. His fingers wrinkled and cracked, his saggy skin the colour of work.

'Davey, you're like a king on a throne,' Jock says.

'Feel more like Robin Knox-Johnston.'

'How do you think you'd have coped with a life of luxury?' Jock says, smelling his expensive whisky and looking out over his hometown.

'The rich are missing out, just like these young-folk. What's the point of life if you don't have to struggle? It makes you strong.'

'These guys must struggle to keep awake if they do this every night,' Jock says.

'They don't have to get up at the crack of dawn to go to work. When I was in the steel works, I'd go to bed at eight.'

'What? As a lad?'

'No, maybes not. Towards the end. It gets harder the older you get, doesn't it?'

'Aye. Did some road work after the fishing. Digging a hole in the road for the Water Board when you're sixty-three was like digging out the North Sea,' Jock says.

'That rhymes.'

'Aye. They say we Orcadians have poetic souls. Always wondered what it was like on one of these gin palaces.'

'Why do you think Rick had so much trouble getting us on board. Don't want the likes of us on here. If the likes of us really knew how the other half live there'd be a revolution,' Davey says.

'Aye, but money talks, eh? I was surprised that Rick put up such a fuss.'

'Aye. Rick's got the best cabin on board and he'll probably be good for a woppa tip at the end of the cruise.'

'My Mabel was a waitress and she told me that the rich were the worst. They leave the smallest tips. Free with the drink, mind,' Jock says, toasting Davey, touching his cut glass tumbler to Davey's dainty champagne flute.

'Your hand's too big for that glass. You look like King Kong holding Fay Wray at the top of the Empire State Building.'

'Used to box a bit, once. I think the more you clench your fists the bigger they get,' Davey says, looking at his glass. 'Used to love a pint, me. Generous, but I still have the taste for seventy shilling and bubbles won't ever take its place.'

The East Pier is still lit up. Behind it, the ragged silhouette of Kirkwall is cut from black crepe paper and dotted with citrine jewels.

'Hard to credit I've lived here all my life and never seen it like this before.'

'Could happily stay here a while,' Davey says.

'What's going on down there?' Jock says, noting the activity on *Bonxie*. 'Surely they're not off to sea?'

'Don't know, but I have a mind to find out,' Davey says.

## (Algiz)

*'A fortunate new influence.'*

Lionel puts his phone away just as Sigurd gets to the car with a case of beer from *Bonxie.*

'Checking in with the missus?' Sigurd says.

'I met a lady called Catriona earlier, outside the Bothy Bar. She bought me a drink.'

'Does your wife know?'

'Lillian's fast asleep. She got fed up with me ogling women.'

'Catriona?'

'No, the barmaid in Helgi's, earlier, last night, yesterday – it seems a lifetime ago. She has a band and I told her where we're going. Maybe they'll all come and we'll have a bit of music.'

'It's three a.m.,' I say.

'I don't think Catriona is the going-to-bed-early sort of girl,' Lionel says.

'You could feed an army with this lot,' Brian says, joining us with more supplies.

'They are a Viking army. My dad's liege men,' Sigurd says.

'I thought that was just history,' Brian says, looking a bit puzzled.

'We won't get them all in,' Lionel says, looking at the three cars and trailers loaded with provisions. The crew, who have materialised out of thin air, milling around the quay passing bottles of whisky like they were rugby balls.

Sigurd encourages his men to squeeze into the cars.

'Incredible,' Brian says, watching me load the car with another two men. I seem to have been nominated driver as I am the most sober. If only they knew how little I drive, but it's exciting and not many people trust me so readily. The men are crawling onto the laps of the three already in the back. I'm going to put Lionel in the front seat beside me, where I can keep an eye on him.

'Aye up, me ducks,' Davey says behind us.

'Where did you come from?' I say.

'Me, I'm Davey MacDonald. Just wanted to introduce myself properly like, and this is Jock,' he says, pointing at a small grey man standing a little back.

'Hi Jock, but Davey, we were introduced earlier,' I say.

'Sorry, one of the pitfalls of old age. I can remember everything I did as a lad but nothing from the last 24 hours. Anyway, used to be names like Peter and Ruth and Christopher, Jane and Jack, now everyone is giving their kids names from TV.'

'Pandora, but you can call me Panda,' I say, as it's clear he has forgotten our names.

'I'm Sigurd, and this is Brian and Lionel,' Sigurd says, nodding towards them in turn.

'Can't say I've ever met a Pandora before. Can I call you Dora? Panda's not much of a girl's name, is it? It's short for Dorothy, but I guess it could be short for Pandora too.'

'I've done worse,' I say, thinking that if I can rename Cathleen, Martin, he can rename me too.

*Dora isn't too bad a name. Maybe someone will mistake me for Dorothy.*

'Anyway, where *did* you come from?' I say. Reminds me of my grandfather, the only time I met him. Cantankerous old sod, but I liked that. Maybe all grandfathers are alike: angry at being old, dilapidated, and slowly melting away, but they know their own mind.

'Been entertained on the royal yacht,' Davey says. 'Look up there.'

Davey points to a cabin high up on the side of the *Highlander* and he waves and a group of people on a balcony wave back, as if they have been watching his progress, keeping an eye on him.

'I've been sitting up there, as if I was someone important reliving the finer moments of my life. Been doing that a lot lately, looking back, trying to make sense of it all.'

'Nothing wrong with looking back. Anyway, who says you're not important?' I say.

'All my life I've been made to feel that I'm not. We're having a bit of a do on the royal yacht but I had this urge to see what you was up to and that you were okay?' Davey says, looking at me.

'Again?' I say.

'Aye, I'm feeling paternal. Just checking on you.'

I smile a 'yes' and nod to answer him.

'I've got daughters and I never liked it when they were down. They think I'm a gypsy now, mind, on the move. My wife is gone and they've settled down. My time now, right?'

'I'm fine, Davey. In fact, I'm better than I've been in a long time. They may be right about there being something in the air tonight, or maybe your poem cast a spell on me.'

'I wish it was a spell,' Davey says. 'I'd like to think I'd helped. Most young folk just ignore me these days. Think that life is all about new stuff and not what you learn as you live it.'

'I got your message. Live life to the full and keep going, as long as I can.'

'Really? That's grand. Really grand,' Davey says, and I can see a tear forming in the corner of his eye.

'Oh, stop that,' I say, and reach out to brush it from his bristly cheek.

'First time I've cried since Mathew died,' he says.

'Mathew?'

'My lad; he was only eight. Wonky heart. Always wondered if he inherited it from me,' Davey says.

I can't help myself and take a step forward to give him a hug. Smells of Old Spice, like Thomas.

'Thought I'd no heart left, that it had shrivelled up, but I'm crying, right? Some emotions left in the old sod yet,' he says, wiping his cheeks.

'We're going to have a sunrise party of our own on Inganess beach,' I say.

'Can anyone come?' Davey says.

'Only inviting important people and you are on my VIP list. Davey MacDonald VIP.'

'Makes me sound like a politician. Now, hang on,' he says, looking back towards Harbour Street, 'Davey MacDonald MPP, that's me, now.'

'MPP?'

'Yes, Member Pierhead Parliament, over there. I think I'm probably a member, for tonight at least,' he says, turning to Jock, his shadow, who smiles and nods.

'I think you make a good MPP. We need people who have lived, not theorized about life,' I say.

'I've lived. Have I told you about my time in the Army?'

'No, you haven't, but Davey MacDonald MPP VIP, you and your friends from the royal yacht are all welcome at our party,' I say.

'Not sure if they'll be up for it. Hard to pull themselves away from all that luxury for any longer than they have to. I think tonight has been a shock for them. Do you know that they have this suite with a huge bed, pink silk sheets, and a mirror on the ceiling?'

'Call of the wild, might be enough to attract them.'

'I was going to Shetland in a few days but after tonight I'm not too sure. Never knew a place could be as friendly to strangers and so much fun as Kirkwall. It took me years to make friends in Corby but no here. People say I talk too much.'

'No, really?' Lionel says.

'Try us in February, it's not so nice then. Anyway, it's easy to be friendly to people who are friendly themselves,' I say.

'Okay. Yes, I like to meet people, me, but I can be a bit grumpy. I will try it in February. If I'm still here, I will,' Davey says, and turns and walks back towards the *Highlander*, smiling to himself, with Jock beside him.

'I.N.G.A.N.E.S.S?' Davey says, spelling out the letters, after turning to look back a few metres on.

'Aye, Inganess Beach,' I say.

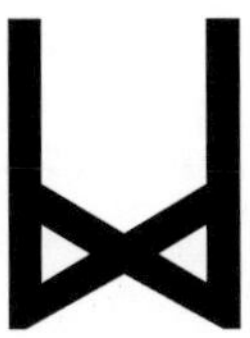

## (Mannaz Reversed)

*'Isolated, lonely – no help coming.'*

Walk across the narrow road to the top of the beach and look out to sea, as everyone else struggles out of the cars.

The moon has fallen into the water, still wobbling gently with ripples from the splash. A wreck firmly aground just offshore seems to be motoring towards the beach on a wake of moonlight, which extends to my feet. In the shadows, on either side, tiny waves break into flames from dancing firework shrimp, on the edge of the sand.

*No more excuses for my fancy words. Decided to embrace my love of language. It's what makes me, me, not someone else. You've had plenty time to get used to me by now.*

Jenny and Johnno come and stand beside me, holding hands. I nearly ran over them on the way here; they were kissing in the middle of the road. They've invited their friends too. The crew have wriggled free from the cars and are now unloading behind us and making a din.

'Bloody romantic, isn't it?' Johnno says.

It is a beautiful sight. The sandy beach in front of us is speckled with small rocks, like nuggets in gold dust.

'What a place for a sunrise barbecue,' Lionel says, walking up behind us.

'Nice place to die,' Brian says, as he arrives.

We coax the last of the Vikings out of the cars, the ones in the deepest sleep, and begin to carry things down the beach. Lionel and Brian bring piles of dry wood and shape it into a stack and in no time it is a giant flare. The Vikings are bringing the logs used to roll *Dreki* earlier down to the fire. There is a smell of diesel in the air.

'Got enough charcoal?' I ask Brian, who is still carrying his burner.

'Maybe that should be my funeral pyre?' Brian says, to Lionel as he passes the fire.

'No way, we'll bury you later, that's for burgers.'

'I need a tarpaulin, or something to put this in so that the fumes concentrate and, you know, I suffocate.'

'Where in hell's teeth are we going to get one at this time of night?' Lionel says.

I'm behind them and overhear the question.

'There used to be a discarded tent up at the top of the beach, beside that World War Two mine. There was a rough sleeper there a while back,' I say.

'Really? Maybe that's a sign. Do you think it was put there for me?' he says.

I shrug.

'Okay, I'll go and get it. Do you have a torch?' Brian says.

'You won't need one. Tonight, the moon is your torch. Just follow the yellow brick road,' I say, pointing to the trench of moonlight that has been dug across the beach.

Lionel and I watch as Brian shuffles through icing-sugar-soft sand, before disappearing from sight.

'There was a bike beside it, padlocked to the mine and a lot of rubbish fell out when I pulled it up,' Brian says, arriving back ten minutes later with a ball of orange cloth trailing tentacles of string, like a beached jellyfish.

'It's a community service clearing up abandoned crap like that,' Lionel says.

'Should do well, this, not too big, but it looks pretty airtight,' Brian says.

'What's that smell?' I say.

'I think it's the tent,' Brian says.

Lionel and I grimace in unison and leave Brian to it. Join a human chain across the beach bringing the food and the booze, most of which has come from *Bonxie.*

## (Berkana Reversed)

*'Family problems and domestic troubles.'*

Split opens the small wooden chest. He takes out a chequered board made of light wood, the black squares crudely charred. He lifts out two bags and carefully removes one piece from each and hides them in his fists. Swift Eye chooses one of them. On Split's open palm sits a human finger bone with a small white dot.

'You are white,' he says, passing Swift Eye the 'white' bag.

'As is custom, I will now greet my ancestors who will help me in this night's battle,' Swift Eye says, sifting through the pieces to pull out seven similar finger bones.

'These pawns are fashioned from our father's hand. May he guide me.'

He then sets up his board piece by piece, speaking as he does so. All those watching hold their fingers together, as if reciting a prayer.

*The Castles, from the shoulder bones of Botolf The Stubborn.*
*The Rooks, from the arms of Einar Buttered-Bread.*
*The Bishops, from the feet of Arni Pin-Leg.*
*The Queen, from the skull Ingirid, wife of Einar Vorse-Raven.*
*The King, from the skull of Einar Vorse-Raven.*

It is then Hooky's turn. He takes out his pieces one at a time and places them on the black and white board.

'These are my wife's grandfather's fingers and may they guide me,' he says.

*The Castles, from the shoulder bones of Eindridi the Young.*
*The Rooks, from the arms of Eirik Stay-Brails.*
*The Bishops, from the feet of Erling Wry-Neck.*
*The Queen, for the skull of Ingibjorg Finn's-Daughter.*
*The King, from the skull of Half Dan-Long-Leg.*

'It's time for the berserkers to fight, naked, biting their shields. Unleash the dogs of war,' Swift Eye says, moving his first piece boldly out onto the battlefield.

(Hagalaz)

*'Unexpected disruptions, limitations and delays.'*

Brian starting to put the tent around his charcoal burner. Places it far enough away to be discreet, close enough to feel the presence of others.

'You okay?' I say. Brian is crouched over the charcoal burner in the centre of the tent with a box of matches in his hand.

'Can't get the bloody thing to light.'

'Don't you need some of that gel stuff? Or, get some charcoal from the fire once it burns through the wood. If you can wait for that.'

'I can wait. Do you know I read about these two blokes on the Atlantic convoys who couldn't bear the agony of being adrift in a lifeboat any longer, so they decided to throw themselves into sea, but they both had a kip first. Don't you think that is strange?'

'Yes, weird. Anyway, you'll need a drink. The guys in those suicide rooms in Japan say that a drink helps.'

'Got any sake?'

'Who knows. Nothing would surprise me the night. Or I could get you some of Martin's little blue pills.'

'Who?'

'Martin, over there,' I say, pointing to her. She has just arrived miraculously on the beach, as if I had wished her into existence, rather than texted her. She smiles when she sees me.

'Martin?'

'She's really called Cathleen, but I call her Martin.'

Brian seems puzzled by that, but he has other things on his mind.

'I feel that you have let me down,' Brian says.

'So, we're quits. You lied to me about your age.'

*I don't want this conversation.*

'Don't you think it will set the tent alight,' I say, looking at the charcoal burner.

'Don't know. Never tried this before.'

'Lionel told us about the scouts and the terrorist police.'

'They both got commendations for bravery. The scouts got some sort of special woggle and the policeman got a medal. They invited me to the ceremony in the scout hut and I had to give a speech. I thanked all the parents too.'

'Drink first then?'

'Why not?'

As we walk towards the fire, now burning fiercely, a thinly bearded man in tracksuit bottoms and a tee shirt is coming towards us.

'That's my tent,' he says.

I laugh. I can't help myself. He looks so puzzled.

'Sorry, I thought it was sort of abandoned, it was empty,' Brian says.

'I was having a shit in the field,' the man says.

'Are you from Holland?' I say.

'Yes, I am, but what about my tent? Aren't the Dutch allowed to sleep here, in bloody Norway Scotland?' he says.

I must look puzzled.

'We call Orkney, Norway-Scotland.'

'Really?

'Well, me and my friends do. You're all so bloody odd.'

'I need it, mate, I can't do what I want to do without a tent,' Brian says.

'Then why didn't you bring one? I want mine back; and what happened to all my stuff?'

'What stuff?'

'The things in my tent?' he says, looking around the beach for his belongings.

'Look, it was dark and I thought it was rubbish. The way it smelled.'

'What do you mean, "the way it smelled"?'

'It just looked abandoned.'

'Well fuck you. Fuck you. I'm taking it back, what the hell has it got in it?' the Dutchman says.

'A charcoal burner.'

'Why?'

'I'm planning to kill myself.'

'With that?'

'Yes.'

'What, in my tent? Are you mad?' the Dutchman says.

'Possibly, but I like to think of it more as suicidal.'

'What's your name?' I say.

'Luuk.'

'Okay, Luuk, how about a drink?'

'How about a drink? How about my bloody tent back?'

Brian turns and walks back towards the tent leaving me with Luuk. 'Lovely night,' I say, then burst out laughing.

'Fuck you too,' he says, before following Brian and beginning to pull at the sides of the tent, even though Brian is inside on his hands and knees looking for something in his rucksack. Luuk's tracksuit bottoms are sliding down, revealing a builder's bum which he tries to cover with one hand while still pulling on the tent with the other.

'Luuk man, how about I give you this?' Brian says, now standing and looking down at Luuk still on his hands and knees.

Luuk stands up too and looks at Brian's hands now holding a bundle of fifty-pound notes.

'You want to buy my tent from me in the middle of the night when I am in my pyjamas?' Luuk says.

'Yes, I think so. There is three thousand pounds here. Where I'm going I won't be needing it and I have done you a disservice, sir. What do you say? It's nearly dawn anyway, and with all this going on you're not going to get much sleep,' Brian says, pointing to the growing crowd of people around the bonfire. The word has got out and anyone still awake in Kirkwall seems to have found their way here.

'It's a lot of money,' Luuk says.

'It's a lot to ask.'

'It is. It bloody is.'

'You can easily buy a new tent tomorrow and hire a car, no more of that biking around,' Brian says.

'I like biking around. I am on a biking around holiday. I didn't check my bike, you didn't take it too, did you?'

'No, man. No need for a bike, just a tent. What do you say? Three thousand pounds and as much food and drink as you want. Look, Luuk, it's nice and warm by the fire,' Brian says.

Luuk is pacified by the cash and happily makes his way across to the fire where Lionel hands him a bottle of wine and he stands politely in the small queue already forming for a burger.

# MY DIARY

---

PRIVATE. YOU SHOULDN'T BE READING THIS.

# STAY AWAY FROM ME

## STRANGE FRUIT

You have just found a woman hanging from the tree in the garden. She is wearing Mummy's clothes, but she isn't Mummy. She isn't Mummy. It is covered with pink blossom that matches Mummy's socks, the tree is. Why is the woman in the tree wearing Mummy's socks? It isn't Mummy. It isn't Mummy.

Daddy grabs you and turns you around to look into his face. He is white. I mean his face is whiter than usual, as if he is wearing a sad clown mask, or someone has thrown flour over him, for a joke, but he didn't find it funny. But you don't think this is a joke. Behind him you can see the reflection of the woman in the tree in the patio door. She is moving from side to side a little in the breeze as if she is swaying to music.

'Pandora,' your father says.

'Yes,' you say, but he doesn't answer you. He just closes his eyes as if he is trying to hide, or to make you go away. You then know that you are alone. That whatever has happened is the end of everything, that nothing will ever be the same again.

As he begins to cry he holds you close, so that it begins to hurt and you only have his stale air to breathe.

'Daddy,' you say, and he releases his grip and stands and drags you into the house and he closes the curtains as if it is night-time and time to go to bed, but it is just the start of another day. You have only just had your breakfast. In the car, on your way home.

---

ᚨᚦᚾ

(Ansuz. Thurisaz Reversed. Nauthiz)

*'Listen and learn, take advice. Be careful, now is not the time to make hasty decisions. Delays, be patient, face your fears.'*

# 18. CONTRITION

The fire now crickling and crackling and swooshing. A monster raging against the lonely terror of the infinite night sky.

'Isn't it funny how we are drawn to flames?' Lionel says. We are standing side-by-side, watching the wood in front of us explode into life, as if combustion had released its spirit and returning to its natural state it was dancing with joy.

'Existential,' I say, and Lionel smiles.

Sticky lava flow of new arrivals sliding down the beach towards the brightly burning beacon. Among them, some of the Up Helly Aa crowd: a Dorothy with a cowardly lion; and the men dressed identically in red dresses wearing plastic Gloria Gaynor masks, but now carrying their high heels.

'Them too,' Lionel says, glancing up at the tiny flutterings above us. Flashes of dusty wings tumbling around in the turbulent clear air. Some resting on logs close to the fire where I can identify them better. Common Marble Carpet – with a light patch in the centre that looks like a face on the log in front of me. Larch Tortrix, and a Barred Red with its pinky-flesh colours, and there are clouds of

Magpie Moths – black, white and orange flashes – dancing in the air above.

'Must have mistaken it for a candle,' Lionel says, following my gaze as I try and spot other species.

'Big candle,' I say. Fire now thrusting its tongue high into the darkness with the force of a passionate lover. Bats emerging, barging through the moths, knocking some aside as they feed on others.

*Are they tearing families apart? Is that what happened to us, a blind monster emerging from the darkness to feed on our grief?*

'Pipistrelles,' I say.

'How do you know?'

'Thomas's nature walks. If you had taken one of them instead of the flatty you would know the difference between them and the Nathusius you get in the Spring and Autumn. Probably see it from Kirkwall – the glow in the sky. Like gas being flared over at Flotta.'

'Mount Etna from Naples. We went there once when it was smouldering and you could see it glow at night from our hotel room. Number forty, I think, Italy.'

'Your room number?'

'No, the fortieth country we visited.'

We both stare at the new arrivals, as others are following Dorothy and the Glorias down the beach.

'We should have sold tickets,' Lionel says, shaking his head as he looks around the fire and sees just how many people have come to our impromptu party.

'At least they seem to have brought some supplies. My God, what is he doing here?' Lionel says, looking at an old guy who has just arrived.

'Who is he?' I say, following Lionel's gaze.

'DQ Jack – Double or Quits Jack, is what I think they call him. Gambler, but his wife won't let him bet anymore.'

'I wonder what odds he'd give me on a happy life?' I say, watching Jack standing unsteadily on the soft sand. Not clear if this is from old age, or booze, or both.

'Don't go soft on me now. Life isn't a game of craps, it's up to you. I keep telling you that we can all choose to be happy, or unhappy.'

'You make it sound easy.'

'Look, unhappiness is a choice we make. We are only unhappy if we decide to be. But unhappy people get stuck leading their lives under the misapprehension that anyone else really cares a damn if they are suffering. They wear their unhappiness like a badge of honour when, in fact, it is just a suppurating wound. We only pretend to reward suffering with pity. We don't really care, no matter what we say, we are preoccupied with our own struggles and we all find it something of a relief to see people unhappier than us. We're all voracious parasites feeding off each other's misery, like those bloody bats. If everyone else was happy we'd all be miserable.'

'Bloody hell, where did that come from?'

'It makes me angry, thinking about what you were planning to do. I'm scared that recidivism is raising its ugly head and you'll change your mind,' he says.

'Lovely word.'

'I think the drink is wearing off and I'm getting serious. I just made all that up.'

'So, you think Brian enjoys being sad,' I say, looking towards the fire and seeing Alex, my neighbour, of all people. He waves and I wave back and then I watch Brian.

'Oh, you mean Party Brian swigging back the whisky and laughing with that girl.'

'Yes, him.'

'I think that he finds sadness a convenient refuge. Like a fat person eating more to excuse their lack of activity or success in life. Maybe being unhappy is a sort of lie. It denies that you have a choice in the matter. It's easier to do nothing, plead for sympathy and wallow in your sadness.'

'Well, Brian is off message. He's flirting with my friend Martin.'

'She's young enough to be his granddaughter.'

'You can talk.'

'You sound like my wife.'

'It's what Sigurd has been saying to me too. Brian has forgotten all the crap and why he's here. That's why I don't think he'll go through with it.'

'Me neither. In fact, I'd give you twenty to one that he doesn't barbecue himself to death tonight.'

'I used my wish to join our destinies so if I don't do it, he won't. I got the idea from Sigurd's Viking family. He told me that his cousin thinks that her life is linked to her father and she will die the instant he does. She follows him around all the time to keep him safe,' I say.

'A guardian angel?'

'You're mine. You and Siggy.'

'What about that old guy who keeps popping up?' Lionel says.

'Davey too,' I say, looking back up the beach for Davey, but can't see him.

'I don't think I'd be here if I really thought Brian would go through with it. A few drinks and bit of a dance and then he can sleep it off until tomorrow. Funny, but he told me earlier that for every person who kills themselves there are twenty who try and fail, so your odds are probably not far off.'

'What's that?' Lionel says, looking down towards the water. There is a barking sound, as if someone with a bad cold is trying to clear their throat.

'I think it's something like 15% of the world's population of Grey Seals live in Orkney. They like it here.'

'I expect they want to get some sleep. Do seals sleep?'

'Yes. They do something called bottling. They lie vertically with their noses just poking above the water like floating bottles.'

'In Vancouver, lumber floats like that. We call them deadheads,' Lionel says.

Several people with fiddles and accordions tuning up on the other side of the fire, competing with music being played on a phone with a big speaker. The harsh rasp of the fiddle strings an echo of a coin being dragged down the side of Thomas's car when I was in a foul mood.

'This your friend's band?'

'Sure is. I didn't really expect her to come. Better pop over and say hello,' Lionel says.

'What would your wife think of your new friend Catriona?'

'She'll never know, will she?'

Lionel heads off across the gap between the party and me, which strikes me as a visual metaphor for my life so far.

I watch him say his 'hellos' and then lead the band around the fire to the log pile, where they can sit and play. He is touching Catriona on her arms and back, as if he is testing to confirm that she is real and he isn't dreaming all this. Or is he moulding her, like a potter with wet clay? Or, coaxing her limbs into the most pleasing of shapes, adjusting her posture as if she is being judged at the County Show? Or is he reading something into each slight resistance she makes, or pressure she reciprocates? Can you talk with your hands? But she smiles back as if it is normal to be manhandled so publicly by someone she hardly knows. Does she want to be his Champion of Champions tonight? Or do we just allow men too much scope?

Been alien to me, touch, or to wanting to be touched, but seeing him in action I realise he has been touching me too, without me noticing until now. My forearm still warm from his gentleness. His hand on my knee, which seemed so natural. His arm around my shoulder as we walked along the beach. Unheard of intimacy for me, but natural to him. It seems to be his way of making a connection, as if proximity wasn't enough, contact was essential to really communicate with another. If it is his magic, then tonight it has certainly worked on me.

I remember Sigurd's first touch too. Was he Dr Spock and was he melding my mind? What was he saying to me? Did it get through? Was he encouraging me to give life another chance? Why have I not learnt this tactile language if it has such power? He smothered me with touches while Lionel slept on *Bonxie* and healed me, bringing me back to life, like I was Lazarus.

Surprised to see Thomas.

He has appeared with the woman I saw him with earlier on the other side of the flames. They are touching too, but he takes his hand off her arm when he sees me looking. Denying her like Judas Iscariot denied Christ. Is he fearful of my reaction? Even though it is a bright moonlit night the obsidian sky frames them as a couple in relief against the sand, a cameo deep cut in shell. Something pious and iconic – Mary Magdalene with my father. They are an inverse silhouette shimmering in the hot rising air: the black sky behind them a shroud.

*I must have archived all this Bible stuff for it to reappear in my head. But why has it pushed itself to the front of my mind now? Is this how conversion begins, or is it just proximity to death that drags all this mumbo jumbo out of the collective unconscious?*

Heat pushing us back from the fire; with all these people arriving we need a bigger circle anyway. Only a little wind and what smoke there is goes straight up into the still air. Reminds me of a cowboy book I had as a child, with smoke signals. Wonder if I should send a smoke signal to Thomas, as I have an urge to talk to him, to say something more positive than my last diary entry. Want to retreat. Like a cavalry officer in the charge of the Light Brigade, who has charged through the Russian lines and now needs to get back to where he was, in front of the enemy.

I have been in the wrong and I know it now and want to make amends. Want to smile but can't make my face muscle move.

(Tiewaz Reversed)

*'Lack of fidelity in friendships and relationships.'*

Thomas smiling at me through the haze. I recognise his relief at finding me but also see he is scared of what I will do, or say. A tired dog who fears an unpredictable pup. Says something to the woman beside him and she looks at me. Bonny lass, as they say around here.

She can't disguise her surprise.

Posters around town are a blemish-free version of me, as I always hide my imperfections from a camera. If she spoke, the most likely word to slip between her plumped-up lips would be, "oh". The first time today I have thought about my colourful burden.

'Stigmata,' I say, but doubt she can read my lips.

Most people start their exploration of me with my greatest weakness, the blotch on my face. Perhaps we look for flaws in people so we know how to defeat them, to win the battle of superiority and status. Is it why I dress the way I do? To distract them. Or is it a visual warning that they shouldn't take me for granted?

Sigurd and Lionel didn't seem to notice and Brian said nothing when he saw me at midnight for the first time. Lionel was probably distracted by my tits and Sigurd my apparent sense of humour. Brian seemed to stare at my clothes a lot. But she is looking at my face, not my clothes, just like all the others. I wonder if that is why I have done so well with the new men in my life, they could see beyond my most obvious imperfection.

*It is a mistake to take me, or anyone for that matter, at face value.*

There are more than fifty people here now, making a lot of noise: the heat from the fire has energised them and turned up their volume. Such a mad selection of folk.

'Cacophony,' I say.

Sigurd's Vikings huddled together near the water singing unintelligible dirges. The Lerwick ones, still in full costume, stand and watch, in awe. When they stop, Catriona and her band start up and a few folk try and dance on the beach, but it isn't that easy and some fall about laughing on the sand. The Gloria Gaynors start singing, 'I will survive,' accompanied by a smartphone, to fill in any gaps in the background music.

Lionel has been sitting on the sand alone, resisting the force of the fire, bidding the bubbling flames to retreat like King Canute. His brave face had slipped and he looked forlorn until he saw that Thomas had arrived and then he looked at me and slipped his smiley mask on again. The potential for our reunion seems to have filled him with joy. Like he wants to hug us both, to touch our skin at the same time, as if that alone will reconnect us. If Jesus had risen from the dead in front of him, he couldn't have been any happier.

(Thurisaz)

*'Protection and luck is on your side.'*

I follow Lionel's gaze as headlights announce new arrivals in the thick darkness, like meteors seen from a boat in the middle of the ocean. A minibus and two taxis have just turned up and Davey is getting out with about ten other people. Sigurd and I react at much the same time to go and greet them.

*The Pied Piper has arrived.*

'I hope you aren't expecting anyone else?' Davey says. 'I thought there'd be a few people sitting round a campfire, not a bloody jamboree.'

'Jamboree,' I say, savouring the word.

I like the way it rolls around my head. It sounds like a cake, a Victoria sponge, but smaller.

'We weren't expecting most of them,' Sigurd says.

'Yon farmer up the road has gone and lost his sense of humour. Blocked road with a tractor after us. Says he's fed up with all the noise and he's not letting anyone else down the road,' Davey says.

'Why did he let you lot through?' I say.

'He might have lost his sense of humour but not his sense of enterprise. He was happy to be persuaded with cash. I gave him a hundred of your Scottish pounds to let us through, but he was pulling a tree trunk across the road as we drove off,' Rick says.

'Looks like you're stuck, boys,' Lionel says, to the drivers.

'Aye, I need a drink anyway,' says one of the taxi drivers. 'Nice night for a party, but the first time I've got a lock-in on a beach.'

'I've brought some booze,' Rick says, as he opens the back door of the minibus to reveal several cases of wine and spirits.

'The Purser will be able to retire on the amount that lot cost,' Jock says.

'What's the point of money if you can't share it with your friends,' Rick says.

'Rick, you're an unusually generous person, for an American,' Davey says.

'Davey, thank you, please help yourself.'

Davey picks up a bottle of red burgundy.

'Is it a good one?' he says to Rick, looking at the bottle of wine.

'They only have good ones on the royal yacht,' Rick says.

'Good,' Davey says, and heads off down to the bonfire.

'You never know who you'll meet on Show Night. I don't blame the farmer. He has to put up with all the aeroplanes from the airport opposite during the day and us at night. Not surprised he's fed up,' a middle-aged woman, a local I think, says.

They carry the booze down to the make-shift bar built from a driftwood tree trunk.

'Look, a shipwreck,' Marina says, pointing out into the bay.

'Aye, *The Juanita*, a tanker used as a blockship in the Second World War, but they tried to move it to salvage it after the war and the front bit ended up here,' the same local woman says.

'Blockship? Tell me more, what is a blockship?' Marina says, to her new guide.

## (Ansuz)

*'Listen and learn, take advice.'*

A little wind came, like a whisper from heaven. It swirled around the fire and the smoke plume enveloped Kito, Sandy, and all those now sitting too close, so they had no choice but to move back. Lionel approaches Kito who is melting in the heat haze from the burning logs. When he sees him clearly again it is as if he has been conjured up out of the swirling smoke.

'Kito, it's good to see you,' Lionel says.

'We came to find Panda.'

'Oh, she's here,' Lionel says, pointing to where Panda and Sigurd are welcoming Davey in the flickering shadows at the top of the beach.

'Yes, I know. I saw her. She seems different. I've never seen her talk to so many people.'

'I think tonight has been some sort of rite of passage for her. She seems to have grown up, just like that. But I feel different too. Don't you? Something in the air tonight. It's been a funny night,' Lionel says.

'It's a bit like a dream,' Sandy says, sitting beside Kito and looking around her.

'A Last Summer Night's Dream. She seems to have fallen for young Sigurd, over there. Part of a family who are a tribute band to the Viking hordes,' Lionel says.

Kito looks down at his phone. 'We should tell the police we've found them, but I don't have a signal,' he says to Sandy.

'Them?' Lionel says.

'Yes, they are looking for both of you. Your wife reported you missing,' Kito says.

'Really? last time I talked to her she locked me out of our room.'

'Maybe she's feeling guilty about that,' Sandy says.

'Would you believe that this all started because Brian wanted company when he killed himself,' Lionel says.

'Brian?'

'Yes, him over there, dancing with that crazy woman. He is supposed to be killing himself but he seems to have gotten a bit distracted. He's not good at it.'

'What, killing himself?' Sandy says.

'Says he's too stupid. It goes wrong every time he tries.'

'Doesn't look like he wants to die at all,' Sandy says.

'Panda left a note in her diary about killing herself, at sunrise, and we were worried,' Kito says.

'I think I'd give her a cuddle and tell her you love her and that it, whatever 'it' was, wasn't her fault. Tell her what you told me the other day. Anyway, she changed her mind, or she was just winding you up, who knows what the truth is, eh?'

'You mean she *was* going to kill herself? She is so dramatic and she speaks such nonsense half the time, I don't know what to believe,' Kito says.

'Who knows? But the madness of the last few hours, and that young Viking, and that crazy old guy over there, and maybe even me, have persuaded her that life is worth living for a little longer. Oh, and there may have been a miracle so I'm hoping she's considering becoming a disciple of The Lord,' Lionel says.

'I didn't know she knew so many people,' Kito says.

'I'm not sure she did, till tonight. Brian though, he's a bit more determined. Look, he's got his barbecue set up over there, in the tent, behind that crazy Dutch guy dancing on his own.'

Sandy looks puzzled.

'It's a long story. Bloody good job we got the fire going though, or we wouldn't have the burgers. Have one, they're brilliant.'

Kito shakes his head and looks into the fire, deep in thought.

'Go talk to her,' Lionel says.

'It's not as easy as that.'

'No, it is, it really is, and she seems to be in an accommodating mood.'

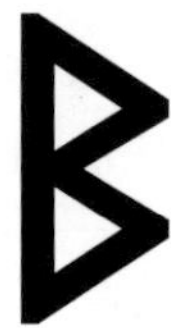

(Berkana)

*'Family, new beginnings, that will bring happiness.'*

My father is talking to Lionel who seems to be building bridges with words, and touch. Lionel sees me looking, smiles, and waves me over.

*Can we just pretend it never happened?*

Kito noticeably winces as I smile back, grab Sigurd's hand and pull him along.

'Hello,' Sigurd says, when we get there.

'Hello, I'm Sandy,' the woman with my father says rather sheepishly. As if the wrong word will detonate me and, like a mine at sea, a huge plume of water will erupt around us and scupper us like the German fleet in Scapa Flow. Or maybe it would be sand, here. She's called Sandy after all.

She seems to be expecting a monster rather than an unhappy nineteen-year-old girl.

'I'm Panda's father.'

'Good to meet you, sir,' Sigurd says.

I look at him with my surprised face.

'We're a polite family.'

'Pandora, let me introduce you to your father,' Lionel says, reaching out and touching my arm. His fingers just caressing the skin, hardly making contact. My arm involuntarily following his lead, and I raise it to shake hands.

*It's like radio control. How often is it we follow others' lead?*

I feel the warmth of his body and the chemical connection between us. Like sister atoms combining to form a familiar substance. His touch more personal and knowing than Lionel's. It reaches through into my inner being and warms my heart. A surprisingly reassuring but unstable thing, but how long before we separate into our constituent parts again? Will it be a second, or a lifetime?

It has been a long time since we have touched.

'I think you've both been hiding from each other and maybe it's about time that you got to know Kito, the real person, not the pantomime villain,' Lionel says.

'You mean Doubting Thomas?'

'No, that is another man, a figment of your wild imagination.'

'He doesn't seem to want to do anything but live in his flat fantasy world that, by definition, excludes all sensible people.'

'Have you read Flatland?' Sigurd says, in an attempt to lighten the mood.

'Is it about a flat Earth?' Kito says.

'Even madder than that, it's about a two-dimensional world where status comes with having more sides. A hexagon is higher up than a square, that sort of thing,' Sigurd says.

I am still holding my father's hand. Neither of us want to let go. Not so long ago, I was hanging over a precipice and he is now reaching out, trying to save my life.

'It's full title is *Flatland: A Romance of Many Dimensions.* It was written by a schoolteacher called Edwin Abbott Abbott in 1884. I always remember because I don't know of anyone else with a double surname,' Sigurd says.

'*A Romance of Many Dimensions*. I love that. It could be the subtitle for the last eight hours of my life,' I say.

Sandy shakes her head and I smile nervously. She seems to have gotten over the shock of my lopsided face.

'Anyway, Pandora, maybe we should talk about, well, everything?' Kito says. 'Things seem to have changed.'

'Some magic in the air, methinks. You have a new friend too,' I say.

Sandy smiles.

'Misery acquaints a man with strange bedfellows,' Lionel says.

'Even I know that's Shakespeare,' Sigurd says.

'Ah Shakespeare, you know this could be the setting for *The Tempest*. That's it, think of yourselves as being washed up on this beach after a terrible gale at sea. You've survived, now it's time to rebuild your lives, but you need to sort out a few misunderstandings first. I, Prospero, call Ariel to put a spell on you both,' Lionel says, seemingly intoxicated by all this, or touched by God, who knows.

'Life-wrecked,' Sigurd says.

'I want you to think of him as someone new, that you haven't met before; not the monster he was this morning,' Lionel says to me.

'Until now you've been under a misidentification spell. You've been in love with yourselves, rather than each other. You've forgotten who you really are,' Lionel says, to both of us.

'Are you a UN Special Envoy or something, or a missionary sent out by the Canadian government to sort out people's family problems?' I say.

'What a nice idea. It would be nice to think that all the agony I went through had some useful outcome for others,' Lionel says.

'Canada, the home of The Rockies, not rocky relationships,' I say.

'Oh, I don't know about that; my wife has locked me out of our room,' Lionel says.

'Why?' Sigurd says.

'Cowardice. I think I like helping others because I don't have the courage to face my own issues. I'm just like that cowardly lion over there when it comes to my personal problems,' he says, pointing to the Up Helly Aa gang now sitting in a ring by the fire.

'Perhaps we all are,' Sigurd says.

Lionel's face serious now, his joyful mask has slipped.

'I can't bring myself to tell Lillian that I'm struggling with growing old. I'm afraid of death and don't want an old man's life. I want what I had before. I'm afraid to tell her that I don't know how to deal with that and how my feelings have changed. Perhaps, it is easier to distance myself from her and let her believe that I don't love her anymore.'

I step forward and hug him. No one could be more surprised than me in both his words and my reaction. There is a pause and Lionel sniffs back a tear.

*It seems we are struggling with the same problem. Perhaps everyone is.*

'Kito, you'll find Panda isn't the person you were expecting either,' Lionel says to the man I used to call Thomas, over my shoulder, between sniffs, carrying on as if nothing had happened.

There is a pause. How should you respond to such candour?

'We were worried about Panda,' Sandy says to Lionel who is facing her. 'After what she wrote in her diary.'

'You read my diary?' I say, letting go of Lionel and turning to face her.

'Your father was worried and didn't know what to do, so he asked me to help,' Sandy says.

'And who are you?' Lionel says, composed again.

'Just a friend,' Sandy says.

'We don't have any friends,' I say.

'You do now,' Sigurd and Lionel say at the same time and I smile, because, they are right, I do.

'We met on Match.com,' Sandy says.

'So, your first date with my father has been spent searching for his mad suicidal daughter?' I can't help laughing at the idea of this being their first date.

'Second date,' Sandy says.

'You are a glutton for punishment,' I say automatically, but regret it straight away.

'It's hard to ignore a cry for help,' Sandy says.

'He managed to ignore all the others,' I say, then turn to Lionel and reach for his hand.

'You said he had something to hide?' Sandy says, but I ignore her.

'What others?' Sigurd says.

'Suicide, revenge sex, murder, all my little diary fantasies,' I say.

'I didn't know what to do,' Kito says, on the verge of tears and I feel sorry for him. For the first time in a long while honey flows from my compassion gland and pools around us both. Is it The Lord at work? Or St Magnus? Or, perhaps, my second wish, for reconciliation, may have come true after all.

'Contrite,' I say.

'Ditch the past, accept that the future is unknown and live for the moment,' Sigurd says.

'It's his philosophy of life,' I say.

'Sounds good to me,' Kito says.

'Me too,' says Lionel.

'Really, I have never seen any sign of it,' I say to Kito.

'I can change too,' Kito says, as if he were another man.

'Can you?' I say.

'I told your father that it was a cry for help and it was about time he helped,' Sandy says, 'that's why we are here.'

'I seem to have uncovered the hidden psychologist in all of you.'

'No, just the human beings,' Lionel says. 'So, will you give each other a chance?'

'Yes,' Kito says immediately without thinking.

'Oh, this is all a bit overwhelming, I need a drink,' I say, and pull Sigurd away, back towards the fire. It is just too much. A tear is forming deep inside me, looking for a way out.

*Disoriented.*

We walk up to the top of the beach and cross the road, where the light from the fire is stretching out to grasp the fence in front of us with its fingertips. A tiny owl is sitting on a fence post. Tengmalm's Owl, sometimes known as the funerial owl and thought of as a bird of ill omen, foretelling death with its loud screech. I look at the owl and then back down the beach to Brian's tent. He is standing beside it now, looking down at his feet and I wonder what he is thinking and if the appearance of this tiny, rare owl is a sign.

## (Sowelo)

*'Victory, health, success – relax, you can do it.'*

'That's your thirty strokes,' Hooky says to Swift Eye. 'You know there is time for just thirty oar stokes before you have to make your move?'

'Aye, I know well enough the customs of the game,' he says, before sliding a piece of Botolf The Stubborn's breastbone diagonally across the board, alongside a piece of Arni Pin-Leg's foot.

It is clear that Swift Eye is feeling the pressure. His daughter now fast asleep beside him on the floor but his sons are at his shoulder spurring him on. The game has brought them together and their proximity has distracted Swift Eye and made him late with his move.

Swift Eye looks down at his daughter, and Split, who is standing behind Hooky, speaks. 'Does she still think her life is bound to yours?'

Swift Eye is concentrating on the game but he looks up and nods.

'She hardly leaves your side.'

'What will you do with the land if you win?' Patrick says to Split.

'It will be allowed to rest,' Split says.

'What about the money you could have made? The laird has already raised a levy for a bulldozer,' Patrick says.

'This is about honour and principle; we have enough money.'

'I could do with more money.'

'Then earn if for yourself, don't steal it from your kin.'

'Didn't our ancestors steal all the time from their kin?'

'They may have, but it generally led to bloodshed,' Hooky says.

'The black and white game is better than bloodshed,' Swift Eye says, involuntarily scratching his missing eye, waiting for Hooky to move, which he does swiftly, removing his opponent's second rook from the board.

'Are you ready to concede?' Split says.

'No, there is fight in me yet.'

(Perthro)

*'Mystery, secrets, the occult – a revelation is coming.'*

# 19. INVASION

'So, you believe the earth is flat,' Siggy says, as he approaches Kito, who is now sitting alone by the fire, deep in thought.

'Do you think I'm mad like my daughter does?'

'No, not really, I actually think it's cool. It's okay to be different. I'm from a family of wannabe Vikings and they believed we all live in a tree.'

Kito looks interested enough to hear more.

'Yggdrasil – the tree of life. An eternal green ash tree that carries nine worlds on its boughs. Odin hung himself from it for nine days and nights to understand the meaning of runes, symbols that spring from the well of Erd – the source of fate. He impaled his heart with his own spear. A flat earth is comparatively sane.'

'Is that why all your guys have rune tattoos?'

'Runes aren't just a *futhark*, an alphabet, they all have inherent meaning. A means of communication between the natural and supernatural, and my family think they act as spells for protection, or success.'

'I didn't know that Vikings were so interesting.'

'Look, half my extended family would be happy to go along with you.'

'Maybe I should start a Tree of Life Tour too?'

'Go for it. Why not?'

'Well, for one thing, it infuriates my daughter and I'd like to stop annoying her.'

'I think she may be mellowing. But you might want to back-off the alchemist's stones you sell; she really is crazy about that.'

'It's my main source of income.'

'Cross your fingers and wish for a headhunter to ring.'

'I've already made my Last Summer Night wish,' Kito says.

'Aye, that storytelling guy over there was telling me that you can make a wish, or cast a spell or undo a necromancer's curse, any time until dawn on the last night of summer.'

'That's what they say,' Kito says.

'So, we didn't need the miracle.'

'What miracle?'

'Oh, just something crazy that happened earlier.'

'You seem to have cast a spell on my daughter.'

'And her on me.'

'But will all this magic last past dawn?' Kito says.

'Hope so.'

'Maybe Lionel's right, we came under someone's curse. Like Nick Bottom, we need to wake up from our dream.'

'You don't have any tall posts near your house with a horse's skull on it, do you?' Sigurd says.

'There is a pole, but no skull, why?'

'The most common way for a Viking to curse someone was by planting a scorn post. One of the Sagas has someone putting a farting curse on a family, but it can be far worse.'

'Panda doesn't like it when I fart, but I don't think that's a curse.'

'That doesn't mean you're not under someone's spell.'

A rifle bullet crack comes from the fire and they look up. One of the big roller logs from *Dreki* has split open and everyone has turned to look at it. The fire huge now, branding the night with its intensity.

'Well how do you get rid of a curse?' Kito says.

'It's normally a chant of some sort, or declaiming a verse.'

'Maybe I should cut the post down?'

'Perhaps if I just kiss your daughter again the spell will be broken and you'll both wake up.'

'Again?'

'Yes, you need to do it several times to break a really strong spell.'

'Okay, but you're not kissing me.'

'Kito, I'll leave that up to your fair lady,' Sigurd says, looking at Sandy walking towards them, eating a burger.

# I

## (Isa)

*'On hold wait for improvements.'*

Zander, the storyteller, arrived with Catriona, much to Lionel's displeasure. He set himself up at the edge of the light from the fire and told a story or two in between songs but now he has moved closer to the fire.

'Ladies and gentlemen, I am the Kirkwall storyteller,' he says.

'Self-proclaimed,' he shouts. 'I thought I'd get that in before anyone else does.'

'I should also say that I'm no traditionalist. I love stories, but never liked Chaucer, so although my stories are old, my language isn't.'

People move towards Zander and form a semi-circle, looking at the fire with the sea and moon behind him. He stands to one side so his face is side-lit and full of depth and character. He has chosen his spot carefully, to show himself off to best effect.

'Who would have thought that my biggest crowd today would be on a beach at four o'clock in the morning?' he says, modulating his voice, like a street-hawker, in order to encourage an audience to form around him.

'Gather round, I have a story to tell about a gentleman and his bride. It's based on an ancient story from North Ronaldsay, called the *Gentleman of Wastness*, but I've given it my own little twist. Like to think I've brought it up to date. Come, gather around, listen to my story, of love and sorrow, and the power of both, and the magnetic attraction of the sea you can see in front of your eyes on this wonderful night.

'Our hero was a bit like Mr Fitzwilliam Darcy. A farmer though. Rich, handsome, young, and *in possession of a good fortune* – if you forgive me for quoting Miss Austen – but did he want a wife? No, he didn't. That is until one day he spied this sweet young thing sunbathing naked on the rocks by the sea with several of her friends and family.

'When they see him, they all put on their seal coats and dive back into the sea but the young girl is a bit slower than the rest and he gets to her before she can do the same and he snatches her fine seal skin from her and walks home with it.

'If you look out to sea where the moon is lighting the water you may see a few seal-folk, Selkies, watching us right now. I think I heard them barking at the moon just then. Some say that there are as many Orcadians under the sea as there on the land. They like to keep an eye on things. Well, anyway, the girl had to follow him, naked as the day she was born, and she cried so loudly it disturbed the beasts on the ground and the birds in the air and the folk in the sea, who all cried, together.

'But our Mr D'Arcy was a hard-hearted man and led her home. He could not bring himself to give her back her coat because in an instant he had fallen hopelessly in love with this beautiful creature.

He told her that she had to stay and that she would be his wife. What all the other women of the island of North Ronaldsay couldn't do, this seal-woman had done. Of course, she had no choice. She had to stay and eventually she agreed to be his bride.'

## ᚢ

## (Uruz)

*'Strength and good health, your wish will come true.'*

'Do you remember when I told you the story about the selkie bride, when you were small?' my father says.

Sitting together on the sand, in semi-dark. Pulled me away from the storyteller as he started to speak and led me by the hand and for once I followed him. Can now only hear that Zander is talking, not what he is saying.

I feel nervous about being alone with him, but Siggy told me I should, and I have grown to trust him. Perhaps all philosophers are wise. Lionel said that it was important too, that he had something to tell me and I should give him a break. So, here I am with my feet in the energetic surf, twinkling with ice crystals of moonlight that are tickling my toes, the water alive with silvery eels.

'Turbidity,' I say.

'Do you remember?' Kito says, looking towards Zander and his audience.

I nod, remembering the stories he used to tell me when I was a child.

'I think I owe you an apology,' he says.

'That's right. Probably more than one,' I say, a little surprised at what he is saying, but don't want to show it.

'I apologise for doing all the things that have made you hate me. I was doing what I thought was best. I apologise for bringing you here, I know you hate it and it was wrong to wrench you away from your friends. I apologise for not making it clear to you that what happened to your mother had nothing to do with you. It isn't your fault that we lost her. It was in her nature, she didn't have any real choice but to do what she did. If anyone is to blame it is me, for not being a better husband, a better father, a better man, or a better person, or whatever it was I should have been doing to stop it. It had nothing to do with clothing, it had everything to do with her.'

This is not my father talking. Perhaps Kirkwall *has* been invaded by Martians tonight and they are taking over everyone's bodies.

'Is that it?' I say, embarrassed, hearing him speak like this.

'No, not really. I also want to apologise for all the flat earth stuff, and the stones. I haven't handled it well and I think I have been a little mad.'

'You're bonkers and you put me on medication. You don't have to take pills like me.'

'If there was a pill for it, I'd happily have taken it.'

'I've thrown mine away.'

'Perhaps that's for the best.'

'After all the sermons you've given me about my medication?'

'I don't think drugs, or chanting, or science for that matter can help either of us. We are just lonely sparks of life trying to make sense of it all and sometimes there is no sense,' Kito says.

'I think that too, now.'

'Lionel tells me you have discovered hope.'

*I think he's right. My life was grey and hopeless until tonight but now I have discovered a new, more colourful world.*

'I don't know what it is, but something has changed,' I say. 'I'm even thinking of getting rid of Mummy's statues in our field.'

'Sandy said I should smash them up, but I told her you won't like that.'

'I'm going to bury them. It's probably time she returned to the soil.'

Kito looks relieved, as if I have finally said the right thing.

'I think I'm in love,' I say.

A question mark on his face.

'Siggy.'

'You've only just met him.'

'True, but I hope it's love.'

'I loved your mother and I love you too. And it makes me unhappy to think that you hate me.'

'I was angry and lost, and thought it was your fault.'

'I was lost too.'

'Why did she go?'

'I don't know. She sent me a postcard a month or so later to say she wanted to start a new life, on her own, and not to try and find her. She didn't have any family and I never knew her friends, so couldn't really search for her.'

'Did you tell the police?'

'No, not after I got the postcard. In a way it didn't surprise me. I always knew she was capable of doing extraordinary things.'

'Maybe she was ill?'

'I would have tried harder to find her if I thought that. I think she was just bored. She had a low threshold for boredom.'

'It's hard to accept that she is gone, even now, at my age. I think that is what upsets me. It follows me round like a stray dog, the guilt.'

'You don't have anything to feel guilty about. It was her, not you. Perhaps it was my fault, but not yours. In her own odd way she loved you.'

'Really?'

Kito nodded and held my hand.

'I think she thought that her job was done. That you could stand on your own two feet and didn't need a mother anymore. She wanted more excitement than family life could give her.'

'I was a child.'

'We are still here and maybe it's time to move on. Do you want to go back to England?' Kito says, shaking his head as if what happened is still a mystery to him too.

'Really?'

'Yes, why not?'

I look around the beach, at the confusion of humanity we have brought together tonight. Some in old clothes, fancy dress, most of them I have never seen before. Like they were apparitions, inhabitants of some other, past life, or perhaps people I could become. Up Helly Aa Dorothy, wearing shiny red boots is on her own in front of us. As I watch, the ginger-haired man dressed in a blue-and-white gingham dress, with a wig and ribbons in his ponytails, taps his ruby slippers together three times and falls backwards onto the sand, laughing.

'There is no place, like home,' I say.

'Where's that?'

'After tonight, I think it might be here,' I say.

Kito laughs, my animosity towards him now gone; I laugh too.

'Oh my God', Kito says, looking out to sea. A Viking longship, silhouetted against the growing blood moon, is coming around the headland and sailing into the bay. Men at both bow and stern with lighted torches. Split at the helm carrying a sword, or at least from here it looks like a sword, and Hooky at the bow. A small group of others, including Swift Eye, in the centre of the boat. A rather beautiful, awe-inspiring, sight.

*'Dreki.'*

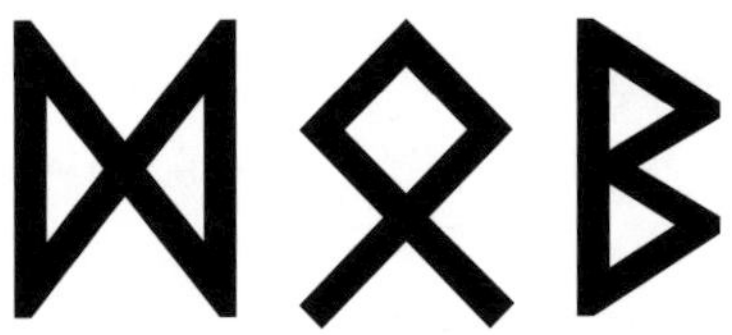

(Dagaz. Othala. Berkana)

*'Dawning of a new day – slow and steady growth and progress. Things you have or will acquire, or inherited. Family, new beginnings, that will bring happiness.'*

# 20. BEACHED AS

Sigurd joins us as we move back to give *Dreki* room to run aground. Hooky at the bow, his arm wrapped around the dragon head's golden mane and smiling down at us as the prow ploughs into the soft sand at the water's edge and the engine of war comes to a halt.

'How will they get it off?' I say.

'Don't worry, the tide is coming in,' Sigurd says.

Split now standing beside Hooky.

'We need you, son. Hooky won the black and white game. He won our share of the land back, but the oath has to be pledged before sunrise,' Split says.

'Isn't this a bit dramatic, couldn't you have called?' I say.

'Too dramatic for you? Really?' Sigurd says, laughing.

'No phone signal, you took all the cars, no taxis, and they say the road is blocked anyway,' Hooky says.

'Yes, good job we had *Dreki*. Anyway, what's the party in aid of?' Split says.

'Hope,' I say.

Sigurd doesn't say anything, he just looks at me and his father raises his eyebrows. His uncle laughs.

'We have a deal with Swift Eye, as long as you can still recite the oath I taught you. Can you?' Split says.

'What, now?' Sigurd says.

'Yes, and it should really be on-board, on our own territory. Get up here.'

'Dominion,' I say, but no one hears.

Split leans down and helps his son up onto the bow. People from around the fire have come down to see what is going on. The Up Helly Aa Vikings, still dressed in their costumes, shaking their heads. Amazed at the longship because the ones they build and burn each year in Lerwick don't have a bottom; they aren't designed to float, just to make an impressive bonfire.

Probably think they're dreaming.

## (Hagalaz)

*'Unexpected disruptions, limitations and delays'.*

'That's as close as I can get. Bobby blocked off the road again. He does it when people rediscover that it's good fun to party on the beach,' Tommy, their driver, says.

'How far is it to walk?' Lillian says, as she has found her way here too, sharing the taxi with Ewan and his mum.

'Oh, no distance. A mile, maybes. No more.'

'Aye, no distance at all,' Ewan says, getting out of the taxi just as the Lady of The Mists, still wearing a white wedding dress, drifts by on her white horse.

'Everyone's being drawn here tonight. Must be the apocalypse. Or maybe you'll see the second coming of the Lord,' Maggie, the lady on the horse says, walking past them.

'Should be a good night then,' Tommy says.

'Night? It's nearly time for breakfast,' Lillian says.

'Aye, well, have a nice breakfast then,' Tommy says.

Ahead of them the Lady of the Mists stops and turns around before walking her horse back.

'Hi Muriel,' Maggie says.

'Room for one more on Bess,' she says, looking at Ewan, who smiles at his mother and then jumps up onto the back of the horse and wraps his arm around her waist.

'Bloody hell, isn't she old enough to be his mother?' Lillian says quietly to Muriel, then laughs.

'What's so funny?' Maggie says.

'It's not just men then. That want young partners,' Lillian says.

'Never thought of Ewan as a toyboy,' Maggie says.

'My husband is addicted to staring at young girls,' Lillian says, thoughtfully. Her comments creating a space for reflection, as if personal revelation should be given time to echo to test its quality, like cut glass.

'Does he touch them?' Muriel says.

'I don't think so, unless undressing them in his head counts.'

'My husband was ten years younger than me,' Maggie says, turning the horse away and moving off slowly.

'Lionel's one week older than me.'

'Oh my God,' Muriel says, as she watches her son ride off with Maggie.

'What?' Lillian says.

'My runes said that Ewan would meet his match tonight and find true love.'

'Golly,' Lillian says. 'You really believe in that stuff?'

Ewan and the Lady of the Mists head down the lane towards the beach.

'Bye, Ma, see you later,' Ewan shouts out, waving back at her.

'Tommy, it looks like I'm staying too. Need to keep an eye on him.'

'Okay, enjoy yourselves. I'm off to my bed,' Tommy says, turning the taxi around and leaving Muriel and Lillian standing in a puddle of moonlight.

They follow in the horse's hoof prints down the slope towards the shore, together.

'Aye, I do actually,' Muriel says,' believe in what the runes foretell. I do, more and more each year.'

(Fehu)

*'Success, attainment, prosperity.'*

'Are you the captain?' Johnno says to Split, now standing on the beach beside *Dreki,* holding the bow rope, even though the longship is firmly stuck in the sand. Reminds me of the Festival of the Horse on South Ronaldsay, where young boys plough the sand and lead the girls dressed as plough horses by reins.

'Am I?' Split looks around and shrugs his shoulders. 'I suppose I am, but I think of myself as more of a jarl.'

'Is it true that ships' captains can marry people?'

All of the blackening crew laugh, including Fran and Alice, standing side-by-side and arm-in-arm behind Johnno.

'Johnno, that is a lovely idea,' Jenny, standing beside him, says.

'Maybe we can have a double wedding,' Alice says, looking at Fran.

'No, really, can you marry us?' Johnno says to Split.

Everyone is now looking at Split.

'I'm serious, will you?'

Split shrugs again and says, 'Why not? But first we have some unfinished business. Siggy, you must recite the oath and Swift Eye, you and your family have agreed that if it is a true oath, in keeping with family tradition, the land by the water will be allowed to rest again.'

'It should be known by everyone here that in keeping with family tradition, I agree to this,' Swift Eye says.

'Good job too. I'm not sure Kirkwall is really ready for all those executive homes,' I say.

Siggy jumps up on *Dreki*'s bow. He looks wonderful with his face lit up by the flames on either side of him. Behind him, the moon still bright though now noticeably drifting down towards the horizon. The soft sea washes around *Dreki*'s hull, announcing the incoming tide.

*Our ancestors watch*
*over blood-drenched land,*
*where rock throw, and*
*keel-carved tracks,*
*stake Claim.*

*The round-topped mound,*
*Dagger-sharp rocks,*
*skerries furred with death-black sheep,*
*bound the family land.*
*Twice split by death.*

*The youngest son must have*
*half the land towards the blood red sun,*
*whose nightly dive into the western sea*
*clean washes ill deeds away.*

*This is my everlasting claim.*

'Is the oath, true?' Split says, and Swift Eye nods his assent. All the Vikings clap and cheer. Not just Split's men, but Swift Eye's too, as if this has been the right outcome for everyone. Although they might be Vikings, no one really seems up for a fight.

Catriona and her band start up again and a few go back to the comfort of the fire, but most don't. They stay with Johnno, Jenny, Fran and Alice, the wedding party, and their guests, assembled at the edge of the sea.

'Okay, now then, let's get married,' Johnno says.

'It's a good day to get married,' Zander says. 'A couple should be married with the moon growing and the tide flowing. To marry during the wane of the moon is regarded as unlucky, and the couple would be sure to remain childless,' he says, looking up at the waxing moon.

'Will you be our witnesses?' Jenny says to me and Siggy.

It is so romantic. I smile and nod and pull Sigurd towards them.

'Who would have thought that we'd be doing this a few hours ago?' I say.

'Who would have thought I'd be marrying this one.'

'Oh, no,' someone says behind me, and I turn to see Ewan walking past naked and erect, marching into the sea.

'Bloody hell. Is he with you?' Hooky says.

'It's just a man,' Ewan's mother says. 'Just a man in state of arousal. Not much new in that, is there? Natural really. Anyway, I can't stop him. He is compelled to make love to the oceans.'

'Just ignore him,' I say, as the wedding party clamber back up onto *Dreki*, gently rolling and twisting with the small waves now being pushed up the beach by the moon.

## (Kenaz Reversed)

*'An ending or loss.'*

Further up the beach, Davey's party are watching from the relative comfort of the fire.

'Rick. I've never had much time for Americans. But you, you have changed my mind. You're a kind man. You didn't buy Land's End, did you?' Davey says.

'It's easy to be kind when you've got money,' Rick says.

'Most people I have come across with money have been stuck up and mean. Seem to think they were better than everyone else just because they had cash.'

Rick puts his hand on Davey's shoulder.

'I'm tired now,' Davey says. 'Tonight I feel young again. I cried earlier; I've even been laughing with Jock here about all this madness. I'm excited because, I feel real joy that the young girly over here, Dora, that she has chosen to live rather than give up on all this. Until tonight I thought that my heart had shrivelled, and I had no feelings left.'

'Joy can only come from the heart, Davey. It proves you have a heart still and I think you've had it all along. You just didn't realise it. You're a good man, Davey,' Marina says.

Davey yawns and Rick notices.

'I was tired earlier but I've got a second wind,' Rick says.

'All this emotion can be tiring for a young-at-heart man like you, Davey. Why not take a blanket and have a rest?' Lynette says, holding Rick's hand.

'Aye, I might just do that. Last time I slept on a beach was during the Korean War, but then we had men trying to kill us. Didn't dare go to sleep in case we didn't wake up again,' Davey says.

Rick shakes his head and smiles.

'Aye, I've had a long life and I've seen a lot,' Davey says.

'It sounds like you have had a fine life, Davey. I'm envious,' Rick says.

'Really?'

'In many ways, yes,' Rick says.

'That sounds like a testimonial,' Marina says.

Rick nods his agreement to this.

'Well, I'm thinking that old age is the greatest success a man can have, and it don't matter how you pass your time, just make sure you have a long life and do a lot,' Davey says.

'Well, you've done that all right,' Rick says.

'Yes, yes, I have,' Davey says, as he walks over to a pile of blankets from the royal yacht and picks one up before sliding into the nearest shadow doorway, to find peace, and escape the noise and the people.

'I'll just have a short nap. Say goodnight to Dora for me,' he says, looking down the beach towards Panda.

'Good night, Davey MacDonald,' he says to himself, in a hollow in the sand, out of the gentle wind from the sea. He takes a deep breath of ozone as he closes his eyes and has never felt more alive. His invigorated heart beating in tune with the pulse of the universe floating high above his head.

'Good night, Davey MacDonald,' he says again. He has said this to himself every night now since his dear wife Sarah died.

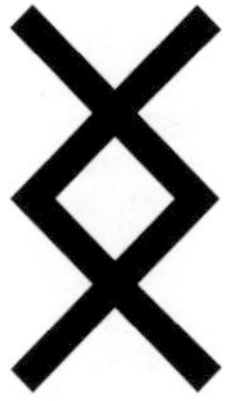

(Inguz)

*'All loose ends tied up, so free to move on.'*

It only took a few minutes to decorate Jenny, and Alice her bridesmaid, with an assortment of borrowed clothes, seaweed and colourful fishing rope from the beach. The band then lead them Pied-Piper-ishly down the beach again, followed by their congregation, to gather in the surf. Both girls have Strandby, and Dead Men's Bells, in their hair, which Panda gathered from the shingle as they were getting ready. The wedding has drawn a crowd and only Lionel and Lillian are now left by the fire, staring into the flames.

'I met a charming young man today; he took me on a walking tour of the past Millennium,' Lillian says, looking at Zander on the other side of the fire.

Lionel follows her gaze and then looks back at his wife.

'Was it good?' Lionel says, following her eyes back to Zander who notices them and smiles.

'Interesting and exciting. I think that's why I got so touchy about the girl in the bar. Anyway, I see you have found a new musical friend.'

'Catriona, yes, she's nice, but she's not my wife.'

Lillian stares into his eyes, as if she can see into his mind.

'Why are you telling me about story-boy?'

'I think I've been a bit hard on you.'

'It's been a revelatory night for all of us and it occurred to me earlier that I haven't been very nice to you lately. Bringing you here, for one thing. I deserve all I get.'

Lillian looks past him to the wedding party on the strandline, as if she was looking back in time.

'I've been a coward. Too afraid to talk to you about how I feel,' Lionel says.

'I've always thought of you as being a very brave man.'

'With some things maybe, but not this,' Lionel says, smoothing the sand beside him with his hand.

Lillian waits for him to gather his thoughts and continue.

'I feel like I'm hurtling towards my death and it's too soon. I want to go back, recapture my youth.'

'Are you bored with me?' Lilian says, her gentle voice caressing him.

'I don't know. I'm scared. I've lost any courage I used to have. I've never dealt with this sort of thing before.'

Lillian asks with her eyes.

'Feeling I haven't done enough, and it's soon all going to be over. Mostly, not being able to tell you how I feel.'

'How do you feel?'

'Scared and confused and lonely,' Lionel says.

'I think it may be normal. Fear of the ultimate journey, which you can only take alone. Perhaps we all start to withdraw into ourselves as we age. Do you know how the week before one of our trips, it's like we are mentally preparing to leave? You start the journey before you start the journey, if you know what I mean. I think it's like that.'

'I'm sorry,' Lionel says.

'It's okay. I understand, but it doesn't make you a coward. It's actually very brave of you to tell me. A lot of men would just let it fester. You know I've always been turned on by your mind. I think you camouflage your courage with wisdom.'

Lionel shakes his head.

'You have plenty courage, for both of us. I've relied on that throughout our marriage. You just need reminding,' Lillian says.

She takes the star-shaped gold locket she is wearing and puts it around Lionel's neck. 'Here, take this. I award you the Star of Courage.'

'I gave you that for our 18th anniversary, it's 18 carat gold.'

'It was the first time you ever told me you loved me,' Lillian says.

'Incredible cowardice. To take so long.'

'Brave to do it. Could have never said it.'

'I still love you,' Lionel says.

'I love you too.'

'I'm giving this back to you, to remind you of how brave you are,' she says, touching the locket on his chest.

Lionel shrugs.

'We have always been honest with each other. Haven't we?' Lillian says.

'Yes, I think so.'

'Well, I like that. It's the foundation on which any relationship has to be built, even for oldies like us.'

'Kito doesn't think that anyone ever tells the truth about anything,' Lionel says.

'He might be right, but we tell more than most.'

'Sorry, for bringing you here.'

'Don't be. I like it here. It's shook me up, brought me to my senses. It's raw and tender at the same time, and I met a guy by the fire who told me it was part of Norway. Brian, that's it, he said it was his first time in Norway, so maybe we can claim our last pin after all?'

'Yes, this is Brian's first time in Norway. Until now he has hardly ever left Leeds.'

'Tonight has been wonderful, it has helped us to talk again,' Lillian says.

'Yes, it's a miraculous place.'

'Look at us, on a beach at four in the morning with a load of drunk Vikings, complete with longship, a puzzle of cross-dressing Gloria Gaynors, all carrying their high-heeled shoes, and the cast of the Wizard of Oz. Maybe Orkney has the power to put a little magic back into anyone's life.'

Lillian reaches for Lionel's hand and pulls him up off the sand and leads him across the beach into the darkness, picking up a blanket from beside the fire as they go.

(Berkana)

*'A fresh start.'*

'This is my first wedding, 'Split says. 'So, I'm going to keep it pretty short. Tell me your names.'

'Wait, I'm serious about the double wedding,' Alice says, pulling Fran forward to join in the ceremony.

'Why not? In for a raven penny, in for a dragon pound, as mother used to say,' Split says, giggling to himself.

'Come, stand side-by-side and it should make this easier,' Split says. 'Pass me the bow rope.'

One of the Vikings uncoils a rope on *Dreki* and brings one end of it to Split. There are wolf-whistles from some of the Vikings as the marriage party expands in front of their eyes.

Holding hands, both couples stand in front of Split. Torch bearers on either side; the backdrop, the folded sail. Split takes the rope and loosely ties their hands together and holds them aloft.

'This is handfasting, it is how I got married, but not with such a big rope,' he says. 'Someone will have to fill in the names at the right moment.'

'Do you…' Split says, pausing for the name.

'Jonathon,' Alice says.

'Do you, Jonathon, take…'

'Jennifer,' Fran says.

'Jonathon, do you take Jennifer to be your wife?'

'I do,' Johnno says proudly and loudly.

'Do you, Jennifer, take Jonathon to be your husband?'

'I do.'

Split then repeats the ceremony for Alice and Fran.

'I do,' they say, in turn.

'In my capacity as jarl, I proclaim that you two couples are now bound to serve each other as you would your lord. To live life to the full and to be happy. I announce to those present with this simple oath that you are both now husband and wife.'

Split then makes this verse:

*Axe smashed skull,*
*or sinking into the deep.*
*Poison, fire, or curse,*
*life is bitter-sweet*
*and short.*

*Man cannot live without,*
*the touch of a maid,*
*the heart of a maid,*
*the arms of a maid.*

*Bring forth heirs,*
*fighting strong boys.*
*Banner high*
*and flashing axe.*

*Enjoy each other and this vibrant life*
*while you can.*

Everyone cheers.

# DRESSING UP

*You are sitting under a tree wearing the fur coat. In hiding. You see Mummy staring out of the kitchen window and there is the smell of bacon. She is cooking bacon, your favourite. She stops what she is doing and slips from the window and opens the back door and walks quickly across the grass towards you. She is swelling up like a balloon the closer she gets. She is a giant now beside you. She looks angry. As if you have done something wrong. You think the wide collar of the coat will hide you, but it doesn't. It seems to have made you even more seeable. 'I used to wear this all the time once,' you hear her say and she takes it from you and puts it on and Mummy disappears. The bacon smell from the kitchen follows her; her normal fragrance, of mimosa, gone.*

# DEAR EDITH, 4

'Botanic garden used to be up there,' Zander said, pointing to a thin passageway and I swear I could see a palm tree poking out between two buildings. The landscape here is mostly devoid of trees. We're above the tree line at sea level. The wind. But in Kirkwall trees hide behind houses. If they can keep out of the scary winter wind they can survive. They have this crazy one on Albert Street. We walked right by it.

'And over there lived a lady who wrote the classics *Delphi* and *Self Control*.'

'Self-Control? Did people need to be told how to control themselves?' I said.

'Well, they were different times. The Church was strong and you got punished for breaking the Commandments,' Zander said.

'Let me guess, Do Not Covet Tourists' Wives.'

'More like, Do Not Commit Adultery, or have sex out of wedlock, unless it was the Lambhas Fair, held behind us, on Church Green.'

I looked back and it was still going on somewhere amongst the rest of history.

'During the Lambhas Fair they had an idea of being Lambhas Brother and Sister for the duration of the fair and then anything went, but at other times you got punished. Just like the lady I said was tied to the Mercat Cross as we walked by.'

'Did you see it too?' I said, as I had seen someone there. I thought it was a girl getting married. They do that here too.

'I told you about it as we walked by,' he said.

'You did a good job,' I said, because I could see it clearly.

'The note tied to her neck said she was an adulteress. She must have been poor. The rich could get away with anything.'

'Not much has changed then. Do you realise most of your stories have involved sex in some way?'

'Maybe that's because most of life involves sex in some way.'

There were a group of men ahead of us with swords, talking loudly, surrounded by tourists watching. It looked like street theatre.

'They're re-enacting Captain Moodie's murder,' Zander said. 'It actually happened back on Broad Street, at Bailie Fea's Gate, but they do it here for some reason.

'Two men were attacking two others, one being the Captain – he was wearing a uniform to make it clear who he was – with sticks and then with swords, but the gallant old Captain seemed to be able to hold his own. A furious man called Burray ordered this servant to shoot the Captain but the first shot missed and hit an on-looker, who screamed as the bullet creased his belly. Then Burray called out, "Fire again, the damned Hanoverian has more lives than a cat." The Captain fell to the ground dead and everyone clapped.

'The murderers went on to join Bonnie Prince Charlie, but one died at Culloden – the only Orcadian there, as it happens – and the other died in a London jail,' Zander said.

We passed the street theatre and Zander stopped to point out two houses, one on either side of the street.

'*Hell* and *Purgatory*,' he said. 'It's what the houses used to be called.'

Further down the street there were a line of beggars standing holding bowls in their hands, just like you see in poor countries. It came as a bit of a surprise to see them here.

'They come from the St Olaf Poorhouse. They are only allowed out to beg on Saturdays, but I'm surprised they let them out on Show Day.'

I smiled at the poor people as we walked by and gave a young girl ten pounds.

'Have your read *The Barchester Chronicles?*' Zander said.

I shook my head.

'I've always imagined it a bit like that here with some churchmen amassing immense wealth. They had one called Bishop Dick here, who was reputed to have discovered the Philosopher's stone. They say he made all his money from usury.'

'What's that?'

'Lending money at exorbitant interest.'

'Like credit card companies.'

Zander walked on and I followed, like I was in a trance, to the end of Bridge Street. 'This is where I live,' he said looking up at the window of a first floor flat above a shop.

'Oh.'

'Do you want to come up?'

'No.'

He smiled and then reached down and gently touched my hand and coaxed me towards the blue painted door between the shops.

It was then that I made what may well be the worst decision of my life, but I am NOT going to tell you what it was.

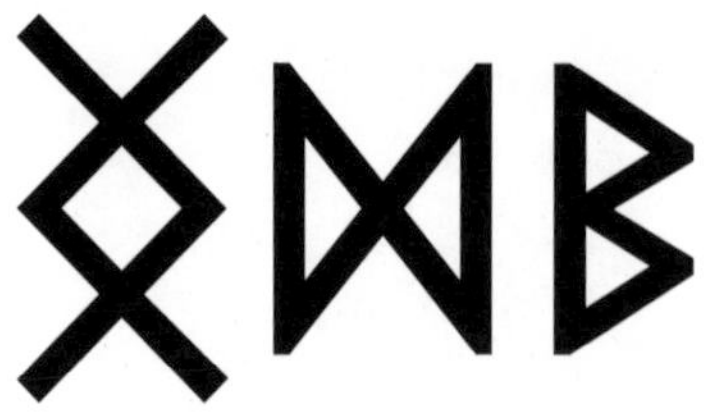

(Inguz. Daguz. Berkana)

*'All loose ends tied up, so free to move on. Dawning of a new day – slow and steady growth and progress. New beginnings that will bring happiness.'*

# 21. RECONNECTION

Sitting beside Kito, on *Dreki*. Everyone else has gone back to the fire. He lingered after the weddings so I have lingered too. I am hopeful that by not dying tonight, by not killing myself, I can find happiness. I also know that I need to forgive him. I need to forgive him for things he hasn't really done. I need to forgive him for being human. Lionel is right, I need to forgive myself too.

Out of the corner of my eye I notice Ewan standing in the surf. His shadow facing out to sea. He is masturbating and spreading his seed into the ocean.

'I can see why his mother doesn't let him out any other night of the year,' I say.

'Yes, rather odd, isn't it, but it's not the main reason he is not allowed out. In spite of all that he's a magnet for the ladies and there are a few disgruntled husbands with a score to settle,' Kito says.

'Really?'

'Some say his father was a selkie, a shape-shifter who can switch between human and seal form, and that is why he is so drawn to the water.'

'Like the Goodman's wife?'

Kito nods and watches as Ewan walks back up the beach to the Lady of the Mists who is feeding her horse.

'You used to tell me lots of Orkney folk tales, even before we came here.'

'I bought a book before you were born with a mind to read them to my children. Long time before you were even thought of.'

'Perhaps it was the stories that drew us here. They were good stories for a child,' I say.

'Yes, you liked them once, until they got too close to home.'

'What was it about the fur coat?'

'I don't know. A trigger, I suppose. It made her remember how things used to be, and being married was just not what she wanted anymore.'

'Nostalgia.'

'Yes, but stronger.'

'Remorse,' I say.

'I think she felt trapped.'

'But she just left us. Do you know how that feels? For your mother to just get up and go and never get in touch again.'

'It wasn't your fault. It was just something in her. Some perversion. A loose wire, or a short circuit in her character.'

'Do you think she is still alive?'

'I do. I don't know why, because I never heard from her again, but I think I'd know if she had died,' Kito says.

'Did you know that I was still alive?'

'I hoped.'

'Sorry.'

'It's okay. Really, in a way I understand,' he says, sliding his arm around my shoulder for the first time in years and holding me tight, so I don't slip the bounds of gravity and fall up into outer space again.

'I don't.'

Zander's tale is still lingering in the air, or maybe this conversation is bringing it back and I can hear it in my head as I sit here with my father. In my head, I have connected my mother's leaving with the Goodman story. It helped explain something that was otherwise inexplicable.

*'The Goodman and his selkie bride lived happily, just like in all fairy tales and they had a fine daughter. One day, the Goodman went out hunting and left his wife and family at home alone. As soon as he left the property his wife started searching the farm. She looked everywhere and when she came to the barn she spotted her daughter watching her.*

*'What are you looking for, Mummy?'*

*'An old fur coat,' her mother said.*

*'I know where it is,' the young girl said, and she took her mother by the hand and led her to the back of the barn, and behind a wooden post was a concealed shelf and at the back of it was a brown paper parcel. Her mother unwrapped it and found the seal skin she had longed for all these years.*

*She kissed her daughter and ran off towards the beach. When she got there, she put on her skin and dived into the sea and was soon reunited with her other family and her husband from the sea.*

*That evening the Goodman went to look for her and saw her head bobbing up and down just beyond the line of surf.*

*'I'd loved you well enough, Kito,'* I thought I heard Zander say she said. *'But I loved my other life and my other man more.' And with that she ducked below the waves and was gone, only to be seen in the distance, whenever her daughter walked along the shore.*

'Do you think Mummy could be in the ocean?' I say, after a long silence.

'I don't know where she is, but I'm sure she'd hope that we could find a way to move on and build a better life.'

'Hope, again?'

Kito nods and smiles.

'Lionel told me to believe in hope, so let's hope we can.'

'I think we can.'

## (Tiewaz Reversed)

*'Lack of fidelity in friendships and relationships.'*

'Fight, fight,' a woman's voice from up by the fire. A group of men grab hold of Rex and one of the Shetland Vikings and pull them apart. The incident like a crackling log: loud and surprising, but over as soon as it began. From the longship we can see the light from the fire spreading wide and tall, rising up to blister the few passing clouds. Band still playing and everyone dancing on the sand, hooting and screaming in unison. Smell of cooking food in the air is slowly wafting down the beach towards the water, like a tidal eddy in the air, pushing the stern of the long ship off the beach so it is floating again.

The blackening gang are united in drink and Ewan is getting dressed, with his mother's help. The Lady of The Mists, still on her horse, watching them. The Vikings swaying together and humming to themselves something old and deep. Lillian and Lionel arm-in-arm in the middle of it all, surrounded by a gaggle of people I don't know talking to our neighbour, Alex. Out of the midst of them all Martin comes walking down the beach towards us, like an emissary from another tribe.

Behind her, at the top of the beach by the fire, the woman I now know as Gladys, but until tonight only knew as The Fortune Telling Lady, is talking to a young woman I don't know at all. They seem to be arguing and then the woman turns away and the girl tries to hold her back but without success.

The older woman then walks in front of the fire to a group of locals who have congregated together, like flotsam in mid-ocean, and she approaches a tall, thin man. When she gets his attention, she slaps him on the face and shouts at him. All I hear are the words, 'Leave her alone, you bastard.' He reacts as if he is going to hit her, but the other men stop him and hold him back as the woman says something to them which I can't hear, then she turns and walks away.

Whatever she has said has an immediate effect. The group fly apart as if the surface tension of their friendship has broken in an instant, with one word. It is like The Fortune Telling Lady's words are magic and they cast an immediate spell. The man is left standing on his own, looking across at the young woman, now in tears, surrounded by her friends.

Gladys introduced herself earlier and told me about her premonitions of the young girl being abused by her father and she asked if it was me. If it was Kito who had abused me.

'Did my father sexually abuse me? No, he didn't, though I accused him of it at times.' There were times, just times when I am in a certain mood, when I am capable of accusing him of anything. Anything that will hurt him. He was just in the wrong place at the wrong time: close to me. 'His abuse, such as it was, was nothing like that,' I said.

Gladys looked disappointed, that her instinct had led her nowhere. She looked up and sniffed the air as if mine had been the strongest scent, but there were other trails to follow and like a bloodhound it seems to have led her to the real abuser. He looks just like any other man. Or is she just another unhappy child, like me, trying to hit out and inflict damage on her father?

My attention is broken by Martin's arrival, out of breath and drunk.

'Hello there. This your dad?' Martin says. Kito is standing beside me watching the proceedings.

'Yes, Martin, this is Kito.'

'Martin?' My father says.

'Yes, Martin, I used to be called Cathleen, but I have decided that I am now a man,' she says, giggling. 'These days that is all that is required, it seems, just say you're a man and you're a man.'

'Hello, Martin,' he says.

Martin leans closer to me and whispers, 'My big boss is here.'

'Where?'

Martin nods towards Jenny and Johnno arm-in-arm looking out to sea.

'Johnno? He's the head of your drug cartel?' I say, a little too loudly, and Kito hears and looks concerned.

'Shush!' Martin says, giggling.

'He's not all that he seems,' she says, in a low voice.

'Evidently. Poor Jenny,' I say.

'She'll know. What harm is he doing? I think he might make a good husband, if he can stay out of jail. Have plenty of money too.'

I shake my head and laugh. I didn't see that coming.

'He's good with babies too,' Martin says, squinting and looking Kito up and down.

'I've never heard a good word about you, Kito, but I don't think anyone can be that bad,' Martin says.

'Well, thank you for that vote of confidence.'

'You think the earth is flat, right?'

'Only sometimes.'

'Stop it. It doesn't help. I keep telling your lovely daughter to get over it.'

'We've had some counselling, or at least I have, and we are trying for a period of reconciliation,' I say.

'Bloody hell. Last Summer Night magic, eh? My gran says that whatever you wish for on last summer night will come true,' Martin says.

'I can vouch for that,' Kito says.

'What about your other plans?' Martin says.

'Oh, I've thought better of it. I've discovered Hope,' I say.

'Hope is the thing with feathers that perches in the soul – and sings the tunes without the words – and never stops at all,' Martin says.

'Who said that?' I say.

'Emily Dickinson,' Kito says.

'Love it,' I say.

'So, no suicide then?' Martin says.

'You know about that?' Kito says.

'Didn't want her to go, but she's a girl who knows her own mind.'

'No suicide,' I say, remembering Brian. 'Shit, where's Brian?'

On the left of the fire, Brian's tent is smouldering gently in the soft light from the bonfire. A thin veil of hot air is leaking out, like it is a mirage.

'Jesus,' I shout as I run up the beach.

# BEFORE

*You look around and she is there: Mummy.*

*You have thought of it as a game: Peek a Boo. You turn and she is there. You turn and she is there, even if you turn quickly and unexpectedly to try and catch her out. You turn and she is there: in the kitchen, in the bedroom, in the garden, in the shop, in the car. Then one day, you turn and she is gone. It is as if you have been born again into a different world, where Mummies don't exist.*

(Dagaz. Inguz. Fehu)

*'Dawning of a new day. All loose ends tied up so free to move on. Success, attainment, prosperity.'*

# 22. BEACH VOLCANO

Sigurd arrives at the tent first, to find Brian lying outstretched at the back, buried in a shallow grave of loamy shadow. It is stuffy and warm inside and the air has a sweet, metallic taste. The charcoal burner is in the way, so he grabs it and begins to drag it before throwing it out of the tent. His hands singed and shaking from the searing heat. The burner sinks into the sand and red-hot clinker tumbles out, sparking like fireflies, as if the tent is a tropical volcano, erupting on this lonely Orkney beach. The scoria hits Lillian's bare feet and she screams.

'Oh, no,' I say, pushing past others drawn there by Sigurd's desperate run and Lillian's scream. Crouching low, at the front, I am the kernel of a swelling nut of spectators. As my eyes become accustomed to the half-light, I can see that Brian's lips are bigger than usual and cherry-red. His body just sand sculpture now; Brian has gone.

'Bloody hell,' Luuk says behind me, when he realises what has happened in his tent.

'Carbon monoxide poisoning,' Catriona says, speaking in a respectful tone, as if she is familiar with the disturbance that death brings to the living. Sigurd is now sitting, slumped, on the sand beside Brian, holding his hands out in front of him, palms up; there are tears on his cheek. The fire is crackling in the background, and the sea is licking the shore like a dog its master, but there is no other sound.

I reach in and grab Sigurd's arm. 'You better come out,' I say. 'You need to breathe clean air.' He looks up and nods and then crawls out, towards me.

'So, he did it this time,' Lionel says, pushing through the others and seeing Brian lying peacefully in his polyester tomb.

'It's all my fault,' I say, once Sigurd is settled on the sand and we have recovered from the immediate shock. Lionel comes across and puts his hand on my shoulder, but I turn away, pushing back through the crowd towards the fire, where I stare into the heat haze wishing that I could go back in time, like Captain Kirk, and change things.

One at a time, others join me, and holding hands we worship the flames and I pray silently for them to keep burning in me forever.

'Brian came to Orkney to kill himself at dawn, in a few minutes' time. I was supposed to be his suicide buddy, but I got cold feet. On the suicide website, he told me he was my age, so it was a surprise when we met for the first time, tonight,' I say, speaking to the fire but others are now praying there too and I seem to be giving the eulogy.

'I hardly know the guy, but I feel like I have lost an old friend. When I saw him drinking and dancing with Martin earlier, I thought he had decided to live too. I really wasn't expecting it to end like this.'

I'm sobbing and can't catch my breath. My father on the other side of the circle, behind a curtain of smoke from the wet driftwood just added to the fire. He looks like he is going to come and comfort me and, for the first time in a long time, I would welcome that, but he doesn't move.

'To Brian,' Lionel says, raising a bottle of wine to his lips and we all join him in the toast. Beyond the flames, the first hint of a new day on the distant horizon.

'It's all my fault,' I say.

'No, it's not,' my father says, through the fog that still separates us.

'I encouraged him.'

'I think it's time to forgive ourselves for other people's choices. It isn't your fault that Brian killed himself, no more than it was your fault that your mother decided to leave us. It wasn't my fault either. It wasn't anyone's fault. It was just choices that they made. They just had different priorities to us,' Kito says.

It takes a while before anyone else speaks.

'Hey, guys. I don't think he would have wanted us to be sad. He would have wanted us to enjoy his wake. Catriona, do you know any wake tunes?' Lionel says, and within seconds the band is playing again and marching in a strange New Orleansy funereal way, elipsing the fire, like an asteroid orbiting the sun.

Sigurd puts his arms around me, but I pull them down to look at his hands.

'Does that hurt?' I say. The skin has melted in lines across his hands, forming long plasticated grooves.

'Yep.'

I pull him away from the fire and down towards the sea, and we walk in up to our knees. I make him bend down and put his hands in the water.

'You're not going to baptise me, are you? Now that you've found religion?' he says, trying to make light of it, though I can see that his hands hurt a lot.

'Could do, I am Jesus after all.'

He laughs at this. 'Really that is funny. That is in fact your funniest line tonight. I think the Church could do with a Goth Messiah.'

'You are the easiest man to amuse.'

'You're my *amuse bouche*.'

'I think that means a tasty morsel.'

'Exactly.'

'Not now,' I say, looking up at the tent and then down at his hands again. 'It's what you're meant to do with a burn?'

'Isn't it too late for that? Anyway, shouldn't it be running water?'

'Who knows? It might help. Doesn't it keep burning deeper and deeper, or something, until you cool it down?'

'Isn't that passion?'

'Really? Calm down. I hope this helps.'

'I don't know, anyway, thanks,' he says, leaning forward and kissing me gently on the lips. I no longer know how many kisses there have been.

## (Kenaz Reversed)

*'An ending, or loss.'*

I wait for the sea water to dissolve the scar tissue on Sigurd's hands. It must hurt now, but it will heal. I look back up the gently shelving beach. Sigurd's Vikings have formed a scrum and I think they are planning a song or something. They must be used to death. Lives were shorter and they ended more brutally then. The scrum breaks and Valter, the Hogweed-armed one, walks down to us.

'Family meeting,' he says to Sigurd. 'Your input is needed.'

Sigurd shrugs, dries his hands on his coconut t-shirt, then walks up the beach and joins the conversation. The circle of Vikings expands and the talking continues. Swift Eye is at the centre and Sigurd's father and uncle are there too.

Behind them, Zander the storyteller is settling down to tell another story, maybe this one, as if nothing has happened, but, as yet there is no one there to listen. Most people are in small groups, probably talking about what to do when someone kills themselves. Do you bury them? Call the police?

The Vikings remind me of those American football scrimmages – if that's the right word – or is it a huddle? You know, where they crouch down to whisper and agree on the next play. Sigurd comes back and stands beside me for a while before speaking. The Viking party seem to be watching him.

'My family have an idea,' he says.

It is hard to take in what has happened and I'm not sure I can deal with much more.

'They think that Brian deserves a proper send off.'

I look at him, waiting for some more information.

'It was Swift Eye's idea, but there is only one *Dreki* and it is ours, so we needed to come to an agreement.'

As I am taking this in half a dozen Vikings walk across to the tent.

'We think he deserves a proper sending off. The Viking way.'

'Yes, you said,' I say, still trying to work out what is going on.

The Vikings crawl into the tent and drag Brian's body out and four of them hoist him up on to their shoulders. They make it look easy, as if carrying a scarecrow, not a man. They start down the beach towards *Dreki*, which is now free, drifting to and fro with the breaking waves, in time with the rhythm of the Milky Way. The two front Vikings are tinted orange by the sun seeping from the crack under the door of night in front of them.

'We thought a Viking burial would be a fitting end for him,' Sigurd says.

'Bloody hell. Is that allowed?' At last I realise what they are planning to do.

'Swift Eye says that Udal law still applies and Viking burials are still legal here. Anyway, he's a local dignitary, so it's up to him what's legal tonight. Dad says he has always wanted to do it and Hooky seems to think it is in keeping with our heritage.'

'But Brian's from Leeds,' I say.

'Grimsby is mentioned in the Orkneyinga Saga. Didn't they get everywhere in Northern England? Isn't it why they speak the way they do up north?'

'Is it?'

'He probably has more Viking DNA than you do.'

The men struggle to lift Brian's body onto *Dreki*, so others come to help. They have to wade into deep water, holding Brian high up to stop his lifeless body getting wet, and then they ease him over the side until his body is straddling two of the benches.

Valter lights a torch from the fire and walks down the beach to stand sentinel at *Dreki*'s bow. The torch flickers in the light breeze, as if it is breathing, and it provides light for the men on board struggling with Brian's body. The music stops abruptly, mid-song, and everyone is now watching.

'It's beautiful,' Lynette says to Rick, clutching his hand.

'I feel like I'm a character in a Hollywood film and any moment Brad Pitt is going to walk into shot, or they'll stop filming and we notice we're in Burbank Studios, not in Orkney after all,' Marina says.

'If this is what happens when you die around here, I want to be buried here too,' Rick says.

'Well, we're certainly not in Kansas anymore,' Lynette says.

(Wunjo)

*'Success, joy, happiness.'*

It takes little time to arrange Brian in the middle of the longship. Wood and hay are carried down and arranged around him. Just two men remain on board to sort out the sail and the others man-handle the hull around so that it is now pointing out to sea, towards the sun now peeping above the horizon.

A bird like a flying door, with broad rectangular wings and a short wedge-shaped tail soars overhead. Of course, this Erne (White Tailed Eagle) shouldn't have been here, but it was probably summoned by the natural magnetism of the occasion. They were a pest once, but now they are rare. It descends towards the boat in a long lazy spiral and then heads out to sea, as if his spirit guide is leading the way, for Brian to follow. Or perhaps it is planning to eat him.

The men on *Dreki* pause and follow the bird's flight, recognising an omen, and then look towards the beach, where Swift Eye, Split and Hooky are making their way down towards them. Together they stop and place their hands on the stern of the boat with their feet in the water. Split places a crate of burgundy and a burger on the back seat.

Together they make this verse:

*Lone traveller*
*be safe without*
*greater offerings then these.*
*No bond women,*
*or tralls to comfort you.*

*Journey to the end of the sea.*
*Blown like a leaf*
*from the Tree of Life.*

*Consumed by the*
*everlasting flame.*

With the last word, Swift Eye nods at the two men still on board. One turns and throws the lighted torch into the hay beside Brian's body and then goes to help the other at the mast. They raise the sail, which gently fills with the early morning offshore breeze. The tiller is tied fast, once they get the boat pointed straight out to sea, and they jump out and help the others in the water to push the vessel out into the bay as the first hint of smoke comes from the stern.

The band starts up and then stops again, as if they don't know the etiquette for moments like this. The sight is astonishing. It takes my breath away and we all stare in amazement as *Dreki* is silhouetted against the small, sectored sun as its first fast emerald rays flash out across the empty welcoming sky and, coincidentally, flames lick the bottom of the mast. It is as if the sun's rays themselves have created the flames and lit the torch. Even without a Klingon firing party, Captain Kirk would have been in his element here.

'Beam him up, Scotty.'

'What?' Sigurd says.

As *Dreki* drifts slowly away from the shore, a flashing blue light mixes with the flames and I turn to see that the police have arrived. Their blue light reflecting off the back of the sail, as if it is pushing it further out into the bay, giving it a photon drive. The two police officers from earlier walk down the beach and stand beside me.

'You must be Pandora? You okay?' PC McTravers says.

'I'm fine. All is well.'

'Can you explain what is going on?' Sergeant Maitland says.

'Just burying my suicide buddy in the old way.'

'What?' PC McTravers says, just as a scream comes from *Dreki* and Brian can be seen jumping around and brushing flames from his beard before jumping into the sea.

'Help, help, I can't swim,' he shouts, as his head bobs up and down 100m or so from the shore.

'Fucking hell,' PC McTravers says, swiftly stripping off her top clothes and diving into the sea, revealing a dragon tattoo across her back.

'But he was dead, his lips were bright red,' Lionel says.

'I think that might have been me,' Martin says. The sergeant shines his torch on Martin's face and I can now see her bright red lipstick. The colour had been lost in the monochrome of night.

'You didn't have that on earlier, when you kissed me,' I say.

'No, it's my party lippy; men love it, makes me seem wild.'

'You are,' I say, and smile.

'Life saver,' Sergeant Maitland says, as he proudly watches his colleague swim out to rescue Brian.

## (Kenaz Reversed)

*'An ending or loss.'*

When she gets to him and we can all see he is safe, the band strikes up again, in celebration.

'Some night, eh?' I say, looking out to sea as *Dreki*, now fully ablaze, sails into the rising sun.

'Always the bloody same, Last Summer Night is mad, but tonight has been the maddest so far,' Sergeant Maitland says.

Brian gets back to shore. In the light, I can see his face is smudged with lipstick and his beard is burned a little, but otherwise he looks fine.

'What the fuck is going on? I had a bit of a snog with Martin here and one of her little blue pills, and decided that life was worth living after all,' Brian says.

'Failed again,' I say, then wrap my arms around him out of sheer joy.

'Told you I didn't have the brains to kill myself.'

He shakes, like a dog, to try and dry himself.

'Isn't your name an anagram for brain,' Sigurd says.

'People are always spelling it wrong on emails,' Brian says.

'There you go, then; you've had all the brains you need all along. Every misspelled email a sort of diploma to your wisdom,' Sigurd says.

'This lovely woman gave me hope that I'm not a total loser,' Brian says, looking at Martin. 'I thought if I could get a snog from her, anything was possible.'

Martin smiles.

'I was a bit tired though, so I thought I'd have five minutes' kip and then get back to the dancing but then I wake up on a bloody Viking funeral pyre. I thought it was a bloody dream until my beard caught fire. Is it always like this in Orkney?'

'More often than most people know,' Sergeant Maitland says.

Rick hands Brian a blanket and a bottle of wine, and Lionel arrives with a burger, which he rather reluctantly gives to Brian.

'Burgers and the Lord his answer to all life's problems,' I say.

'Bloody ravishing,' Brian says, biting into the burger as if he hasn't eaten all day.

'Why, thank you, kind sir,' Martin says.

'Martin, stop it. He's still recovering from the shock,' I say.

'Martin?' Brian says.

'Transgender,' I say, again. I still think it's funny.

'So am I, I've just seen how old he is,' Martin says.

'Me, old? I'm young and happy and haven't had enough of life. Isn't that right, Panda?'

'Aye and he's very clever too. They even call him Brain,' I say.

'Better tell the coastguard that there is a hazard to shipping sailing out into the Strand,' Sergeant Maitland says to himself, before turning back up the beach, leaving his colleague drying herself in towels from the royal yacht. As he does so, it begins to rain.

'Told you,' Double or Quits Jack says to Lionel, standing on the edge of the group. 'That'll soon put it out.'

'Nice tats,' Martin says, admiring the dragon that covers most of the policewoman's back.

'Thanks. I did it after that film came out: The Girl with the Dragon Tattoo. Seems a bit daft now, but it's part of me.'

'The Policewoman with The Dragon Tattoo. They should make a sequel about your life, probably make a good film,' Martin says.

'Tonight would. It really would. Wouldn't it be great if Rooney Mara played me?' PC McTravers says.

'Panda, what about you? Who do you want playing your role in tonight's blockbuster?' Martin says.

'It would have to be Judy Garland.'

Behind us we can hear a horse splashing along at the water's edge. We all turn together to see the Lady of the Mists, still in her wedding dress, with Ewan, naked again, sitting behind her riding side-saddle, facing us. He has his arms around her waist as if he doesn't ever want to let her go.

'Ewan. You know what happened last year. Get some clothes on before we have to take you in again,' Sergeant Maitland says, turning back to talk to him.

'Don't worry, officer, no erection, look,' Ewan says, opening his legs to show his flaccid penis.

'Ewan, stop that,' his mother shouts from higher up the beach.

'Before you arrest him, we need to show you something,' Maggie says. I hadn't heard her voice before, but it is English and proper. She sounds just like a lady.

She turns the horse and we follow her along the beach to a slight indentation in the sand. There is a lump in the middle covered with a blanket, which I soon realise is Davey.

'Davey,' Marina cries out, sensing it first.

'Star nearly stood on him,' Ewan said.

'Oh, no,' I say, hoping that it is a mistake, for a second time, but I know it has happened, that Davey has died.

PC McTravers kneels by Davey's body, looks for his pulse in his arm and neck, then looks into his eyes with the help of the light on her phone. She then does what they do on all good cop shows, and pulls the blanket up over his face.

'He's gone.'

'No, not Davey,' Marina says, beginning to cry.

'That man had a huge heart,' I say.

'He said to say goodnight to you, though he called you Dora,' Lynette says to me.

'Yes, I was his Dorothy,' I say, imagining myself as Judy Garland.

'If you've got to go, there are much worse ways,' Rick says.

'I think he knew he was going. That's why he was telling us everything. Downloading his life to help us. I believe that just after you go, you have time to take stock. To help you decide if it was all worth it,' I say.

'Maybe he's doing that now,' Marina says.

'How are we going to bury him? No long ships left,' Sigurd says.

'You don't get too many parties where two people die and one is resurrected,' Martin says.

'Biblical,' I say.

'Yes, but at least it wasn't three people dead,' Kito says, now standing by my side and it feels good.

'Isn't it strange how death can leave you feeling hopeful,' I say.

'Is that what Sad Guardians is on about?' Sigurd says.

'I still have no idea what that was all about,' I say.

'Great, but what are we going to do about Davey?' Lionel says.

'Nothing, I think the Policewoman with the Dragon Tattoo has it in hand,' Lilian says, now standing beside us.

Sure enough, PC McTravers is walking along the beach talking into her radio.

# THE WORDS

*You are watching Mummy driving past you in the car. She is looking at Daddy and she is saying the words. 'I have had enough of this life; I want to go back to my old life without a husband and without her. I'm not cut out to be a mother. I love my old life better than this one.'*

*It is hard to run and cry at the same time. The crunchy gravel slips and slides, but no matter how fast you run, or how loud you shout 'Mummy', you can't get any closer to her, so you stop and scream. But it doesn't work, this magic spell that normally works with Mummy, and Mummy's car gets smaller as it drives away and then it is gone, as if it has shrunk so small you can no longer see it. But you wonder is it still there? Is it just small now but still there? You can't help crying even though you know it annoys Daddy and he looks at you as if he is angry, that this is all your fault. That if you hadn't been playing with the coat and put it on when Mummy was cooking bacon, nothing would have changed.*

You have only eaten half of your bacon sandwich and now everything is ruined. You love bacon sandwiches.

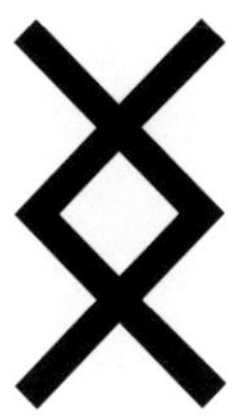

(Inguz)

*All loose ends tied up, so free to move on.*

*These tree-less islands set*
*Where the wild-goose flies*
*Lest men should e'er forget*
*The sea and the skies.*

Robert Rendall